G. F. Newman is the aut
social issues, including *t...*
Obsession and *The Natio...*
Operation Bad Apple whic...
med at the Royal Court.

Mark Porter

March 1984

By the same author

G. F. NEWMAN

Law and Order

PANTHER
Granada Publishing

Panther Books
Granada Publishing Ltd
8 Grafton Street, London W1X 3LA

Published by Panther Books 1984

First published in Great Britain by
Sphere Books Ltd 1977
in separate volumes: *A Detective's Tale; A Villain's Tale;
A Prisoner's Tale*
This revised edition in one volume first published by
Granada Publishing 1983

ISBN 0-586-05783-8

Printed and bound in Great Britain by
Collins, Glasgow

Set in Times

PROLOGUE

'Of course, the ramps and fit ups,' the detective inspector said conversationally over the rim of his glass, 'even the tradeoffs, you have to have them in order to nick a few at times. They're something that most decent policemen deplore.'

There was no irony in his tone, no smile brushing the corners of his mouth even though he was talking with a colleague in The Feathers just along the road from the Yard. What he didn't add but what lay behind his observation was: Especially when the stroke that was pulled came on top and a detective had his collar felt.

'Almost without exception those sorts of strokes are pulled for the good of society. You know what I mean, Tony?'

That was both the public and private justification detectives put forward for whatever they did, and some even believed it, certainly those like Fred Pyle who had been a detective going on fifteen years, and a detective inspector for five of those years.

The second man at the bar nodded and raised the gin and tonic to his lips. He emptied the glass then motioned to the barkeeper. He was a detective chief inspector and had been through the same conditioning process, and had developed those same patterns of thought which helped keep him at his job day after day, and for as long. He was neither a deep thinker nor a philosopher; the job didn't bear thinking about in the abstract sense, for it was odds on you'd quit if you did; and what the philosophy amounted to was: Do it, nick someone, keep your numbers up, keep it all ticking over. Detectives had to believe that was important; not that they were winning necessarily, but that they were keeping about level.

Detectives had always believed that was what was happening, and by all accounts it was, only now they had two very distinct disadvantages. One was C1B2 the department set up within the framework of the Metropolitan police to investigate complaints against themselves. It was causing the CID more than enough aggravation, specifically with the complaints against officers which had to be investigated, and generally with the number of detective-manhours it took to investigate complaints. The second great disadvantage was having a commissioner who was uniform branch orientated and anti-CID, whose intention it seemed was to disband the CID, or failing that, decimate it to such a degree that it was left with no rank above that of detective sergeant and so effectively strip it of its operational power. The commissioner resented the power the CID wielded, also their autonomy; they were a law unto themselves, or always had been. And that was especially so with the Robbery Squad. Their power had been as close to absolute as was possible within the current system; therefore the commisioner's resentment of them and their activities was more marked and was reflected in his appointments and manoeuvres which seldom favoured them.

It was recent action by CIB2 which had prompted this present conversation, and many more like it between many different CID men. These two detectives were both part of the Robbery Squad, and were affected by the activities of CIB2, who were currently investigating complaints against no less than eighteen officers out of a total of one hundred and ten that made up the Squad, four of whom were under suspension. A number of these allegations were a legacy of Operation Countryman, which had brought a whole gang of Dorset policemen to London to investigate wrongdoing in the Met and City police; they had gone home now, ironically to face an investigation into their own wrongdoing by the Yorkshire CID. DI Pyle was one detective who was having complaints against him investigated; the other man was one of the Squad's three detective chief inspectors, who had to bear the brunt of more senior officers' irritation at the state of affairs. Each new complaint added ammunition to the commissioner's arsenal against the CID in general, the Squad in particular; notwithstanding all the other complaints, from that of an over-zealous traffic cop to the very senior policeman who was using the police computer for the benefit of gaming clubs' membership drives.

'The investigation'll have to run its course, Fred,' the DCI said, 'for what it's worth. I don't doubt they'll want a word.'

'They already interviewed me once this week,' the DI said with a straight face.

The DCI smiled grimly now. 'That was in your own right.' The latest complaint being investigated by CIB2 was against the senior detective sergeant on the DI's squad.

'Be the same waste of time,' the DI said. 'You can't wonder at so many villains keeping their liberty.'

'Too many CID earning, Fred,' the DCI said, dropping his voice a couple of decibels. Anyone overhearing that in the bar might not have been aware that he was joking.

'I wish one or two would bung me,' he replied, sharing the joke. 'I'm getting pissed off with being missed out all the time, Tony.' He smeared the last of the egg pie in the brown sauce on his plate and pushed it into his mouth, chewing it only twice before swallowing it, then emptied his neat scotch down immediately after. 'You want another one before I shoot off?'

'No, I got one to meet myself, Fred.' The DCI looked at his watch. 'Well, make it a quick 'un then.'

The DCI was night duty officer for the Squad.

The DI and his squad had the current tour of night duty.

1

'The thing is,' the man said in a slightly didactic manner which
frequently crept into his conversation, 'what chance have you
got with the filth.' It wasn't a question.

The man at the bar with him knew the answer anyway but
that didn't stop Jack Lynn making his point. 'You got no
chance, have you? The slippery bastards'll not only cop a nice
earner off you, they'll go and nick you as well, they want you.'

'Well, maybe they don't want me very much, Jack,' he said.
He had told Lynn how, having been picked up by the CID
with stolen bearer bonds in his possession, he had bunged the
DI and pulled himself clear. It sounded reasonable when he
had said it, but now he wasn't so sure. Maybe he shouldn't
have said anything when he had sought Jack Lynn's company
in the after-hours drinker. That wasn't the reason for seeking
out this villain's company. He had been obliged to say
something, he argued to himself, as Lynn might have heard
how he had been picked up and then released. That, without
some sort of justification, like bunging the filth, might have
been a bit sussy. Even though he didn't see Lynn often,
rumours still flew about. He might have been taken for a
grass, one who had traded a few bodies in order to get himself
a result.

'I wouldn't fancy making a book on it, Dave,' Lynn said. He
motioned to the woman behind the bar.

'I'll get that, Jack.' He finished his own drink. 'When you're
ready, Sal.' He turned back to Lynn. 'Maybe you're right. I
dunno. You gotta take a chance. Know what I mean?'

Lynn gazed around the smoky club, as though not
interested in continuing this conversation. There was a card

game in progress at a table in the corner and he wondered if he had time for a few hands before going off to his meet.

'I mean, what can you do about it anyway? I mean, fuckall, they come back and nick you, can you? You can get up in court and scream about them fitting you – you gotta try that, haven't you. Or you scream that the filth nicked your bit of dough. But you're up the steps before a wrong 'un, you see what good it does you. And Old Bill make sure you go up in front of the right judge, 'worry about that. 'Specially if their case is a bit dodgy.'

Lynn reached round to the bar for the gin and tonic that had been put there and sipped it. "They let you have your bit of liberty, the cunning cunts have done it for a reason, I'd say. And not just the earner you bunged 'em.'

The thought flashed through Dave Roth's mind that this man knew why he had dug him out and was now playing with him. The skin on his face began to prickle with embarrassment. He could brazen out any sort of story put up to the filth, or stand a quizzing from a silk in court, but this situation was different. After all he was supposed to go mates with this blagger, and here he was trying to get information on his activities along with any other villains, so he could make sure of his own liberty.

'Leave off, Jack, for fucksake. That means I'll have to go on the trot.'

'Might not be a bad idea.'

'T'rific. My missus and kids would love that. I might as well be away doing a bit.'

"Talk like a cunt,' Lynn said dismissively. He had a wife and two children and thought no less of them than Roth did of his family but he'd sooner be dodging around the country, avoiding Old Bill, or tucked away in Spain, than having his old lady visit him down at Albany, and lying to the kids about where he was.

'A mate of mine –you know Ray Turner, don't you?'

Roth did

'He was tucking up banks with a Visa card the other week. Having a right good earner. He'd done about six hundred quids' worth, he had. He was just coming out of a bank in Hammersmith, he was, just got into his car, when zoomp! a car pulls right up in front of him. Bang tight like that.' He demonstrated with his hands. 'He couldn't pull away a bit lively. It tops up the geezer who gets out of the car is a DS on the Squad, that's all. He was just driving along apparently, spotted him – didn't know him – just on instinct, sussed something was going off.'

'Fuck his luck,' Roth commented, accepting the story but not seeing its immediate relevance.

'Oh, that's not the best of it,' Lynn said. 'He flashed his ID, the filth did, and nicked every penny off him. Well that's all right, you gotta expect that, I mean, it's a chance you take. He left him the Visacards so he could go and do a bit more for himself.'

'As you say, Jack, s'chance you take. That's how it goes.'

'Right. But what the dirty cunt done then was give him to the Fraud Squad. They went and nicked him later that day. Only he hadn't done enough for them to have an earner too!'

Reacting with prescribed dismay, Roth said, 'Snaky, no-good cunts.'

'You'd be as well to go on the trot,' Lynn advised. He shrugged. 'S'up to you though, innit. I mean you wanna take a chance.' His attention went back to the card table. One of the players got up to leave, unhooking his jacket from the chair. Lynn slid his shirt cuff off his Rolex day-date chronometer – he had given a twoer for the watch and expanding bracelet, both were eighteen carat gold. He wouldn't have time for a game. He'd get involved then have to leave to make his meet at Catford. That would mean leaving whatever he had contributed to the pot. All he had time for was another drink with Dave Roth.

'Sal?' he said, motioning to the fat barmaid.

'What did I tell you? Regular as a geriatric with an enema,' the

10

man said with pride from the passenger seat of a parked car.

Light from the arc lamps around the perimeter of the car park spilled over the few cars that remained. One of them was an old 3.8 Jaguar in immaculate condition. The car belonged to Jack Lynn, who spent a lot of money maintaining it. There was no point in having such a car if it wasn't kept up, he felt. This was one of the last models with real leather seats and walnut facia dashboard.

Jack Lynn was sitting behind the wheel of the car watching the road that ran along the side of the car park. One or two punters late to leave the stadium moved off on foot with no sort of bounce in their gait, having lost their money. What he and the other man in the car were watching, and had commented on, was the security truck going along the road to the main gates of the stadium. Pushing the gates open wider, the white-coated attendant waved to the driver as the truck veered off to the left and ran up the ramp towards the enclosure.

Two guards, armed with night sticks and wearing large, heavily visored crash helmets, climbed from the front of the truck and locked the doors shut before moving on down through the stadium.

'Sometimes we're not quite ready,' the man with Lynn said. 'Depending how much we've taken in during the meet. It all has to be collected from around the stadium, counted and sorted.' He knew the details so well he could probably recite them in his sleep, and did for all he knew. He wasn't sure how the worry of this might be affecting him. If it was, his wife had made no comment. He considered he was justified in doing this, having convinced himself of the rightness of it long before he had met up with Jack Lynn, who had given the idea definite shape.

'What happens if you're not ready?' Lynn wanted to know. Possibly he had been given this information before, but it didn't matter if he had. Lynn needed to be absolutely sure about these things.

11

'They wait. They make themselves a cup of coffee. The money has to go out. It can't stay there overnight.' He hesitated briefly, as though what he was about to say was an impediment to what they were planning. 'You know it was done once before.'

'A long time ago,' Lynn said, vaguely aware that the Tote at Catford dogtrack had been robbed before. He was too young to remember.

'Just after the war. That's why they won't leave it overnight now.' At one time the takings from Tote betting had been left in the office safe from the Thursday and Saturday meetings and banked the following Monday, until the safe had been cut open one weekend. Andy Harrington was old enough to remember; he had gone to work in the Tote not long after the robbery, and had been there ever since, suffering injustices, being passed over for promotion that should rightly have been his. Now he was redressing the balance, taking compensation. Yet paradoxically he told his firm's history with a sense of pride.

'There's no problem if the guards don't appear again within a couple of minutes?' Lynn said, fetching the conversation back to the present. 'Their mate left in the van don't go and call Catford nick and tell them he thinks there's one going off, does he?'

'No, 'course not. I've known them to be in there as long as, well it must have been twenty minutes. When we've had a big night, that is.'

'What's the biggest night you've had since you've been working there, Andy? Can you remember?'

'About thirty-eight grand, I think it was,' – he knew precisely. It had been the Saturday preceding the Spring bank holiday four years ago. 'Just didn't stop coming in that night. No one seemed able to pick a winner that night, no one betting with us anyway. The Tote jackpot was just on four grand, and even that didn't go. They'd like a few more like that, my bosses, I can tell you.'

12

'Wouldn't be bad, would it? Thirty-eight grand for a night's work.' There was a note of expectation in Lynn's voice.

'The average would be nearer twenty-five thousand, though.' He glanced apprehensively at Lynn as though he was afraid that figure might cause him to lose interest, even though he told him at an earlier meeting how much to expect. 'Well, say between twenty-five and thirty,' he added quickly, improving the proposition.

'In nice safe used notes that you don't have to go again on,' Lynn said. 'How bad's that? No problem spending them when you want. No hungry placer taking the lion's share.'

Harrington didn't know anything about that, never having considered the pros and cons of stolen money. Money to him was simply money, he wouldn't have considered the dangers of holding new, recorded notes. 'Look, I'd better be getting back,' he said, glancing at his watch by the light that slanted through the windscreen. 'They might start wondering if I'm too long.'

'Yeah, don't make yourself sussy, Andy, 'n' fuck it all up,' Lynn advised.

Reaching for the rearside door handle, he started out of the car, but stopped. 'The thing is, Jack. When's it likely to go off? Have you got any idea?'

Lynn didn't want to commit himself yet, not to this man anyway. ''S hard to say. The sooner the better I'd have thought.'

That seemed to satisfy Harrington. 'I'd say so – just want to make sure I'm off sick that week, is all.' He smiled nervously, seeking Lynn's approval of such a move.

'Be nice to get a look at that office where the money's kept, 'fore I decide definitely,' Lynn said vaguely. It wasn't essential, even though that was where he was planning in his mind to have it.

'Be a bit difficult, I think.' Harrington was slightly embarrassed at not being able to lay this on for the man. Getting a job as a cleaner or something was the only

13

suggestion he could make.

The look Lynn gave him blanked the proposal, for obvious reasons. He wasn't even happy about Harrington seeing his face; letting everyone in the office see it made him a million if the blag went off.

In an attempt to redeem himself for his impractical suggestion, Harrington said, 'I could get an impression of the key to that door from the corridor, if you like.'

'Be handy,' Lynn said. 'Do them in a piece of cuttlebone. Don't do them in soap.' Soap left traces on the surfaces of keys that forensic scientists could detect weeks later, which would immediately suggest it was an inside job, and soap didn't offer as sharp an impression as cuttlebone. 'S'not bolted, that door, while they're in there, is it?'

'I've never known it.' He checked his watch again. 'Look, I gotta go. You going to pop down Saturday night, are you?'

'Yeah, I'll probably take another look.' He smiled reassuringly at him. 'We'll have a nice little earner here, Andy. 'Worry about that.'

'That's good. I could use it. I'll see you then, will I?' he asked, uncertain and not wanting to push Lynn.

'I'll give you a bell. Mind how you go.'

Lynn sat watching as he went away at a brisk pace across the car park. It faintly amused him that Harrington who had probably been law abiding till then, should at his time of life turn to crime. He guessed Harrington was sixty. He thought briefly about the grievances that had prompted his action in putting the prospect up to him. He wondered how many people there were like Harrington who'd not only been doing their job as long, but resented it and had as much information about money their employers handled. There must have been thousands of them, guys who'd never make the move, never get the opportunity, but would retire finally with the company's thanks and a pension they could barely manage on. That was their loss, he decided.

Such thoughts ceased abruptly as the two security guards

reappeared, each carrying a metal cash container, certainly heavier than when they had been taken in. He knew the routine by heart, not from the couple of times he had seen this operation, but the numerous times he had watched other security-truck collections and deliveries. He was a blagger: patient watching – sometimes for weeks on end – scrupulous noting of details, however small or apparently insignificant, was part of his trade. He had no other trade and made no pretence of pursuing one. He had been lucky in the past, had had some good earners from a few blags. How long his luck would last and the consequences of it failing was something he didn't contemplate. Few villains did. Once they started that they often quit the life, there was little alternative, unless like Lynn they were compulsive villains. However, they were simply better just not thinking about that almost inevitable nicking.

With his nightstick one of the guards rapped the back of the van and a hatch measuring fifteen by twenty inches slid up. The two guards put their containers inside and the hatch closed again. Lynn remained in his car watching as the guards unlocked the cab and climbed in. The glow from a match illuminated the cab as one lit a cigarette. The other filled out his log in respect of this collection.

Almost out of hand Lynn dismissed the possibility of going after the money at that point. Those guards were curious animals who, for the few quid they earned each week, tried all sorts to protect the money they were carrying; he could never understand that mentality. It wasn't their money, why should they give a fuck? But all too often they did. Also doing it there inside the stadium in full view might give others a chance. All they had to do was get those gates shut. There was only one road out, which could be blocked easily with a couple of cars. The third guard in the truck would be on the radio for help while they were blagging the containers off the other two; then the containers themselves, they'd be a dead give-away if they were stopped with those in a car, and some of them automatically destroyed their contents, but only when holding new and recorded bank notes. Going after it up in the Tote office was almost certain to be the best place, Lynn concluded.

Turning the ignition key, the engine fired immediately and surged with power as Lynn's foot brushed the accelerator. High-performance cars had always pleased him, and actually having one that a finance company had no interest in pleased him more. Pushing the gearstick into first, he let off the brake and the Jaguar purred out of the car park in the direction the security truck had gone. Lynn wasn't about to follow it. He was heading north, back across the Water.

The grey 3.8 Jaguar came through the junction at the bottom of Oxford Street from Charing Cross Road and into Tottenham Court Road just as the lights changed. Instinctively Lynn's eyes darted about, looking for police who might spring him. His move wasn't strictly illegal, though he had had sufficient time to stop. He didn't usually take chances when he was driving, preferring not to give the police any opportunities, not even the uniform branch. Making a lefthand signal, Lynn pulled over into a parking space on Tottenham Court Road. It was on a yellow line, but at that time of night he knew there would be no problem, even though he was within sight of the police station. Climbing out, he carefully locked the door and walked round the car checking that the other doors were locked. He had no faith either in the police recovering the car if stolen, or the fact that as he did a bit himself would-be car thieves would leave his alone.

Pausing on the pavement, having satisfied himself that the car was locked, Lynn looked first up the street in the direction of Goodge Street, then towards Oxford Street. Jack Lynn had just turned forty, having arrived there without seeing it, like so many, as a watershed; he didn't consider it such, and saw no reason to change the course of his life. He was having it off fairly regularly and quite successfully, and without thinking about

16

it knew of no reason he shouldn't continue that way for a long time to come. Earning well by his profession, Lynn had a comfortable lifestyle which avoided being extravagant. He dressed well and lived well. A modern well-cut hand-stitched suit covered his well-built frame – there wasn't much fat on him – the taste slightly suspect and wasn't helped by his wife going with him when he chose his suits. He was considered a fairly sharp dresser, and like most villains of his generation, unless out doing a bit of work, he was always suited and booted; he wore large links in French cuffs and slightly too much deodorant. His dark, wavy hair, which was receding slightly, was worn at a conventional length, anything longer he disapproved of. There was little about Lynn's outward appearance that would immediately identify him for what he was, or did. He had a flattish, bland sort of face, his eyes were a little too close set, but apart from that there was nothing particularly memory-jogging about the face. It was a good face for a villain to have when he had to put his face in anywhere. Like so many villains, Lynn was obstinately right wing; he had implicit belief in the status quo and, believing in free enterprise, had voted for the Conservatives at the last election. He was a slight contradiction in terms, and had a contradictory, dogmatic nature.

Easing his jacket and camel-hair coat off his shoulders, as though taking some rucks out of the back, Lynn stepped along the pavement, satisfied that he wasn't being watched, and that his car wasn't going to get towed away. He turned into the unlit doorway of the after-hours drinker where he had been earlier that night. Having decided quite definitely that he was going after that one at Catford, he had to see about putting a firm together.

No light appeared behind the door, but Lynn heard a board creak and knew someone was there. Shortly the door opened, admitting him to the dark, narrow entrance hall. 'Hello, Chas,' he said in a familiar manner to the man who had opened the door. 'How's it going?'

'There's one or two Old Bill in,' he informed him. 'Thought I'd mark your card, Jack. Know what I mean.' He shut the door.

'They fucking well live in this place, don't they,' he said.

'They're just knocking out some Scotch, s'all.'

Immediately beyond the darkened hallway was a small reception area where coats could be deposited; there was a door which led to the lavatory shared by both men and women, a payphone fixed to the wall beneath a soundproof canopy, and crates full of empty beer bottles stacked against the only other available piece of wall. At one time there had been a guest book which had required signing, but it had fallen into neglect and finally disappeared. The room beyond, which comprised the club, was L-shaped, with little more than the bar and a makeshift proscenium arch where occasional entertainment was put on, usually strippers or an off-key singer – once a drag act but the guy had made the mistake of feeling up the wrong villain at the bar. The whole works including the seating couldn't have cost the owner more than a couple of hundred quid to set up.

There were usually a number of what Lynn would call reliable people in there drinking. Most of the patrons were would-be villains, or vaguely connected; the filth weren't slow in using the place, especially as the booze was free to them. At the bar two detectives were drinking with Bernie White, the owner of the place. Lynn went past without saying hello, and stopped at the opposite end of the bar. He didn't want to get involved with the filth. There were a few card games that the chancellor earned nothing out of, nor the off-track betting that went on, nothing terribly illegal, but it all amounted to enough for Bernie White to have to entertain the local Old Bill when they came looking for an earner. The alternative would have been shutting up and finding another location. But it would have been the same there. A place like that couldn't be kept quiet from the filth; there were too many grasses about.

'Gin and tonic, Sal,' he said to the barmaid and turned to check round the club while she poured it. Across the room at the table in the corner the card game was still going but with only one of the players from earlier. Lynn caught the eye of one of the others, and with a gesture offered him a drink. 'What's John drinking there, Sal? Give him one, will you.'

She peered through the cigarette smoke in the unevenly lit room and identified John, then reached for the gin bottle again. Lynn put two pounds on the bar and didn't get any change.

'Nicking a nice few quid, John?' Lynn said, putting the drink on the table in front of him.

'Wish to fuck I was, Jack. Haven't had a hand yet. A ten,' John Tully said to the table, and showed his card, stopping another player going nap and taking the pot.

'Fuck my luck!' the player who had been stopped said irritably. 'I could've fucking well done that the other way.'

'Cheers, Jack,' Tully said, raising his glass. He put another two pounds in the pot, as did each of the others.

'You wanna sit in, Jack?' One of the players asked. 'Might change my fucking luck.'

'Gotta get my bit of indoor money somehow.' Lynn pulled up a chair.

'Gonna stand you in about a score, son,' the player said, doing a quick count of the pot.

'Well, let's see if I can't go and nick a nice few quid.' Lynn's mood was buoyant, the sort of mood that helped a player to win at cards, unless he wasn't able to play the game. Lynn could play. He counted twenty pounds and added it to the pot. Extra cards were added to the limited number used in napoleon to accommodate the additional player. Lynn removed his jacket and put it on the back of the chair and sat. He had a feeling he was going to win, despite the fact that cards weren't his reason for coming to the club; probably because of that he would win.

At the table there were two prospects for the bit of work he had in mind. But of the two, John Tully, was the firm favourite, as Lynn didn't know the other man well enough to want to put it up to him, and probably wouldn't unless he got stuck and couldn't get anyone else. All he knew about him really was that he had it off from time to time – that was probably enough. He had several people in mind who he knew would be good enough, even though he hadn't used them before – the team he had used before on blags were no longer available to him. He would wait till afterwards then put it up to John Tully, he wouldn't mention anything at the table; there were too many grasses around, to say nothing of the filth at the bar. Whispers about one you had planned were picked up all too easily, but there was no way to stop it, not when you were punting around; someone you put it to, thinking he was doing you a favour would mention it to someone else to see if they were interested.

The feeling Lynn had about his luck was accurate. He took a hundred and fifty pounds out of the first pot, and sixty out of the second. There wasn't a third.

'What d'you go and earn there, Jack?' Tully asked as they were driving away from the club in Lynn's car.

The hour was late and there was little traffic about, apart from a few empty cabs plying around with their signs down, working for brasses.

Lynn told him. 'Thought that Tony Holder was gonna block me on that last hand. He was well fucking sick, wan' he.'

'Well, can't say I was exactly pleased, Jack. Know what I mean. Thought I was gonna nick that. 'Been handy, pay the rent.' Tully was shortish, powerfully built, with a large head; he had a fairly large stomach that looked like it had come to him as an afterthought. He was in his early thirties and had been a villain ever since childhood which was spent for the most part in Care or Approved schools.

'Where you living now?' Lynn said. He had offered him a lift, assuming he still lived in his own direction, which was Kentish Town.

'Same place more or less – Swiss Cottage. Got a flat with this married woman – she's got a couple of kids,' Tully explained, as though he had been called upon to justify himself.

'Yourn?' Lynn asked.

'Leave off! – nice kids, though.' He thought about the situation, then added, 'S'pose I am like a father to them. The ol' man pissed off.'

'Happens all the time, John.'

'Yeah. No-good cunt!' Tully said like he meant it.

There was a silence in the car for a moment.

'This is a nice motor, Jack. How long you been running this?' It had been a while since they had seen one another.

'About six months, I s'pose. One of them V12s, is what I'd like. Trouble is you'd go and make too many Old Bill sick driving about in a car like that. They couldn't stand it. Jealous cunts. This does me though. S'not a bad runner, a nice clean motor.' He paused and glanced across at the man next to him, at the road, then at Tully again, as though assessing him. 'What you been doing lately? Been doing any work, have you?'

'Why, you got something in mind, Jack?'

'I expect to have in a little while,' Lynn said. 'Could be very tasty, an' all.'

'Well, I might be interested. But the thing is, I got something of my own I expect to go off soon. Depends what you got in mind, Jack, and when it's going, I s'pose.'

''S blag at Catford dogtrack,' Lynn said.

He looked over at Tully, expecting some kind of reaction. But the villain just stared through the windscreen, considering the proposition. 'I'm light about two, I reckon.'

'I always thought you had a regular little firm, Jack. S'what I heard.'

'No. Nothing definite.' He hesitated. 'Stevie Murry and Terry Hutt got nicked on that one that went off down at London Bridge a couple of months ago.'

'Fuck I! Yeah, I was offered some of that, wan' I.'

'You did well to give it a miss. They were well lollied. The filth are entitled to let them have bail, I would think. Help 'em out. They been stuck down in Brixton for two months now waiting to go up.'

'That's fuck all, is it. Peter Collins has been waiting seven months to go up. 'S fucking murder. You go and do your bit of bird 'fore you even get weighed off.'

A grin spread across Lynn's face. The remand situation while awaiting trial wasn't funny, but a sense of proportion had to be kept. 'This one I got in mind's gonna be worth about six or seven apiece, a bit of luck.'

That impressed Tully. 'As much as that?'

''S got to be there, no problem.' He tried to resist sweetening the proposition. If anyone committed he wanted them to do so on its merits rather than promises he knew he couldn't fulfil.

'Well, the thing is, Jack. I'm sort of committed to this other one. What I mean is, it's all down to when you got it going off like. It's one I was putting together myself over at Romford.'

'I can't say definite, not yet. I gotta take another look on Saturday. But I reckon it's gotta be soon. Soon as possible, really. It's silly leaving it. I mean, if I know about it then someone else might.'

'Oh yeah, you're better off doing it as soon as you can. Look, could you give us a bell at the weekend. M' plans should've firmed up by then, a bit of luck. I'll know definite like. But I do fancy it, Jack.'

'What's your number? – the thing is, I don't wanna leave it much later than Sunday.'

'Well, I'll know, won't I! I'll be able to tell you.' He picked up a business card from the top of the dashboard and scribbled his phone number on the back of it. 'If I ain't in, I'll almost certainly be down the hall. My Ann'll know where I am.' He put the card prominently back on the dashboard. 'Why don't you give Ginger Chapman a bell, you're short-handed? I heard he was looking for something.'

'He's a fucking hippy, 'in he. You can't rely on people like that, John,' he said didactically. 'He'd probably be well doped up.'

'His hair's a bit long, is all,' Tully said. 'Do the next right there, Jack.' They were travelling along Adelaide Road.

''S enough, John,' Lynn wouldn't call the man. He followed Tully's directions to a block of council flats.

'I'll give you a bell on Sunday then.'

'Yeah. Good luck, Jack.'

2

At this stage with organizing a blag half his time seemed to be spent sitting around in cars watching the prospect or waiting to meet someone. If that person didn't show up, or he failed to see what he expected to see, then he began to wonder if it was all worthwhile.

Lynn had spent another Saturday evening at Catford dogtrack and had stayed around right to the end watching as the security truck arrived, waiting for the guards to come out of the stadium with the money containers; timing them; watching them depart. He had followed them out along Adenmore Road, past Catford Bridge station, watched them make a left turn onto Catford Road. He had made a righthand turn into Ravensbourne Park Road and had parked his wife's Austin Metro and switched off the lights.

He was waiting for Andy Harrington to show up. When he had phoned him he had blanked the idea of their meeting in the car park again; someone might have spotted them and got sussy, even though he was in a different car. And Harrington offering another excuse to leave the office might have made him a bit sussy when the blag finally went off. Something might have jolted someone's memory, their recalling his going out a couple of times around about when the money was collected. The filth wouldn't take long to crack him. Lynn wondered about Harrington as he waited, whether he might not be a prime suspect anyway. He didn't know a lot about him, nor how he was thought of in the firm, whether he would be the immediate candidate should one be made there. Maybe there were things he hadn't told him that he ought to have told him before making a decision. What Lynn knew he had in his favour was the fact that the man didn't know him. It would be all right, Lynn decided.

Watching through the offside driving mirror, he saw a red Mini 1000 crawl along the line of parked cars. Lynn put his arm out of the window, signalling to the driver. The car tucked into the space behind Lynn's car and Harrington climbed out, and after nervously glancing about went and climbed into the Metro.

'All right?' Lynn inquired generally.

'Yes, I'm fine. We had a good night.' The profitability of his company might have made a difference to him.

'I'll go round the block,' Lynn said, starting the car. 'Otherwise we'll probably get done for sus sitting here.' It only needed one of the householders in the street to call the local police about two men sitting in a car.

'Well, don't go too far. I haven't locked my car.'

'That'll be safe enough,' Lynn assured him with a grin. 'It's all spades living around here – they only nick big cars.'

Harrington gave him a doubting look, then glanced back at his car a little anxiously. 'We had a good night,' he said again as they drove. 'Took in just over twenty thousand, we did.'

Dividing it by four, with a couple of grand extra for himself for Xs and something for Harrington would give all involved a nice earner. Lynn didn't comment on the take. 'D'you fetch the impression of that key?'

'Oh, yes.' Removing a large wad of tissue paper from his pocket, he unfolded it and produced a four-inch piece of cuttlebone. He handed it to Lynn, who reached up and put on the interior light and inspected the impressions as he steered. They were clean and well formed, and Harrington had had the foresight to take two of each side of the key. 'Are they all right?'

'They'll do fine, I'd say, Andy. You did well there. I'll get my keyman to cut one from that all right. I'll send it to you to test.' He switched out the light.

'Good. That's good.' He smacked his hands together in a pleased, excited manner, as though concluding some business. 'What do you you think, Jack? About doing it, that is?'

'Won't be too long. A couple of weeks or so, I should think. Bit of luck.' He sensed Harrington's disappointment and glanced sideways at him. 'What, you desperate or something, Andy?'

'No! No, of course not,' he replied emphatically, like he believed the affirmative would invalidate him. 'It just seems to be going on forever.'

'Yeah. I know what you mean. But just try not to think about it till it's done.'

Harrington gave a nervous, excited laugh. 'A nice few quid will be handy – they owe it me.'

'You'll get a taste soon enough,' Lynn assured him, and turned the car round to head back.

There was a lot to do in putting one together, besides just getting the firm. Things that he wouldn't even consider telling Harrington. There were tools to get; the right kind for the job, the sort that would have the right effect. There were cars to get; again the right kind. It was no good having any old car dragged off the street so that you went and had your collar felt before you even got to the blag. The cars had to be well rung so that they could be left parked on the getaway route without any problems. There was the getaway route to be looked at and given careful thought. There was never any guarantee what might happen in urban traffic; it was perhaps the most unpredictable part of the blag. But carefully worked out, they could hopefully toe it away without getting snarled up in traffic and nicked as a result. Arranging all that took days. But Lynn's most immediate problem was getting his team; it was pointless making moves towards cars, guns or anything else until he had enough of a firm to go out and do the blag. He was beginning to wonder about that. Names were getting scratched from his shortlist, guys who for various reasons couldn't make it. A couple of them had said straight out that they didn't fancy making one, without even hearing what it was. But many villains were like that. He preferred a straight blank, then he knew it wasn't anything about the blag they didn't fancy. When he got a couple of knockbacks he even considered reducing the number he would need, but finally decided that four, including himself, was the absolute minimum. Five would have been better, but they'd make it all right with four. If he could get that number together. If this other little team hadn't been nicked or Stevie Murry and Terry Hutt had been out on bail while waiting to go up the steps, there'd have been no problem. Both of them would have had a taste, if only to provide for their families while they were away – it was a million they were going to be sent down. Lynn wondered about the blag they had been nicked on, how come he hadn't gone for it when it was offered to him. There had been something about it, he hadn't known what, but he just hadn't fancied it. He always followed his instincts in these things. He was beginning to get a bit of a bad feeling about Catford, but knew it was only because he was having a problem with his firm. If one or two said yes, it would all suddenly look as good as gold.

The Plough on Clapham Common was a popular lunchtime pub, especially at the weekend when they put on some good food. Maybe it was as popular in the evening, Lynn didn't know as he hadn't used it then. He never came south of the Water to do his drinking, and the only reason he was using the pub now was to meet a villain who might be interested in making the blag. All he ever came to South London for, it seemed, was business.

Alan Parker lived not far from the pub and when he had given him a bell it had seemed the obvious place for a meet. But Lynn wondered if it was such a good idea now, as there was barely room to sit down, much less have a quiet chat. The customers in the bar didn't thin as people rushed away for their Sunday lunch; most of them probably lived in bedsitters or had a late lunch.

'Sorry, pal,' Lynn said to a black customer as he elbowed his way out from a short section of bar while the other man tried to get in. Lynn made his way back to Alan Parker, who was pressed into a corner, and gave him his pint. "S fucking murder, this, in' it.'

'Where else have they got, Jack?' Parker said wisely. He was in his early thirties, was about three inches shorter than Lynn and had a deceptive build. Looking at him people mistakenly thought he couldn't do much, but Lynn knew he could in fact use himself very well. He had an older face than he should have had for his years; it looked almost like he had a brief record in the ring, there were blocks of flesh around his vivid-blue eyes that sometimes developed on boxer's faces. His blond hair was fairly long, but Lynn was prepared to tolerate that, for it was meticulously styled – hair hanging in rats' tails like some of the soapy bastards wore it was what he couldn't stand.

Glancing round, making sure no one was consciously listening to their conversation, Lynn said casually, 'You looking for a bit of work, Alan?' There was no need to qualify it; Parker knew what he did for a living, knew what the work would be. He showed no surprise, even though Lynn had given no indication of what he had in mind when he had phoned him and arranged the meet.

Without any prelusive inquiries, Parker said, 'I don't think so, Jack. I mean, I wouldn't do you no favours getting involved – I'm getting a lot of aggro from the filth on account of some videos I done a couple of weeks ago.'

'Fuck a duck!' Lynn said in dismay. He had been convinced that Alan Parker would have had some of it. 'I thought there was s'posed to be a recession on.'

Parker scoffed disgustedly. 'You wouldn't think so, would you. You try moving a hundred videos and see how you go.' He sipped his drink.

Lynn considered him for a moment, then said, 'I'd take a chance, 'you fancy it?'

'No, I don't think so. I mean, I got Old Bill calling round my place every other day, they worry the life out of me. Just cause

28

you a lot of aggro, Jack. "S all.' He drank some beer. 'You stuck?'

'Can't get no cunt to work with me, can I. You'd think I was a fucking grass or something.'

'And 'Arris is under the bed, sir . . .' Arris is under the bed!' Parker interjected. They both smiled, recalling a joke about the grass who grassed himself. 'Sorry, Jack. I'd like to have had some of it.'

'That's all right.' Lynn swallowed his drink decisively.

The bottom of the list hadn't been reached but it was getting close. Lynn began to wonder about the job, whether the difficulties he was having putting a team together were an indication for him to give it a miss. Such thinking gave an opening to those negative feelings about the blag, feelings he usually responded to. Still he chose to ignore them, push them aside. The blag was going ahead until such time as he had exhausted every possibility of getting a little firm.

The telephone bell was barely audible at the best of times beneath the sound-proof canopy near the bar. Anyone playing on the tables had no chance of hearing it, especially if there was more than one game in progress. Certainly John Tully didn't hear it, and wouldn't have attempted to answer it if he had.

Since the coming of snooker on the TV, Sunday lunchtime was no longer fairly quiet at the snooker hall – nor any other time come to that. There were games in progress on most of the fifteen tables that transversed the badly lit room. Not much light got through the soot-coated opaque windows, and the lamps over the tables were designed to light only the playing area.

'John!' Peter Wright, the man who ran the hall called, bending to look beneath the hood. 'Telephone, son.'

John Tully heard him but didn't respond immediately; he played his shot. He straightened and watched the ball run. It didn't go where he intended it to. 'Fuck it,' he said. He moved along the side of the table, where his opponent Micky Fielder was leaning on his cue, and started toward the phone.

'What's your old lady chasing you for –dinner, John?' Fielder said, and stood off his cue.

'Probably,' Tully said good-naturedly. ''S what comes of being in love, Micky.'

Fielder watched him as he went to the phone, curious to know who it was. There was no way he was going to find out standing there. He turned back to the table and considered the balls. White had been left awkward on the yellow, which was next – there were no reds left. He wasn't snookered, but knew he wasn't good enough to make that shot, not without a little help. Fielder stooped and carefully lined the shot. All he could do was give his opponent an easy shot to come back on. Pausing with the cue poised, he glanced round in Tully's direction, then with the end of his cue pulled the yellow out to an easier position where he could make the shot.

Even though he knew it wasn't possible to make the one Lynn had offered him, John Tully hesitated. Despite what he had going off himself he wanted to say yes to Lynn's. Certainly he'd stand to earn more than he would on his own one, but that fact alone wasn't enough to persuade him to put his own blag back. It was his blag, and that was important to him. The fact that it was worth less than the other one was only a minor consideration. It was his own and he wanted it, and doing the two just wasn't practical.

'Sorry, Jack. I'd like to help you out. But this other one I've got's going off. I mean, I do fancy that one of yourn strong. Sounds like a right good earner.'

'Oh yeah, it should be,' Lynn said down the phone, trying to conceal his disappointment.

'I don't suppose there's any chance it's gonna be put back a bit?'

'No, I wouldn't have thought so, John. It's gotta be done.'

'Yeah, pity that,' Tully said reluctantly, half-tempted by the offer.

'Still, that's the way it goes. Another time, John.'

'You want me to put anyone in touch, I hear of anyone?'
Tully suggested.

'No. Well, you hear of someone tasty. Mind how you go. Be
a bit slippery.'

'Yeah, you too. See you, Jack.' He replaced the 'phone and
ducked out from under the canopy. He paused thoughtfully,
then assured himself that he wanted the blag he was planning
more than Lynn's.

Fielder was meticulously chalking his cue like that was the
object of the game and gave the appearance of not being aware
of Tully's return. 'Oh,' he said when he noticed him, 'I nicked
the yellow, brown and green.'

'Down to me, is it?' He retrieved his cue and considered the
three balls left on the table. 'Not got a lot of chance here, have
I? What's in it, Micky?'

'About six.' Fielder watched him line up the blue. 'D'you
get your marching orders?'

'It was Jack Lynn,' Tully responded conversationally, and
played his stroke, taking blue. 'He has one going off down at
Catford – he's a bit lighthanded.'

'He's a nice fella,' Fielder remarked. 'You having some of
it?'

'Wouldn't mind.' He moved round the table to look at pink.
'I've got enough on my plate. You wanna be put in, Micky?'

'Me? Do I fuck. Not my game, is it, blagging.' Fielder
watched him stoop for pink, but he didn't make it. His
instincts were like antennae when it came to what seemed
worthwhile information going on offer. They were fully
stretched now and probing. What Jack Lynn might be having
sounded interesting and Micky Fielder would endeavour to
get whatever details he could. Information was the stuff by
which he lived. The casual, ingratiating way he had with
people made it quite easy for him to get his living. As a rule
villains would tell one of their own everything and anything,
including the structure of the crap they had that morning.
And Fielder was one of their own.

3

'So I gave her a pull,' the corpulent detective sergeant said, and hitched his trousers which had slid off his large waist. It was a frequent habit and most of the time DS Eric Lethridge wasn't even aware that he was doing it. Lethridge was standing by one of the thirty or so desks placed in lines in the main Squad office. 'Well, we get back to her flat, this place she's using anyway – I mean, a real rat's nest, but you know, you don't care when you got one about sixteen on the firm. 'S all she was, I promise you,' he put in as if to dismiss any doubts. 'So she says, she says, "do you want to make love to me?" just like that. Well, I said, it's either that or I nick you, love.' A smile started across the DS's face in anticipation of the conclusion of the story. 'So it winds up me giving it one. I'm giving it a right seeing to when she says, "Oh, I s'pose I ought to tell you, I'm attending Charlotte Street clinic for this discharge I get" ... ah, it slaughtered me!' As Lethridge reached this point in his story, his awkward hipgrinding movements, resembling those of too large a dog on too small a bitch, ended and he pulled violently back, arching his spine as though withdrawing suddenly from the infected girl.

The audience was very appreciative, exploding with laughter. The four detective constables whose ages ranged from early twenties to mid-thirties, were standing around the desk where one of them, Ray Jenkins, was halfway through typing a report which was getting none of his attention now. They were all part of the night duty relief of the Squad, which was made up of ten separate squads, each employing ten men under a detective inspector.

The Squad office, on the fourth floor of Scotland Yard, was

about forty feet long by twenty wide, and crowded with furniture. The desks, which belonged to no one detective, were littered with typewriters, wire trays, some full of reports, pastel-coloured folders. The huge duty book stood chained to a desk near the door: in it were entered all investigations and movements of detectives. On other tables at the side of the room were telephones; eight more with soundproof canopies were affixed to the wall; also jammed around the walls were metal filing cabinets, which got a lot of use with detectives continuously digging out files for cross-reference when keeping the paperwork moving, or for current searches. The whole area had a desolate, impersonal, neon-lit look, and was relatively deserted now with only the night duty squad on, and that not at full strength. There were only seven men in the office.

A telephone on one of the side tables started ringing, and usually telephones were answered quickly, as invariably a call meant a job away from the hated paperwork. But that evening no one jumped. It wasn't because the DS's story was more important, for not even DC Warren Salter, who was sitting typing a report at a desk quite close to the ringing phone bothered, nor the seventh detective farther along the office with his feet on a desk reading a paperback. Tonight they were all waiting to go on some raids and no one wanted to get involved elsewhere.

Finally when the laughter from the detectives died, Eric Lethridge gave a thin, satisfied smile, and moved across the office to answer the phone.

Glancing at DC Salter as he raised the handset, he said, 'You lazy bastard, couldn't you answer this?'

Salter, who was the only one doing any work, looked up, his fingers continuing to hit the typewriter keys – he realized he had made a typing error and swore. 'Sorry, skip,' he said. 'Didn't hear it.'

'Robbery Squad,' the DS said into the phone and waited through the paypips. 'Sergeant Lethridge.' A voice down the phone asked for his governor. 'You've got the wrong office, old son. You want the detective inspector's office ... I don't think he's in.'

'The thing was,' the man's voice said, 'I was supposed to meet him.'

'Well hang on a minute, I'll go and check.' Lethridge laid the phone down and moved out of the office past the Squad's now deserted radiophone booth, hitching his trousers.

Eric Lethridge was forty years old, large and overweight despite his active existence. Like many detectives he had a tiredness about him that wasn't entirely accounted for by his work routine. He actively pursued women with the dedication that he pursued villains, the former with the exclusive intention of fucking them, though nicking the latter wasn't always his single objective. Despite the hierarchy's edicts concerning detectives and their relationships with the felonry, Lethridge, along with most of his colleagues, still associated with villains: that was the way they kept their ear closest to the ground. He wore a serious, almost permanently disdainful expression on his fleshy face, which only occasionally broke into a smile. He had been a policeman a long while. Having been a detective sergeant for three years he had every expectation of making DI, an expectation that wouldn't be fulfilled. For detectives had to go back into uniform to take promotion then reapply for CID, and returning to uniform, at whatever rank, wasn't a promotion as far as Eric Lethridge was concerned, but most decidedly demotion. No CID chose to go back into the uniform branch. Lethridge had dark, straight, sleeked-down hair, with a high, off-centre parting that made him look a bit like a 50s ad for hair cream. His clothes had an outdated appearance, like he was waiting for fashion to come round again – some of the younger detectives wore more up-to-date clothes, but none exactly stopped the traffic. Separated officially from his wife, Lethridge often found himself at a loose end, even though before their separation he had never diligently gone home. There had always been various reasons not to, such as one to meet somewhere; still were most of the time, only now excuses weren't necessary. Sexually he was very hungry – his appetite for most things was large – and it was said that if it moved Eric Lethridge would stiff it. He took a certain amount of pride in having that said about himself.

Detective inspectors on the Squad worked out of a communal office along the corridor. It was smaller than the main squadroom, with just four double desks to serve the ten DIs who worked out of there at various times during the twenty-four hours – rare indeed would be the time when all the DIs on the Squad were in the office at once and requiring desk-space. Like all the offices on the fourth floor, and most of them in Scotland Yard for that matter, it was cluttered with filing cabinets, and had that impersonal look which offices belonging to no one person invariably had.

Detective inspector John Redvers was the only person there, and he knew he shouldn't have been, but at home instead trying to get ahead on sleep in readiness for later on that night. He was seated at his desk in his hat and overcoat, having been on the point of leaving for the past hour, but allowing himself to be delayed by the backlog of reports he was checking. Scotch in a styrofoam cup stood on the desk close to his hand as compensation for his unsocial hours; the bottle was safely tucked away in the bottom drawer. None of the governors on the Squad objected to the drinking that went on around the offices, but they most certainly would have objected to a bottle of Johnnie Walker left on the desk advertising the fact.

DS Lethridge's large frame filled the open doorway. 'Fred around, guv?' he asked. 'Guv' was how most detectives addressed senior detectives, even when Christian names were more familiar off duty.

'Had one to meet, didn't he. A snout, I think.' Redvers said, lifting his eyes from the report.

'Got him on the 'phone now, I think – thought he might

have popped back.'

'Maybe he's stuck up some old tart somewhere.' Redvers finished the scotch in the cup. 'You want one downstairs, Eric?'

'Aren't you going home?'

Redvers glanced at his watch as though not aware of the time. It was past ten. "S hardly worth it, is it.'

'Let me get a number from chummy. 'S not exactly hectic in there.' Spending an hour or so in the Tank, the policemen's bar on the ground floor, would help relieve the monotony of the night.

Rising with a dismissive laugh that amounted to one note, Redvers said, 'The time the night tour find anything more than their pricks to pull, Eric . . .' It was said without rancour. There was little animosity between the individual squads, certainly none between the one DI Redvers ran and that which Lethridge was on; they worked together too often. 'I'll see you downstairs.'

When Lethridge got back to the phone, whoever had made the call was gone. He dropped the handset back on the rest, and dismissed the call from mind.

4

Underground train meets with grasses were often favoured by the CID, for trains were casual and anonymous and frequently the safest place either party could suggest. People rarely noticed their fellow passengers on the Underground, even though most of the seats were arranged opposite one another; people could have epileptic fits, break a leg, get raped, and most travellers would immediately avert their eyes rather than risk the possibility of getting involved. Occasionally if eye-contact was accidentally made across the aisles eyes were instantly turned away. Who was likely to take any notice of two men casually meeting?

The Circle line was favoured by Detective Inspector Fred Pyle for his meetings; the train passed through St James's Park station, which was only a short walk from the Yard. Like so many of his contemporaries, Pyle avoided unnecessary expenditure of energy, otherwise he'd never have got through the sort of day he all too frequently put in. The only trouble with these meets was, Pyle thought as he waited on the edge of the platform, they weren't always reliable, with the train service being what it was. He checked the time, then glanced along the platform to the opening of the tunnel. The signal at the tunnel behind him showed green, but as every commuter knew from experience that in itself didn't mean much. There was no indication of an approaching train. His eyes moved on to the three other people waiting on the platform, his brain automatically registering details about them. Two were Asians, who weren't together; the third a woman, a secretary he guessed, deciding she had worked late for her boss, then turned down his subsequent offer. He couldn't think why, she didn't have too much going for her, leastwise he wouldn't have bothered. His gaze moved on across the tracks, the prospects were no better over there. He looked up the tunnel again, feeling no inclination to pace out his growing impatience.

At forty-three Fred Pyle had an inclination towards heaviness, due both to the amount of scotch he consumed and the kind of food he ate – snacks at irregular hours were what kept him going, he would grab something and eat it quickly rather than miss altogether, figuring that way he avoided an ulcer. His height of five-eleven helped to carry his extra weight, but his fleshy face and thickening jowls added to the overall impression. He still had all his own hair, a fact which pleased him, especially as some of the younger CID on the Squad had lost half theirs. It was a grey-sand mixture and he wore it short. His clothes, as with his hair, showed he wasn't concerned with current fashion, most of the time he wasn't even aware of it as such; he dressed conservatively, wearing a small knot in his Squad tie, M & S shirts, charcoal or dark blue suits which his wife usually bought for him off the peg from one of the multiple-stores outfitters; he had never dressed as well since following the time on Division when he and another DC had nicked a couple of villains after breaking into an expensive men's outfitters, but the tone of those clothes he had kept for himself had been mute. He wasn't one to brag about what he had earned, but strove constantly to keep a low profile, which for the most part he managed to do. Like most detectives who had been in the job as long as he had, certainly his colleagues on the Squad, his face was often expressionless. It was a trick he had developed over the years, learning to detach himself from emotional involvement. With this came the ability to control his face muscles, especially those around his mouth and eyes. Eyes were the most revealing part of the face, and Pyle overcame betraying his thoughts by perfecting a cold glaze. The fact that he often worked long, exhausting hours helped him to achieve this, but as a result whenever his face did become mobile it was mechanical. Perhaps the most revealing thing about detectives was that they revealed nothing, not good ones. Pyle rarely smiled, apart from at the odd joke or the wry humour of the CID, and then never dropped his guard. When he showed anything resembling feelings, it was probably a ploy to gain advantage with a suspect or witness. He had got married as a young constable to a young WPC, who subsequently resigned, and they stayed married despite the strains the job put on marriages. Their two children, now in their early teens, helped keep them together. If asked he would say he was not unhappily married rather than happily married; it revealed nothing and they weren't planning a divorce. Family had always been forced into the inferior role through his application to work; that wasn't a conscious choice, but simply the way of things, which both parties accepted.

Automatically Pyle checked his watch as the west-bound train burst out of the tunnel. He had been waiting around twenty minutes now, and if his grass wasn't on this train he'd give him a miss and make another meet. Carefully he watched the carriages as the train slowed towards him; it was relatively easy to see whether his party was on board, for the train was almost empty.

Pyle gave no sign of seeing his contact but boarded the leading carriage and walked the length of it to the front, checking out the other four passengers who were zombie-like and showed him no interest. The train had started by the time he reached the grass, who was sitting at the far side of the carriage, which put the door on his left – a simple precaution against anyone springing him. Without greeting him Pyle lowered himself into the empty seat next to Micky Fielder, who by comparison was almost flamboyant. Fielder was about the same age, and had a mop of dark hair, with greying sideboards. He troubled over his appearance; his hair had been sculptured and lacquered. He had on an expensive, dark brown, three-quarter suede coat, which was now looking a little grubby and shiny in places. His lamp-tanned face was very mobile and his eyes darted nervously the whole time.

'Did you miss one, Micky?' the DI asked conversationally. Their meet had been set for as close to ten o'clock as the train passed through St James's Park station.

'They cut a bastard out, didn't they. No fucking sense of responsibility, London Transport.' His disgust was as close as he'd get to an apology.

'I could've been doing something better with my time. Thought you'd blanked me.'

'I wouldn't do that, guv. I tried giving you a bell ...'

Pyle didn't say anything, but watched him. He needed little prompting to tell all he knew, but then compulsive grasses rarely did. Some of them really had to be worked at, all sorts of strokes had to be pulled to get them to impart their information, and sometimes it was only achieved by the most effective pressure, a definite threat to their liberty. Most grasses who worked for the CID did so because of such threats; that was how Fielder fell under Pyle's sphere of influence. He had been nicked for a breaking and bargained for his liberty. Pyle always listened to such propositions, it made no difference to him whether or not villains like Fielder went down. Although he was undoubtedly a part of the criminal fraternity, Micky Fielder enjoyed his alignment with the CID, especially this Squad DI: it gave him a sense of power and immunity – all the while he offered information.

'Picked up a nice little whisper, didn't I? Very nice.' Fielder waited, expecting the DI to acknowledge his efforts. Pyle never responded in that way. 'Ever hear of Jack Lynn? Comes out of Kentish Town.'

The name meant nothing to Fred Pyle even though he was a detective who managed to keep a whole catalogue of villains and their deals in his mind, some stretching back years. 'What's he do, Micky?'

'Armed blags is what I hear – s'posed to be one or two nice little tucks down to him that he didn't go for. He keeps well active. Someone told me he's putting one together now. He's a bit short-handed still, looking to get another couple, he is.'

'You in line?' It was a perverse compliment to which Fielder responded.

'Me, guv? Leave off, I'm not in his class. Robbery's not my line, is it?' He flexed his shoulders, adjusting his coat. 'A bit of screwing does me. You go pulling blags with other villains you wind up being grassed, know what I mean?' Fielder said without being at all aware of the irony.

'What's he putting together? Did you find out?'

"Course... well, I heard a whisper. Supposed to be the Tote down at Catford dogtrack. 'S what I heard. I'd say it was about right.' He believed the source to be sound.

'That's a bit ambitious I'd have thought, Micky – be a nice little taste if they have it off.' He glanced round as the train slowed in the tunnel for a signal, then picked up again.

'Oh, he's a bit near the mark, this guy, guv ...' He saw the DI's look. "S what I heard. He could get it done, this one. You any idea what that could come to, guv? That Tote? It was done once before, just after the war, if you remember. It was worth about thirty grand then.'

Pyle remained purposely unimpressed. That way he extracted the maximum information from the grass. 'In those days though, Micky, they only banked their takings about once a month. Securicor'll collect it now after each meet, regular as clockwork.'

'Well, it's still got to come to a nice few quid,' Fielder said, only slightly deflated.

'When's it supposed to be going off?' Pyle asked.

That question caused the grass to shift uncomfortably in his seat. The reason being that he hadn't got the most vital piece of information for the detective to move with greatest effect – capturing the blaggers bang to rights.

'Ain't got that for you yet, guv. My party didn't give me it.'

"S not a lot of value then, son, is it?' He couldn't conceal his disappointment. 'What d'you think the chances are?'

Immediately responding to the challenge, Fielder said, 'Oh, should be a doddle. Just mean punting around a bit more.

Should be able to get it all right.'

'I'd appreciate that, Micky. Be a nice little earner off the insurance, if we nick them.' There was a pause as the train ran into Victoria Station. Both men watched the doors slide open. Two passengers climbed in at their end of the train but walked up the carriage away from them. When they were underway again and the rattle of wheels on the tracks was almost drowning out their conversation, Pyle said, 'You okay for a bit of dough, are you?'

'Oh yeah,' Fielder promptly replied as though not wanting to impose on their friendship. 'I had it off the other night, didn't I?'

'Pleased to hear it, Micky,' Pyle said casually as if not at all interested in the details. 'Anything worthwhile?'

'Wasn't bad. Tucked this office up over in Putney.' He gave him the location of the breaking. 'A bit of cash and some American X – all unsigned, of course. It was a doddle, they might have put a sign out, know what I mean. I get those travellers' cheques placed it'll have been a right good 'un.' He hesitated and glanced at the detective. 'The thing is, guv, could you do anything with them?'

Pyle considered the question. There was a time when he would have taken them or found a buyer for them, but not any more. American Express travellers' cheques were too much aggravation to mess around with nowadays. But he went through the motions for the grass's benefit. 'What do they come to?'

'There's just on two grands' worth.'

'What were you expecting to earn? A monkey?' That was an optimistic figure; knocking them out for goods rather than cash, a twoer would be more reasonable.

'Wouldn't be bad, would it?' the grass said.

'I'd like to help you out, Micky,' the DI said, his tone extending some kind of hope, even though he had no intention. 'I'll have a word with someone. But mind how you go, if you do them yourself. I don't want to have to drag down to some local nick to spring you. Specially if you haven't dug up anything more for me on this Catford blag.'

Fielder grinned sheepishly at the DI, believing he was joking. He had a lot to learn about Fred Pyle and would never grow old enough to know the half of it.

5

The fourth floor corridor of the main block at Scotland Yard was a seemingly endless neon-lit square tube with a labyrinth of offices off it. Those along the left-hand side belonged to the Squad, and most of their doors remained open as if to invite anyone in. Occasionally the DCS's door would be shut if he was having a meeting that he didn't want advertised; sometimes the two superintendents' door would be closed, but not often. The corresponding doors on the opposite side of the corridor were shut and marked Keep Out, some were even locked. These offices were used by C11, Criminal Intelligence, who were more obsessive than most about guarding their information. Their inquiries frequently went on for months and months before they came up with enough for anyone to move against target villains; after that amount of work it was disheartening to have the suspect given prior warning by some CID earning. It happened.

Fred Pyle stepped from one of the lifts and turned wearily along the corridor. Since leaving his grass earlier he hadn't thought much about the information he had been given; he had been in an after-hours club drinking, hoping to see another villain about something that might have been coming up soon, but the man hadn't been there. Now that he was back at the Yard Jack Lynn was occupying part of his thoughts. Perhaps it was his age, he reflected, or perhaps he had drunk too much scotch since he had come on duty, but night-duty lately was leaving him more and more tired. Possibly it was only the fact that his kids had woken him too early that afternoon. Teenagers, even his, little appreciated that he had to get through the long night and needed sleep.

Turning into the DCIs' office he found it deserted. He

wanted to talk to Tony Simmons about the possible blag at Catford. All the lights were burning in this office, which was about the same size as his own, but with only three single desks, on for each of the DCIs, and more filing cabinets. Also there was more noticeboard space, all of it filled with announcements about vacancies in various constabularies, papal-like edicts from the commissioner, angry memos from different departments about reports or forms or tests sent in incorrectly, wanted posters, circulars – it was a whole week's reading. Dominating the wall to the right of the door was the Squad manpower availability board. Its multicoloured tabs with the name of each member of each of the ten squads showed who was available, and if they weren't on duty, whether they were on holiday, sick leave or loan somewhere.

The DI was unconcerned that the night-duty chief wasn't around: what he had would keep. As he started away the telephone on Simmon's desk rang and the DI answered it.

'Chief inspector's office.' A man down the line asked for the DCI. 'He's just stepped out. Can I take a message?' The caller wanted to know how long he would be. 'Can't say.' Pyle wondered if he was a grass, but doubted it, for DCIs were rarely that active. 'Tell him Terry called.' Pyle replaced the 'phone and scribbled the message on the pad along with the time, two-twenty.

In the Squad office there were now more detectives besides the night-duty squad. Men on John Redvers's squad were creeping in like somnambulists having reluctantly stirred from their slumbers, especially to assist the night-duty squad with Method Index raids. The eleven men so far present weren't particularly busy; only three were, taking the opportunity during this lull to catch up on some paperwork. All of them had paperwork outstanding, but that was something to be put off to the very last moment: most of them sat around talking or reading paperbacks, or wisely slept, employing the trick that most CID developed of sleeping sitting upright in a chair.

'Haven't any of you got homes to go to?' Pyle said as he passed a group of four detectives on his squad.

'Chance'd be a nice thing, guv,' DC Ray Jenkins replied. It was a familiar complaint.

'Well,' Pyle said in a friendly, dismissive tone, 'you'd only sleep, or give the old lady some,' – what they were currently doing was far more worthwhile.

The obliqueness of the DI's remark was neither lost on his men nor resented. He could make such remarks simply because whatever was their lot was his too. He continued along the office to where Jack Barcy, the second DS on his squad, was at a desk aggressively hammering out a report on a typewriter.

Jack Barcy would rather have been hammering a statement out of a suspect. He was tall, lean, hungry-looking, with cold, emotionless eyes. There was no doubt about the position he held on the squad, he was the violence specialist, always ready to give stick to any villain or witness who didn't respond the way he wanted them to. Paperwork for him more than any other detective in the entire Metropolitan CID was something to put off.

'Found your true vocation finally, Jack?' Pyle inquired with open mockery.

Barcy scowled as his fingers continued to smash down on the keys. He slammed the carriage along like he was trying to break the typewriter. Because of his poor application to paperwork Barcy was never going to rise above his present rank, and he was aware of this. It was only through better than average results that he held onto his place in the Squad. A lot of CID had been transferred out for much less than Barcy got away with.

'Where's the duty chief?' Pyle asked. 'He out?' The DI assumed he was from what the man had said in The Feathers earlier that evening, but imagined he would have been back by now.

'I think he popped over the Middlesex Hospital. Giving a

nurse one, isn't he?' It was no secret.

Automatically Pyle glanced at the clock on the wall. 'That probably means a late start on these raids.'

'What you got one to meet then, guv?' Barcy asked, now leaning back in his chair.

'Me? I'm a respectable married man, Jack.'

'You say your prayers too, don't you?'

'I've got to get promotion somehow, son.' A smile appeared briefly. 'D'he say what time he'd be back?'

'Not to me he didn't.'

'Couple of hours sleep before court tomorrow would be handy.' That wasn't a prospect if they didn't make their raids as planned. 'There's an active party called Lynn. Jack Lynn, with a double "n", I think. He's a blagger out of Kentish Town. Have one of the lads slip down to the third floor and draw his CRO file, will you? I'm going to get my head down for an hour or so.'

Barcy watched his governor move away, then glanced about the room for someone to send on the errand.

Behind the wheel of the large grey Ford Granada the Squad driver dozed uncomfortably. He was a police constable out of uniform assigned to the Squad, and despite the fact that driving was all he did, and had done for years, he still hadn't got used to sleeping in cars. He was parked along the road from the entrance of York House in Berners Street, which was one of the Middlesex Hospital's nurses' homes. His governor had said he would be out at two o'clock, but was probably down for second helpings. The r/t set fixed just below the dashboard was switched on, but was barely audible; it crackled with static and odd snatches of messages of no interest to the driver.

There wasn't much going on. Apart from the odd taxi that juddered by the morning was quiet.

The driver woke with a start as two nurses wrapped in their cloaks crossed the road in front of the car. He stretched and watched them let themselves into the building with a key. One of them was black, the other was plump. He liked plump women with heavy thighs. Idle thoughts of pursuing nurses with fat legs slid away and he checked the time, but didn't stir. He was a driver and had to be ready to drive at any given moment. A hotdog vendor went by, pushing his rattling cart, doubtless heading across Oxford Street for Soho where he would find more prospective customers at that time of morning. The driver wouldn't have minded a hotdog but thoughts of food disappeared with the soapy-looking vendor.

After a while the door of the nurses' home was unlocked and DCI Tony Simmons appeared in the lighted vestibule with a young woman in a plaid dressing-gown. He gave her a perfunctory kiss goodbye as she let him out, like he was embarrassed or didn't want to be seen.

Simmons, who was in his mid-forties, wasn't noticeably or more fashionably dressed than his subordinates. He was tall and balding and had a slight stoop as if trying to disguise his height. He wore an expression of faint disapproval, even his smile invariably seemed to be deprecating.

The driver grinned collusively as the DCI climbed into the car next to him. Simmons glanced at the man but didn't look back towards the nurse, who waited in the doorway.

'I didn't say a word, guv,' the driver apologized.

'Let's get back, Charlie. We've a heavy morning.'

The car started away along Berners Street. Still the detective didn't glance towards the woman or give any indication that he was even aware of her.

6

Twenty detectives were crammed into the DIs' office; they had all drifted along there for the briefing because that was where DIs Pyle and Redvers were, when it would have been far more convenient to have briefed them in the Squad office. They were divided into four squads, as they were to raid four separate addresses, though in that confined space it was difficult to tell who was with who.

'There's a bit of bustlebunching going on here,' Ian Middlewick, a DS from Redvers's squad, who was leading one of the raids, had said humorously. Pyle, Lethridge and John Redvers were leading the other three raids. The briefing, like most at this level was informal; it was Pyle's operation so he did it.

'It starts to get light around a quarter to six, for the benefit of those who aren't usually awake at that time,' Pyle said. 'So we'll be hitting these addresses simultaneously at around five thirty. There'll be little chance of resistance at that time, I wouldn't have thought.'

'Well, what if one of them's got up for a leak, guv?' Warren Salter asked with a grin. The DC was young and heavy with thick sideboards and more than enough to say for himself.

'I suppose that might conceivably be armed resistance,' DCI Simmons put in. 'You could nick him for that.'

'But make sure he has it in his hand,' Pyle added in the same vein. There were amused chuckles from some of the detectives who felt more loyalty to the DI than the DCI. 'John, you're liaising with the DI over at Paddington. Frank Polden's his name.'

'They going out with us?' Redvers wanted to know. That was the usual procedure with visits on a divisional DI's

49

manor. Although the Squad had carte blanche to go where they wanted and had right of veto, courtesy dictated that they cleared such moves with the local DI, unless there was reason for not doing so.

'I don't think he's very concerned, John. He might expect to send someone along,' Pyle said. Then turning to DS Middlewick, 'Ian, Paddy Kennedy over at Acton'll hold your hand. Our two are both over at Holloway,' he said in the general direction of Eric Lethridge, even though he had been in on every stage of planning the raids.

'The DI out there's not a bad sort,' Simmons said. Holloway had been his own sub-division before coming to the Yard.

'What's this then,' Redvers asked, 'a bit of favouritism?'

'Well, your squad has gone and drawn the easy ones to nick,' Pyle countered. 'Oh, what channel are we on?'

'Channel six,' Lethridge informed them hitching his trousers onto his stomach.

'Remember,' Simmons said, 'this is only a Method Index raid. There is no guarantee that any of these four were involved on the blag last week.' That said, the DCI added, 'But of course they are all villains, so you don't have to be too polite.'

Villains had no rights at all when raided. They were targeted from information in the Method Index files, which relates to the type of crime that had been committed; the files were searched for the most likely candidates, preferably with some connection to the others, however tenuous. The Squad hadn't found the connection between these four villains but each was individually the most likely candidate.

As the assembly of CID began to disperse, DC Roger Humphries, who was the newest recruit to Pyle's squad, approached the DI. 'Guv, 's it all right if I take my own car up to Holloway – I've got that one at Watford magistrates' court in the morning. I could shoot straight off then, if that's all right?'

'Yeah. That's okay, Roger,' Pyle said. Most detectives wouldn't have asked.

"'S that something I didn't see?' Simmons wanted to know.

'From when I was on division, guv. The suspect's only just got out of hospital.'

The DCI accepted his information with a nod. 'Shouldn't hit them so hard.'

'Leave your car at the nick, Rog',' Pyle said, seeing that the young detective wasn't certain whether the night-duty chief with his deprecatory expression was serious or not.

After dismissing the DC, Pyle turned to his desk by which he was standing and picked up a pastel-coloured foolscap file, which he handed to Simmons. 'There's something a snout gave me earlier. Jack Lynn. He looks like he might be a worthwhile suspect. He's supposed to have one coming off down at Catford.' He gave the DCI the details as he glanced through the CRO file. It was thick and well established.

'He's not been idle, has he?' Simmons said.

'From what I hear there ought to be a few more down there. We missed him on a couple.'

'One of your regular grasses, Fred?' The DCI was weighing up the prospects.

Pyle nodded. 'A right good 'un an' all.' He watched the man as he read on briefly, then decisively shut the folder.

'Okay. Start a file on it, Fred. See if we can't get something on him this time. He looks as if he might be due.'

'Overdue, I'd say, guv,' Pyle said emphatically.

It was Lynn's turn to go. He didn't know the man personally, but even from the limited information he had gathered since talking to his grass there was no doubt in his mind that it was the felon's turn. Such moves were almost like a game the CID played with the felonry, both parties being aware that sooner or later the spotlight of police attention would swing in their direction. Each felon strove constantly to make it later rather than sooner when all manner of ploys were tried: other bodies might be traded, more worthwhile crimes,

51

or simply money on the table. But occasionally when the CID decided it was someone's turn none of those would do – a decision often arrived at arbitrarily, sometimes out of anger or disgust with the crime or manner in which it had been committed, or sometimes mere perversity. Whatever the reason prompting the CID's actions, at the bottom of the line there was always a clear-up rate, which they strove to keep as high as was reasonably expected. Within the general rate detectives were obliged to keep their own numbers up and justify their existence, especially those on the Squad. Fred Pyle had no problems. Jack Lynn would go, he had no doubts about that.

As far as anyone knew none of the villains they expected to find at the addresses they were going to raid would be armed, so the detectives weren't issued with guns. But what they did take along on such raids were a number of baseball bats and saw-down snooker cues. They would give the CID the advantage which their numbers might not if any of their raids turned into a roughhouse. DC Peter Fenton, who was in his early thirties, and not averse to putting some stick about, emerged from the Squad office with a bundle of bats and cue ends badly wrapped in brown paper. Other detectives were collecting last-minute things such as coats, briefcases – they didn't expect to return to the Yard on this tour of duty. Fred Pyle moved out of the office and along the corridor after them. John Redvers fell in step alongside him.

'What's the DI like out at Paddington, Fred?' Redvers asked. 'Frank Polden, isn't it? You know him?'

'Yeah. Lazy bastard, you won't have any trouble with him at this time of the morning.'

'Pity. Thought perhaps we could leave it all down to him.' They stepped into a lift that a DC held.

The DI at Holloway was waiting for the arrival of the Squad, as were the night relief and a number of detectives from the previous relief. The local governor, DI Bartman, was amenable and didn't protest when Pyle told him he

52

wouldn't need his lads. He simply said. 'Pleased to hear it. Most of them have had a long day.' He told his DS to send home those who had stayed behind. With Pyle and DS Lethridge he went through the details of the target addresses, but told them nothing about the location that they couldn't have got from the area map.

The address which Pyle was raiding was in Nicholay Road, a street of Victorian terraced houses built for the lower middle classes, tradesmen who aspired to neighbouring Hampstead but couldn't quite make it. The houses all had a sameness with their tiny front gardens, where motorbikes or broken cars were lodged behind bits of shrubbery, their crumbling façades, windows hung with net curtains; Habitat couples were moving into the street but their influence passed barely noticed beneath the harsh sodium street lighting.

Parked without lights like all the other cars in the street was a blue Cortina 2.0. All that distinguished this in the line of other vehicles were the four policemen sitting in it. This was the car DI Pyle had at his disposal most of the time he was on duty. In the car with him were two DCs and his regular driver. They had a couple of minutes in hand before the hour that the raids had been synchronized for; it was unlikely that a minute or two either way would make much difference, but on some raids it could, so they waited. On the ledge under the rear window some of the baseball bats lay, though none of the CID believed they'd have much need of them here. There was no conversation in the car. Earlier there had been an animated conversation between the two DCs and the driver about a case of a dentist who'd been stiffing his patients when anaesthetizing them. His nurse had been involved also. Finally they had agreed that the *News of the World* probably employed writers who made up such cases week after week.

Pyle glanced at his watch. It was twenty-eight minutes past five and it hadn't started to get light yet. 'Give us that, Frank,' he said to the driver, reaching across the front seat for the r/t handset. Then into the 'phone he said, 'You awake back there?'

'Just about,' Jack Barcy replied after a moment. Exchanges on the air between detectives on the Squad were casual; they had all but forgotten the formal procedure. 'So quiet you'd think no one was at it.' His glance swept the backs of the houses from where his car was parked by the playground of Scholefield Road school.

'About two minutes, I reckon, Jack.' Pyle stared down the road towards the house they were going to raid. Suddenly the lights in the street popped out as they did a little before dawn, then the first glimmer in the eastern sky was noticeable. 'Okay, we're going in now.' He handed the phone to the driver who would stay with the car. Pyle and the other two detectives climbed out.

They walked abreast at an unhurried pace across the road and down to the house, which was in total darkness. They moved up the short path and steps, three sinister early morning callers. Pyle hammered the door-knocker, then stabbed the bell push shattering the morning stillness. Before the noise had died the Squad car had swept across the road and stopped at the gate.

In the main front bedroom of the house a man started awake. It was neither that nor the noise at the door which woke the woman next to him, but their baby who cried immediately afterwards. That was the sound her ears were tuned to. The baby was only five months and demanded a lot of attention.

Somewhere along the street a dog barked.

The doorbell went again. A long, insistent ring that demanded an answer. The man sprang out of bed in his vest and underpants and crept to the window. There were only two sorts of people who'd come visiting at this hour of the morning. One might be villains calling to kneecap him as a punishment but he had nothing like that due; the others were the police. He had no real need to go the window to confirm this. The doorbell went again, then the hammering. They'd crash the door if he didn't open it. His mind was coming slowly awake, trying to find a solution.

The baby was wailing now.

'What is it, Cliff?' the woman in bed asked. 'Russ'll never go back to sleep now,' she informed him irritably. Soon he'd wake the other kids.

'I think it's the filth,' he told her. 'Turning us over.'

'Jesus Christ, won't they ever leave you alone?' She sounded bitter.

'Oh, fucking hell,' he said less calmly, fully awake and realizing the consequences of the raid. That was the worst possible moment they could have chosen, and as he stepped into his trousers to go downstairs, Clifford Harding wondered if he had been grassed. There were more than enough about.

'Took your time, son, didn't you?' Pyle said, pushing straight on into the hall, followed by the other detectives. 'Thought perhaps you were going to try legging it. Heavy night?'

'Here, look, what is this?' Harding said. He was an active villain; they were detectives, and he knew there was no real point in protesting. It would gain him nothing.

'All right,' Pyle said to the other detectives. 'Let's make it thorough. Give Jack and the others a shout, get them in.'

'Look, you got a warrant, have you? Coming here upsetting my family this time of morning. You're well out of order.'

Pyle looked at him, then nodded calmly. 'Keep it up, son, and you'll get plenty of stick.'

Harding could see the detective meant business. This wasn't local filth and he knew he'd have to be especially wary because of it. He was in trouble and saw no immediate way out. Russell, his youngest kid, was screaming his head off upstairs like he realized the danger, and Harding could hear the other three awake also, their mother trying to reassure them. His thoughts leaped on to the outcome of this raid and what it might mean to his family, and suddenly Clifford Harding was very frightened. He watched three more detectives troop in through the kitchen. Their appearance did nothing to reassure him of his future or that of his family.

Not a mile away in a similar street DS Lethridge carried out his raid in much the same manner, only the suspect Terry Clark wasn't so obliging as to open the door, and they had to crash it open. But not before the villain had legged it. He took flight at the first knock. Leaping out of bed and sweeping his clothes into his arms, he went through the bedroom window and down over the corrugated roof of a lean-to immediately below, moving as fast and as silently as he could. The two detectives positioned at the rear of the house watched, and smiled as he came barefoot along the garden path, hopping painfully as stones dug into his feet. The detectives had difficulty preventing themselves laughing when Terry Clark clambered up on the garden fence. It was then he saw them; panic enveloped him and he hung there undecided before trying to go back the way he came. He left that decision too late. The detectives reached up and pulled him down.

'What's this, a bit of sleepwalking, Terry?' DC Salter said dryly.

'What ...? Fucking hell! What's it about!' It wasn't a question.

There was an air of desperation in his words, but his actions reflected greater desperation, he threw a punch in a defiant bid for freedom. The blow connected badly, catching Warren Salter in the ribs but didn't even sting through his layers of clothing. It was the wrong move. Although Clark was solid and muscular, he was short and no match for the two detectives as they retaliated. Salter threw a couple of short jabs, and when Clark tried to resist and prevent a beating, DC Jenkins put a couple in from the other side. Clark cowered, trying to protect himself.

'All right, leave off!'

'Stand up then. What's the matter with you?' Salter said, bringing his knee into the man's groin. 'Stop resisting, will you?' There was no longer any resistance. 'Leave it out, we're police officers.' He hit the man again.

Along with the other lights that began to appear at the rear of the terrace, there was one at Clark's bedroom window, and DS Lethridge stuck his head out.

'He's scarpered,' he called. 'D'you see anything of him?'

'Yes. We've got him, skip,' Jenkins shouted. 'Stay there, we'll fetch him up.'

Terry Clark was a villain and regardless of whether or not the Squad established that he had any connection with the robbery they were investigating, his immediate prospects were no better than those of Clifford Harding.

The detectives went through Clifford Harding's house very thoroughly, though not very tidily. Carpets were taken up, some floorboards too, loose skirting boards removed, cupboards emptied, even dismantled, anything and everything that looked like it could hide something, anything; money most likely, part of the proceeds of the robbery that had taken place at Barclay's Bank in Walthamstow last week as Securicor was collecting money from the branch. One of the guards had been beaten severely when he had refused to part with the sack. Forty thousand pounds had been blagged that morning, all in old unrecorded notes, none of which had been recovered. The local CID had got nowhere with their initial investigation, and the Squad's subsequent involvement hadn't pushed it much further ahead. The only positive development to date had been the injured guard coming off the danger list.

Pyle stood in the living room, where he provisionally questioned Harding about his suspected involvement in the blag, and watched dispassionately as the house was systematically taken apart.

The villain who had dressed in anticipation of being taken in was less than dispassionate, but totally impotent. As something broke or was spilled he would say, 'Look, for fucksake. Tell 'em to leave off, will you?'

The man's protests were limp compared to his wife's, who followed the detectives around the upstairs part of the house, clutching her youngest child as she hurled abuse at the men. 'You no-good bastards!' she protested. 'Coming here upsetting my children. You lousy sods, I'll swing for you bastards.' The only peace the CID got from her was when she went to comfort her other kids.

The orange and purple carpeting in the hall was taken up, but nothing found. The CID didn't replace it, but simply moved on.

Harding watched in utter dismay. 'Look at that fucking mess.' He resumed an earlier tack. 'You haven't got a warrant, I know you haven't,' – as though believing it would gain him something.

'Don't be silly, Clifford,' Pyle said in a reasonable manner. 'You don't think we'd take a liberty like that and search without one, do you?' It was a standard reply, regardless of whether or not they had a search warrant; here it was mocking. They had warrants for all four raids this morning. He paused and measured the suspect. Harding was thin-framed, with round shoulders and a bad posture. He was about the same age as himself, Pyle guessed, though there the similarity ended, apart from that one between most CID and villains. Often it was chance, a quirk of fate that put a villain on one side, the CID on the other; basically they weren't so very different when they started out as kids. Some of them, like Pyle, scraped through without getting themselves nicked or taken before the courts, others weren't so lucky. Perhaps that was how it had been with Harding, but it wasn't really of much interest to Pyle one way or the other now.

'Of course,' he said, 'You could save yourself all this aggravation ...'

'I already told you. I weren't nowhere near Walthamstow last week.'

''Course you weren't. Your alibi sounds terrific,' Pyle said sarcastically.

'Guv!' There was excitement in DC Fenton's tone as he came in. The reason was the shooter he had found.

'Handle it carefully, son,' Pyle cautioned, finding a felt-tip pen and pushing it down the barrel to take hold. 'We'll want his fingerprints off it or his brief'll get up in court and say we planted it, 's a million. Where was it?'

'The cupboard under the sink. Beneath the floorboards there.'

A humourless smile parted Pyle's lips when he turned back to Harding. 'This is it, I'd say. Wouldn't you, son?'

The villain didn't say anything. There was nothing to say then. The gun made him bang to rights.

7

The compound in Holloway police station, formed by the surrounding buildings, was deserted. Two sodium arc lamps fixed up on the building spread patches of light and shadow across the area. The place was still except for a Panda car parked with its lights on and static issuing from the radio. After a while a uniformed policeman, who had all too recently put on more weight than his uniform wanted to accommodate, emerged unhurriedly from the building, letting the door bang. He went across to the Panda car, not particularly interested in the blue Ford Cortina that turned into the yard. He was aware that the Squad was visiting, but their presence wouldn't affect him, unless to run errands for them, so he was making sure he wasn't around; he was on a promise from a widow who he had paid a visit to after a disturbance a couple of nights ago.

In the back of Pyle's car Clifford Harding, like most villains at this point, was facing his moment of truth, living his biggest regret. If only he could have turned the clock back. Although the process he was going through was illogical, impractical, impossible, there was no way he could prevent it. The shooter had been found at his house, he was bang to rights, a million to do a nice piece down the road. He had been nicked this time even before he had it off. That hurt.

But once he was over this initial feeling he would begin to think more practically, try and find some solution. Maybe there was a way out. Maybe there wasn't. Something had to be tried.

The car stopped outside the rear exit to the old brick-built Victorian police station. Pyle climbed out, and leaving the other two detectives to bring the prisoner, moved the short ramp into the station.

The interior of the nick was as seedy as the exterior suggested, two of the traditional colours of green and cream prevailing and badly in need of repainting at that. The furniture, what there was of it in the back reception area, had seen a lot of service. The overall impression was enough to depress those who worked there, had they had any time to spare to be concerned about their surroundings or sufficient sensitivity left, in fact, to be affected by them. Necessary overtime, now officially cut to only sixty hours a week, still tended to leave policemen dulled to the finer needs of existence.

Pyle went in through the back reception to the charge room, which was narrow with a high ceiling and no windows. There was little furniture; a tall charge desk stood in the centre of the room like an obelisk in honour of some distant epoch, while opposite was a long bench fixed to a wall. There was nothing that could have been picked up and used as a weapon by a suspect.

The two DCs followed with Harding.

'Sit down,' Pyle said over his shoulder, indicating the bench. 'It's going to be a long night.'

Harding didn't move. 'I want to call my brief,' he said calmly, as though believing he had some kind of rights.

When he lifted his head to speak, his face catching the light, Pyle noticed how gaunt he was, how prominent his bones were. They were the kind on which sparse flesh opened easily when struck.

'You're going to need more than a solicitor, son. A miracle's what you need to help you out.'

Still the suspect remained standing, as if to challenge the detective's statement.

'Sit down,' DC Fenton said, putting his hand on the villain's shoulder. Harding didn't argue.

'Slip up and find the DI, Roger. Tell him we're here.' Pyle moved off across to the duty sergeant's office. It was one of several doors beyond the charge room. His going to see him was more than mere courtesy, the sergeant was the duty officer and ran the station at that time of night. Everything that went on there he was supposed to know about. 'Have you got a minute, skip?'

The duty sergeant climbed out of his comfortable chair; he was a man who had gone pear-shaped with too much sitting around, his biggest activity nowadays was shifting paperwork from one basket to another. 'Morning, sir,' the uniform said. 'Your lads got here a short while ago. They're in the cells.'

Pyle didn't acknowledge the information. He had had word from DS Lethridge earlier about their nicking. 'Got another one spare, have you?'

'You can take your pick,' the uniform said with an apologetic smile. 'We've only a couple of drunks in. We can soon throw them out. Save giving them breakfast.'

'An interview room'll do for now.'

The duty sergeant indicated a door at the side of the large room, it opened into a windowless cubicle about eight feet square. There were two such rooms, one either side of the corridor that led down to the cells. Both were painted in dark green and had a scarred table and two straightback chairs.

'That'll do fine. Come on, son,' the D.I. said to Harding, who was now encouraged to rise by DC Fenton.

The local DI appeared from the back reception with Humphries. He glanced at Harding as he was taken into the interview room. He had stayed on, but wasn't sure why. 'A busy morning,' Bartman commented.

Pyle was seen to protest. 'I won't be sliding off to bed in a hurry.'

'He the one with the shooter?'

'Under the sink.' There was a smile on Pyle's face. Some of the hiding places villains used often amused him.

'They get a fucking sight sillier, I swear they do.' Bartman shook his head. There was a pause. These two men had little to say to one another; one wanted to go home, the other wanted to get on with the job he was there for. 'Wasn't anything else you needed us around for, was there?'

'I don't think so. Thanks for your help.'

That slightly embarrassed the local DI. 'Well, make yourself at home – use my office if you want. Most of the night relief are upstairs if you need any of them. I s'pect I'll see you around sometime tomorrow.'

'I expect so,' Pyle said and moved off towards the interview room.

Before departing Bartman said to the duty sergeant, 'I'll be in late tomorrow, Wilf. Anyone wants me, tell them I've got one in court.' It meant he could lie in till lunchtime.

'What about that brief?' Harding said to the DI as he came in. He might have been promised his solicitor. 'I'm supposed to be allowed a 'phone call.'

Pyle looked at him for a moment. 'Who told you that? It's a fairy story. You've no such right, Clifford. You're a million, you were caught bang to rights. Weren't you just.' It wasn't a question. 'Sit down, son.' The felon remained standing. 'We'd better understand each other,' Pyle warned him, 'it'll save a lot of aggravation, I promise you. Whatever favours you get now, son, are because I want to give you them, and for no other reason. So sit down like you're told, and we'll see how you shape.' Still Harding hesitated, but finally he sat. 'That's it. Now in order for us to progress in the fastest and easiest manner possible, there's certain information I want from you, son. Like your whereabouts last Monday week. Who you were with on that blag, who had the dough off you, and where you got that shooter from.'

Harding's mouth fell open in amazement. 'Oh, is that all?' he asked sarcastically.

Pyle surprised him when he slowly shook his head. 'That's just the start. I'm going to know a hell of a lot more about you and that blag before we're through. I'm going down the cells to see your mate now ...'

'What mate?' Harding interjected.

Pyle smiled tolerantly. 'You're going to have a little chat with these lads. When I come back I'll expect some answers. Right.' Harding simply looked at the DI. 'You'd better know it's right, son.'

Pyle glanced at DCs Fenton and Humphries: the look might have given them the licence to give the suspect whatever treatment they saw fit. Although there was no certainty that he had been connected with the armed blag at Walthamstow last week, the gun they had found at his house indicated that he was heavily involved in something, so information about that would do instead of Walthamstow; however, the assumption that he had taken part in the blag was a good enough starting point.

Terry Clark, the villain who Lethridge had picked up, was still in his underpants when Pyle pulled open the door. He was sitting on the edge of the shelf bunk in the bleak brick cell, which measured twelve feet by six. There was a flushing toilet in the corner at the end of the bunk and a barred window high in the end wall opposite the door, but nothing else, apart from the chair which Lethridge was sitting on. DC Jenkins was leaning against the wall, another DC, Brian Neal, was sitting on the bunk near Clark.

Pyle's arrival made the cell crowded. He sniffed the stale air, the dominant smells were disinfectant and the wc which probably didn't flush efficiently.

'Well, don't look at me, guv,' DC Jenkins said, as if being accused of causing the smell.

'How's it going, Eric?'

'Usual old story. Don't know nothing,' Lethridge said mockingly. 'Do you, Terry?'

'Fucking right I don't. What about my fucking clothes? Sitting around like this in this fucking pisshole. I'll catch m' death of cold.'

'They were your choice of going away clothes, weren't they?' Lethridge said. 'Running down the garden like that.'

'Going to pop into one of the neighbours, were you, son?'

From the end of the bunk Pyle lifted a folded blanket, which smelled of disinfectant, and offered it at arm's length to the prisoner. 'There you are.'

'Piss off! I ain't putting that soapy thing around me.' He flexed his shoulders as if to menace Pyle.

There was an arrogance about this man that Pyle didn't care for. His manner wasn't merely defensive, like that Clifford Harding had adopted, but aggressive. The DI thought this suspect might come in for a bit of stick before they got what they wanted from him. Perhaps he didn't have what they wanted, but still he would get the treatment if he wasn't very careful.

'Suit yourself,' Pyle said and let the blanket drop. 'Can't say I blame you. Wouldn't be so bad if they were washed after some of those drunks were through vomiting over them. So what about this blag then, Terry?' Pyle's tone was reasonable and stayed that way, even when he was putting pressure on villains. 'D'you want to put your hands up to it? Save a lot of trouble.'

'Some fucking chance, I should think.'

'All right, let's do it step by step. Where were you the Monday before last?' Pyle asked.

'That was a long time ago, I have a short memory.' There was a smile on Clark's face.

Pyle regarded the young man for a moment, then glanced at Brian Neal, who was a large-framed detective with a bright red beard. There was an implicit threat in the gesture. ''He gives you a couple of rabbit punches he might jog your memory a little.'

'It'd fucking well need about four of you an' all.'

'He's a hard man all right, guv,' Lethridge said.

'Or just thick. Can't even remember what he did eight days ago.'

Clark adopted a thoughtful pose. 'Oh yes, I remember now. I was with my solicitor. Why don't you give him a bell and ask him?' He smiled again, like he had said something clever.

'I'd say you'd better have another think about that, son.' Pyle's tone was unyielding. 'I'd say you were over at Walthamstow tucking up that bank.'

'Not me, pal. Not my game, is it. Ask your mate.'

'You'll do all right,' Lethridge said, as if going back on some former agreement. 'Your alibi's not worth a rub, and you know it.'

'I got no worries. All you done is give me a pull on my form. What d'you think, I'm up from the country?'

'It's a bit more scientific than that, Terry,' Pyle told him, feeling certain in his mind that they'd find something for this flash bastard, even if it wasn't the Walthamstow blag. 'Not much, I grant you, but a bit.'

'Oh yeah? Well I don't fancy your chances when my brief gets to work.'

A note of mocking laughter parted the DI's lips. 'He must find your faith in him very touching. You cunt, you *sound* like you're up from the sticks. You'll be weighed off almost before you even get to see your brief. Who is it he wants, Eric?'

'Gladwell, guv,' Lethridge informed him. 'He's supposed to be well bent.'

"S what I heard. Even less of a problem then, especially if we work him on the list before someone like Morgan-Stevas. I mean, he's tried so many strokes, he's about lost all his credibility, especially with that judge.'

Terry Clark smiled, trying to prevent his confidence becoming too brittle. 'You can't do that.'

Pyle didn't bother enlightening him, but there was nothing easier than making sure a villain went in the lists before a certain judge if that judge's known bias was likely to favour the detective's case, all it needed was the DI to have a quiet word with the clerk of the lists. Judges themselves had their clerks juggle the lists when they wanted to try a certain case where they could vent their bile, just as defence lawyers pulled strokes in court in order to get their clients off certain judges' lists.

'It might sound all right when Gladwell gets up in court and slags us off, Terry,' Pyle said, 'but when it comes right down to it, son, it only impresses villains. You add up his results, see if you find them quite as impressive.'

Doubt entered the villain. He flexed his shoulders as if to dispel it. 'I'll take my chances.'

'You really could save us a lot of time and effort,' Pyle said. 'You won't find us unappreciative. We've got homes to go to. You think these lads don't want to go home rather than fuck around here until you crack?'

'They don't mind, guv,' Lethridge put in. 'Looking forward to a couple of days away from home.'

'You gonna call him for me or what?'

The four detectives merely looked at Clark.

'I want to know how long I'm going to be kept here.'

'I told you, until we crack you,' Pyle leaned in closer to the man, an air of quiet menace in the gesture. 'As far as anyone out there's concerned you don't exist anymore. Not until we say you do.'

'Leave off, I know my rights. You can't keep me here indefinitely.' There was an edge of anxiety in Clark's voice. He had had enough experience of the CID to know what they could do and get away with.

'This is the Squad that's nicked you, Terry, not some silly woodentops. You pulled a right stroke with that security guard, you wicked bastard. So don't whine to us about your fucking rights, because you haven't got any. Not now you've been nicked by us. What you've got, son, is information we want, and you'll stay tucked up here assisting with our inquiries for as long as it takes to get it.'

'Yeah. We'll see about that,' Clark said, and flexed his shoulders again in an instinctive, defensive action. 'Don't cost me nothing sitting here ...'

'Then stand up!' Without warning and without anger Pyle's hand shot out and seized Clark's genitals. As he pulled him up Clark was compelled to rise in order to alleviate the sudden, crushing pain. Rising, however, didn't relieve much of the pain or prevent him crying out.

'What's that, painful, Terry?' Lethridge inquired soliciously.

Clark clawed tensely at the air, resisting pounding the detective who was responsible for his suffering. There were four of them and no sound would escape from the cell, and certainly there was no one to take any notice. Even in his suffering the villain remained aware of his position and wasn't taking any chances.

'Ah, leave off, for fucksake. Leave off, you bastard ...'

'Oh now that's not nice, Terry, is it,' Pyle said. 'I'm not a bastard, am I, Eric?'

"Course not, guv. You've impeccable credentials. You're a policeman. He should show you the sort of respect that's accorded your office ...' All the while the felon was having his balls squeezed.

'About right.'

'Le' go, will you ... Le' go ... fuck you ...'

'That's not respectful, Terry. Let's have a little respect.'

There was a sharp rap at the cell door, and a uniformed constable pulled it open. He waited.

Clark finally cracked. 'Please,' he said in as polite a tone as he could muster.

Releasing him, the DI turned to the uniform. 'Inspector Redvers is on the 'phone for you, sir.'

'Good luck.' Pyle turned back to the felon, who had sunk back to the edge of the bed and was holding his bruised balls, protecting them from further assault. Pyle watched him for a moment. 'I think you'll find you've a lot to say to us, son.'

He went out leaving the interrogation in DS Lethridge's capable hands.

8

Activity wasn't exactly brisk in the front office where Pyle went to the telephone, nor was it likely to be until the six-to-two relief came on, and the DI doubted it would do much then. N division wasn't anything like the busiest in the Met. There were just two policemen present, besides the lad that had brought him to the 'phone, one of them being the duty sergeant; Pyle would have bet money on their drinking tea.

'John,' Pyle said, picking up the handset. 'How did it go?'

'Nothing doing.' The detective inspector on the other end of the 'phone sounded disgruntled. 'The bastard had skipped. He wasn't long gone though. I reckon he must have got a bell from someone down here.' He was at Paddington police station.

'Yeah, could be.' Pyle was unconcerned; the prospect wasn't worth expending unnecessary energy on, no matter what the potential value of the suspect. There was nothing he could do about it now. 'How'd the other fella go?'

'They got him all right,' Redvers said. 'I'm on my way up there to see how he shapes. What about that end? Any good?'

'We claimed them both.' He told him about Harding and the gun.

'That sounds worthwhile, Fred. Going to be a long morning for you.'

'With luck we might get what we want a bit lively. I'll see you later, John. Cheers.' He replaced the 'phone and stood by the table for a moment and thought about Clifford Harding. Harding was afraid of the prospects before him, and not a little desperate, but that didn't mean he'd necessarily take the easy option.

'All right then, Clifford,' Pyle said, back in the interview room. 'How about it?'

The two DCs had taken him through his story, but they hadn't progressed. His minding the gun for a man, was what he said it amounted to.

'Well, what do you want from me,' Harding said sarcastically, 'a signed statement?'

The detective inspector wasn't put off at all. 'Be handy. And to have you plead to it in court.' He paused and watched him. 'Let's start with a few names, shall we?'

'What names?' Harding tried.

'You know the names we want, son. You've got them all right. The names of those lads who went on the blag with you last week. What do you think I'm talking about?'

Harding remained silent, like he was lost for an answer. He was. He didn't have the names, quite simply because he wasn't involved on the robbery. Not that that small fact would make much difference to the CID now.

Pyle glanced at the two detectives with him, then back at Harding.

'Says he hasn't got any names,' DC Fenton said. 'He was at home with his wife and kiddies, guv.'

Pyle scoffed with disappointment. 'That's the very worst place you could have been, Clifford. Terry Clark, Brian Finch, Dennis Cooper,' he informed him, putting up his thumb and fingers for each of the other men who had been raided that morning. 'They'll do nicely. Oh yes, we might as well stick up Jack Lynn. He was involved as well, wasn't he?'

'Sure, for all I know. You might go and nick them for that blag,' Harding said. 'But I wasn't on it, I promise you that.'

'Don't talk silly, Clifford, you were seen.' The detective had a way of saying things that made them sound like irrefutable facts, and it worried Harding. The sense of desperation he was feeling took firmer hold. Pyle watched him closely, saw all his problems.

"Course I was, by some slag you just stuck up to lolly me. By some dirty cunt you told it was me!'

70

Slowly Pyle shook his head. 'No need to pull strokes like that. Not here, for fucksake.' He dragged the second chair over and sat opposite the villain. 'What about the shooter we found at your place, Cliff? You fancy trying to say it was ours? We planted it there?'

Harding didn't make any reply. There was nothing he could say in answer to such an invitation without it would cost him something later.

'I have been known to carry around a pocketful of guns to lay on suspects, guv,' Fenton said.

'He doesn't believe that, do you, Cliff? Sure you don't. You know we don't do those sort of things.' He smiled, playing with him. 'You know what that gun's going to get you, with your form? Ten years, without us even trying, son, especially if I put you up before Morgan-Stevas.' He was the stick to beat villains with; no judge currently ruling over an Inner London Criminal Court had such an open loathing for the felonry in general, displayed such an unremitting bias when summing up and subsequently sentencing them. Villains, both innocent and guilty of the current charges, dreaded going in front of him.

'You realize you were grassed, son, don't you?'

Harding raised his eyes to meet Pyle's, something he resisted doing often. 'I don't think so,' he said quietly. 'That's just a CID ramp.'

The DI didn't give him anything. 'No such thing, son. Your mate down in the cells put you right in it. The only sensible thing to do when you're nicked.' He shook his head in mock dismay, a smile of sorts accompanying it. 'Fancy keeping a shooter in your own house. Who ever heard of anything more stupid, especially for a professional villain.'

'Well, who said even professional villains have to have any sense, guv?' DC Humphries commented, still not quite sure of himself.

'That isn't just lacking sense. It's insanity; especially when you go mates with grasses.'

71

What was being said here wasn't very important in itself, but as a conversational tack it was important and effective; the design was to undermine the suspect's resolve to resist the CID. Harding was becoming nervy and irritable; having his sleep interrupted in the manner it had been did nothing to induce calm, but having this detective, who had all the advantages anyway, mock him as well only made him feel worse, and would cause him to welcome finally any reasonable alternative he was offered.

Little chips began to fly off Harding as he started to crack. The DI was waiting for it to happen, but gave no sign of satisfaction when it did.

'All right,' Harding said, 'so you done me for the gun. It was stupid, I was like some fucking jumbo. But that's all you got' – as though it was an advantage point to him.

'But it's enough, son. More than enough. That would be about the last thing you ought to be done for.' There was a pause while he let the words reach into and work on the man. Harding had previous with the use of firearms, one of the reasons he had been on the Method Index raid. 'Give me the others on that blag last week and I'll drop the firearm charge.' The proposition was made in a quiet, undramatic tone. 'Drop it right out.'

A bitter note of regret escaped with Harding's laugh. 'I can't can I? I mean, fuck I, I don't even know the guys you stuck up, do I?' He hesitated, seeing the detective wasn't impressed; maybe contrary information was on his record. 'Well, one of them, but not very well. Lynn, Jack Lynn.'

Still Pyle remained purposely unimpressed. 'Then you're in trouble, my son. Bang in trouble.' There was an air of finality in his words.

The war of nerves was continuing, and Harding losing. He watched anxiously as the DI rose, he glanced at each of the DCs then back at the DI. He didn't want to have to give anything, but didn't want negotiations to close. 'I'd like to be able to help you.'

'Help yourself you mean. I don't need any help at all to get you sent down for a nice long while.' He waited now as Harding glanced at each of the DCs again. The chances of Harding giving him something if they were alone would be better, he figured, than in front of these two; if a villain was going to put up names then the last things he wanted were witnesses to his grassing. 'Pop down and see how he's getting on with the other fella, Peter, will you?'

'Yeah, sure.' DC Fenton knew what was going on. He went out.

'Haven't you got to shoot off soon, Rog'?' Pyle inquired, catching the second DC's eye.

'If I could, guv,' Humphries said, but didn't stir.

'Well you'd better shoot off then, hadn't you – time you get up to Watford, have a word with your witnesses.'

It was too early, Watford wasn't that far by car . . . finally DC Humphries got the message.

'What did you have in mind, Clifford?' Pyle said when they were alone.

With a vague shrug Harding said, "S up to you, guv.' He waited, hoping the DI would take the initiative and put the proposition. But he didn't. He went on hesitantly, as if believing others might be outside listening. 'I could put a nice earner into you. Be well tasty. I mean, if that charge could be dropped out – the shooter like . . . know what I mean.' The fact that Pyle didn't react made the villain more nervous; he would like to have seen some promise. 'The dough would be double safe. There'd be no problem on that score. I mean, what's it worth, d'you think . . .?'

Pyle held his silence for a moment more as he considered the man. 'It's a bit late to do it that way, I think. I mean, my entire squad's involved, and most of another squad. That's about twenty CID. They'd all want a taste, and not just fivers and tenners.' Pyle wasn't at all adverse to having an earner off villains if the circumstances were right; these were far from right. 'You wouldn't have enough to go into us all. Even if you had the lion's share out of Walthamstow.'

'I wasn't on that. I told you. That's straight, guv, I promise you.'

'About as straight as a dog's dick.' He smiled thinly. 'You've no reason to lie, have you, Clifford' – mocking once more. 'Who was then? Jack Lynn?' The suspect didn't answer. 'You want the firearm charge dropped out you've got to be practical, son. Your money's no good to me; so you've got to offer me something else. Something I can use. Give us the villains who did that blag.'

'I can't. I really can't. I haven't got them.' There was an air of desperation about the man now.

'Well, what have you got? You go mates with Jack Lynn. What's he having these days?'

'His old lady, I s'pose. I haven't seen him for years.' It was a lie and he suspected the filth knew it, but he didn't go mates with Lynn. The few times he had seen him in recent years were merely by chance. Lynn didn't mean much to him, no more than most of the other felons he knew on the same terms, but still he didn't want to lolly him, because he knew the result of grassing, which the CID could never fully appreciate when they casually asked villains to do it; Harding knew what it was like to spend time in prison and wouldn't wish that on anyone, especially someone he knew. But then the spectre of his own loss of liberty loomed frighteningly close. He wanted a deal and hoped the DI might come around to taking an earner. He'd part with every penny he could scrape together to keep his liberty.

'He's supposed to be very active,' Pyle said, like the matter was of no importance. 'That's the word.'

'I heard that,' Harding found himself saying. Then, as if to retrieve the situation, 'But I didn't get no offers.'

There was a rap at the door, and DS Barcy opened it and put his head inside the room. 'Guv. Got a minute?'

He stepped back to allow Pyle out, then pulled the door to, excluding the villain. Barcy had remained behind at

Harding's house with another detective to complete their search. 'Nothing else there,' he said, 'apart from these.' He produced a plastic bag which contained six bullets. 'Up behind the sink they were.'

'Good hit, Jack.' He took the bullets and considered them. 'The right size, are they?' They were; had they not been then he might have found the right size and substituted them. His thoughts moved on. 'Not even a bit of bent gear at the house, a colour telly or anything?' The more pressure he could get on Harding, the better the final result.

'Nothing worth a look, guv. His old woman screamed like a maniac after you left. Set all the kids off, she did. A right upset; thought they were never going to see their Dad again.'

The fact registered in a corner of Pyle's brain. 'She tell them that?'

'Wound them right up, like there was something I could do.'

'Did she telephone anyone, Jack?'

'No. She tried calling a solicitor, but all she got was an answering service.' The DS anticipated his governor's next question. 'Wasn't any of the little outfits likely to cause too many problems; just a straight brief.'

'Good. All right, hang around. I'll probably want you to do a bit of visiting, start checking some alibis. See how things shape with him first.'

Pyle went back into the interview room, closing the door. 'He just came from your place,' he said in an apparently concerned manner. 'It seems your kids were a bit upset.' He watched Harding as he gave him this information, suspecting that through it he might find a more immediate pressure point; villains were often perversely sentimental about their kids, Pyle found. Harding was no exception.

'What? What's wrong with them? – fucking upsetting them like that. You were out of order.'

'Poor little buggers. They're missing their Dad, that's what's wrong with them, son. Still, all you villains are the same, don't think nothing of your kids, do you?' The words were reaching into Harding and affecting him, but the detective wasn't about to let the pressure off. There was only one way Harding was going to get off the hook. 'They'll miss you for a very long while from what I can see of it. Probably even forget you altogether – happens all the time, son.'

That piece of information, indicating the prospects, did nothing to comfort Harding. He kept his head down as if to hide the display of emotion charging across his face, reactions that he had no control over. The DI saw it all.

'What about the gun?' Pyle asked changing the tack. 'What d'you have in mind for it?'

'Nothing,' Harding said abstractedly, his thoughts still worrying about his family. 'I was just minding it for someone.'

'Someone you met in a pub, I bet. 'S always the way, son. What about these then?' He dropped the plastic bag of bullets on the table in front of Harding. The DI's manner during interrogation changed frequently and with the suddenness of gear changes on an accelerating automatic car. The villain didn't respond. 'You'd better come up with some answers, son, if you want a deal. Good answers, the sort I want to hear. Otherwise you'll be a long time away from your family, I promise you that.' There was a pause, another gear change; Harding barely noticed it, the pressure on him was so great. 'Right, where d'you get the shooter?'

Harding hesitated, struggled to surface through his emotions, and said, 'Can we have some sort of deal?'

'Depends what you give me,' Pyle replied, extending the promise as though there was nothing easier for him to do than fulfil it.

'The gun dropped right out, that is?'

'I'd say my governor would agree to that, if you put the right sort of stuff on offer, Clifford. 'S up to yourself entirely, son. I mean, you've got nothing at all to lose, have you?'

Still Harding resisted, as if thinking perhaps he did have something to lose; maybe some part of personal integrity. 'I don't know about that Walthamstow blag. I mean, those fuckers what pulled that, they deserve nicking, hurting that guard like that …' He hadn't given anything and hesitated again, not wanting to go on. 'But Jack Lynn, if you're really interested … if he's at it, I could probably go and get what he's having for you.' He wasn't exactly sure about that, there was no reason Lynn should tell him anything of his plans. From the little he did know of the man he thought him half-shrewd, having had it off with a couple of nice touches. But it was worth a try.

'That means you'd have to be out before I get a result,' Pyle said flatly, though he wasn't perturbed about such a move. Suspecting how Harding felt about his family, Pyle knew he wasn't likely to have it away without them; so subsequently it wouldn't prove too difficult to pick him up again if he didn't come through.

With a sense of desperation now, trying to impress upon the DI his genuineness, Harding said, 'I won't have it away, I can't. I mean, I can't, can I, there's no point. What about my family?'

'Your family ties might impress a magistrate when granting bail. That's about all.'

Harding ran true to type. 'How could I have it away? I mean, I couldn't take m'family on the trot, even if I wanted to, could I? I just want to get myself out of trouble.'

'Oh, I believe you, Clifford. Then I'm a trusting sort of bloke. But it isn't down to me; it's up to my governor. He's the one has to be impressed.' He paused and considered Harding as he registered this new impediment to his freedom. 'As a gesture of faith you'd better give me the dealer you got the gun from, hadn't you?'

That final point of commitment to the CID, after which there would be no turning back, caused Harding to withdraw slightly. It was a bridge he was having great difficulty in crossing, despite the alternative. But finally he nodded. 'Wally Marks …' The words almost stuck in his throat, making him feel like all kinds of a bastard. Wally Marks wasn't any sort of a friend, they had done some business together, that was all, but he was one of his own and consequently he felt he owed him more than the money he had given him for the gun. He told himself the gun dealer would have traded him had their situation been reversed, but it didn't make him feel any better. He was a grass now. 'He has a greengrocery business over at Finsbury Park. He does a bit of dabbling on the side ...'

Pyle looked at him but didn't comment. The information was a start; he didn't despise Harding for grassing any more than he would have admired him for holding out. As far as he was concerned all Harding represented was a means to an end, the end being the capture of a few more villains, and what he gave him would probably have little bearing on his final result. For he was a villain and active; the fact that he had a shooter suggested he had something planned. He would eventually go for that, along with those whom he had it planned with. There was no more integrity between CID and felon than was generally found between felon and felon. If you put enough pressure on them, Pyle knew, offered them something, almost always there was a result to be had. He'd have a result here, he reflected, there was no doubt.

9

Pyle's step wasn't exactly springy with enthusiasm as he came along the fourth floor corridor at the Yard. It was turned nine o'clock, past the end of what should have been his tour of duty, and he wanted to go home and go to sleep; but there was little chance of that in the immediate future, not before his court appearance; he had a lad whom he had nicked for robbery going up. He felt crumpled and unshaven and at times like these was inclined to regret being a policeman, especially one on the Squad. He ought to have been out of the race, at division running a CID office with comfortable nine-to-five hours. Despite himself it wasn't a serious considera-tion; he'd be transferred out of the Squad soon enough – no one ever did more than a couple of years – and would doubtless regret that when it happened. Maybe he wouldn't stay the course, maybe he'd get the boot as a result of the current complaint he had against him that CIB2 were investigating, have to go back into uniform. Not a very inspiring prospect, he thought, for a tired Wednesday morning. He doubted there was much real chance of having the complaint substantiated, even though there was substance to it. He had gone into the villain all right for an earner in order for him not to oppose bail. The villain had been badly advised, if advised at all, to make a complaint; it would gain him absolutely nothing when he came up for trial. Pyle had taken the man's money and had done what he had offered to do; it was a simple business transaction and should have ended right there. The fact that he had subsequently drawn a complaint didn't cause him to regret his action; it was simply another of the problems he had daily to contend with in the job.

There was a lot of activity on the fourth floor, it being daytime. The other squads, and both uniform policemen and civilian personnel were moving around, some of the detectives at a slightly frenetic pace getting last minute papers and reports sorted out to go to court with. Most of the movement came from the paper-carriers, shifting the bumf from one office to another.

'Morning, Fred,' said a fresh-looking detective in a shortsleeved shirt, who had huge, sagging ribbons beneath his eyes.

'Have it in last night?' Pyle asked casually as he went past.

'Not even in my hand.'

His thoughts caught up with him and Pyle spun round. 'Graham!' he called after the detective, who stopped at one of C11's doors and waited for the DI to come back to him. He was DI Graham McHale, one of the few detectives on C11 who wasn't totally possessive about information that Criminal Intelligence managed to gather. 'D'you have anything on a villain called Lynn? Jack Lynn. He comes out of Kentish Town?'

McHale thought for a moment, then shook his head. 'Doesn't ring any bells. What's his line?' Pyle gave a précis of the villain's CRO file. 'I'll have a look for you, Fred. You going to be around later today?'

'Looks like it. Good luck.'

There were four other DIs in the communal office, bending to their hated paperwork, and each glanced up and greeted Pyle as he moved along to his own desk. Alan Welch was sitting typing a report on his side of the double desk. Pyle's arrival seemed like a reasonable excuse for him to stop what he was doing.

'Morning, Fred.' Welch fished out his tobacco tin to build a cigarette. 'Hear you had it off last night.'

'No, nothing much,' Pyle said modestly. His arrests rate was sufficiently high for him to be as modest as he chose. 'One looks halfway promising,' he said as an afterthought, aware that Welch was leaning back in his chair waiting for something more. Despite the fact that he had the lowest arrest quota on the Squad Alan Welch was quite highly regarded, mainly on account of the efficiency with which he dealt with his paperwork; it was always where it should be, always in order. His presence wasn't so much an inspiration to the other detectives, more a vindication; he bore out what most detectives vociferously maintained, that while they were hamstrung as they were with all the paperwork that fell their lot they couldn't move forward and operate at maximum efficiency, capturing villains. Although Pyle managed to cope adequately, if grudgingly, with his paperwork, he didn't deny the possibility that one day he might fuck up on it; that was a rock on which all too many policemen perished.

Pyle remained standing at his desk in his overcoat and sorted through the paperwork that had collected in his 'posts' trays. There were reports for his attention, memos for his information; reports that had been written by him and sent back because there was inadequate information, others with the approval of senior ranks and for Pyle to now take on to a further stage. None of it held his attention, it would keep until he came back on duty that evening, it would have to for he certainly wasn't going to come back after court to clear it, not when the trays would be just as full again by his next relief. He slid the paperwork back and reached into one of his drawers for his electric shaver. The batteries were running down and the blades seemed to turn reluctantly, giving him an indifferent shave. The wasp-like buzz of the machine was added to the general noise of conversation, typewriters and telephone bells which pierced the thin dividing walls. The confusion distracted no one on the Squad.

'Some brief 'phoned you this morning, Fred. Gladwell his name was. Wanted to have a word about his client you nicked last night. Clark.'

The information pleased Pyle. It wasn't an infallible guide, but when villains' solicitors were as quick off the mark as that it usually meant their clients were at it. It was fairly obvious what Gladwell wanted, but despite the fact Pyle said, 'D'he say what he wanted?'

'Wants you to call him the moment you get in.'

'He's got some chance, I should think.' Pyle wouldn't be in a hurry to talk to the brief, and would also keep him apart from his client for as long as he reasonably could.

'He probably wants to go into you, Fred.' Welch was alluding to an earner.

'Be handy. I could use a taste,' he said lightly.

He continued shaving, picking up the 'phone with his free hand and dialling his own number. As he waited for his wife to answer he watched another detective come into the office. He was Maurice Head, a DI with the Squad who had been under suspension for a little over three months now: he had been named in bribery allegations by a villain who had been nicked. At the time of his arrest the villain, who had run a number of clubs in the West End and a lot of brasses, had threatened to take as many CID with him as he could if he went down, but whether or not the threats had impressed anyone, he had been too involved not to go. Subsequently he had carried out his threat, causing an enormous upset. Maurice Head had been only one of about twenty detectives named, and one of fourteen who had actually been suspended. Some of them had had the sense to resign before the investigation that CIB2 currently had underway was concluded. The consensus was that the result wasn't going to favour the CID in general and especially not those actually under investigation. While he was suspended DI Head wasn't supposed to enter the building, no policemen under suspension were, but it wasn't an insuperable problem, and Head popped back in from time to time. Pyle watched him stop and exchange a few words with the DI at the desk near the door, before coming on up the office. Pyle felt a bit sorry for his colleague, it was too easy to simply dismiss him because he was at it and had come on top, it could happen to anyone. He thought him foolish for hanging on as he was, but understood why he did. Head had put a lot of villains away in his time, he liked being in the CID, it was a way of life that couldn't be let go of lightly. Pyle knew he would probably do the same in similar circumstances, despite what commonsense told him.

His thoughts ended abruptly as his wife answered the phone. 'Edith, 'S me,' Pyle said. 'Yes, still here, only just got in.' The woman had little to say; he didn't tell her specific aspects of his job so she couldn't enquire how it went. All she could ask was how he was, where he was, when he'd be back; that information he willingly gave her. 'Be back later this morning ... oh, not sure when. Depends what time I get finished in court. Shouldn't be long...' He acknowledged DI Head with a nod as he stopped at the desk to speak to Alan Welch. Pyle's wife was telling him she might be out shopping. 'All right. I'll see you later ... bye, love.' He replaced the phone. 'How's it going, Maurice?' Pyle asked, knowing it was an inane question. An enormous cloud had been lying over Head ever since his suspension.

'Well pissed off with hanging around, I am,' he moaned, his thick hands tightening in frustration on the ends of the patterned silk scarf he was wearing. 'Just looked in to see if there was any word.' That was as close a justification a detective like Head would make; the real reason he looked in as he did was because he was feeling lost, strung out under suspension as he was, out of touch, even lonely; though that was the last thing he'd admit.

'I was just saying,' Welch put in, 'I've not heard a thing, Fred. You?' If anyone was likely to hear it would almost certainly have been DI Welch. His ear was closest to the ground around the Yard. Even rumours of what went on over on the seventeenth floor of the tower block where CIB2 were, reached him first.

'Not a whisper,' Pyle said. He finished with his shaver and blew the head clean. He put the machine away and removed his black standard briefcase from the bottom drawer. He looked up, his eyes meeting Head's. As much as he sympathized with the DI's position, he wished he wouldn't keep showing up like he did. Despite himself Pyle found himself saying, 'I'll tell you what, Maurice. That investigation going on as long as it has, there's no way you're not going to wind up nicked ...'

'Oh, good luck, Fred!' Head said, startled.

It was the best advice Pyle could give him. Head knew as well as his colleagues what his logical move was. 'Sorry, son,' Pyle said. 'But it stands to reason ...' He paused and regarded the thickset, ginger-haired man. He was about to debate the matter, but thought better of it. It was old ground which they had been over before. 'I'll see you later.'

He went out and along the corridor to the DCI's office. 'Is Tony still around, guv?' he said to Trevor Watson, the DCI who had the day relief. The third DCI on the Squad was currently on sick leave, and hadn't been replaced; his two colleagues were coping with his work, under protest.

DCI Trevor Watson was short enough barely to have made the minimum height required for service in the Met, and he looked more like a bank manager than a detective in his neat three-piece suit and starched collars. He wore a silver chain across his waistcoat with a silver Omega which he claimed belonged to his grandfather. He had sharp, pointed features, a slightly pedantic nature and wasn't popular with the lower ranks as a result, as it often meant his returning reports to them for redrafting or retyping if there was anything wrong with them. Not the smallest mistake got past Trevor Watson.

'Just missed him,' Watson said, pausing and marking the place to which he'd read in the report. 'He's gone out to Barnes on that complaints inquiry.' He wasn't sure that the DI was aware of the complaint that DCI Simmons was investigating but didn't qualify his statement. Despite the ever-increasing size of CIB2 most senior detectives were from time to time called upon to investigate complaints, albeit reluctantly; any who did it with cheerful willingness usually applied to join CIB2. 'Was it urgent, Fred?'

'It'll keep. Just a development with one of the bodies from this morning's raid's all.'

There was a detail connected with that raid which had fallen into this DCI's field of concern: the solicitor, Gladwell, had first been put through to the DCI's office. 'Did you talk to that brief?'

'Not yet.'

'Didn't waste much time, did he? Is his client involved, would you say?' Watson knew as well as the DI.

"S odds on. I left Eric up there – I got this one in court,' Pyle reminded him. 'Did you see Maurice Head?'

'He looked in,' Watson said dismissively, like he wished he wouldn't look in but didn't want to categorically tell him not to. 'I advised him to resign. About the only advice I could give him, hard as it is. But it'll save him being nicked, and save his pension. The commissioner'll accept it all right if he gets it in now.' That was almost standard in the police force; the last thing the hierarchy wanted was the attendant bad publicity when policemen were arrested, charged and sent for trial, especially policemen as senior as Maurice Head. Far better was the alternative in letting them quietly resign with all their pension rights and with the tacit understanding that they wouldn't subsequently be charged.

'Maybe I ought to stick mine in,' Pyle said, alluding to the complaint investigation he had against him.

Watson merely grinned as he turned away to answer the 'phone. 'DCI's office. Watson ... I drafted the report yesterday,' he said in a tone which suggested he was talking to his boss. 'It's just being typed ... doesn't look like it'll be much of a result, guv ... Yes, soon as I get it back.' He replaced the phone.

Pyle said grudgingly, 'They're wasting their time and mine. Chummy'll get a result, and that'll be that as far as the complaint goes.'

'CIB2 like to make themselves busy, Fred. Incidentally, what's happening with that lad you have going up this morning? Any chance he'll plead to it?'

'I'm hoping he will, guv. It'll mean sodding around at court for a couple of weeks if he don't – the witnesses aren't all that.' The Director of Public Prosecutions' office had been far more confident about going to court on the evidence they had than Pyle ever was; then he didn't really think them very shrewd, and having something thrown out of court was far less of a reflection on them than on the detective in charge of the case. 'I suppose if it's put to him right.'

'Offer him something, why don't you?' Watson said pragmatically.

'It's his liberty he wants, guv,' Pyle replied.

'Yes. Don't they all? See what he says, Fred, might save a lot of time and effort.'

10

Cells below magistrates' courts were little different from those at police stations. They provided as standard a bench-bed, usually without a mattress, though rarely a toilet of any kind; walls were scarred with graffiti, names and legends of those gone before, who expected a result or had been weighed off. Like most cells there was room for about five paces, depending how tall the prisoner was.

David Shepley wasn't particularly tall, and looked slightly uncomfortable in his suit, which had obviously been donned on the advice of his solicitor to try and create the right impression during his court appearance; he had been wearing jeans and a flying jacket when DI Pyle had nicked him. He paced agitatedly, sometimes getting in five, sometimes six strides as he considered the proposal the detective had made, and tried to weigh the pros and cons.

'... I don't know. I just don't know, do I?' Doubt was like a heavy cricket bat someone was beating his head with. 'The thought of pleading guilty, here this morning, it really does me up. It's ruining me.'

Pyle wasn't at all moved by Shepley's visible distress. 'Well, let's be practical, son,' he said. 'You know you've got some coming, don't you. About eight years, unless you're very lucky.' Shepley knew all right, even though he tried to resist the prospect. 'I mean, you can go and gum up the works by electing to go for trial now. That's your right, David, no one'll deny you it. But it's going to piss everyone off. And what'll happen, you'll be remanded down to Brixton for about six months before you ever come to trial.' He paused to let the words sink in. The picture wasn't very bright, but it was accurate. There were interminable delays in getting prisoners up the steps from the magistrates' courts, the lists were seemingly endless and villains simply had to stand in line, whatever they were going up for. 'It's your best bet, David, a summary trial, you pleading to it here today. They'll have to send you up to the sessions for sentencing anyway – again that's going to mean a delay of months. But meanwhile you can get your liberty, on bail – I won't object. You could even go and do a bit more villainy, provide for your family while you're away.' The offer was far more appealing than the alternative. Pyle waited.

'You make it sound easy, don't you,' Shepley said, still uncertain, trying to cling to that slender possibility of his getting a result, if he were to plead not guilty.

'It is, son. You've got to have a little faith, 's all. He added cream after the sugar: 'When you finally go up for sentencing, I'll be able to tell the court, I'll say you were most co-operative. And I'll leave out all the poison. That alone'll save you a nice piece. But the thing is, David, I want an answer now.'

Still Shepley hesitated. 'Jesus. It's just the thought of pleading to it. It slaughters me, it really does. I mean, I got no chance then, have I?' He ceased his pacing, his look appealing to the DI for something better. He didn't get it.

'You think you have anyway? With a brief on legal aid? I s'pect he told you to elect trial.' Immediately he saw from Shepley's expression that that was so, as if suddenly believing the brief was part of some conspiracy against him, which he was, in effect. 'They get a bigger fee for taking it up the road. They're not interested in the final result, doesn't make any difference to them. But then you have to be realistic about this. You can't really expect the system to provide an adequate defence for those who offend against its canons. It's not reasonable. The system works for them, David, not you.' That all presupposed the guilt of anyone in those circumstances, in need of a lawyer to defend him; then that was how the system tended to work. Pyle knew it, all he wanted to do was make Shepley aware of it. 'Just think about it. Then ask yourself what chance you have. I mean, what chance?' He shook his head. 'You've no chance, son.'

'My brief's up in court expecting me to plead not guilty,' Shepley said hesitantly, as though this was likely to prove an insuperable problem.

'You'll want him down here then, to tell him.'

'Bail won't be a problem, will it?' Shepley asked, seeking some final reassurance. 'There are a few things that need sorting out at home. Be handy.'

'I'll have a quiet word with the magistrate,' Pyle lied smoothly. He wouldn't, but didn't anticipate any problems. 'There won't be any trouble.'

Shepley grew easier now. 'I'd better have the old wanker down then.'

'Best thing you could do, David. You help the system, it helps you. See if I'm not right.'

The man's decision would save the detective a lot of work that might all have finally amounted to an acquittal – he would give him what help he could in return. But Pyle's expression as he considered the prisoner reflected nothing of his triumph.

The eleven-plus exam had him completely baffled. Pyle read and reread the questions a hundred times and drew a blank on each of them, they were meaningless to him; they were written in plain enough English but it might as well have been Sanskrit. He floundered on briefly before pulling himself into wakefulness, though his mind was reluctant to let go of sleep. He hadn't had anything like enough rest for him to function at an easy pace through his next shift. His muscles ached and his eyes hurt, there was a pain in the back of his neck which crept steadily up under his cranium now he was awake. It all amounted to little that a couple more hours' sleep wouldn't cure, and he wanted nothing more than to roll over, adjust the covers and go back to sleep, even though his mouth tasted foul and his bladder was distended to a point close to bursting. But he couldn't go back to sleep, he had already done that once since his alarm clock had woken him; now his wife had come into the bedroom. Her presence had woken him the second time. He watched her move to the side of the bed and set a mug on the night table.

'Fred ... It's past five, love,' she said quietly in her permanently hoarse voice. She went to the window and opened the curtains, which were of a flimsy floral patterned material and unlined, keeping little of the daylight out. The bedroom wasn't large, then nor was the post-war semi-detached house which Pyle had still only half paid for. Their tastes were floral patterned wallpaper to go with the curtains and lilac nylon quilt cover, or rather they were his wife's tastes, which Pyle didn't resist. He didn't take a great deal of interest in the house, certainly no practical interest, if something like decorating needed doing, then either a decorator was got in or Edith Pyle did it.

She was in her late thirties. Her hips had thickened slightly, so too had her stomach, but in her dark, neat face, framed by her short black and grey hair, were traces of the woman who had first attracted Pyle. She watched him a little anxiously as he sat up, groaning. He rubbed his eyes and went on to massage his face, which felt as if all the blood had drained from it.

'Jesus,' he said, like he was in agony. 'I can hardly open my eyes. 'S that the time? Only feels like I went to bed a few minutes ago.'

'You ought to sleep longer. You were late getting to bed.' Instinctively she knew this wasn't the best time for what she had in mind and he was offering excuses before she had even suggested anything. Maybe he knew by instinct too. Yes, she thought, he always knew such things, just by looking at her. She was only the wife of a detective and couldn't mask her feelings in the same way he could. Despite the hours he put into his job, probably because of them, she had to reach out for everything in their relationship whenever she could. Out of necessity her needs had become less and less acute, but she did still have needs.

'Ah, my back hurts like a bastard,' he complained, reaching round to knead his spine. He saw the mug on the night table. 'What's this, tea?'

'I was just having a cup ...' the woman lied, and not at all easily. 'I thought you might want one. Thought it would help you wake up.'

He looked at her, his eyes, it seemed, even in their sleep-weakened state, were seeking to disprove the validity of her statement. He knew it wasn't the whole truth, that she had an ulterior motive for doing what she did. The gesture she had of nervously smoothing her skirt, which she was doing now, told him as much.

'The kids have gone to the cinema,' she informed him as she moved back to the bed. The information was for no reason other than to reassure him that they wouldn't be interrupted. 'It's a rock film they've gone to see. Sooner them than me. They'll probably come back half deaf.'

Pyle didn't respond other than to sip some of the tea before reaching up to massage his neck and his tense deltoid muscles.

'I'll do it, Fred,' she offered. It was the excuse she wanted. At his side she began to knead his neck and shoulders. She had done a good bit of it over the years and was quite skilful.

'Didn't they have any homework?' Pyle asked. He thought it important that his kids got good results at school, and assumed that was why he dreamed of failing the eleven-plus.

'They managed to get it finished before they left school,' she said.

'Well, when did they do their schoolwork?' he said testily.

Hesitantly she eased herself down on the bed behind him and continued massaging his shoulders. Pyle leaned forward as if to avoid her, he didn't want to make love to her now; at the best of times he didn't enjoy that when he woke up. First he would need to have a shower, wash his mouth out, and to have

91

slept at least eight hours. A feeling of desperation sprang through Edith Pyle as she felt her husband, along with the opportunity, slipping away from her. She threw her arms around him suddenly and held him close, pressing her face against his head. But the gesture was to no avail, he didn't respond. There was a pause; both of them tensed, hating the demand, the contact. Edith Pyle leaned back, releasing her husband, despising him for this rejection. She accepted that his hours were long and arduous, but somehow the excuse was no longer good enough. He chose to do what he did.

'It's been a long time, Fred...' There was a note of regret in her voice.

'I'm tired, love. I'm too tired ... I can't even manage tea when I first wake up. You know that.'

Her knowing didn't make any difference.

Pyle pushed the covers back and swung his legs over the edge of the bed. Reaching round behind him, he massaged his back, more for her benefit than his own relief. He groaned as he rose. 'I've got a few days' leave soon.' The information was extended almost as a promise, but Edith was unimpressed. There would be other excuses then, or his leave would get cancelled. It had happened so many times before, that call to duty ruining their sex-life. She knew she shouldn't allow it to upset her anymore, but still it did. She sighed and leaned against the headboard of the bed as her husband shuffled out to the bathroom. She remained there pensively hearing the noises he made from the bathroom, hawking, peeing; the lavatory flushing; cleaning his teeth. The shower running. The walls were thin and every sound crept out. She didn't know why she was sitting there, there was no point, and there were a number of things she could be getting on with, but still she didn't move. Thoughts idly trailed back. Fred Pyle hadn't always been like he was now, he had had more energy than most; they had had some really good times together. Her thoughts didn't help her at all, they simply made her more aware of her needs.

The hot water through the shower helped Pyle wake up and as he stood under the steam he found himself getting an erection, which carried his thoughts back to his wife. It was a while since they had had sex together, he reflected. He doubted that she had answered her needs elsewhere, and wondered if the day would come when she would seek to; then he was curious to know how he might react. Not as well as he liked to tell himself he would. Maybe he ought to go back in and make a show. He still quite enjoyed having sex with Edith, but he was tired, and he was running short of time – not that he had to clock-on at the office. He decided to see how he felt after shaving, though probably she would have gone back downstairs to get his breakfast.

Pyle was surprised to find his wife still in the same position on the bed when he returned to the bedroom, and surprised to find he still had a touch-on.

'Edith?' he said, coming to her side. He put his hand on her head and pushed his thick fingers through her hair.

She looked up at him and smiled thinly. 'I must get your meal,' she said, but didn't move.

Crouching on his hams in front of her he put his hand on her knee, she wasn't wearing tights and the flesh was smooth and soft, and the feel of it excited him a little, especially when he slid his hand between her thighs. He didn't enjoy the feel of nylon covered legs. The flesh on her thighs had begun to crêpe, but he didn't mind that. She didn't move as he reached in farther under her skirt, but eased her legs slightly apart to permit him access. By the time he got to the apex of her legs he had an erection, which on discovering that she wasn't wearing any pants, grew more intense. She sighed as his fingers eased her thighs apart and his finger stroked through the short hairs. She was wet and very responsive. It was worth avoiding sex for a while to have her achieve this state, he thought.

After a while he rose and untied his bathrobe; she twisted herself round on the bed and wriggled her skirt up round her waist. She pulled him on top of her and helped guide him into her.

Pyle would be a little late getting into the office. It wasn't important.

11

Work was the last thing Pyle felt like then, and he had a long way to go through the night. Having just come on duty, he was sure he wouldn't get through to the end, especially not if something broke, demanding a lot of effort. With luck there'd be a quiet stretch and he'd be able to get his head down for a couple of hours. Tony Simmons the night duty officer wouldn't mind; he'd probably be out visiting his nurse anyway.

Moving along the corridor towards his own office, Pyle passed the open door of the superintendents' office when his name was called. He had noticed that the light was on, but not whether either of the two superintendents had been present. Pyle moved back to the door. Detective Superintendent Ernie Jeymer was standing by one of the desks in his coat, he was putting papers into his briefcase. Although the office was the same size as most of those along the left-hand side of the corridor it had only two desks, which gave the two superintendents the amount of floorspace relative to their status.

'Evening, guv,' Pyle said.

There was no greeting or preliminary comment from Jeymer. 'What's happening with those villains you nicked this morning, Fred?' he wanted to know. He was a big man with a bristly grey and brown beard and spiky eyebrows and a brusque manner. He tended to get upset easily, especially if he wasn't kept completely in the picture by his subordinates. However, he soon got over his explosions and wasn't a man to harbour a grudge, leastwise not with colleagues. Whether the hierarchy ever upset him Pyle didn't know, he suspected they did, like most working policemen, but he never heard the man complaining; then probably he wouldn't, for he was the sort of detective who accepted that those above him in rank were there because they knew better than he and as a result accepted their edicts.

'Still assisting with our inquiries as far as I know, guv,' Pyle explained. 'I've only just come on.'

'One of their solicitors has been trying to reach you most of the day – Gladwell. He's been threatening a writ of habeas corpus unless Terry Clark is either charged or released.'

'There's a good chance he'll be charged, the way he was shaping, guv.'

'Pleased to hear it. Gladwell sounded like he was full of piss, but why upset him unnecessarily?' It wasn't a question. 'Keep me posted, Fred.' He turned back to the papers in his briefcase, summarily dismissing the DI.

Pyle stopped by the DCIs' office to talk to Tony Simmons about the case. Trevor Watson was there on his own and he didn't seem very pleased, whether because he was still there or as a result of his telephone conversation wasn't clear.

'. . . Well, stay on watch there,' he was saying into the phone. 'I'll try and get someone out to take over . . . I can't say when. Just stay put.' He replaced the phone irritably.

'You got shares in this little firm, guv?' Pyle asked.

'Didn't show much of a dividend last year, Fred.' He clicked his tongue in disgust. 'I was supposed to be taking the old lady out to dinner this evening.'

'What's it, her birthday?'

'Something like that,' Watson said, as if admitting taking his wife out for any other reason was a sorry admission.

'Is Tony in yet?'

'No.' That was the sore point with the DCI. 'It's him who's holding me up.'

A uniformed messenger, one of the whole battalion who floated around the Yard, came in to collect the 'posts' from Watson's desk. The DCI snatched a pink folder from the top, before the uniform bore it away.

'Not that one, son.' He passed it to Pyle. 'That's yours, Fred. Jack Lynn's CRO file. Looks as though he might be worth some time.'

'Aren't they all,' the DI said wearily. Apart from the one-off criminals, those people who committed a crime of some sort, got caught, got scared, learned their lesson and never went for another taste, Pyle suspected that any file could be drawn from CRO and the villain it belonged to would be worth looking at; almost certainly he would be having something, have had something since the last entry or would be planning something. He had great faith in the belief that most felons were recidivists, and no matter what lengths one went to in an attempt to reform them they'd always revert to type. But there just weren't enough detective manhours to continually be checking through files and looking villains up, you simply had to wait for one to go off then look up the likely suspects. Proceeding the former way would probably get them into a lot of problems over the infringements of civil rights, there was always someone to shout about those on behalf of the villain; rarely did anyone do so for the victim. Most detectives didn't worry too much about villains' rights, believing that most of them gave those up when they went in for villainy; most detectives felt they were quite able to keep their own sense of proportion in these matters, and did of course! Villains had no rights, it was as simple as that; and detectives had too little time to give them the attention they would have liked.

Detective Superintendent Jeymer came into the office and dropped a pile of pastel-coloured folders on Watson's desk. 'Get Tony to have a look at those. And don't forget that request from Staines. Get someone out there to assist them as soon as you can. I'll leave you to it, Trevor.'

'Sounds like something for the Regional Crime Squad to me, guv.'

'Wouldn't give them the satisfaction.' Jeymer started out. 'I'll be in the Tank for half an hour or so,' he said over his shoulder. It was an invitation to either detective.

'Night, guv,' Pyle said politely.

Watson turned to answer the phone on DCI Simmons' desk 'Chief inspectors' office. Watson ...' He waited, glancing round at Pyle as he did. 'How are you fixed for going out to Staines, Fred?' That was how work, other than that which detectives found for themselves, tended to be allocated, to whoever happened to be on hand. Watson turned his attention back to the phone before Pyle could reply. 'Hello, hello ...' There was no reply and the phone went dead. 'Obviously didn't like the sound of my voice.' He replaced the phone. 'They've a couple of robberies they're getting nowhere with.'

'I'm not exactly scratching for work myself, guv.'

'Well, see if you can't do something.'

The prospect didn't inspire Pyle. When he reached the DIs' office the place was deserted and the phone on his desk was ringing. He answered it hurriedly, only to feel slightly disappointed when the caller identified himself. It was Alex Gladwell, Terry Clark's solicitor. 'Oh, good evening,' Pyle said. 'I was just about to ring you ...' Nothing was further from his mind.

'What is the current position with my client?' the brief asked in a detached manner.

'At present he's at Holloway police station, helping us with our inquiries into the robbery at Barclay's bank last week,' Pyle responded formally.

'Has he been charged?'

'I haven't charged him.'

'In that case I presume you are aware, inspector, that you have no grounds on which to hold my client,' the solicitor tried. It was worth a try when you were getting paid for it.

There were no legal grounds for the police to detain a suspect unless he was charged, other than under the Prevention of Terrorism Act, but few people knew that or were in a position to enforce their rights once in a police cell; while solicitors knew that it wasn't necessarily in their client's interest nor their own to force the point.

'We're not holding him, sir,' Pyle offered evenly. 'He's simply assisting us with our inquiries.'

'Voluntarily?' the solicitor wanted to know.

'I'd say so.' He opened his briefcase and lifted out papers uninterestedly.

The solicitor leaped on that as if in a courtroom. 'Taken at six in the morning, and held for fourteen hours? Come on, inspector. You seriously believe that's reasonable?' He didn't want an answer. 'Why hasn't Mr Clark been allowed access to his solicitor?'

For a moment Pyle thought Gladwell was talking about a third party. Then he said simply, 'He made no request to contact you, 's why.'

'This is most unsatisfactory. Now I'm giving you fair warning, inspector ...' he paused as if he couldn't find the name he wanted, 'Pyle. Unless my client is either charged forthwith or released, I'm going to apply to Mr Justice Houghton this evening for a writ of habeas corpus.'

'That'll be perfectly in order, sir,' Pyle said in an unperturbed fashion; he might have been looking forward to it, but guessed instead that the brief was bluffing. 'Just present it at Holloway police station.'

The DI had guessed right. The solicitor's tone changed. 'I see. Then you are charging my client?'

'That's your conclusion. But I'd say he has a good chance of being charged, Mr Gladwell.'

'I'd like to see him if that's possible.' The demands were gone.

''S not a problem,' Pyle said, and paused, before adding, 'if he wishes to see you.'

'Just between ourselves, inspector. What do you think?'

Pyle had a relationship with some solicitors where they could ask those sort of questions and get a straight answer, and who could then ask straight away, what was to be done. Alex Gladwell was one of those, but over the phone both he and DI Pyle behaved quite correctly, 'Our inquiries are incomplete, sir,' the DI said.

Realizing he had reached out too far, given too much, the brief tried to regain control of the situation. 'Well, thank you for your trouble, inspector. I appreciate it.' It sounded as though the DI had given him all he needed.

When he replaced the phone, Pyle found DS Lethridge in the office by the desk. He looked like he had been on the piss all day, rather than off sleeping like any wise detective on the nightshift.

'Eric,' Pyle greeted. 'In early, aren't you?' Leaving him to conduct the interrogations that morning, he hadn't expected him in until around midnight, depending what time he got through. But apart from sleep, the DS had no real reason to stay away now. 'What's the position over at Holloway?'

'Clark stuck up an alibi. Doesn't amount to much – his old lady and some villains,' he said dismissively. No one would believe any of those if they were put up in court; everyone knew that wives of villains and friends of villains were inevitably liars! 'The lad with the shooter, well, it's fairly obvious that he was going after something, but it doesn't look like Walthamstow was down to him.'

'I'm not worried about that,' Pyle said. He had other plans for Clifford Harding, which his going for the Walthamstow blag would mess up. 'What about that lad John's squad picked up?'

Lethridge shook his large head. 'He's not shaping at all.' At best that sort of average was to be expected from Method Index raids. Pyle nodded thoughtfully. 'Maybe we'll find something else for him.' It seemed a pity to have spent time on a villain only to have to let him go. 'Round up some of the lads, Eric. See if we can't nick that one John missed. 'S no hurry. I want a word with the chief about Harding.'

'You think Brian Finch might be a prospect, Fred?' DCI Simmons asked, welcoming this interruption to push aside the huge pile of paperwork he was diligently working at as if in atonement for arriving late and delaying Trevor Watson's departure.

'Make it look like we were winning, wouldn't it?' Finch was the fourth villain on the Method Index raid, who had avoided DI Redvers' squad. 'The way he scarpered, someone out of Paddington must have given him the bell.'

'Yes. John was telling me. A fact of life, Fred,' he said philosophically. 'I mean what can you do, complain to CIB2? I daresay we've all done one a favour like that sometime.'

'Still pisses you off,' Pyle said despite himself. There had been any number of times when he had earned from villains for a timely phone call in just such circumstances.

'Give the local CID a miss when you turn him over this time,' DCI Simmons advised. 'Try that girlfriend of his as well, Fred. He might have slid in there.'

'Yes, I had planned to,' Pyle said. 'What about Harding? What do you think about a deal?' The climate in the CID was changing to such a degree that he could no longer make these decisions entirely on his own; at one time he would have, and certainly on division. But now strict supervision was the game which the hierarchy wanted playing, having as many senior detectives involved on such decisions as possible. It was a lot of nonsense as far as Pyle was concerned and he believed it did little more than reduce his overall efficiency.

'Can't say I like the idea of dropping him out altogether. Mind you, I don't mind if he's led to believe that's what'll happen.' He considered the matter; he was duty officer, there was none on the Squad higher than him at that moment in time, unless he liked to call one of the supers or the chief superintendent back, and he wasn't likely to for a decision such as this, even though it might have made him easier. 'What do you think yourself, Fred? Is he really going to come up to scratch?'

'Difficult to say. I mean, he's well placed. It wouldn't be hard for him to find us something worthwhile on Lynn.' Pyle shrugged. 'Depends what he's offered, I suppose.'

'What about C11? They have anything for you?'

'To be perfectly honest, guv, I haven't checked back with them yet.' It wasn't that he had been too busy to do so, for he'd simply have sent someone, but he'd forgotten. 'I think Jack Lynn might be more worthwhile out of the two. The other fella might only have been minding that gun, like he said.' He didn't really believe that, but did believe it was worthwhile having Harding at liberty to punt around, and so chose to soft pedal.

'With a firearm charge on the sheet, a magistrate would expect us to object to bail,' Simmons said, suggesting that course rather than coming right out and saying it. He didn't really want to take a chance, but didn't want to be seen to be afraid to. 'He wouldn't be much use to us down in Brixton.'

'Unless I had a quiet word with the beak,' Pyle offered.

Simmons looked askance at the DI. 'That's what Eric tried, didn't he. Now he's got CIB2 down his neck.'

'He was unlucky.' Pyle knew it was no more than that. DS Lethridge had done nothing more than most detectives did from time to time; he had gone and had a quiet word with the magistrate in favour of a grass who was doing a bit for him, only there was aggravation between the magistrate and his clerk and the latter had made a complaint against the DS.

'He'll be lucky not to get disciplinary action taken against him. Still it's a chance you take.'

Pyle conceded the point. 'Unless we leave Harding out altogether.'

'Be nice to have some kind of hold, Fred.'

'It's there, guv. Only be a matter of finding him again. Wouldn't be too difficult in his circumstances.'

'Got a family?'

'Four young kids,' Pyle said. 'Thinks the world of them. He wouldn't go far.'

That lessened the risk. Simmons considered this for a moment. 'How did it go with the gun dealer he put up, by the way?'

'We've got him down at Holloway. From the way he's shaping he'll go all right,' Pyle said. 'And one or two more besides, I shouldn't wonder.'

'Good. All right. Harding's worth a chance then, I suppose,' he said grudgingly. 'See if they have anything across the corridor first.'

The offices across the corridor used exclusively by C11 were much like the Squad's offices, too small for their requirements, impersonal, overstuffed with filing cabinets and desks. A very prominent feature in the main office was a large noticeboard which took up almost entirely one wall. It somewhat resembled a bizarre family tree made up of photographs of villains with arrows and information connecting them to other pictures. Most of them were in conference or nightclub-type settings, some in long shot, others in closer; some had been circled.

DI Graham McHale pointed to a circled photograph for Pyle's benefit. 'That's Jack Lynn,' he said. 'The most recent picture we have of him. Taken about six months ago. You see that?' He indicated the prison mugshot that was arrowed clear of the centre group. 'He's changed a bit.'

'Good living, I suppose,' Pyle said.

He was grateful for that vanity which made villains unable to resist having their photo taken in such circumstances, in nightclubs with hostesses hanging on their arms, but he resented the apparent good times they had, however transient.

'He was with a villain called George Bennett. This one here.' McHale pointed out a squirrel-like man in the picture. 'The Regional Crime Squad nicked him for a job out in Bromley. A bank. It was suspected that Lynn was involved, but there wasn't enough to nick him. You know what they're like,' McHale said with a note of disapproval.

Pyle nodded knowingly. The Regional Crime Squad were notoriously cautious before moving on anything, painstakingly careful before making an arrest. 'They still interested?'

'They have a nibble now and again, Fred. The way they work it'll be another two years before they bite.' The DI from Criminal Intelligence yawned. He kept mainly daytime office hours, and it was only because some of the detectives in C11 had something going off that night that he was around at this hour.

'What else you got? Anything?'

'Another rumour is all. A security van blag out in Wimbledon which might have been down to him. Around about that time he was seen in bad company. He was seen going mates with a lad called Alf Kitchen, who was believed to have been involved.'

'Was he nicked?' Pyle wanted to know.

'No. Only one lad was for that job. One or two more were pulled in. But later released.'

'D'you think he sold the Regional Crime Squad two bodies?'

'Appears that way.'

'Looks like he's had a good run.' He paused and thought about Lynn. 'Yes, he's well overdue,' he said, as though responding to what he was thinking. 'How did he stand? Was he putting those blags together?'

'I'd say that was possible, Fred. We've heard nothing to the effect.' McHale waited. 'That's all we have. The rest is on his CRO file.'

'Makes him a bit more interesting. Good luck.'

McHale seemed disappointed. 'You got anything for us, Fred?'

Pyle measured the DI with a look, then shook his head. 'Only a whisper that he's putting one together. 'S all. Not where or when.' He wasn't about to give C11 his information for them to give any CID who came looking for it. He came up with Lynn; he would nick him.

12

The block of flats where Brian Finch's girlfriend lived in West Hampstead was fairly modern, built within the last ten or fifteen years. It might easily have been council property, but then it might as easily have not: probably it wasn't, there weren't any prams parked in the entrance hall or on the landing and there were no graffiti on the walls. There was no lift and the flat they wanted was on the top floor. That was six flights of stairs.

'Wouldn't you know it,' Pyle said to DC Humphries as they started up the stairs.

'Keeps you fit, guv,' the DC replied.

'I'd say I was fit enough, Rog'.' By the fourth landing he wasn't showing much sign of fitness.

Access to the building had been easy enough, there was a caretaker who had admitted them, and was then summarily dismissed. The old man seemed disappointed at the CID's attitude, obviously believing he was going to be privy to a choice piece of gossip. Both the exits were covered. DS Lethridge was sat in his car at one; two detectives were at the back of the building.

The block was built in an L-shape with open walkways. The door to the flat they wanted was open, which made Pyle wary; maybe someone had left in a hurry. Maybe the woman was a fresh air fanatic or simply getting rid of cooking smells. As the DC rang the bell, so a dog immediately began barking. It was an Alsatian and it came bounding along the short hallway and stood at the threshold, baring its teeth and barking at the two men like it meant business. DC Humphries edged back, but Pyle refused to be intimidated, especially not by an Alsatian. He had done a course with dogs when he had been in the uniform branch, and he knew the breed well. He simply stood his ground and snarled back.

'Go on, you bastard, 'fore I break your arms!'

The young detective grinned nervously, not trusting the dog, but not too sure about his governor now either.

'Stop it! Stop it, Judge, there's a good boy. Be quiet now,' a woman said, appearing along the hall. The dog quietened and she caught hold of the choke chain he had on. 'You're very brave,' she said to Pyle. 'Most people run from Judge.'

'Of course I'm brave, I'm a police officer.' He said it like a recruitment handout, with an expressionless face, and might have been deadly serious for all this woman knew.

The woman appeared nonplussed, and didn't respond for a moment. She was in her late twenties, and was attractive in a tired, greasy-skinned sort of way; her face was good, with strong bone structure, but had a slightly vacuous expression, a look of the lonely and haunted. She had a good body as well, Pyle noticed; she was dressed in a pair of jeans and a shirt without a bra beneath it. The DI had a simple means of categorizing women: those he'd give one, and those he wouldn't. He'd give her more than one if he had the chance.

'Is that who you are?' she said. 'The police?'

"S Brian Finch ere, love?'

She started to shake her head, but Pyle was pushing into the flat past her, as though he had been invited. Humphries followed.

'Do you have such a thing as a warrant, by any chance?' The protest was feeble, knowing it would do little good. The dog's protest was nonexistent.

'Of course,' Pyle said over his shoulder. He reached into his pocket, as if to produce the appropriate paper. 'Roger ...' He indicated a room off the hall for Humphries to search. It was the bedroom. Pyle went into the other room without producing his warrant, for he hadn't one.

There was a lot of stuff in the small livingroom, but nothing that would conceal the body they were looking for.

Pyle could see that at a glance. Humphries was equally brief searching the bedroom. Both detectives swiftly reappeared in the narrow hallway where the woman waited. That left only the bathroom and the small kitchen to search, which took them just a few seconds.

'Now perhaps you'll believe me,' she said hostilely.

Pyle looked at her, feeling himself respond to her hostility. There was always something about angry women that touched pockets of sexual interest in him, it never failed, especially if they were halfway attractive. 'Slip down and check with Sergeant Lethridge,' he said casually to the DC. 'He might have got out ahead of us.'

The DC moved carefully around the dog and went out.

'Well, where's that warrant?' the woman wanted to know, still bristling.

'What warrant's that, love? Didn't you invite us in to search? Oh, I thought you did,' he said dully. 'I thought you said, come in, have a look round.'

She simply glared at him. Pyle could feel her anger, and could feel himself getting aroused. Having a hard-on twice in twelve hours was unusual for him.

'How long's he been gone, love?'

'How long has who been gone? Who are you talking about?' Her attitude was imitative of his over the warrant.

'Going to make me work for the bit of info', are you? All right, love, what's your name?'

'What's it to you?'

Pyle shook his head. 'Keeps the paperwork straight,'s all.'

'It's Finch. Elizabeth Finch. Brian's wife.'

She was lying. Pyle would have known that even had he not previously visited Finch's old woman over at Paddington, everything about her manner told him; he had, after all, cracked some of the best liars around. 'If you really want to be difficult, love, we can go to the local nick. But somehow I don't think you'll like that. A right pisshole it is.' There was a pause. His eyes bored into her, and she avoided meeting them.

'If you're his wife then he'll have to be done for bigamy as well. We just left Mrs Finch. Nice woman. Her mouth's a bit big, shouts a lot. Especially when she knows he's been at it with other women.'

The detective's words surprised her. 'Brian's not married,' she said, but without any confidence.

'Not to you, he's not.' He watched her closely, observing that his tack was having an effect. 'What are you wasting your time with a villain like that for? A nice girl like you. Brian knows he's got some coming. A lot of bird. 'S why he legged it like he did.'

'He didn't tell me he was married,' she said, vaguely disappointed.

'Why would he? I don't think I'd tell you I was married if I was looking to give you one.' In fact he'd make a point of doing so; she was obviously the sort of woman who appreciated that kind of honesty, and that kind of honesty was easy enough. 'What's your name? Your proper name?' He knew, of course, but the answers to such questions were the starting point for all successful interrogations.

'Libby Howard,' she answered.

Pyle nodded, 'About right. What are you doing with him, Libby? Slags, they're about his mark.' She didn't respond. 'Oh, I suppose he has a certain attraction. Most villains have. You'd be surprised some of the women they manage to pull.'

The Alsatian, which had been lying near the woman's feet, raised its head and began barking as DC Humphries returned.

'There's a good dog,' the DC offered nervously. 'Good doggy.'

'He's more sense than to bite you, Rog',' the DI assured him. 'Any sign?'

'No, nothing, guv.'

'He wasn't here,' Libby Howard said, yielding a little now, 'not today, he wasn't.'

Pyle nodded, then inclined his head at the DC, indicating for him to leave. 'Tell Eric to get over to Holloway. I'll see him there a bit later.'

The dog growled some more as Humphries went out again.

'D'you train him to do that?' Pyle asked. 'Bark at detectives?'

Finally she was unable to suppress a smile.

'What's this? A little smile – thought I had struck rock there for a moment. Always comes as a bit of a surprise to find you've been kipping with a liar.' She gave him a curious look. 'Well, that's what you were doing, wasn't it?'

'I don't think I can help you,' she said, resuming her detached manner.

'Come on, you haven't really tried, have you?'

'I can't help you – I have rather a bad headache.'

'I promise you the local nick won't improve it. Make yourself a cup of tea. Take a couple of those.' Pyle produced a flat silver foil pack of Disprin. 'Policemen get headaches too, you know. I'll have a cup with you.'

She hesitated and looked at him, then took the tablets.

In the kitchen Pyle casually picked up letters that were placed between a storage jar and the wall at the end of the shelf and glanced over them while Libby Howard waited for the kettle to boil. She turned and saw him and became a little alarmed.

'Hey, they're private letters!' She reached for them, but Pyle pulled his hand back keeping them out of reach.

'You shouldn't have secrets from me, Libby,' he said lightly, and returned the letters to the shelf. She immediately retrieved them and jammed them into her jeans pocket.

'How long have you known Brian Finch?'

She shrugged and switched off the boiling kettle. 'What do you want him for?'

'You trying to tell me you don't know?'

'I don't. Why should I?' She seemed genuinely surprised.

'Villains have a lot of bunny. They never leave off telling people what they've done. That's why we catch so many, not because we're geniuses.' He saw her take up a pale green tea packet. 'What's that, China tea?'

'It's the only sort I have.' It wasn't an apology.

'Better make mine coffee.'

'Are you always so presumptuous?' she wanted to know. But reached down a jar of coffee.

'Is that what I am?' He nodded vaguely. It might have been an apology; he didn't mind her thinking that. 'I suppose being a policeman as long as I have, that makes me like it. You don't even realize at times.' He nodded again.

Libby Howard was surprised, not expecting this change of attitude from the detective. She paused and considered him, not recognizing the ploy, not realizing that if you gave a little of yourself, as Pyle had done, you made the person you were dealing with beholden to you; however, she responded instinctively. Brian Finch had told her what detectives were like, but somehow that didn't correspond to this man.

'Is he in serious trouble when you find him?' she wanted to know.

'There's a bank robbery down to him.'

That surprised Libby, but she tried not to show it, not wanting this man to see quite how gullible she had been about Brian. She had known he had been a criminal, but was way off on her definition, naively thinking that that meant little more than his living by his wits. 'Oh well, banks have loads of money,' she tried lightly.

'More than I've got, that's for sure,' Pyle said. 'But a guard was hurt this time, and pretty badly hurt. Still, that's nothing to do with you.'

'I'm sorry. I didn't realize ...'

"Course you didn't. Why would you?'

She was silent, regretting her flip remark. She offered him black coffee without thinking about what she was doing.

'You got some milk for that, love?' She got it from the fridge. Pyle watched her, not considering then whether or not he might get to stiff her, but deciding how best to manipulate her. He changed tack slightly, deciding that she hadn't quite written the villain off yet. 'He can help himself, of course. It's not all down to him. Fact is, I think very little of it was. Only that's not how the other guy we nicked is telling it,' he lied. 'He says it's all down to Brian. Everyone tries to save himself when he's up against it. A fact of life – never was any honour among thieves.' He shrugged, as if apologizing for having disillusioned her. He sipped his coffee and waited. 'Did you take your tablets?'

She retrieved the foil tray from the draining board and handed them back. 'I have some of my own, thanks. It's not that bad now, anyway.'

Pyle nodded, like her relief was his doing. His eyes circled the kitchenette. Earthenware pots and crockery were neatly arranged on the pine shelves. She was an orderly person and he was curious about her relationship with Finch, involving herself with the obvious chaos surrounding his life.

'What do you do for a living, Libby?'

'I'm a windowdresser,' she said. 'Women's fashion.' Pyle smiled. It was the first time he had done so.

'Don't you believe me?'

'Course I do. Why would you lie? I was just thinking about a lad I knew who kept a couple of those mannequins. He was a bit of a sad case – never could pull one. He ended up in Broadmoor finally. Poor bastard. He couldn't be helped at all.'

She considered him for a moment, trying to work him out. 'Will you help Brian when you get him?'

'I don't like seeing villains taking stick for other people's villainy. But I honestly can't say, love. I mean, I'll help him if he lets me. First we have to find him.' He paused to allow the words to make their mark. 'You any idea where he might be?'

Finding herself on the horns of a dilemma, Libby Howard hesitated. She was disappointed with Brian Finch for being what he was, for deceiving her, but still wanted to help him. She believed this detective might help him, but remembered what her lover had said about all policemen. Then his outlook was biased, and even if he was right about a lot of policemen, she decided finally, he was wrong about this one.

'There are a couple of people he mentioned from time to time. Friends of his. I don't know the people, but he could be with them, I suppose.'

Pyle didn't say anything. He waited for her to put up the names, knowing she was going to give him more than a couple of names.

13

'Some of us have done a day's work here, guv,' DS Lethridge said on encountering the DI, who came in through the back reception area at Holloway police station with DC Humphries. The corpulent DS pointedly checked the time, then hitched up his trousers.

'It's results that count, son,' Pyle said. 'That right, Rog'?'

'Yes, guv,' the DC said awkwardly.

'How d'you get on?' Lethridge asked.

'Oh, she came round all right. Put a couple up.' He produced his notebook and considered the names he had been given before giving them to the DS. 'Send a couple of the lads out visiting, Eric. A chance Finch might be there.'

'You were up there long enough,' the DS commented. 'D'you give her one?'

'To be honest, I wouldn't mind. Wouldn't mind one little bit. I will have to pop back, for a statement,' Pyle said. Ordinarily a DI wouldn't bother but simply send someone.

Lethridge grinned, feeling an irrational stab of envy. 'Old slags can come to the station and make their statements! What's she like? Any good?'

'I've fucked worse. A lot worse,' the DI said, giving nothing. 'How are the bodies here shaping?'

'Clark's still whining for his brief. He put one or two up. So did the gun dealer.' He handed the DI the statement in the folder he was carrying. 'Jack's out visiting now.'

'Good. What about Harding? What's he have to say?' He was glancing through the pages.

'He's missing his family.'

'About right. I'll have a word with him.' He shut the folder decisively.

'My governor wasn't very interested in doing business with you, son,' Pyle told Clifford Harding when he went to see him in his cell. It might have been some cruel game he was playing with him, but in fact there was more to it than that.

'Jesus,' Harding protested. He was visibly distressed. 'I mean, I give you the gun dealer, didn't I. You said if I give you the gun dealer.' He began to pace the cell. A tray of unfinished supper was sitting on the bench. The congealed fat from boiled bacon, blackening potatoes and dried carrots didn't exactly look appetizing, but then it would only have been a little more appetizing when first served. 'Fuck I! I mean, I give you the man, didn't I, I thought we had a deal . . .'

'I appreciate what you did, Clifford, don't think otherwise, son,' Pyle assured him as though that in itself was worth having. 'But he thinks that shooter makes you a more interesting proposition.' He paused, leaving Harding on the hook. What Pyle was doing was letting him taste that sickening alternative to the help he had promised for help in kind: only then did the DI believe he would do the business he wanted him to do. 'I mean, personally, Clifford, I'd take a chance on you myself, regardless of what my governor said – if I was really convinced you were going to come up with the goods on Jack Lynn for us.'

A glimmer of hope got airborne, and Harding reached for it desperately. 'But I can though, can't I? I can. I'll do the business.'

'You think so?' Pyle said doubtfully.

'Oh, fuck me, guv, I've got to. I mean, I've got to, 'in I?'

'Unless you want another taste, a long one that is.'

'I'll do the business for you. You just gimme the chance. I won't let you down, I won't, straight.' The felon was so urgent in his appeal that he ached with apprehension.

At first the detective appeared unmoved. Then he nodded slowly, letting Harding off the hook. 'If you do, son, then you'd better leg it. Get as far away from me as you can . . .'

'I can't. I mean, what about my family . . .?'

No criminal might ever have run out on his dependants.

Pyle looked at him, unimpressed by his argument, but knowing that Harding wouldn't be too difficult to capture again if he didn't come through. A little effort was all that would be needed.

Tentatively, Harding said, 'What about the shooter, guv?'

Pyle knew what he was asking, but was purposely obtuse. 'What, you want it back!' he said sarcastically. 'It's been left pending. I'll see how you shape, son.'

After he had released Clifford Harding, with a few more threats, Pyle spent some time on both Terry Clark and the gun dealer, Wally Marks; then when DS Barcy returned with two more suspects whom Marks had put up, he interrogated those. The last two in would probably be nicked for possessing firearms and conspiracy to rob, and with the help of the gun dealer that would be no problem. But Pyle probed deeper. He'd sooner have past deeds, actual robberies that had taken place. Results were always more impressive if some figure, blag or recovery was attached to them. Ideally he would have liked to have tied Terry Clark up with Marks somehow, and put that possibility to the gun dealer, but they weren't in fact connected. Clark still hadn't been allowed to see his solicitor, and nor would he be until he was taken before the magistrates for remanding. There was little doubt that he would be charged in connection with the blag out at Walthamstow last week. Pyle guessed he would find some means of cracking him. There would be something he would want, some pressure point he'd yield to. One thing was for sure, the CID had all the advantages now.

As the night wore on and the interrogations became more specific, Pyle knew that by the end of this investigation he'd wind up with some nice results to his credit. That was part of what made it worthwhile after all.

Some detectives, so rumour had it, were supposed to work nonstop until they cracked the cases they were working on; if there were or had ever existed such policemen, Pyle had never met them. When it was time to finish or take a break or he had had enough, that was it, he stopped at the next most convenient moment. He often left the detectives on his squad to work on after his departure, but knew they applied the same rules. Those super-detectives with an unflagging capacity for work only ever existed in works of fiction.

Travelling south from Holloway in the back of the blue Ford Cortina, Pyle shut his eyes but wouldn't go to sleep. DS Lethridge was in the back of the car with him.

'Bit swift, wasn't it,' Lethridge remarked casually, 'letting Harding go like that?'

'I dunno. Depends if the wrong people get to hear of it, I suppose.' He stretched and rubbed his eyes. 'He'll come eventually. He has to, he's too active to be left loose. I'd say he was going to make one with that shooter, wouldn't you?'

'Certainly looked that way.'

'See what he comes up with on Jack Lynn first. I'd like to see him nicked. You want dropping anywhere, Eric?'

'No, Cocoa'll do. I haven't got a meet tonight. Thought maybe I'd shoot up to Soho, give an old tom a pull.' He grinned.

'About your mark, you fat bastard.' There was a pause. Pyle wanted to change tack; he didn't want to discuss Eric Lethridge's sexual or marital problems. Lethridge still hadn't got over the surprise of his old lady leaving him, but the DI didn't think he had too many problems finding other women to stiff. 'I have an interview with CIB2 on Friday,' Pyle informed him.

'Oh, yeah – been at it again, Fred, have you?' Lethridge said lightly, knowing the reason for the interview.

'Right at the fucking start of my leave. The bastards do it for the purpose. Be as well to get it straight what you want me to tell them.' Pyle was being interviewed in connection with the complaint against the DS. Lethridge had gone into the magistrate on behalf of a felon who had been nicked but had previously been doing a bit for him. If proven it could cause

116

the DS a lot of problems.

"S like we agreed. He wasn't my grass.' Lethridge considered the senior detective. 'That's best, Fred, isn't it?'

'Probably. That wouldn't have given you any reason for going into that magistrate.'

Pyle, as the DS's immediate governor, was supposed to be informed of all and any snouts that were used. This knowledge, the hierarchy believed, acted as a kind of safeguard and prevented subsequent charges against detectives involved; Pyle in his turn was supposed to inform his governor about his grasses.

'But I didn't, Fred, did I? I mean, I wouldn't go into a magistrate to try and get favours for a criminal, would I?' He grinned knowingly.

"Course you wouldn't, son.' Pyle grinned. He'd give the DS whatever help he could.

14

There were about thirty men crowded into the first floor gym
of the Grapes off Bethnal Green Road. There were some
professionals sparring and shaping up with would-be
champions; there were old pros who hung around doing what
they could for whoever they could, simply because they
couldn't leave the game alone. There were managers and
would-be promoters standing around the ring, some
earnestly discussing fighters' prospects; there were people
who had simply wandered up from the bars below when they had
shut, people with nothing else to do when bars shut; people
with tenuous connections in the fight game, if only by instinct.
There was a smell about the place familiar to most gyms; it
hung in the slightly humid atmosphere, that sour smell of
damp leather and stale seeds of sweat caught in unlaundered
clothes.

Jack Lynn had no connection with the fight game, though
knew a lot of villains who had. Not even as a kid did he do a bit.
He could use himself in a fight when put to it, but saw little
sense in actually doing it for a living. A lot of kids started
boxing as an alternative to villainy and for a lot of the kids he
grew up with those two pursuits seemed about the only two
alternatives. Perhaps there were other opportunities, but he
wasn't any more aware of them now than he had been then.

Stopping inside the doorway, Lynn stretched onto his toes
over the crowd to try and locate the man he was looking for.
He saw him on the far side of the gym, working out on one of the
punchbags. Bobby Shaw had been low on the list, simply
because Lynn hadn't known if he was out of prison. He had
run into Shaw's brother about a fortnight ago and was told
that Bobby was due out, but anything might have happened to

prevent his release.

Several people greeted Lynn as he made his way across the gym and he responded in a familiar manner, despite drawing a blank on some of their names. Lynn stopped on the far side of the room and watched Shaw slam his fists into the heavy bag. Bobby Shaw glanced at him as one fist followed the other down in a series, but he didn't speak.

'You look like you're staying fit, Bobby,' Lynn said.

Shaw stopped hitting the bag and looked at him. 'I didn't recognize you for a minute,' he said, pleased to see him. He stabbed almost disinterestedly at the punchbag now, using his right fist only. 'You gotta keep yourself at it, son. All that bodybuilding inside, you go fat as a pig' you leave off.' Shaw was in good shape, having been doing a lot of working out inside; there was little else to do, and the weights got a prisoner out of his cell.

'When d'you get out?' Lynn asked, leaning his weight against the punchbag as the boxer started pounding it again.

'Last Friday.' His breathing became heavy with exertion.

'I saw Terry, d'he tell you?' Shaw didn't reply. 'He reckoned you was getting full remission.'

'Was a good boy, Jack, wan' I. Yes, sir, no, sir, three bags full, sir!' He slammed his fists into the bag now as if trying to relieve his frustrations over the prison system. Lynn could feel the weight of the blows jarring his shoulder through the bag. 'Got the right pox of that fucking place.'

'You must be about ready to do a bit of work, I'd've thought,' Lynn suggested.

'Be handy. This don't earn me nothing.' He stopped hitting the bag. 'What you got in mind, Jack?' There was a glistening film of sweat across Shaw's muscular arms and shoulders.

'Something very tasty. You want to turn this in?'

'Yeah. I'll take a chance on getting fat.'

'You fat bastard,' Lynn said lightly. 'What d'you want to be slim for anyway?'

'You gotta stay in shape, you wanna pull a few. Know what

I mean, Jack?'

'Pulling my prick's about all I can manage nowadays, Bobby.' Without warning Lynn drove a right hook into Shaw's shoulder while his guard was down. Shaw responded out of surprise, but it was too late. Lynn had moved back, 'Got you, you fat bastard.'

'Ah, you cunt, you done m' shoulder right up,' Shaw moaned exaggeratedly.

Lynn laughed, his mood was buoyant. Those bad feelings he had been getting about the job had vanished. 'That's just to show you who's the guvnor at this boxing game.'

'Leave off, Jack,' Shaw said, going along with the sport. 'You're the guvnor.' He'd bide his time and get Lynn back with a good 'un. It was a game, irrelevant, pointless, even banal, but enjoyable, even when you forgot, lowered your guard and took one.

When Lynn outlined the bit of work he had in mind, Shaw committed straightaway. He had been living on Social Security since getting out of prison, and Social Security was the only prospect for the future other than villainy. He didn't fancy getting a proper job, even if he had been able to find one. And prison hadn't exactly rehabilitated him. There wasn't a lot of call for sighted basket makers these days! He had one or two suggestions of people who might fancy going to work. One of them, Billy Braden, was already down on Lynn's list. He simply hadn't been able to reach him but had been leaving messages about getting in touch.

Bobby Shaw was most impressed when Lynn took him down to Catford dogtrack to watch the collection operation by the security truck. It was as though until actually seeing that truck arrive and then the two guards emerge from the stadium some fifteen minutes later with the cash containers he had never believed it. He believed it now. The vein of excitement that ran through him made him almost glow at the prospect.

'It'll be a right fucking doddle, Jack, won't it?' Shaw said.

'Yeah. Won't be hard at all, I don't reckon.'

'We'll want some shooters though, I'd think.' The last blag he had been on, the one he had been nicked for, they had only had pickaxe handles, which impressed no one. A few skulls were knocked in, but that didn't stop people having a go.

'I s'pose they would be handy,' Lynn conceded, even though he had been planning to use guns. 'They're not gonna be a problem.'

'Got someone in mind to get them, have you?'

'Yeah, little firm over my way should do them all right.'

''S not Wally Marks, is it?' It was an instinctive guess. 'You hear the Squad nicked him?'

'No. What, the greengrocer out of Finsbury Park?'

''S what I heard, Jack.'

'Fuck I! I didn't hear nothing.' Lynn was a bit dismayed. 'As it happens I did have him in mind. I mean, well, it wasn't definite. He was one of them.'

'He was well bubbled up. 'S what a lad who does a bit told me. Reckons it was down to Clifford Harding.'

'Leave off. Cliff's as good as gold,' Lynn protested. 'Least, he wouldn't put no one away.'

'Well, how else could you go and get your liberty after being nicked with a shooter, Jack?' Shaw wanted to know.

'By putting a nice earner into the filth. That's what I heard. Got one on the Squad straightened.'

The argument was academic. Whether or not Harding was a grass didn't affect them. The only difference it might have made was through his having grassed the gun dealer, but that was easily remedied by going elsewhere. There was no reason Lynn should be doing Harding any favours by defending him anyway. He quite liked him, but although he worked regularly he hadn't thought of him for this blag.

'You could be right,' Shaw said grudgingly. 'I always liked the man when we was in the Scrubs together. I mean, I wouldn't wish no cunt back there. Probably even pull one or two diabolical strokes myself in order to stay out. Know what

I mean, Jack?'

'Cliff's all right,' Lynn announced, not wholly convinced but not interested in pursuing the matter.

There was a brief silence in the car as they watched the two security guards climb into the truck and start it up.

'Where we gonna do this precisely? Just there?' Shaw asked.

'I was figuring inside. In the office. I got a key to the door,' in I.'

'Oh, we'll definitely want shooters then, Jack. The way some of them cunts are. One or two of them have to have their kneecaps done before they realize it ain't worth having a go for someone else's bit of dough. Not when it's insured and all. Know what I mean?'

'As it happens I do, Bob. Shooters won't be a problem. I can see about them tomorrow.' Lynn knew three men who dabbled in guns, including Wally Marks, who had done the most and had been the handiest. But Lynn guessed he wouldn't be doing anything for a long while, however he came to have his collar felt. The second dealer he couldn't reach. The third, Trevor Foley, was around.

He lived out at Willesden, which wasn't too far. When Lynn phoned him he told him to come up and see him, but to give him a bell when he got up there. That made sense, Lynn thought. He hadn't done business with the man before, but had met him a couple of times and knew him to be a cautious bird; that was the way he kept his liberty, and he couldn't be faulted for that.

From the phone box outside the post office in Harlesden Road, Lynn rang the gun dealer again. The phone was answered almost immediately but no number was given. Lynn pushed the coin in the box.

'Trevor? 'S Jack ... all right?'

'Yes,' the voice down the line said, though he didn't seem too certain. 'You didn't take long. Where are you?'

'Just down the road. What d'you want me to do? Come up?'

'Here? No. I'll meet you. You know Roundwood Park?'

Lynn didn't, but Foley gave him explicit instructions, then repeated them, just so there was no mistake and they didn't miss each other.

Roundwood Park was only a couple of minutes from the phone box, so Lynn was the first to arrive. Sitting on the bench on the path as described, Lynn felt a bit conspicuous as he waited for Foley. The weather was damp and cold, not the sort of day on which people sat around in parks. The few people he saw were mostly walking dogs and moving briskly. The park looked quite nice, Lynn thought, with the carpet of red and brown leaves that had fallen. Some of the leaves had been cleared into piles, one of which was smouldering. The tarry smell of smoke hung in the air where the leaves were either too wet or too green to burn properly. Eddie Aldiss popped into Lynn's thoughts, he was an arsonist he had done sometime with. Aldiss could have made those leaves burn in a torrential downpour. He was able to make anything burn.

Lynn's attention suddenly went to a man who turned onto the path with a dog. It was Trevor Foley. He would have recognized him a mile off in his trilby hat, his clipped moustache and thick-lensed National Health glasses. He stopped and let the dog off its lead, then approached Lynn on his own as the dog ran off to have a sniff round and see what was on offer.

'Fuck knows what we're meeting like this for, Trevor,' Lynn said as Foley sat on the bench with him. 'We can get done just as easily for conspiracy here like this.'

'It's a nice fresh day,' Foley observed.

'We'll probably get done as a pair of flashers or something.'

'That'd be a turn up for the book, Jack,' he said cheerfully. 'You want to take a walk?'

Lynn huddled deeper into his coat in the corner of the bench. 'Can't say as I do.'

'Trouble with you people living down in all that muck,' Foley said. 'All so unhealthy.'

'Willesden's not exactly fucking countryside, is it.'

'I don't know,' Foley said, looking around the park. 'It has its good points.'

Lynn smiled. 'You're still doing a bit, Trevor, are you?'

'You have to do something, Jack, 'pay the rent. Social Security doesn't go far these days.' He checked around to make sure no one was within earshot. 'What sort of shooters are you after, any idea?'

'Something impressive,' Lynn said decisively, 'so we won't have to use them. But not too big – there won't be a lot of room to manoeuvre. A couple of sawn-off shotguns and a couple of .38s should do it all right, I'd think.'

'You want ammunition?' Foley asked. The question wasn't as silly as it seemed. Some villains wouldn't take ammunition for fear of shooting someone.

'Be handy,' Lynn said sarcastically. 'Cutdown cartridges, we'll want.' When fired from a sawn-off shotgun or even a full length barrel for that matter, they didn't carry so far and consequently did less damage. The lead shot fanned immediately on leaving the barrel and peppered a whole area, but would rarely kill anyone unless they were right in front of the gun. It was effective in scaring people witless.

'When d'you want them? You in a hurry?'

'Well, as soon as possible, I think. It might go a bit lively. 'S that all right?'

The gun dealer thought about it. 'Yes. That should be okay. Give me a ring in a day or so. I can let you know definitely. Mind you, they'll come to a nice few quid, Jack. About six and a half, I'd say.'

'Fucking hell! What are you doing, manufacturing them.'

'It's the world situation that's the problem, Jack,' he explained. 'People are frightened to dabble nowadays in case they get done as a terrorist.'

'Still a bit strong, I'd have thought, Trevor.' Lynn accepted that he was going to have to pay that sort of money. 'You want to have a taste of it, what we earn?' he tried.

Foley shook his head. He wouldn't consider such a

proposition. 'I'll take them back off you, you get out without firing them.' He considered the villain, then stared across the park at his dog sniffing around another. 'You hear about Wally Marks?'

'I heard he was grassed,' he said, hoping Foley might offer some information. He didn't.

'Wicked, wasn't it. Can't trust anyone any more hardly. Did you try him?'

'Did I fuck. D'you hear who it was, Trevor?'

'Some no-good cunt, that's for sure.' He thought about that, then shook his head, dismayed by the sad state of affairs. 'I'll have those ready for you, Jack.'

'I'm relying on you,' Lynn said.

'Give me a tinkle, just to make sure.' He rose off the bench. 'Patch! C'mon, boy,' he called to his dog. 'Mind how you go, Jack.'

'Be lucky.' Lynn watched him move away, stooping to catch and leash his dog as he went.

15

The kitchen had never been large enough, but lately it seemed to be getting smaller, closing in on Dolly Lynn, pressurizing her, trapping her; a kitchen four times the size wouldn't have made any real difference to those feelings as she stood at the sink, and listened to the two girls bickering. One teased the other and of late no matter what she said to them they took no notice. In the short time since they had started that morning she couldn't remember what it was that had set them off – a pop singer one of them liked and the other pretended she didn't, nothing more serious. Normally their squabbles went over her head or she resolved them with either a few words of comfort to one or by chiding the other. But now she just couldn't cope. It was nothing to do with the girls or the way they carried on, they were healthy, normal kids, who carried on no differently to the way two sisters should, but even so they had to bear the brunt of her irritation. Aware as she was of the injustice of it all, Dolly was unable to help herself shouting at them, or even giving them a slap. Not that it seemed to do much good. It was as though they were aware of her anxiety, the uncertainty that was undermining her, and were made edgy by it themselves. Their Dad was the only one they took any notice of nowadays. She didn't resent that, only wished she didn't feel as she did.

What it was that had happened to her in the past few weeks she didn't know; she knew the cause, only couldn't understand why she was unable to cope. She had before, on many occasions when her husband was getting involved, even while he was in prison she had been okay. For five long years that had been. But now the thought of him going away again terrified her, probably because she was older and had too much to lose. She didn't know. Maybe it was just her age, the strange period she seemed to be going through at thirty-eight. She hadn't reached menopause, and felt she would like another child before it was too late, but suddenly the uncertainty of the future made her feel ambivalent about a third child.

The bickering behind her reached a pitch when Sandra, the youngest at eight, shouted at her sister, 'You bloody well shut your face, Carol!'

'Hey, now that's enough of that, miss, or I'll put my hand round your bloody face,' Dolly said, turning from the sink where she was cleaning their shoes for school. These days she tended to be less tolerant of Sandra than she might ordinarily have been, simply because she was her father's favourite. It was wrong, she realized, but she couldn't help herself. She wasn't malicious to the child or spiteful, just didn't let her have her way.

'Well,' Sandra retorted, 'you should tell her to leave off. Saying my friends have got fleas.'

'I never!' Carol protested. She was eleven, and large boned like her mother.

'Well, just pack it in the pair of you,' Dolly said. She saw the comic Carol was standing at the breakfast table reading. 'Oh c'mon, Carol! Help your sister will you, or you're gonna be late for school.'

'Well, she won't finish, will she,' the older girl retorted. 'Look, she ain't even eaten her Rice Krispies yet.'

'You didn't get me no sugar like I asked,' Sandra said.

Impatiently Dolly reached into the cupboard close to hand – in the small modernized kitchen all cupboards were close to hand – for a jar of sugar and banged it on the table. 'There! Now come on.'

'I don't like them very much, anyway. They're all soggy.'

'Well, you get and eat them. You've hardly eaten anything.'

'She dawdles and plays with her smelly friends – I'm gonna go without her,' Carol announced, closing her comic.

'Here, get those on,' Dolly said, reaching the girl's shoes off the drainingboard and dropping them on the floor in front of her.

'Can't Dad take us to school by car?' Sandra wanted to know. She knew better than to expect her Mum to take them.

'He might as well,' Dolly said irritably. "'S got nothing else to do. Go and get him up, Carol – get your shoes on first.'

'I will,' Sandra said, leaping up from the table.

'You finish your breakfast ...' Dolly began but realized it was a mistake, the youngest girl didn't take any notice. All she could do was scream at her or drag her back. There was no point taking it out on either of the girls.

'I'm going to get Dad up,' Sandra insisted as she rushed out.

Carol's attention went back to her comic until her mother saw her.

'Carol! Will you move yourself,' she snapped. 'Put that comic away.'

'Bloody hell! I'm not doing nothing. Taking it out on me.'

'And less of your cheek or you'll get my hand round your face.'

Carol and her mother glared at each other, the girl not in the least bit impressed, the woman sensing she was losing control.

Lying in bed Jack Lynn listened to the raised voices as they came through the ceiling, but didn't attempt to disturb. He had had another late night last night. Anyway, he knew what was going on. His eyes trailed round the modern bedroom, from the daylight emerging through the curtains, over the built-in dressing table and wardrobe units to the door as it opened. He immediately closed his eyes and pretended to be asleep.

Sandra came into the room and moved cautiously along the side of the bed. 'Dad? You awake, Dad?' she said, stopping at the bed and reaching over to shake her father.

Suddenly opening his eyes, Lynn grabbed her and pulled her onto the bed and kissed her. 'Got you.' He squeezed her against himself. 'Ah, come in to bed for five minutes and cuddle my back.'

'Can I?' she said eagerly. She liked getting into her parents' bed, especially when her Dad was there. But she hadn't been given the opportunity lately.

'You gotta go to school, haven't you,' he said, and saw his daughter's nose wrinkle in disappointment. 'What was your Mum shouting at just now?'

'Oh,' Sandra responded vaguely, as if having forgotten. 'Carol won't get herself ready. We're gonna be late for school. Will you take us, Dad?' She pulled at the buttons on his monogrammed pyjama jacket.

'What's the matter with walking? You lazy little bugger.' He resisted her playfully.

'We're gonna be late though. We'll get the stick if we're late.' It had the desired effect.

'They'd better not bloody well give you the stick, sweetheart. Or I'll be down that school and give them the stick.' He paused and looked at her feeling a slight quake of emotion in his chest that resembled a palpitation; that was how much he loved his kids, and he couldn't look at them without feeling that. 'Haven't you got a kiss for your old Dad, then?' She had. She placed her lips against his and locked her arms around his neck. 'Oh, only one?' he said in mock disappointment. She giggled and kissed him again. Her lips were soft and eager against his. 'All right, just one more now and I'll consider getting up and driving you to school.'

It was a game which Sandra enjoyed, and would have been happily delayed by all day. She was a bit disappointed when he kissed her finally and eased her off the bed.

'Right! I'm coming down right now. Tell Carol she'd better be ready.'

Sandra went across to the door and stood with it open, not attempting to go out as her father climbed from the bed. She hung on the two door handles, placing her face against the edge of the door and looked back as he started out of his pyjamas.

'I don't feel like going to school, Dad. I got a tummy ache.'

Lynn gave her a doubting look. 'You sure about that, Sandra?'

She avoided his eyes and fiddled with the doorknob. 'I have, Dad,' she said quietly.

'Come 'ere then,' he said, yielding. He stooped to her when she sidled up to him and rubbed her tummy. 'How 'bout we go to school in my car and see how it is when we get there? Hey, lovey?'

She didn't say anything, not wanting to have to commit herself. But Lynn accepted her silence as assent.

'Good girl. Down you go, love,' he said straightening up. 'Tell Mum I won't be long.'

Both girls rode in the front of the grey Jaguar as their father drove them to school. Sandra was next to her Dad and most of the way offered ploys to distract him so he shouldn't take them. Carol was quite happy to go, and as soon as the car drew up outside the school gate she jumped out, throwing a perfunctory 'Bye, Dad' over her shoulder.

'You all right now, sweetheart, are you?' Lynn asked, putting his hand on the younger girl's head. She nodded. 'There's a love. C'mon, give us a kiss or you'll be the biggest dunce in the class.'

Sandra kissed him, then hesitated, holding open the door. 'You gonna get a job today, are you, Dad?' she asked seriously. She was concerned that he did. Their Mum had been going on about it at breakfast and was quite cross, she thought; that was why she hadn't really wanted to go to school.

'Yeah, 'course I am, darling,' he said lightly, a little surprised by her question. 'Otherwise we won't be able to pay the milkman, will we.'

That prospect didn't interest her. 'Mum won't get cross then, she won't.'

Lynn thought about that as he considerd his daughter, touched by her concern. He guessed all kids were concerned that their parents got on. He remembered he used to worry a bit when his parents rowed, tried to help them make the peace, felt uncomfortable when they didn't. Kids didn't change.

'What sort of job would you like me to get, Sandy? Would you like me to be a policeman?'

Sandra shook her head, knowing instinctively that a policeman's life was not the life for her Dad.

The schoolbell sounded. Both father and daughter reacted to it.

'Come on, there's the bell.' He kissed her. 'Don't worry, love. I'll get a nice job. I'll see you lunchtime.'

'Will you come and meet us?'

'Don't think so. Be a good girl. Bye, darling.'

She climbed out of the car and started into school. She paused at the gate, as if hoping for a reprieve, then turned and went inside.

Lynn sat pensively looking after her for a moment, thinking about what she had said, how she'd reacted to the current situation with Dolly. He knew the sort of state his wife was getting herself into. He knew why, yet couldn't really understand it — it wasn't as if they hadn't been here before. However, he knew he ought to try and do something about it before it really upset the kids.

Dolly didn't react when he let himself into the kitchen. She was at the sink, washing up there. At least eighty per cent of her working hours seemed to be spent in the kitchen, mostly at the sink, though she didn't object or resent the fact. Instead she rather enjoyed keeping the house nice, until it started to become a strain, that was; until anxiety caused her to question what the point of all the effort was when Jack was putting everything at risk.

Gingerly Lynn felt the teapot on the table. It was cold, but he didn't really want any tea, even though he hadn't had anything that morning. Almost as gingerly he moved in behind his wife and pressed his hips into her soft rump. Her ass was getting a bit bigger, he noticed, since getting her own car, but he didn't really mind. He wasn't exactly encouraged in his gesture, but then she didn't give him a straight blank, so he persevered. He made a grinding motion against her, feeling himself getting an erection. He reached round her and forced his large hands down the front of her skirt.

'How many pints today, Mrs Lynn?' he said, knowing she was avoiding a smile. He managed to get one of his hands into the top of her pants, feeling the soft flesh of her stomach, the coarseness of her pubic hair.

Despite herself she shrugged him off. 'Don't mess around, Jack. I'm not in the mood.'

'Oh, t'rific,' he said, appearing hurt. His manner suddenly hardened. 'Well, how about a bit of breakfast then?'

'You know where it is.' She didn't even turn from washing up.

'All right, Dolly, you got the hump. What's the problem then? What's wrong, hey?' It would have given her too much of a tactical advantage by immediately acknowledging what he knew to be wrong with her.

'Oh, you make me tired, Jack. You make me bloody tired.' The words suddenly burst out of her. She turned to confront him. 'You keep on, don't you. You keep pushing your luck. You can't be like other men, you won't be satisfied, will you.'

Still he refused to yield ground. 'What the fuck are you on about?'

'You know. You bloody well know,' – her voice going up slightly. 'You make me tired. Well, just don't expect me to be waiting for you when you get done again. I'm not gonna wait around twenty years till I'm an old woman ...'

'You having a brainstorm or something, Dolly? I should think you fucking well must be.' The momentum of the argument carried him, making him feel selfrighteous. 'I should think you fucking well must be,' he repeated.

'Oh don't take me for a complete idiot, Jack. I know you're

at it again.' Tears were building behind her eyes now, but anger was keeping them.

'What makes you think that?' he demanded. 'C'mon, what makes you think so?'

'You think I don't know you after all this time? Don't know how you behave? You're putting one together all right. I can tell.'

'You ought to be a fucking detective, that's what ...'

'I'd be a sight better off,' she retorted. 'You can't be like other men. You gotta be at it the whole time. 'S like a disease with you ... Well, I won't be here, Jack. I promise you. I'll take the kids and go.'

Lynn realized it was no use lying to her, that she knew him too well. In order to try and gain ground he changed his tack. 'Well, who d'you think I do it for, then?'

'You!' she said. 'Who d'you think.'

'Talk fucking silly. You think you'd have a nice home, two cars, and a bit of spending money? You think you'd have all that if I was working down the road in a factory?'

'I don't know, Jack. Other people seem to manage all right. Least they know their husbands ain't gonna go away for twenty years. The thought of it's too much, Jack. I can't stand it.' She was appealing now rather than badgering. 'I get so frightened when you're out nowadays. One time, well, one time it almost didn't matter, there didn't seem too much at stake. We were younger and could cope better.' She had become quieter, anger subsiding; tears were at the brim of her eyes, waiting to tip down her face.

Pausing and looking at her, Lynn was moved by her urgent concern. 'You really want me to go and get a job?' he asked, almost expecting her to recognize what a punishment that would be for him.

'You could do, Jack. I know it wouldn't be easy at first, not even with the sort of money you'd get. But we've got everything we need, 'in't we. You could go mini-cabbing with Tommy,' she suggested.

That idea had been mooted before. In fact, occasionally he helped her brother out when he had a lot on. He accepted there were worse ways of earning a living: at least you were more or less your own boss mini-cabbing.

'Yeah, I s'pose that won't seem too much like collar,' he said. He liked the way his wife responded.

'You mean it, Jack?' she said, coming to him. 'You do mean it?'

'I tell you,' he said evasively, 'I weren't having too much luck putting this one together. The way it was going I'd do myself a right favour giving it a miss. I'll give it a try with Tom, 'he can put a bit my way.' He put his arms around her as if in confirmation of this, and felt her relax. 'But the thing is, Dolly,' he began, like the thought had only just occurred to him, 'I'm a villain. 'Something a bit near the mark comes up, I'll have to have it.' Alarm came into his wife's eyes as he held her, it was as though he had pushed on a switch. She was about to wrench away from him when he smiled. But in fact that statement which he passed off as a joke was a very accurate reflection of his attitude towards life and work. He was a villain and couldn't resist a worthwhile prospect, regardless of need. 'No, I'll give it a miss.' His words had a ring of conviction in them.

Dolly wasn't sure. 'You promise me, Jack? It's for the girls' sake as well. I mean, think of them.'

He told her how their youngest daughter reacted to his suggestion about becoming a policeman.

'You'd be no different,' she said. 'The only difference is you'd have a licence to go thieving.' She had no time at all for the police.

'How about some breakfast then, love?' Lynn said.

'You promise me now, Jack?' She didn't want to move away from the issue before being absolutely sure.

'Yeah, promise,' he said.

She seemed satisfied; she kissed him. 'What would you like?'

He smiled. 'Well, how about a little taste of this?' He pressed his crotch into hers again as he held her. Because of the tension that had been simmering beneath the surface it had been a while since they had made love. Lynn was less inhibited than his wife and wasn't concerned that they were in the kitchen.

'I've got my gloves on,' Dolly said, as if they made the proposition impossible.

'Leave 'em on. They might be all right,' he said lightly, and pulled her hard against himself. He heard the sucking noise behind him as she pulled the gloves off. Reaching down behind her, he caressed her buttocks; then raised her skirt up and ran his hand between her thighs. She didn't have any tights on and he was glad. He eased his hand into the side of her pants and stroked her vagina from behind her; he discovered her need was as great as his.

'Not here, Jack,' she said. 'Someone might come to the door.' Her protest was feeble, as if she was afraid he would stop and break the spell that had brought them together.

Lynn didn't heed her words. The idea of having sex in the kitchen suddenly appealed to him. It was reminiscent of sex on the back seats of cars: he had had more than enough there. He had first made love to Dolly on the back seat of an old Ford Consul he had owned, and a lot of times subsequently. He had some good memories of those days, and felt a soft yearning for them; what he was doing now reached out to meet it.

Unfastening the catch at the back of her skirt, he unzipped it and eased the garment over her hips. Another faint protest he stifled with his mouth. His fingers quickly undid the buttons on the shirt of his that she was wearing, but he didn't remove it. Instead he reached round and unfastened her bra. She had large breasts that hung low on her chest when unsupported. She didn't protest when he eased her back onto the kitchen table, but she seemed a little surprised, with a small, sudden intake of breath when the naked part of her back touched the cold surface. Lynn removed the pink woollen pants. She was still worried in case anyone should call at the kitchen door,

135

but was distracted from her anxiety when he eased her legs apart where they cut over the edge of the table and knelt into her, kissing her vagina. Quiet, slightly inhibited words of endearment emerged on her quickening breath.

When he stood unzipping his trousers, his penis found its own way out of the tangle of pants and shirt-tails. Kicking his trousers and pants off, he walked forward into the vee of his wife's legs and pushed into her, feeling as grateful then as he knew she felt.

It was at such moments as this that he knew there was too much at risk to be leading the sort of life he led. He loved his wife very much, despite their occasional bits of domestic; he loved his daughters very much. The problem for him was that such moments were only fleeting and bore little relation to the outside world. Jack Lynn knew he wouldn't change, probably couldn't change; and when it came right down to it he got more than a little enjoyment from going at risk.

There were a lot of faces in the snooker hall, mostly youngsters who got there early to get their tables booked, none of them serious players. Clifford Harding hadn't been looking for a serious game of snooker, but for someone who might be interested in a bit of work. He wasn't in urgent need but wanted to test the water, see whether he had any credibility after his recent result. Nowadays there were always enough kids around the hall who fancied they could play, and were prepared to lose a couple of quid. Harding didn't know the lad who propositioned him; and from his game he guessed most of the man's experience around a snooker table was from the television. He beat him on their first game and offered him another try to get his money back. He was ahead on the second game as well, not by much, but enough to make it clear who the four quid on it was going to go to.

Seeing Jack Lynn crouch to look under the lowstrung lamp hoods two tables away, as he was about to play his shot, didn't exactly cause him to miscue, but he was startled. The ball didn't go where it was supposed to go. Lynn was obviously looking for someone, and Harding automatically assumed it was himself, that he had somehow tumbled what he had in mind, what the filth demanded of him for his result. They somehow knew he was at it and that the DI who had nicked him with a gun in his possession gave him back his liberty on the sole condition he got some info' on Lynn. It was something Harding didn't fancy doing at all; but then his liberty was at stake, and there was nothing more important to a villain, especially one who, like Clifford Harding, had had a little taste of prison.

'Jack!' Harding said impulsively, like he had something important to tell him. 'How's your luck, son?' He straightened and moved to the end of the table.

If he hadn't spoken Lynn would have turned away as though not seeing him – it wasn't Cliff Harding he had come looking for. After what Bobby Shaw had told him about Harding's result Lynn was instinctively wary. He didn't want to believe it, but he was a realist and couldn't avoid those slight doubts now.

'Terrible,' Lynn replied to the man's question. He moved between the tables and joined him. 'I heard you had your collar felt – didn't expect to see you around.'

'Yeah, more aggravation than enough, wan' it – oh unlucky son,' he said to the man down the table as he tried but didn't make a shot. 'Watch me nick this now.' He moved along the table and took the blue.

'The Robbery Squad, weren't it?' Lynn said casually, while Harding chalked his cue.

'Yeah. There was a nice one I was going after,' Harding said, protesting a little too loudly, as though that would affirm his innocence in the subsequent events. 'What happened was I went and got a pull on my form, that's all. They went and found a fucking shooter at my place, they did. Silly as a fucking goat.' He scoffed and lined up the pink, which went for him. 'That do you?' he said to his opponent.

'I'd say so,' the man said, and uncrumpled four pound notes

137

from his pocket.

'You wanna double it? Have a chance to get it back?' Harding offered.

'No, I gotta shoot off.' The man moved away to rack his cue.

'Four quid, it might be the end of the world,' Harding said as he rejoined Lynn.

'He thought it was going to be your four quid, Cliff,' Lynn said with a grin. He was beginning to feel easier about him now. 'You did well to pull clear of that other bit of trouble, didn't you?'

'Did I fuck! Didn't come to enough, did it, bunging the Squad. They all wanted a taste, didn't they, the hungry bastards – well, according to the DI. That weren't all though, Jack. It fucked up this one I was going after, that's the nause.' He let his anger bubble through the words, trying to dispel any doubts.

Lynn shrugged; prospective blags were always easy enough to find. 'Still, you kept your bit of liberty, that's the important thing.'

It was the most important thing, but Harding didn't want it to appear that simple.

'Sure I did. But it's like the fucking sword of Damocles over my head, even though I bunged that DI. You can't trust them cunts, can you.'

'I wouldn't like to rely on it,' Lynn said, acquiescing. 'I'll see you later, Cliff.' Lynn started away.

A sense of desperation leapt through Harding. He was afraid Lynn hadn't been convinced, believed instead that maybe he had traded a few for his liberty. 'You fancy a game? – the table's paid for.'

'Just want to see if Billy Braden's been in,' Lynn said over his shoulder.

Doubt crept into Harding's mind. He wondered if that was just an excuse. He watched him go to the bar. Maybe he was straight, he argued, for if he thought him a wrong 'un he'd have almost certainly have blanked him right off. He turned back to the table and started retrieving balls from the pockets.

The man Lynn was looking for hadn't been in this evening, Peter Wright, the hall manager, informed him.

'His mate Alan was in this afternoon,' the bald, round, sweating man said. 'Nicked a nice few quid off a couple of punters, he did. I thought there was going to be trouble.'

The information didn't help Lynn at all. Braden had half committed to the blag, and he was looking to get him firmed up. He didn't want his mate. His thoughts moved on.

'How old are they, Peter?' he asked, indicating the sandwiches neatly stacked in the glass case on the counter. 'Drawing a pension yet, are they?'

'She only made them this afternoon,' Peter said. 'You want one?'

'Do I fuck. Tell Billy I was looking for him,' I don't see him, will you?' He went back to the table where Harding was, collecting a cue.

Winning the toss, Lynn let Harding break. He put white carefully against the pyramid of reds, but not carefully enough. Following on, Lynn managed to nick a red. He went on to black and got it.

As the game progressed they talked, and Lynn relaxed his guard, became less wary. The gaunt, stooping figure that was Harding talked and acted no differently from the way he had done previously and by the time he said, 'What are you up to these days, Jack? Got anything in the pipeline?' Lynn didn't even think that he might be a grass.

'A little taste across the Water it comes off,' he replied casually, then suddenly brought himself up. 'A bit iffy though. Still punting around, you know,' – trying to render it a vaguer prospect than it was. He leaned across the table and potted the blue. 'Getting a lot of stick from my old lady to get a job. Be perfectly honest I'm thinking about it.'

'What's her problem? Menopause?' He reached the blue ball out of the pocket and respotted it.

'Probably,' Lynn said dismissively. He hadn't really

thought about that.

'I might have a bit of work soon. Some silver bullion out of an air freight firm out at Hounslow. Could be worth about nine or ten grand to you, you fancy some of it.'

Something told Lynn he was being perfectly straight in his offer, which tended to cancel out those earlier doubts. If he went and blanked him out of hand it would seem like he still had doubts.

'Don't sound bad, Cliff. I'll keep it in mind. But I want to see how this one down at Catford goes.'

'Well, there's no rush, like,' Harding said.

Lynn had committed information to him and although it wasn't likely to cause too many problems, even if he had gone the other way, because of it he reverted to his original opinion of Harding, deciding he was as good as gold.

He played a decisive stroke and watched the ball rattle around the table, striking a red which he didn't make. He looked up at Clifford Harding, who was watching him. He only hoped he was right about him.

16

Paperwork was an ache for most policemen. That included Fred Pyle, who was back in the office after four days leave when changing from night duty to the day shift. He was typing a legal aid report for the DPP's office, the purpose of which was to help the DPP to decide whether the villains involved could be successfully prosecuted. It irked DI Pyle that the DPP's office wanted a better than fifty-one per cent chance of conviction before they prosecuted. Everything he was involved with had paused during his absence, and now his desk was littered with reports which he had to give attention to, either reading them or typing them – mostly typing it seemed, though possibly because he could read faster than he could type. Some of the hated paperwork had become urgent, but at that moment he would have welcomed an excuse to leave it; there were people for him to see, suspects, witnesses; phone calls had been made, messages left, but nothing that was more urgent than that paperwork.

Other detectives around the office were also bending to their hated paperwork; two more DIs were discussing a policewoman both knew and one was stiffing; another was talking on the telephone about a robbery that might be going off. Ordinarily Pyle wouldn't let any of this background noise, which the DIs' office was rarely without during the day shift, affect him, but today it irritated him. His fingers dropped aggressively on the keys.

'Trying to break that machine?' DCI Watson said, stopping by Pyle's desk with an armful of reports.

'Fucking thing,' Pyle said, continuing to type. 'Feel like tossing it out the window. 'Bout time we had some word processors in here. Let those lazy cunts upstairs have some of the rubbish.' He was referring to the civilian typists who were employed at the Yard.

'You look like you're winning, Fred,' the DCI said placatingly.

'I'd like to believe it.' He finished typing the paragraph.

'That was a bit of a result Eric got, wasn't it?' Watson commented. The result of the CIB2 inquiry was that the complaint was unsubstantiated.

'I had my doubts for a time there, guv,' Pyle said. 'Mind you, CIB2 were well out of order in the first place.' Nothing was likely to make him change his opinion of CIB2, unless he was seconded to that department, which was quite likely.

'It did sound a bit swift, Fred. The beak's clerk obviously thought he was at it with that grass.'

Pyle looked askance at the DCI, wondering if that had been a slip of the tongue, or whether he was simply being knowing, the whole point being that the man wasn't supposed to have been working for Lethridge. 'He might have thought so, guv. Doing a bit of trading, I s'pect,' he said, not wishing to appear to treat him like an idiot. 'Worth a try. Unless you're let alone to do the job you won't get anywhere.'

'Try telling that to the commissioner. Still, he got his result.' He laid some reports on the desk. 'Bit more for you, Fred. Have your lads go through those again. The spelling's atrocious. I can't put them up to the governor like that.' Nor would he attempt to.

Pyle glanced uninterestedly over the reports. 'They must have slipped past.' He sighed despondently.

'Have them do them again. Especially that one Shields wrote. He always struck me as a literate sort of lad.'

'I'll go through them myself, guv.' The prospect didn't inspire him.

'And it's diary day tomorrow. Make sure they've all got their details corresponding – Alec!' The DCI saw one of the DIs slinking out, and pursued him with some reports.

Pyle pushed the typewriter away and glanced over the top

report. There probably wasn't too much wrong with it by ordinary standards, but Trevor Watson would have all reports perfect.

The telephone on Pyle's desk rang and he answered it quickly, hoping it was something that might urgently drag him from this work. 'Oh, good morning. How are you?' he said when the man down the line identified himself. He was an insurance loss adjuster. Detectives were always civil to such people, who were after all on their side. With the help of one of his grasses, Pyle had nicked a little team about eight months ago and recovered most of the money they had blagged. They had been convicted, but had appealed only to have their sentences upheld. But true to form the insurance company hung on to their money as long as possible, and had now decided it was time to weigh on. The grass would have to go to their offices in the City for his money. 'This afternoon?' Pyle said. It was a bit short notice. 'It depends whether I can get in touch with my informant, sir ... Four o'clock ...' There was no real point in debating the matter until he had tried reaching Billy Little, the grass. 'Okay, we'll leave it at that. If I can't make it I'll phone you back ... Look forward to it. Cheers.' Pyle replaced the 'phone feeling cheerful. All he had to do now was try and find Little, of course!

Sometimes the detective didn't bother with putting the actual grass up to the insurance loss adjuster regardless of whether or not they were going to get the reward; some grasses wouldn't allow themselves to be put up anyway, even though it was an innocuous process. The insurance company simply needed someone other than the detective to hand the money to and sign the receipt. Pyle would try to get the minor villain, who was due the reward money, or part of it, before he tried putting anyone else up; that would be less complicated. He rang Billy Little's number and the grass answered. He asked him how he was, what he was at; told him about the reward and arranged to meet with him later that day. Replacing the phone Pyle turned back to his paperwork with renewed interest.

'If you spent less time playing with your prick, Tony, and bent to this a little more,' Pyle told DC Shields when he eventually got round to passing back the reports the DCI had returned, 'you might have less mistakes.'

'What d'you mean, guv!' the DC said indignantly. His protest was more over his not playing with himself than the state of his report. He looked over the paperwork Pyle handed him. 'What have I done, left a comma out? – he's a pedantic sod.'

'Don't worry about Trevor Watson,' Pyle said, out of a sense of loyalty. 'He's still a very practical copper.' Feeling no inclination to debate the matter, Pyle wheeled on Peter Fenton, who came along the busy Squad office looking for a free desk. 'Peter. Did you get that statement from that witness yet?'

'No. She wasn't in when I went down this morning, guv. She's coming in this evening,' the DC said.

'Well keep on at her, for fucksake. It's been over a week now.' Pyle moved on to DS Lethridge who was at one of the sergeants' desks at the top of the room. 'Have the typist do these again, Eric,' he said, depositing the rest of the reports on the desk. 'He wouldn't sign them.'

'He does go on a bit about a few fucking mistakes.'

'Yeah, well, you know what he's like. And don't forget it's diary day tomorrow. Make sure they get all their details corresponding. I don't want him screaming about any discrepancies over joint actions. Go through them yourself, Eric.'

Once a week all detectives' diaries were handed in for checking by the DCI; it was a disciplinary matter if diaries weren't kept up to date, recording all the details of a detective's actions as they more or less occurred. It was rarely that diaries were written that scrupulously by detectives. Lack of attention to the writing of their diaries was the single thing that most frequently got detectives into trouble.

The building that housed the firm of insurance loss adjusters

144

in Old Broad Street might have housed any company from a merchant banker to a solicitor, and probably did. There were several brass nameplates either side of the solid mahogany doors. Also there was a uniformed porter, from whose neatness a line of dandruff across his shoulders detracted.

The porter watched the black taxi draw up outside the building, but didn't step forward. He didn't usually, certainly not for people arriving in cabs.

Fred Pyle stepped out of the cab and settled the fare. He was followed by a grey, furtive-looking Billy Little. He lived up to his name, being only about five-feet-five – and that was with his three-inch-heeled boots. He looked decidedly unsteady in them. He'd have had no chance had he to leg it a bit lively, Pyle had thought earlier. For a man, like most in his situation, who had to be as inconspicuous as possible, he had an odd choice of clothes; someone half his age would have blended with fashion-conscious youth dressed as Little was, but a man going on fifty tended to stand out.

After settling the fare, Pyle turned to the grass, who was waiting on the kerb uneasily, his eyes darting nervously about in case anyone who knew him would happen past and recognize him.

'Don't look like that, Billy. You won't have any problems,' he assured him, even though he had been through this number before. 'He'll simply ask your name, get your signature and give you the reward money. Just stick up a wrong 'un, of course.' He unhooked Little's shirt collar which was turned in behind the enormous knot in his tie. 'Terrific,' he said with mock approval and patted his shoulder, before leading him up into the building.

The insurance loss adjuster was a pink-faced, striped-shirted, well-fed man in his late twenties. He showed Pyle and Little into a tiny, steel-partitioned office with only a small desk, two wooden chairs and a calendar on the wall. It was the sort of office where job applicants filled out personnel forms.

'Just the usual formalities, inspector,' the adjuster said,

laying a thick folder on the desk and removing forms from it. 'Won't take but a few moments.' He had a bouncy, buoyant manner that well-fed people often had. He glanced quickly at the grass as though to look at him too frankly might have given offence. Certainly it would have worried Little. 'Is this the gentleman who supplied the information leading to the arrest and conviction of David Thomas and Laurence James?' he asked formally.

'Yes, sir, it is,' Pyle replied.

'If I could just have a few particulars then. For the record, nothing more,' he assured the grass. 'Your name and address is all.'

Billy Little hesitated, he looked at Pyle as if uncertain whether to proceed. Then said quickly, 'It's Smith. It's Billy Smith. 100 Old Kent Road's where I live.'

The young man smiled tolerantly at the fiction as he committed it to paper. 'That's SE1.' He wrote quickly in a small, round hand. 'Well, Mr Smith. There was £28,400 recovered as a result of your information. Also two convictions, of course. Under the insurance reward agreement you are due ten per cent. £2,840. Along with the company's thanks, though I'm sure that's of no interest to you.' His round, pink face showed an official smile. 'I'll need two signatures from you, if you'd be so kind. One there and another there.' He indicated the place on two separate forms. And as Little scribbled the name, the loss adjuster reached an envelope from the folder. 'They are all old notes of mixed denomination. You're perfectly at liberty to sit and count it if you wish. But I'm sure you'll find no discrepancy.'

All the grass wanted to do was take the money and get out of the building. He wouldn't have been able to concentrate long enough for the count. Conversely it was times like this when he wondered if being a grass was worthwhile.

'I'll take your word for it, squire,' he said and stuffed the envelope into his jacket pocket.

Back on the street again with the grass, Pyle said, 'That was painless enough, Billy.'

'Fuck I! It only wants me to go and get seen with you now, guv.' That wasn't Billy Little's only reason for wanting to part company with the DI as quickly as possible. There was a chance he'd get away with all the money, not much of one though.

Pyle searched around the street and caught the eye of a taxi driver who was plying. As he waited for the cab he glanced at the grass and shook his head. 'Billy Smith,' he said mockingly. "S that the best you could come up with, son?'

'Well, I couldn't think, could I? I always go blank when I get in places like that. But I mean, it did, didn't it?'

'For all the fucking diff it makes. Wasn't a bad day's work.' And the initial effort on both his and Little's part hadn't involved a great deal as he recalled. Also, along with Eric Lethridge and Jack Barcy, he had had an earner out of the money recovered at the time. Not all of it had been entered in the back of the charge book and it was simply assumed that Thomas and James, the two villains involved, had knocked out the shortfall.

'Nice little touch, guv,' the grass said. He hesitated reluctant to broach the subject, but guessed the DI wasn't likely to have forgotten. 'Eh, how much were you looking for, guv?'

Pyle gave him a blank stare as the cab drew up. 'I think we agreed on half, Billy.' There was no doubt, and the figure was standard and wasn't open to negotiation. He held the door of the cab for the grass, and told the driver to take them to Charing Cross. In the back of the cab Pyle took the envelope and divided the money. Fourteen hundred and twenty pounds in safe old notes decidedly improved the day, Pyle found. And his grass wasn't too put out about the deal. Not sufficiently not to want to do business in future. The DI wasn't that inept at handling people.

17

Both lifts in the block of council flats were out of order. That was a million, Tully thought as he started through the graffiti-scrawled hallway and up the stairs. It was a banker's bet also that the lifts in the other four flatblocks on the estate would be out of order. Colin Coleman only lived on the second floor, but living in a block of flats himself, Tully automatically tried the lifts, even though he could never recall those in this block working when he had been here.

The kids on the estate must have nicked more than enough aerosol paint. There was a thick, snakelike trail of it up the stairs and along the wall on the second floor, cutting right across windows and doors. It ended a few doors from Coleman's flat. The front of that flat had come in for some stick for some unknown reason. Tully considered for a moment what he did instead of aerosol graffiti as a kid. Something as destructive, he guessed.

He rang the bell a second time and turned to lean on the walkway parapet to watch the kids kicking a large cardboard box around on the bald patch of grass that was imprisoned by the flatblocks.

'The idle bugger's still in bed, John,' Mrs Coleman said when she opened the door. She was thin and middle-aged and looked like she did a lot of fetching and carrying. She was fastening her coat, her handbag and shopping bag over her arm. 'See if you can get him up, love. I'm fed up with trying. He was s'posed to be at the social security offices at ten.'

She stepped out across the threshold and let Tully into the flat.

'And tell him not to eat all them eggs for his breakfast,' she said as a parting shot.

In the small back bedroom Tully found the woman's favourite son – despite her complaining – in bed, curled into a foetal-like ball under a duvet. He considered ripping the cover off him but would probably have had a fight on his hands. Cole Coleman went into blinding rages at the drop of a hat, especially at times like first thing in the morning – his first thing. So instead Tully reached under the cover and grabbed his cock. 'Caught you! Playing with yourself,' he said.

The young man in bed was startled. 'Fuck off, you dirty bastard!' he screamed.

'Come on, get up. Your Mum said you gotta see the social security. You won a long service award.'

Now he was awake Coleman quickly became reasonable. He stretched his arms out of the duvet and took a look at the day, then at his grinning visitor. 'Ah, it's a bit nippy,'innit?' he said and put his arms back in. 'She getting my breakfast, is she?'

'Yeah, 's bout ready,' Tully lied. 'C'mon. It's eleven o'clock; we got a day's work to do.'

Cole Coleman wasn't pleased when he rose and discovered that not only his breakfast wasn't waiting for him but there was no one to cook it. He went without.

There had been a minor setback in John Tully's plans, one of the villains who was going to work with him had to drop out on account of his old Mum getting a stroke and being put on 'open visits' in hospital. She wasn't expected to live, and surprised everyone by hanging on as long as she had. Still, he could understand Ernie Johnson wanting to be available. There was another prospect to take his place, he was sure the man would want some of it.

Sitting in the kitchen of Phil Hayes's flat with Cole Coleman, Tully outlined the blag. Like Coleman, Philip Hayes had been got out of bed, only his wife was around to cook his breakfast, which he sat eating in front of the other two.

'What's it all come to, John?' Hayes asked, pouring himself

149

some more tea.

Almost unobserved Coleman reached across the small table and helped himself to the food on Hayes's plate.

'About eight or nine grand. A bit of luck.'

'Sounds nice enough, dun it. 'Ere leave off, Cole! That's my fucking breakfast.' Hayes might have let the sausage go without comment, but thought it a bit much when he bit half of it then dipped it in an egg.

'Ah, what I got, fucking germs or something?' Coleman protested.

'Fucking cook yourself some, you wan' it,' Hayes offered.

The prospect didn't appeal to Coleman, who could have done that at his own flat. He would rather go and eat in a café than have to get a meal for himself. 'Can't your wife do some for me?' He was serious.

'Yeah, hang on a minute,' Hayes said sarcastically. He looked at the young man and shook his head. Somehow it was hard to resent the liberties Cole Coleman took. He had an easy, likeable way about him. 'Who else is gonna be involved, John?' he said, turning back to Tully.

From habit Tully hesitated, even though he had already committed a lot of information to Hayes. He studied the man, who was in his late thirties, though looked older, even with his dark curly hair. His face was old, and lined, especially around his eyes. 'Only Cole here doing the driving,' he said at last, 'and Benny Isaacs. He's got the shooters.'

'Well, as it happens, John,' he said ponderously, 'I do fancy it double strong. When's it going off?'

'Pretty soon, I reckon. The thing is, it's there. It might as well be done. Know what I mean?'

They both knew exactly what Tully meant.

The plan was all more or less set in Tully's mind. There were one or two arrangements still to make, minor things that he could do himself; but something that was important was making sure this little firm were all set in their minds just how it was going to go. That meant visiting the proposed blag. This they did in a Ford Transit van that Isaacs borrowed from his father-in-law. Coleman drove the van over the getaway route, deciding where best to park the changeover car. Finally they stopped in Leyton Street, a little away from the entrance to the offices of the Gas Board. Only Coleman remained in the front of the van; the other three climbed into the back, from where they could look out through the windscreen without easily being seen themselves.

The office block was a purpose-built brick building with three wide steps up to the main entrance and railings protecting bare concrete flower tubs. A seven foot wall to the left of the block extended some forty feet to gates to the works and service department beyond the offices. Glass doors off the main entrance let onto a small foyer with stairs that could be seen at the end of it.

Leyton Street was a fairly long road whose dwellings comprised mainly pre-war terrace houses with bow fronts extending beyond the building line. The street was reasonably busy with traffic, it being a bus route.

'Here it comes now,' Tully said.

The attention of the men went in the direction he indicated. Along the street a security truck nosed out of the side turning to Bushgrove Road, which was about fifty yards or so from where the van was parked. It crossed the traffic lanes and started down towards them, but signalled left and turned in through the gates to the works yard.

'Where they going?' Hayes wanted to know. 'I thought you said they delivered to the office across the street there?' He seemed disappointed.

'The money goes up to the first floor,' Tully explained. 'But they go in the back way.'

A woman who might almost have been watching out for the security truck, her timing was so close, came down through the foyer of the office block and locked the glass doors.

'That's a regular touch,' Tully said. 'Those doors get locked every time the payroll arrives. They come along that corridor there and up the stairs.' He paused as if expecting the two security guards to appear on cue. They didn't. 'They'll be along in a minute' – as if to dispel any doubt creeping through their minds. 'What we gotta do is go through those doors and get the money off them as they reach the stairs. Then they ain't got no chance of legging it.'

'We'll do them easy with a flogging hammer,' Hayes suggested.

'Might be a bit sussy climbing out of a motor and running up with a hammer,' Isaacs said. He knew what Tully had in mind but wasn't about to steal his thunder. 'And it might take a few swings to do all that glass clear in those doors.' Benny Isaacs was very practical, and unlike most villains didn't push himself forward the whole time, but quietly did what was required of him. He was short and slightly swarthy, with a very badly pockmarked face, it wasn't a face he liked putting in too often as it was easily remembered. He had muscular shoulders and was very strong, though did nothing either to promote or maintain his strength.

'Well, what we gonna do it with?' Coleman said, pursuing the prospect of smashing the door in. 'A gas stove?'

'As it happens that's just what I had in mind,' Tully said.

Cole Coleman laughed, thinking it was a joke. Hayes was a little puzzled.

'I mean, what could be more plausible,' Tully went on 'pulling up in the road and offloading a stove to the Gas Board? It's a million. No one'll even look twice. Take it up those steps and zoomp! Straight through that door, it's done. Know what I mean? There!' He indicated the two guards who passed through the hall.

The four men watched in silence as they disappeared.

'Why not have it in the yard as the van pulls up, John?' Philip Hayes suggested.

'I don't think so. There'll be too many cunts around likely to have a go. A gas fitter comes after you with a bit of lead pipe, you gotta shoot him. Can't odds it.'

The prospect caused another silence. Hayes didn't pursue the matter.

'What about cars?' Coleman said. 'We'll want something a bit tasty, John.' He didn't have to mention reliability; they all knew the stories about the cars used in making one that wouldn't start.

'No problem. I've got a man who should be able to do something for us straightaway.' He smacked his hands together in a decisive manner. 'It'll be a doddle, you see.'

The thought of going into those offices across the road with shooters and blagging the wages held no fear for any of the four men. The moral question of the act wasn't even considered.

The car ringer Tully had in mind for the two cars he would need had a car-breaking business down at the Elephant and Castle. He had done one or two things for Tully before, including losing cars that were no longer of any value that he reported stolen then claimed insurance on. Del Rogers was just one of the many contacts who enabled Tully to get a living as he did.

Signalling right under the bridge on New Kent Road, Tully made a right-hand turn on to the narrow, unmade service road to the businesses conducted beneath the railway arches. The road was full of ruts which had filled with water from recent rain. The car-breaking operation Del Rogers ran occupied two full arches, which were littered with salvaged parts, scrap metal, old tyres. In the arches themselves there were pools of black sump oil in the uneven surfaces instead of rainwater.

Del Rogers, a lithe, ginger-haired youth, whose pores on any exposed part of his body seemed clogged with oil, was cutting up the body of a car with an oxyacetylene torch when Tully pulled up in the newish Cortina he was driving. Tully stepped out carefully between the puddles.

'Can you cut this one up a bit lively for me, Del?' he joked.

'Old Bill's right up m'daily.'

A grin broke over Rogers's greasy face and he scoffed. 'Just what I fucking well need, my son.' He turned off the lamp and came across to Tully, but was more interested in the car. 'That's not bad, is it. Yourn, John?'

'Till they snatch it back,' Tully replied. He was kidding, he was up to date on the HP payments so far, but he could never guarantee staying that way. He glanced across the yard to where two other men working for Rogers were breaking cars. 'Doing plenty, Del?'

'Quite a bit,' Rogers said evasively. He knew what Tully meant.

'Any chance you can do a couple for me?' He had called for a specific purpose and saw no reason not to get straight to it.

Wincing at the difficult prospect Rogers said, 'I don't think I can, John.'

'Fuck I, Del,' Tully said with some dismay. 'I was relying on you. I thought you was a stoneginger.'

'Well, the thing is, John, I got a lot of stuff to cut up.' He seemed embarrassed, and not without reason.

'I mean, what's it gonna take you? Half an hour to drag a couple off the street and stick different plates on them? That'll do.'

'Won't you want them resprayed or nothing?' Rogers seemed a little surprised. Most villains he rung cars for wanted a proper job doing, so they weren't likely to be driving along the street and get a routine pull from a uniform. That meant a respray, changing the external features of the car, mirrors, racks, etc., sometimes the interior trim; grinding out engine and chassis numbers and putting on new plates. It all took time and put him at risk while he had such cars on his property.

'I'll take a chance if you're that pushed.' Tully would do so reluctantly. The alternative was going and dragging the cars himself, which he didn't fancy. He never had been much of a car thief. His first adult conviction had been for taking and driving away.

"'S not just that, John. I been cutting up one or two dodgy ones lately. I've had the filth down from the Stolen Motor Vehicles branch. Been sniffing around, giving me more aggravation than enough.'

'Oh, what do them cunts know?' Tully said in disgust. 'They don't know fuck all. Just looking for lost chassis and engine's numbers, is all. It's worth a twoer to you, Del.' He paused and considered the uncertainty in the man's greasy face. But appealed to his sense of honour. 'Don't let me down for fucksake, son, will you. Or I'm bang in trouble.'

'Well ... I'll see what I can do.' Rogers committed reluctantly, despite himself.

Tully took his response as a firm promise.

After they had discussed the details and the blagger had left, Del Rogers was even less sure about the proposition. He was in trouble with Old Bill already, that wasn't just a get out on his part. He sat in the tiny battered office caravan that was wheelless and propped against one of the arch walls and stared vacantly through the grease-smeared window. He knew what he had to do, knew how it would help him get a result, only was reluctant to do it. But as if he wasn't in control of his responses he found himself reaching out for the telephone and making the call. Instinctively he glanced about himself to make sure no one was listening when the voice down the line said, 'C11.'

He hesitated, his manner tense, apprehensive. He almost put the phone back. 'Inspector McHale, I want,' he said. The voice asked him to hang on. He said he would.

He wished he hadn't.

The pub they agreed to meet in at Waterloo was a halfway house for both. It was an old Watney's house that was tenaciously hanging on through surrounding redevelopment, but its old clientele, if it ever had one, showed no such tenacity. Nearly all the customers in the bar were demolition workers; local office workers obviously preferred to spend their

LVs in the smarter, plastic remoulds.

Del Rogers sat with his back against the wall and stared vacantly over the bar, feeling depressed, his pint hardly touched, the cheese and tomato sandwich untouched. He saw Detective Inspector McHale enter the pub and nose up to the bar, but didn't acknowledge him, not even when he turned and motioned to offer him a drink. He was thinking about what he was doing, whether it was going to help him; whether he should quit. It seemed he was never going to get ahead. He didn't think about such things often, having recognized a while ago that there was no value in doing so.

The detective arriving at the table almost startled him. He looked up at McHale, who was quite short and quite fat and whose hair had all but fallen out, leaving a few strands trailed across his pink scalp.

'What are you daydreaming about?' McHale asked, pulling up a chair and sitting. 'I offered you a drink.'

'Oh, I'm all right, thanks, Mr Mac.' He sipped his beer.

'Been here long?' The DI said, checking around the bar again.

'No, a few minutes, is all.' Rogers's eyes followed the detective's briefly. Then searched the table top again.

'Well, cheer up, Del. 'S not the end of the world yet, is it.' The DI looked no more cheerful than the car-breaker, but simply because like most detectives he avoided displaying his feelings. 'How's that sandwich?' he asked, as if considering getting himself a round. But he didn't; he simply helped himself to one of those on Rogers's plate. Half of it disappeared in one bite. When after a couple of chews he had room to push some words out, he said, 'What is it you've got for me?'

Rogers looked directly at him for the first time, and hesitated. 'I gotta ring a couple of cars for a little firm,' he informed him in a low voice. 'A fella by the name of John Tully. Comes from across the Water.'

'What is it they've got going off?'

With an apathetic shrug, Rogers said, 'Dunno Just two cars is what he wants; a bit tasty. Estate cars of some kind he wants.'

'They must have something going off pretty soon, then,' the DI speculated.

'Dunno.' He wasn't very interested, only in what the information benefited him. He drank some more of his beer. 'What about those lads of yourn from Chalk Farm, Mr Mac?' That was where the Stolen Motor Vehicles department was.

'They're not my lads,' McHale said vaguely, as though they had no bearing on this conversation.

'You said you'd straighten them for me, 'I got you something.' The words came out like a betrayed whine.

'Been down again, have they? Looking a bit too closely at those you've been cutting up?' A mocking smile danced over the detective's face. Sometimes he fulfilled the promises made to potential grasses, but it wasn't a point of honour. It depended entirely on whether he thought the man would be of any further use to him. He believed Rogers would be, certainly to the conclusion of this current prospect. 'You shape up all right, Del. I'll have my governor call the superintendent on C10. You'll get a clean bill of health.' For a few weeks was all. 'Where are you parking those cars for them to pick up?'

'I don't know yet,' Rogers said. 'I got to phone him when I done 'em.'

'You'd better phone me immediately after then, Del, hadn't you?' The look the DI gave him sufficiently emphasised the point. He smiled again, and took the second sandwich from Rogers's plate.

C11, the department at Scotland Yard that McHale worked for, didn't investigate or get involved in crimes in the same manner most CID did. They dealt with criminal intelligence. Detectives of C11 had powers of arrest the same as other detectives, and did occasionally get to feel a collar, but usually, having collected sufficient evidence for an arrest to be made, they handed it over to the appropriate squad or Division. The Squad being situated just across the corridor from them tended to get whatever was important.

Ordinarily McHale wouldn't have dreamed of involving the Squad on the little he had so far from Del Rogers. But C11 were so overstretched currently with potential robberies they were following through on that they hadn't the men to spare to give this one the attention it would need. He was optimistic in assuming the Squad would be any less busy. Certainly Fred Pyle's squad wasn't, and it was DI Pyle he approached.

Sitting on the edge of Pyle's half of one of the four double desks in the DIs' office, McHale tapped the thin folder on his thick thigh, and talked the prospect through, trying to make it sound more attractive than it was.

'The thing is, Fred,' McHale was saying, 'it definitely looks like something is going off.'

'I'd say so,' Pyle acquiesced, without committing at all. There were other DIs in the office, most of them involved with their hated paperwork.

Sensing the DI's resistance, McHale laughed, slightly embarrassed. 'Well, the thing is this, Fred. Can you spare a couple of your lads to put down there on watch?'

'I wouldn't have thought so, son. I mean we've got so much going off ourselves that I'm even going to have to go out and feel a few collars myself.' It was Pyle's idea of a joke; he was one of the most active DIs on the Squad. 'Haven't you got anyone to spare? You must have someone, for fucksake.'

'We're in the same boat as the Squad.' McHale shook his head ponderously. 'Seems a shame to have to give it a miss. I think there might be a nice one going off here.'

'Yeah,' Pyle said, regretting the situation. He didn't like to know about crimes going off by default. 'Couldn't you stick a lad down there with a camera?' he suggested. 'You must have a lad – I'd try and find one, but the thick cunts'd probably fuck up the photos.'

'Doesn't look too clever, something goes off, does it?'

'Better'n fuckall, I'd have thought.'

Reluctantly McHale agreed. He'd find one of his detectives who knew his way around a camera. It would be a thin sort of cover, but at least the job would be covered.

18

Normally Detective Superintendent Ernie Jeymer wasn't a man who moved at any great speed. Notwithstanding his brusque manner, he had a methodical, plodding mentality that was directly translated to his actions. But he moved fast enough now as he strode along the corridor and swung himself around the doorframe of the DIs' office. There was an urgency about him. Fred Pyle was the first detective his eyes lit upon; so the job that was the cause of Jeymer's burst of energy became his.

'Fred! There's a shout for help from the Terrorist Squad. Holborn. Get your lads over there right away. You too, John,' he added, seeing John Redvers. 'Get instructions on the air. And you'll need shooters.'

Both DIs moved fast, it might have been no more than their paperwork they were running from. Fred Pyle went along to roust detectives out of the Squad office while Redvers went next door to the DCIs' office to get the firearms organized.

Five-shot Smith & Wesson .38s and ten rounds of ammunition for each detective were dispensed casually, but quickly now, in the DCIs' office by Tony Simmons. He reached them out of the metal filing cabinet directly behind his desk and passed them up to the queuing detectives, who hurriedly scribbled their names in the book. The standard procedure was for the detectives to load the guns in his presence; most of them did so before grabbing a holster from the cupboard by the door and hurrying out, but the DCI could give the operation none of the attention he was supposed to. He was keeping his eye on the book, which everyone being issued with a gun had to sign, regardless of rank.

'Looks like we gotta pull the cunts out of trouble again,'

Pyle commented as he collected his gun. There was a slight smugness in his tone; they never called on the Terrorist Squad for help.

'Yeah. Shoot the fuckers, Fred,' Simmons said, and meant it. On straightening up he saw one of Redvers's DCs slinking off without signing the book. 'Oi! Sign the book.'

The DC came back and did so. 'Sorry, guv.'

Over the air the four cars with both Pyle and Redvers's men in them were directed first to Holborn, then immediately redirected to Bloomsbury. There they rendezvoused with Brian Shilling, a DI on the Terrorist Squad. He was directing the operation and sent them to take up positions where they were keeping tabs on a blue Fiat Mirafiori carrying two suspected PLO terrorists whom they'd been tipped off about.

Pyle's car was parked in Great Russell Street, the narrow road alongside the British Museum, which at that time of the evening was jammed with people and traffic. All he hoped as he watched them bustle past was that nothing went off or it would be chaos. They wouldn't be able to manoeuvre at all. To add to their problems a wooden top came sauntering along and tapped the window to DC Fenton who was in the front next to the driver.

'You can't park here,' the constable said when Fenton ran down the window. 'It's a restricted area.'

The DC looked round at Pyle, who said, 'Tell him to fuck off and nick some motorists for illegal parking.'

'Sir?' the constable said stooping further to look at the men in the back.

'We're on a job, pal,' Fenton explained. 'Just make yourself scarce, will you?'

The wolly looked blank for a moment as if he was considering this; then finally the penny dropped. 'Oh, sorry, sir,' he said addressing his apology to Pyle.

When the uniform had moved on, Pyle said, 'Fuck knows what they wanted us for with him around.'

What they were needed for anyway Pyle didn't know.

Certainly there seemed no great urgency about the shout now. He guessed the Terrorist Squad had seen their parcel on the move and had panicked.

'Give us that,' he said reaching across the front seat for the r/t. The driver passed it back to him. 'Brian...'s Fred. What's the word, son ...?'

'Where are you?'

'We're still sat here,' Pyle said slightly defensively, as if the detective running the operation was implying he had proceeded contrary to instruction. 'We haven't moved. 'S no sign of the parcel ...'

'I think we've lost it,' the Terrorist Squad detective said. 'Anyone see anything.'

'Not a thing,' a voice Pyle didn't recognize said.

'Nothing this way,' Redvers said.

'Hang on ...' a voice with excitement edging into it said. 'A blue Mirafiori. Turned into Montague Place. 'S heading in your direction, John.'

'Not ... wait a minute,' Redvers said, 'Yes, I've clocked it.'

There was silence on the air for a few moments, save for the crackle of static. The detectives in Pyle's car waited tensely, even though none of them was convinced they were going to see any action.

'What have you got, John?' DI Shilling asked. 'Anything?'

'No. A couple of old ladies, that's all – they couldn't bomb anything.'

There was another silence, longer this time.

'There, guv!' DC Fenton suddenly said pointing to a blue Fiat that turned into Great Russell Street from Bury Place. There were four dark-skinned men in it.

'This looks like it might be it,' Pyle read off the number. 'It's turning into Montague Street.'

As it did so it accelerated like the driver believed someone was after them.

'I think they might have tumbled something. They're accelerating...' Pyle informed the others over the air.

'Fuck it!' the words from Shilling exploded angrily over the r/t. 'All right, let's nick them.'

The driver started the car and accelerated away along Great Russell Street, and as he cornered hard into Montague Street in the direction the blue Mirafiori had gone he almost ran down a party of school kids who had been to the museum. The ones in the front leaped back on the toes of those behind.

'You mad fucker,' Pyle said as he looked behind, making sure no one was hurt. The car didn't slow at all, but wove in and out of traffic and pedestrians alike.

Despite their breakneck speed they weren't the first to reach the suspects' car. Three other CID cars were there before them, two Terrorist Squad cars and one of Redvers's. Pyle wasn't at all upset about that. Those sort of villains weren't at all shy about producing guns and blasting away. Their car was trapped in Russell Square, and two of the suspected terrorists tried to run. The other two had no chance. Lethridge, coming into the Square from Bedford Way, cut them off. Once all seven CID cars had converged on the blue Mirafiori in Russell Square there shortly followed an enormous traffic jam, which the detectives couldn't have cared less about. It simply meant a few people would get home a little later than usual that night, but at least they would get home; someone might not have done had the four terrorists got to do what they had planned with the explosives that were in the boot of the car. But doubtless the inconvenienced road-users didn't appreciate that at that moment. All they knew was that the traffic was snarled and the police were doing nothing to cope with it.

Relief that they hadn't been shot or blown to pieces by people who drove around London with a car full of guns and explosives rarely took the form of detectives thanking God, or saying how pleased or lucky they were to find themselves still in one piece. But it manifested itself in other ways. It bubbled out in their words, in their actions, even though they tried to repress the feeling, lest it should betray them, reveal that human weakness which they tried to deny.

Having helped the Terrorist Squad capture the four Arabs, their assistance wasn't required further, so there was nothing for DIs Pyle and Redvers to do but debate the result, along with DS Lethridge and Ian Middlewick. The four men came noisily along the otherwise deserted fourth floor corridor. They were like the local rugby team returning home in triumph.

First the guns and ammunition had to be returned. The two DSs had collected them from their respective squads and DCI Simmons checked them back in. He too became infected by the same feeling that had got the returning detectives.

Pyle had a bottle of scotch in his desk drawer along with a pack of styrofoam cups. He preferred scotch, but in similar circumstances detectives would drink whatever happened to be available, even sherry.

'Did you see the look on that fucking driver's face when we pulled him from the car?' Middlewick said. They were safe now, they were back home.

'Wicked. I saw it. Fucking good job that one didn't have a shooter handy, Ian.'

'That ought to be a nice result for them,' Pyle said, splashing scotch liberally into the cups.

'Got the Terrorist Squad right out of trouble again. The cunts.' Redvers raised one of the paper cups. 'Here's to it.'

'No thanks for it, of course.'

'One of those'd do me every day of the week,' DCI Simmons said coming into the DIs' office after shutting the guns away. He brought a real glass. 'I don't care a cunt about getting the credit. Just so long as we get them all nicked and locked up out of harm's way.' The subject for Simmons as for most policemen, was an emotive one.

'The Arab had to be trying something,' Lethridge said. 'With those accents, said they'd just rented the car.'

'Firms are always hiring out cars full of explosives,' Pyle commented.

'A bit simple,' Simmons said earnestly, 'but they can shoot you just as dead.'

It was a sobering thought.

'Yes. Sure they can.'

There was a silence in the office as the detectives considered this. DI Frank Brickman came in. His squad were the current night duty squad.

'What's this, a wake?' Brickman asked, looking round at the solemn faces.

'Yeah, something like that, Frank. Have a drink.' Pyle straightened a cup and poured Brickman some.

'Your old woman phoned, John,' Brickman informed Redvers, 'Said I didn't know what time you'd be back.'

'Better give her a bell, I suppose.'

Pyle thought about ringing his wife, but didn't.

'How's that other fella shaping, Fred?' Simmons asked. 'Do any good yet?'

'Not yet,' Pyle said. 'I'll give him a day or two, then look him up if I don't hear.' He figured a week was long enough for Harding to have got started had he any intention of so doing.

Pyle finished the scotch in his cup and poured himself another. The party would go on until the bottle was finished. Pyle knew that what he ought to be doing instead of standing around drinking was shifting some of the paperwork that his visit out had interrupted. And what he ought to have done afterwards, instead of what had occurred to him, was go home and eat the dinner his wife would have cooked.

Going down in the lift with DI Pyle after the party had broken up, Lethridge said, 'You fancy going on somewhere, Fred? Having a few, maybe pull one?' Like a man separated from his wife Lethridge was always making such proposals.

'Not tonight, Eric. Got one to meet.'

There was disappointment in the fat man's expression. 'Oh, give her one for me, will you?'

Pyle smiled flatly. He didn't even know that he was going to give her one himself yet.

19

Light was showing at the frosted glass of the bathroom which was on the open walkway, adjacent to the front door. That might be a good start, Pyle thought, having her half undressed. He pushed the doorbell and waited. The dog barked from within, but there was no other sign of anyone stirring. Pyle shifted the wrapped bottle of scotch, which he stopped off to buy, to his other hand and pushed the bell again. The thought that Brian Finch might be there crossed his mind fleetingly: he didn't give the possibility serious consideration.

Finally Libby Howard opened the door. She was wearing a white bathrobe with a towel wound around her hair. She was a little surprised to see the DI. The Alsatian dog, which was at her side, remembered him: it had stopped barking.

'A bad moment,' Pyle said. 'I should have telephoned first, I suppose. Don't think I took your number, though.' He had it, in fact. Pyle was in no way embarrassed by his intrusion.

'He's not here, if that's what you want,' she said, matter-of-factly.

Pyle looked at her, as if considering the unintentional alternative in her statement. 'Isn't he?' He stepped across the threshold as she blandly invited him to enter with a sweeping arm gesture that almost lost her the head towel.

'Least the dog's friendly this time – knows a friend. Hello, Judge. Good old fella, good boy!' He shaped up to the dog playfully.

Libby Howard observed this, still puzzled by Pyle. 'Were you expecting him to be?'

'Bet you've not even seen him,' Pyle said, casually. 'Have you?'

'As a matter of fact, I haven't.'

'Well, as a matter of fact, love, I came to see you.' Pyle watched her closely to measure her reaction.

She considered the bottle in his hand. 'A new tack?' she asked, giving nothing.

'What's your problem, Libby? Some uniform nick you sometime for offensive behaviour?'

She laughed nervously, not quite knowing how to react, trying to resist the instincts which were urging her to yield ground. 'You could doubtless get me dropped out if you wanted.'

Pyle thought about this, then shook his head. 'You've been listening to too many villains,' he said, 'that's your trouble. Policemen don't do those sort of things.'

Libby didn't protest. It wasn't an argument she thought she could win. She wasn't a person who argued much anyway; rather she turned inwards when she disagreed, tried to resolve things there. She didn't always succeed.

'We going to stand here all night? You must be getting chilled like that.' He wasn't particularly concerned that she didn't invite him in, but moved along the passage, patting the dog.

There was an air of resignation about her as she watched him turn into the livingroom. She wondered briefly what would happen if she protested, told him to go; she wondered also what would happen if she didn't. Finally she shut the door and followed him.

'D'you want me to take the dog for a walk while you're finishing your bath?' Pyle said. 'Or shall I help you with that instead? I wash a nice back.'

She was uncertain about her next move.

'Looks like I'm being blanked, Judge,' the detective said to the dog, as if eliciting his opinion.

Resigning herself to Pyle's propositioning manner, Libby said, 'Are you married?'

'The world's full of married men, haven't you heard?' She

wasn't impressed; then it was an evasion and he recalled she didn't like evasions. 'Of course I am. Two lovely kids.'

Libby nodded wearily, she knew he would be. 'Why don't you go home to them?'

That irritated Pyle. Having her react this way, he felt like slapping her in the face. But nothing of this feeling surfaced. Slowly he shook his head. 'You don't want me to go, do you.' It wasn't a question.

'You really are the most incredibly arrogant man ... Oh, I forgot, your profession makes you like that.'

Pyle didn't say anything, only the current position of their relationship prevented him doing anything. He wanted to fuck her; had he already have been doing so he might have hit her. He set the bottle down on the coffee table; then when she didn't press the attack he went after her. 'You'd better visit the local station, love, for that statement ...'

The words suddenly shattered her. They had been talking about possibilities between them, now he had changed like the wind and it was business as usual, his business. 'You fucking bastard ... you really are.'

'A fact of life, love. All policemen are – cunning bastards. I thought everyone knew that.' This change of attitude, from arrogance to as close to frivolity as he could get, threw her once more.

A bemused expression covered her face. 'Does this visit have anything to do with Brian?' she asked tentatively, trying to feel the ground before she stepped forward.

'Him? Who's interested in him any more? We'll pick him up eventually. Won't be too difficult.'

She nodded. She felt a little relieved, felt he was being honest; decided not to resist her instincts any longer. 'I've never been out with a policeman before.' It was a silly thing to say, she thought, an instant later.

'You don't know what you've missed, Libby,' Pyle was relaxing. He knew he was going to make it. 'Take off the uniform and I'm just the same as anyone else.'

Libby smiled, still a little uncertain. 'I'm not so sure.'

'Take my word for it, love.' He took off his coat; then his jacket and unfastened his tie. She watched him a little amazed.

'What are you doing?' she said.

'Well, you were never going to get around to inviting me to take off my coat; relax, have a drink, Fred – got another bathrobe, have you?'

'Oh, my God!' she said, stalling for a space in which to consider this sudden surge forward rather than because she was shocked by his precipitate action.

'What's the matter? Changed your mind?'

She didn't respond, and Pyle knew from experience that all the moves were his to make. He wouldn't have got this far if basically she didn't want to go further. Having removed his tie he stepped in close to her and placed his mouth against hers without prelusive niceties. Perhaps she wanted those gestures, Pyle thought, for there was no response. However, he persevered. Gradually she gave ground: it was like a sandbank giving way before a wall of water, once it had started yielding there was no holding it back. Her lips lost their tenseness, they parted, inviting his tongue into her mouth. She closed her arms around him and held him like she wanted to be reassured by his presence. She squeezed him tightly and Pyle didn't resist. She pressed her cheek against his and bit his ear.

Finally she said, 'Shall I get some glasses?'

She felt the need of some kind of formal bridge between the position they were currently in and the one they would eventually adopt. A drink was the obvious choice. Pyle needed no such device.

'Not yet,' he said quietly, and kissed her again. She responded readily now. A smile wrinkled in the corner of his mind. He eased back from her slightly and unfastened the belt of her robe; she resisted him, but he wasn't deterred. Parting the robe he found the woman completely naked, and his look openly appraised her. She had good tits, firm and round, and

169

a very bushy cunt. He liked that. His wife cropped hers, but he never told her his preference. 'Go and put on your underwear,' he said quietly.

This precise instruction puzzled Libby Howard at first. She hesitated as if she hadn't heard. He told her again.

'Just my underwear?' she asked.

'That's all.'

Finally she did as she was told, with a more curious than bemused expression.

Pyle followed as far as the bedroom door, where he stood removing his own clothes. His cock was hard now and struggled for a way out through the tangle of clothes around his crotch as he watched Libby step into her tiny pants and tuck the pubic hair in beneath the elastic; she did this with a certain coyness which suggested she wasn't used to such performances. It was the same when she retrieved her bra off the bed and pulled the garment on over her breasts; reaching round behind her under her bathrobe, she fastened the bra in one easy movement. Pyle remained motionless for a moment and looked at her. Bra and pants always made breasts and vagina far more exciting for him. He suspected it had something to do with conditioning from childhood and the taboos that were always associated with the areas that always had to remain covered.

Libby waited, a little embarrassed, not knowing what the next move was. She pulled her bathrobe close about her. Pyle didn't mind that. He moved across to her and embraced her and kissed her mouth, her face and neck. How good a lover he was he wasn't sure. He was quite practised at fucking, then most policemen were one way or another, but suspected they were two entirely different things. Opening her bathrobe, he said, 'That's nice. I like that, Libby. You're terrific, you know that?' He accepted that she probably did, and wouldn't tell her again. He ran his hands over the outside of her bra, gently caressing her breasts through the material. She was curious to know why he didn't prefer the feel of actual flesh – she did – but refrained from asking him. His hands moved on down over her waist and round to her buttocks, and he slid his fingers into the top of her pants; his hands moved deeper, fondling the firm flesh of Libby's buttocks. He got intense enjoyment from the sensation of his hands being enclosed there. The smooth nylon garment reacting on the hairs on the backs of his hands. His strong fingers pushed down further between the cheeks of her ass to gently stroke her vagina. She intoned her pleasure as one finger found an opening. She was moist there, a fact which added greatly to his urgency. Her clitoris was too high for him to reach comfortably from his present position: he would have to approach it from the other direction.

His tongue worked equally as attentively in her mouth, caressing first beneath her tongue, then deep into her with darting movements. With his hands behind her he drew her pelvis hard against his erection. He could easily have pulled her pants down and thrust into her, but decided she wasn't ready. Instead he slid her pants onto her thighs and lowered himself to his knees before her; his tongue entered through the clearing of pubic hair, that his thumbs turned aside, and found and caressed the clitoris. As he increased the pressure there he caused her to moan with pleasure more than just a little.

'Oh dear,' she said as if apologizing. But that was all she said. It was enough.

Fred Pyle enjoyed doing this as much as she enjoyed his doing it, and knew he could quickly take them both past their peak. He eased her back on to the bed and stood before her and finished undressing himself in purposely slow movements. She raised herself to assist him. When she started to remove her own pants he stopped her halfway; he wanted them left just where they were on her thighs. His penis wasn't very large, but it didn't matter as it slid into her. It was big enough, he had always found, and the pants, around her thighs, restricted her, preventing her spreading her legs. She enjoyed the constriction as much as Fred Pyle.

Afterwards he lay unmoving on top of her, his full weight unsupported, not exhausted, merely idling. He was quite contented, reflective. His penis was slack, but still inside her and she felt reassured; she hoped for something more, not just his making love to her again, that in itself wasn't important, but his not rushing off straightaway was. Instinctively she felt that was what he might do; he had after all a wife and two children, a home he should go to. Awkwardly she reached out and caught hold of the bedcover and eased it over them. There was a slight chill in the room after their passion. She continued to hold him, moving her hands over his back in a smoothing gesture. Her fingers found a thick slab of flesh around his kidneys; Brian Finch popped into her mind, his body was hard, spare, without surplus fat. She dismissed him and went back to thinking about Fred Pyle. It was curious, she found, that despite his having made love to her, and her having had an orgasm – something she didn't do easily at the start of a relationship – and his closeness now, she felt that he wasn't touching her. Quite definitely she got the impression that he was holding too much of himself in reserve, the vast part of him that no amount of passion from her would draw forth. Having started this relationship she would work at it because she would have hated to have got into a situation where she was going to bed with men no more than once, but she would do so in the almost certain knowledge that he would give her little, apart from enjoyment on that superficial level. The thought depressed her slightly; she hoped she was wrong. She hugged him closer to her, trying to convince herself.

20

Grasses were more trouble than they were worth.

It was a thought Pyle often had when things didn't go to plan or there were problems with his informers. The stick he had got from his old woman when he had got in this morning wasn't exactly Micky Fielder's fault, but it had obviously been prompted by Fielder phoning, only to find him out when he wasn't at work. Edith knew he had been seeing another woman last night, despite his emphatic denials and threats to take any wicked oath she chose to stipulate. If he was to go on giving Libby one, and he wanted to, then he'd have to be a good deal more careful to cover himself and get home at a reasonable hour. He hadn't said anything to the grass when he had finally reached him at his office that morning and arranged a meet, there was no point.

'Sorry if I put you in it last night,' Fielder said straightaway as Pyle joined him at the end of the carriage.

The grass was obviously full of remorse over what he had done. He was in his usual place in the front end of the Circle Line train. The carriage was less deserted than it usually was when they used the venue for a meet in the evening but passenger traffic had slackened after lunch and hadn't started its buildup towards the rush-hour yet. The other passengers were mainly Pakistani, or from points farther east. There were two Japanese girls sat almost directly opposite the detective and the grass. Pyle looked them over but didn't consider them any sort of threat.

"S all right, Micky. Couldn't be helped,' the DI said, letting him off the hook. Then he added, 'You cunt.'

The grass smiled a little sheepishly, uncertain whether he was serious, and finally decided he wasn't. 'Have one on the firm, did you?'

- 'Wish I had,' Pyle said dismissively. He glanced at the two girls across the aisle, then said. 'What about Jack Lynn? What's the word, Micky?' He wasn't really in the mood to make the full circle with him.

'Going off soon now's what I heard. Still the Tote at Catford, of course.' He paused briefly for effect. 'But I heard something else. About a blag that went off in Bromley that was supposed to be down to him. A bank he done, oh about nine months ago now.' He waited, as if expecting some comment from the DI. 'There was some bearer-bonds of some kind what went missing apart from the cash.'

Pyle nodded like he knew all this, but didn't say anything.

'Well, I was told that the fella what placed them was Gerry Davis. Well, he's not your average placer. He's got some very smart offices in South Street in Mayfair. Apparently he used to do a bit with longfirms over Camden Town. S'posed to be well involved now, he is. He dabbles in all sorts. Especially a bit of video porn.'

The suspect sounded interesting, but Pyle guessed he might have to go carefully. 'How reliable is that, Micky, would you say?'

'Oh, pretty good. I mean, I'd say that was about right.'

'What else has this Davis done, d'you hear? Anything?'

Micky Fielder was sorry at having to disappoint the detective, if he could have invented some worthwhile business for him he would have done just to please the CID. 'Dunno,' he said, 'apart from the longfirms, that is. He's supposed to be share-dealing now. Well, I mean, you got to be well bent to go and get a living there.'

'He sounds like he might be worth chasing up,' Pyle conceded, much to the grass's delight.

The train pulled into Victoria station and both men fell silent. They watched as the doors opened and an Indian in traditional dress got in at their end.

'Fucking swatzers!' Fielder said, unable to hold his silence.

He was as much an anglophile and as right-wing in his views as any villain. 'Look at that, not a white man in the place. I tell you, you start to forget what white men look like.'

'About right, Micky,' was all Pyle said. He took his point, but didn't let foreigners irritate him too much, whatever their colour.

After the doors had shut and the train restarted, Pyle said, 'How d'you go with those American X? Any good?'

'Ah, a right rubout, guv,' Fielder said defensively, and adjusted his coat on his shoulders. 'I found a man to take them all right. But you know ...' He made a brief gesture to toss himself off, completely disregarding the girls opposite. 'Bits and pieces's how he wants to weigh on. What can you do ...?'

It was a standard ploy. Pyle smiled tolerantly.

'You weren't looking for a taste, guv, were you?' the grass inquired hesitantly.

'I wouldn't earn much by the sound of it, Micky. Not even enough for flowers to sweeten the old lady.' Pyle considered him for a moment, wondering fleetingly why Fielder pursued the life he did. He doubted that those few brief moments of glory were worth all the aggravation. 'Just keep listening for what Jack Lynn's having. It's his turn, Micky.'

Pyle rose to get off at Sloane Square. He'd get the first train back. He still had a stack of work in the office.

'Malcolm!' DC Salter shouted emerging from the Squad-office and seeing a uniformed PC from A1 going along the corridor. PC Malcolm Larkin turned and waited for the DC to catch him up.

He was a policeman in his early twenties who hadn't long finished his initial training before attestment when he applied for and was transferred to A1 which among other things dealt with obscene publications. Until a few years ago that was all handled by the CID's Dirty Squad until too many of them were caught at it. The uniform didn't automatically make it straighter as some of the hierarchy seemed to think it would: what happened was that the earlier nickings made them more careful.

'Been looking for you,' Salter said. Then, glancing round and lowering his voice, he went on. 'Any chance of some videos? There's a party tonight. Looks like being a bit near the mark.'

The PC could be very accommodating if he wished. Supplying confiscated cassettes of hardcore films for a showing or to have copies run off wasn't difficult. 'How many did you want, Warren?'

'Two or three should do it, I would think. If that's all right?'

'You had better put me in then, hadn't you?' PC Larkin suggested. He would have to take care of the property.

'Won't be difficult. They'll have to be good 'uns though. No rubbish.'

Rising to the challenge the uniform said, 'We nicked a lad last night with some terrific stuff. I tell you, Warren, it even gave my governor a hardon.'

'They'll do ...'

Pyle emerged from one of C11's offices in time to catch the tail end of the conversation. He could guess the rest – he'd been invited to the party but couldn't make it, the way his old woman was – but wasn't concerned. 'Slip down to CRO, Warren,' Pyle said, 'see if you can find any record on Gerry or Gerald Davis. There might be something.' It was a chance, though a slim one. C11 had heard nothing more than a whisper about him and his connection with the blag in Bromley, but it didn't even amount to enough for a visit.

Pyle went along the corridor and turned into the DCIs' office. Trevor Watson was there with one of the Squad's DIs whom he was advising about a prospective charge – unnecessarily Pyle thought, though he didn't say anything.

'I don't think those plates will be enough, Mark,' Watson was saying pedantically. 'His brief'll probably stick up a fanny about you planting them.' He glanced at Pyle.

'The age-old problem,' Pyle interjected. ''S Tony about?'

'He's still out investigating complaints.'

'He ought to join CIB2.

'We'll all be in CIB2 before much longer,' the second DI commented.

'Daresay they could use a bit more help. You want to look at what I've got, guv?' Pyle offered.

'I'm not exactly scratching, Fred,' Watson said. 'Get the super to have a look, will you?'

'Yeah, sure.' Ordinarily Pyle might not have bothered, but Davis looked half-respectable, even if it was only a front, so it was as well he proceeded carefully with him.

Knowing how cautiously Superintendent Jeymer would likely want to go about things, Pyle decided to try and firm up his info' a little more before putting it to him. He made a phone call to Bromley CID. 'Inspector Allen?' he said when he was put through. But he was told he was out. 'When's he expected back?' Pyle asked. The voice down the phone wasn't sure. 'Well, have him ring me when he comes in, will you? Inspector Pyle ... C8. It's about that bank blag that went off on your manor last year ...'S man called Davis I'm interested in ... Cheers.'

Pyle replaced the phone and watched Warren Salter move along the office towards him.

'No trace, guv. Not wanted either, not as Gerry or Gerald Davis.'

'It was a stoneginger not to be that easy,' Pyle said. 'Thanks, Warren.'

All he could do was put it to the super as he had it, but he could almost guarantee how Ernie Jeymer would react. Anyone wearing a suit costing more than ninety quid and with an accent that wasn't decidedly working-class then Jeymer called them 'sir' and treated them deferentially. He was someone who liked to readily identify villains as such and was a little disturbed when they slipped over into that – as far as he was concerned – area of middle- and upper-classes where the ramps were slightly more genteel and less readily pursuable.

With his arm resting comfortably over a filing cabinet in the superintendents' office, Pyle watched his boss as he considered the proposition he had put up to him about Davis. He could almost hear the questions being posed in the superintendent's mind. Sure it was a bit thin, but at least worth a visit, Pyle thought.

Jeymer pulled his well-trimmed beard thoughtfully between his thumb and forefinger, then said, 'Rumours that he may or may not have placed those bearer-bonds, or that he may have been running long firms a few years ago. They don't amount to much, Fred, do they?'

'I don't know, guv. I thought they might. That's why I wanted a word.'

'Davis is really quite respectable, isn't he? He's always on the financial pages.' Jeymer had about two-penn'orth of shares so he read the financial pages; he hadn't been taken for a ride yet so he had great faith in the wizards who were knighted for their stockmarket manipulations.

Pyle was about to say how he didn't feel that was important, but merely shrugged.

'You know yourself, Fred, what he is as much as what we've got determines how we go after him. And what we've got doesn't amount to a rub, does it? We can't just pull him down the road and give him the treatment like some villains.'

''Course not,' Pyle conceded. 'But I thought he might have been worth a visit. I s'pose I've less faith in the financial Establishment than you, guv.'

Jeymer gave him an oblique look. Then said, 'How good is your snout?'

'He's pretty reliable. He's the lad who gave me the stuff on Jack Lynn in the first place.'

That made the superintendent pull thoughtfully at his beard again. 'Even so, I think we'd better give Davis a miss for now, Fred. Concentrate on Lynn.'

Pyle moved off the filing cabinet and collected the folder from the superintendent's desk. 'He's more a prospect, I daresay.' His manner reflected nothing of his disappointment. He had quite enough to do without looking for work, but he thought it silly concentrating merely on one side of an investigation, the readily identifiable villain who was going to come sooner or later anyway. If he had more time he might have taken a chance and pursued Davis anyway.

'Incidentally, are you going to Staines to give a hand?' Jeymer asked.

That visit had more or less fallen his lot. 'I don't know when, guv,' Pyle said, hoping it would get passed to someone else.

It didn't. 'Try and make it soon, Fred. They've been on again.'

'Where the fuck was I last Monday?' DC Ray Jenkins asked, leaning round from the desk where he was sitting in the Squad office. Such inquiries were familiar from detectives who hadn't kept their diaries up to scratch when they were due to be handed in for the DCI to check them.

There were a lot of detectives in the Squad office. Most of them were bending to their diaries now like they were sitting an exam.

'I expect that was when you were stuck up that old tart, Ray,' a detective nearby suggested.

'Chance! Wouldn't that be a nice thing. Was that when we went and nicked chummy with those forged logbooks?'

'No. That was on the Saturday,' DC Peter Fenton said. 'Wasn't it? That was when I put it down. It's not in the Duty Book. That just shows obo both days.'

'I think you're wrong, Peter. I'll have a look in Jack's diary.' He rose and moved up the office to Eric Lethridge's desk where some of their squad's diaries were in awaiting collection. The DS looked up as Jenkins came to the desk explaining what he wanted.

'You should fucking well do it as you do it, Peter,' Lethridge said. That was expected of the DS, but it wasn't likely to result in trouble for the DC; an incomplete or incorrect diary would.

For all his loathing of paperwork, Jack Barcy's diary was

always written up accurately and ahead of everyone else's and could always be relied on.

Fred Pyle took no more notice of his detectives corroborating their details than the DS did. He stopped by the desk and proffered Lethridge the slim folder he'd brought. 'Davis. He's not worth too much attention after all.'

'Oh – surprised. 'What's the SP then?' Lethridge asked. He wasn't particularly concerned one way or the other.

'We mustn't upset him – might spoil his image on the financial pages.' Pyle smiled; he remained philosophical about the priorities they had in the CID. 'Check through his known associates anyway, Eric. Might give us something useful for when we get around to nicking Lynn. And ring Inspector Allen down at Bromley. He was going to phone me back.'

'Any particular hurry, Fred? I'm up to my ears at the moment.'

'No. Whenever you can,' Pyle said uninterestedly. 'I don't suppose it'll help us much anyway.' He searched around the office. 'Where's Jack Barcy? I want him to go out to Staines ...'

'Will you get away with sending him?' Lethridge asked. He'd have used the same argument had the DI suggested his going.

'He can take the seconds. Tell him I want a word.' He collected up the diaries from the desk.

'D'you see that new typist along the corridor? Has she got some form!' Lethridge said. 'Wouldn't mind giving it one.'

'You got some chance, you fat bastard. I heard Tony Simmons was giving her a seeing to.'

'Dirty lucky bastard.'

'Fred!' DI Welch called up the Squad office. 'You're wanted on the blower.'

It was Paddington CID informing him that they had picked up Brian Finch.

'Good luck,' Pyle said into the telephone. 'Where d'you find

180

him . . . I'll come over and interview him,' he told them. 'I'll be a couple of hours at least, I'd say. Still, the wait'll do him good – the chasing around he's caused. Don't let him make any phone calls or see anyone . . . no, especially not his brief. Cheers.' He replaced the phone and sat at his desk with the pile of diaries.

DC Shields came along the office with his diary. 'Want to have a look at this one, guv?'

'Up to date, Tony, is it?'

'Just about, guv.' He waited as the DI glanced over the entries uninterestedly. 'I saw this snout earlier. I have him doing a bit for me – gave me a couple of nice things on division, he did,' Shields explained. He waited as if expecting some comment, but all he got was the DI's attention. 'He's put me onto a little ramp at the Sanyo television factory out at Acton. There's a regular touch each week apparently. Two or three sets going.'

It didn't sound of much interest to the Squad. 'What's it come to so far? Any idea?'

'Not really, guv. Couple of grand. I s'pose.'

'Reliable, is he?'

'He tries, guv, you know. Like I said, he's put one or two nice things my way.'

'Bung him?' Pyle wanted to know.

'A tenner.'

'Unless we have it off you'll lose that,' the DI said with a grin. Money was drawable from the Informers' Fund by detectives where it was related to a job or investigation. Shields' information didn't amount to that. 'It doesn't sound all that, Tony, does it. A couple of tellys a week. Tell him to keep his ears open though. If they decide to have a lorry load, well . . .' The Squad had to keep a sense of proportion. 'Unless you wanted to pass it onto division, did you?'

Shields dismissed the prospect out of hand. 'Acton wasn't my manor, guv, was it.'

Pyle nodded his approval. 'About right, son.' He understood the need detectives felt to protect their information, even when it meant the continuance of the crime involved. He not only condoned such practice, but actually encouraged it. Such a state of affairs helped create in detectives a sense of independence; it was in that manner that detectives were at their most efficient, despite what the hierarchy believed. This was one of the areas DI Pyle was convinced he knew better than those in offices he would never attain, simply because he was in close contact with crime detection at street level while the hierarchy were no longer in sight of it. The priorities of the Squad were such that they couldn't pursue every job that came their way, and Sanyo could probably afford the loss anyway. If such practices as the DI had just approved became known to the hierarchy then disciplinary action might have resulted, but that was a chance most detectives were prepared to take to preserve their independence.

21

D division was one of the busiest in the Met, and the divisional HQ at Paddington was a large, relatively new building equipped with most of the modern aids available to the police. But despite the high degree of technological efficiency both the building and the division were still operated by policemen and policewomen who could be helpful or unhelpful, efficient or inefficient as perversity dictated. They were governed by whim and loyalty to colleagues and sometimes no amount of pressure would cause them to shift.

Many times during his so far short career, Alex Gladwell had run up against all human factors governing policemen. Sometimes it had helped him to achieve his end, sometimes it had merely hindered him. It was hindering him now as he waited on the public benches at Paddington police station. He was waiting to see his client Brian Finch, and had been there over an hour and had no intention of moving. He knew the police were being wilfully obstructive, and was well able to guess why. It would have been on the instructions of the Squad detective inspector who was in charge of the case and whose arrival they were awaiting.

Alex Gladwell was at twenty-nine a solicitor who, in the two years since he had started in practice had made a considerable reputation for himself. Most of his clients were villains who came to him not because they were innocent, but because they were guilty. Gladwell made no moral judgements. Anyone, no matter what their crimes, was entitled to a defence, and his clients were equally entitled to the best result he could get them, no matter how he got it. Some of the means he employed would not only have got him disbarred but also criminally prosecuted, along with a number of policemen. But so far he had escaped unscathed, and hoped to continue to do so.

He was a short round man, with a plump boyish face; his hair was slightly receding and he had a mousy-coloured moustache, neither of which detracted from his youthful appearance. Nor his grey pinstriped three-piece suit which had the look of the legal profession about it.

Although he hadn't wasted the time he had been kept waiting, having read a number of reports that were necessary for him to brief counsel in a fraud case, he had now completed all his reading and subsequent note-taking, so was growing impatient. He was still determined not to quit without seeing his client or getting some satisfaction from the detective handling the case. He rose from the wooden seat and strode across the terrazzo floor to the public desk, which was like a large serving hatch. The uniformed constable who was sitting at one of the desks in the area beyond, looked up. He was embarrassed by the solicitor's presence and the fact that he was unable to accommodate him. His blush of embarrassment was hardly noticeable among the spots and boils that peppered his face.

'He's on his way, sir,' the constable said apologetically.

Gladwell merely stared at the young man for a moment, believing he was lying. He wasn't convinced they had even telephoned to inquire when Inspector Pyle was likely to arrive. Swivelling on the balls of his feet, Gladwell marched back to the seat and lowered himself. He looked at his watch, then opened the briefcase he had with him and checked through the notes of the details he had taken from Mrs Finch.

Although the DI and the solicitor had met on a number of occasions, Gladwell didn't openly greet him when he came through the glass door with a second man. Instead he followed their progress to the public desk.

'Inspector Pyle,' the DI said to the constable without attempting to produce his ID.

'Yes, sir,' the constable said, glancing beyond him to

Gladwell who was now approaching. 'Inspector Polden said he'd like a word ...'

'Inspector Pyle,' Gladwell said as the constable moved away to the telephone. 'My name is Gladwell. Alex Gladwell.' The solicitor introduced himself as if they were strangers.

Pyle said, 'We talked on the phone the other day about Terry Clark.'

'You're holding another of my clients here, and quite illegally again. Unless of course Brian Finch has been charged, or your powers to detain a suspect have been increased without my hearing about it,' the young brief said with mild sarcasm.

'Not unless I haven't heard about it,' Pyle replied mirthlessly. 'You're a busy man, Mr Gladwell.'

'Seems that I've been waiting around here all week,' Gladwell said. 'You left instructions that I wasn't to be allowed to see my client. What is he being charged with? Or is that a police secret?'

Carefully Pyle said, 'I can't tell you what it'll be until I interview him. But probably robbery, along with malicious wounding, same as the other fella.'

The constable came back to the desk. 'Inspector Polden would like to see you in his office, sir. You can take the lift to the first floor.' He pointed to the lift across the front reception as though Pyle were only partially sighted.

The DI accompanied by DC Unwin, moved away towards the lift. Gladwell pursued him.

'Inspector. I would like to see my client,' he said firmly.

'Of course, Mr Gladwell. But not before me.' He watched the younger man a moment. Pyle knew how safe his ground was; this solicitor was a hustler, a dealmaker, he wasn't going to scratch or bite or kick up a storm for his client just yet, that wasn't the way he operated. The DI nodded, as if concurring with his own thoughts, then turned away into the lift.

Detective Inspector Frank Polden looked more like a gentleman farmer than a policeman; his crumpled lovat wool suit seemed to complement his florid complexion and bushy grey eyebrows. The almost standard bottle of scotch was brought out for Pyle's visit. Peter Unwin wasn't in the office with them. He was left to get the witnesses organized.

'You have any trouble picking him up?' Pyle asked as Polden poured a drink.

'Came as good as gold – a neighbour gave us a call.' He gave Pyle his drink. 'We turned his drum over – he had about two grand there.'

Pyle didn't comment, but wondered if that was the amount the detectives had found or whether they had had an earner out of it. It wasn't really important.

"S down in the front office,' Polden said, ignoring the question running through the DI's mind. 'It's all old. He stuck up the usual fanny about winning it racing.' He scoffed, a little dismayed. 'I wish some of my horses would run as well, I really do.'

'Funny that, the luck some villains have on horses,' Pyle said dismissively.

'Was that one at Walthamstow definitely down to him?'

'Be handy. Who called his brief? One of your lot?'

'No idea. He showed up a while ago. Got a bit upset when he was blanked.' Polden found that amusing.

'He's supposed to be well bent. 'S what I heard. I daresay one of your lads is earning a couple of quid.'

Completely unconcerned at the prospect, Polden simply said, 'I wouldn't be surprised.'

Pyle wasn't concerned. He nodded, 'I've had the witnesses brought over. You got somewhere handy to put him up for an ID?'

'You're not parading him?' Polden said like he didn't wish to be inconvenienced.

'I wasn't planning to.'

'We'll find you somewhere nice and quiet – we'll have to be a bit slippery though with that brief downstairs,' he added as though Pyle wouldn't have been aware of the problem.

Officially identification parades should have been conducted in a manner which was in no way likely to prejudice the witness against the suspect. For that reason identification parades were always officially held within the confines of the police station and within the precincts of the front office, and this procedure was always conducted by the uniform branch, with the duty inspector in charge. However, practice was another matter, and convenience was often a determining factor. No policemen, whether uniform or CID, liked the inconvenience of parading suspects, it wasted a lot of time for a lot of people, not least of all the police.

Brian Finch was brought from the cells and put in an interview room and sat unsuspectingly facing the door, which by the merest chance had a fifteen inch square window of clear glass.

Singly the two witnesses who had been collected from Walthamstow were ushered along the corridor by DC Unwin and reintroduced to Pyle. The DI told them in a quiet voice what he wanted from them.

'Now there is no doubt about this being one of the robbers,' Pyle said reassuringly to the first witness, a man in his mid-fifties. Then to show that he was in no way biased, he added, 'But I want you to be quite certain in your own mind, okay?'

With a precise nod, like someone quite used to taking instructions, the witness, a messenger at the bank that had been robbed, said, 'You just want me to look into the room and see if it's him. I understand, sir.'

Offering an encouraging smile, the DI patted his shoulder and sent him towards the door. He watched as the witness paused outside the door and peered in. There was no immediate recognition on his face. He continued on past the door; then came back towards Pyle, peering into the interview room at Finch again. There was a perplexed expression on his face as he stopped before the DI.

'What d'you say, Mr Higgins?' Pyle said doubtfully.

'Well ...' he began hesitantly. 'It could be him, I suppose, but I'm not saying it is, mind.'

'Perhaps if you were to have another look,' Pyle suggested. 'Take your time.'

'I don't think that would help, sir,' Higgins said. 'I really wouldn't like to commit myself, to be perfectly honest. I'm sorry I can't be of more help, inspector – when I think of what they did to Charlie. I'd like to help lock them up and throw away the key.'

'That's what we're trying to do here,' Pyle told him.

The bank messenger looked back towards the interview room, adopting a thoughtful expression, then finally shook his head. 'No, I can't say as that's him, sir.'

His face set in a grim expression, Pyle nodded, concealing his disappointment.

The next witness, Ellen Mellish, who was a customer of the bank's was equally disappointing to the DI. She was put through the same motions with more or less the same result. She couldn't say with any degree of certainty that Finch was involved. Pyle could imagine what the villain's silk would make of their testimony in court. There'd be more chance of a conviction if they weren't called.

A prospect Pyle had to face at this stage was the distinct possibility that Finch hadn't been on the Walthamstow bank blag. But if not then what? For it was odds on that he was involved in something. His swift departure just prior to his house being raided the other morning suggested as much. But then Pyle couldn't imagine any villain who, regardless of whether or not he was currently at it, would choose to wait around for a dawn visit from the Squad. Then there was the two grand the local CID had found at his place. Pyle didn't really believe it had been won betting. Although he was a sufficient realist to recognize that he might not have enough eventually to charge him with the Walthamstow blag, he wasn't about to completely rule out the possibility, not yet anyway.

Brian Finch was a square-jawed, sand-haired – what there was of it for he wore it closely cropped – villain in his late thirties. His eyes were a little too close set and his mouth was too small for him to have been called good-looking, though Pyle suspected he was possibly being biased; before he wouldn't have considered such aspects.

The villain rose expectantly as the DI entered the room. Pyle indicated with his head for the uniformed constable to leave, and closed the door after him.

'What's this then,' Finch wanted to know, 'the treatment?' He was arrogant but not demonstratively so. It was as though he believed himself innocent and knew therefore that it was only a matter of time before he was released.

Not for a moment did Pyle imagine that a professional villain could be so naïve. 'We'll see how you shape, son.'

'You're jumping the gun a bit. I'm not saying nothing until I've seen my brief.'

Pyle laughed. 'What the fuck d'you think he can do? You're bang to rights.'

'Oh yeah? Should be dead easy for you then, shouldn't it?' He wasn't giving an inch.

'About as easy as taking a leak, you see.' Pyle was judging this man as Libby Howard's former lover, wondering how efficient he had been in that area; whether she had enjoyed Finch fucking her more than him. He was younger, so maybe he was more efficient. 'You might as well put your hands up to it right now, Brian,' the DI said pragmatically.

'Oh yeah. That's what you reckon, is it?'

Pyle adopted the same mild approach. 'The sensible move, son. Gets you some help. You were grassed. Cliff Harding put you right in it. That's why he's out and you're nicked, of course.'

'Never heard of the man,' Finch said. 'Who is he?'

'Just a villain who puts his liberty above yours. Then why shouldn't he? That's the sensible thing to do.'

'What am I supposed to do now then? Grass a few I don't know, and go and get myself some kind of deal. 'S that what this is all about?' He believed it was and was surprised when the DI shook his head.

"S no value, son. We can't go on trading villain for villain indefinitely. We've got one in the book that someone's got to go for.' He stabbed his thick index finger at Finch. 'You've been elected.'

That caused Finch to change his approach slightly. 'You'll think different when my brief has a pop at you ...'

'A little kid with a wispy moustache?' he said like he hadn't met Gladwell. 'He's here now. Flapping around like a queer penguin he is.'

'Oh well, come on. I want to see him, don't I? I've been asking to see him for the last two hours.'

'You'll see him all right, Brian, when I'm ready. Now that'll just depend on what you give me. You put up as much as Terry Clark did, we'll get on splendidly.' He smiled. 'So sit down, make yourself comfortable, son.'

Finch looked at the DI, then sat. Pyle drew up a chair opposite him.

'Right, we'll have a nice little chat about blags and blaggers, shall we.' It wasn't a question.

The interrogation took the DI no more further forward than the two witnesses, simply because the villain wilfully resisted him, and Pyle refrained from putting the pressure on. Rather he conveyed the impression that it didn't much matter one way or the other what Finch offered, the result would be just the same. The fact that he apparently wasn't trying only served to confirm this. If Brian Finch gave the CID nothing, then Pyle revealed less of his true hand to the villain.

'It's going to be a long wait, Mr Gladwell,' Pyle informed the solicitor, who was still waiting in the public area of the station. 'He's well stitched up.' Alternatives were jostling in the DI's mind, most of which would benefit him personally. It wouldn't be difficult having it off here, he decided.

'But you are going to permit me access to my client, inspector?' the brief said formally, endeavouring to imply that the consequences of his not doing so could cause him a great deal of trouble.

'Now I didn't say I wasn't, did I?' He smiled politely. 'You'll almost certainly see him at Bow Street tomorrow.'

This slightly surprised the young solicitor, whose attitude promptly shifted to the line of least resistance. 'Your case is that good, inspector?'

'Both you and Finch know it, Mr Gladwell – 's why you're here.' Or they knew something he didn't know, Pyle was convinced of that.

The solicitor pursed his red lips with a thoughtful, accommodating smile. Cautiously he glanced about the reception area, making sure no one else was within earshot. He was sufficiently experienced with the CID to know that almost anything could be put up to detectives provided one didn't do so in front of witnesses. 'Is there any possibility of latitude here?'

A smile started in Pyle's brain, but he stopped it before it transmitted itself to his facial muscles. He recognized how the young man was shaping, but merely considered him, without saying anything.

'Certainly it might be to our mutual advantage,' the brief suggested. He was empowered to make those sort of deals on behalf of his clients; it was why a lot of them came to him in the first place, and not with a Legal Aid certificate.

'What d'you have in mind?' Pyle asked vaguely.

Again Gladwell checked about him. 'Perhaps we could talk somewhere less public?'

They used another interview room, which differed little from that which Finch was in.

Despite having done business together before, each proceeded warily, sounding the other out initially as though what they believed they were doing, were interested in achieving here, was strictly legal.

'I think my client might be interested in a lesser charge,' Gladwell suggested.

Pyle nodded studiously. 'I'm sure he would.' Then asked,

'Pleading to it?'

Parrying the proposal, the solicitor committed himself a little further. 'He would be more interested in some alternative arrangement ...' He hesitated there.

The DI waited. But saw that the brief wanted commitment for that in kind, 'That's always a possibility. What are you suggesting?'

'Some financial arrangement. We're both practical men, after all.'

'I'd say so. But it still depends on what you're looking for,' Pyle said.

'I'm sure something very beneficial could be worked out ... I would first need to see my client.'

After considering this for a moment, Pyle nodded. 'That's not difficult, Alex.'

The solicitor needed to consult with his client to ascertain what he could afford, rather than what his involvement may or may not have been. For that had little bearing compared to what the police had or chose to find if they decided he should go. Gladwell wasn't long in coming back with an offer of twelve hundred pounds for having his client dropped right out. That struck Pyle as a reasonably good deal, but he sought and got fifteen hundred, which struck him as an even better deal, especially as his evidence wasn't such that he could have charged the villain for the Walthamstow blag, certainly not to have got a conviction. Had he been able to obtain that, he would have blanked the offer on account of the beating the security guard took. He wanted to see the villains put away for that job. But now Brian Finch probably wouldn't be one of them. However, his not being nicked for the Walthamstow blag was about the only thing Fred Pyle's earner would guarantee. He had been at it somewhere, that was fairly obvious from the way the offer was made. What the DI would do, once he had his earner safely tucked away, was give C11 the word that Finch was having something and see what they could sniff out. That was the price of being a villain and having a bent brief.

192

22

The DCI had been on to him several times wanting to know what was happening with Harding, whether there were any developments. He was worrying about it, while for his part Pyle would just as soon have let it run on, let the villain get what he could in his own time; the levers he had under him were good enough. But then it wasn't entirely his decision how the informant was handled, and with his boss getting on to him he had to get on to Harding.

The meet looked like a pretty safe one. Harding had suggested it, having a legitimate reason for being at the makeshift community playground, which was fenced off from the street in a holey fashion – more kids went through the holes in the fence than used the gate. The area was littered with brightly painted rubbish; a profusion of empty oil drums, old timber-and-doors climbing frame, old tyres, rope swings. The kids there seemed to love it, and swarmed eagerly over the ramshackle apparatus in a noisy, reckless manner, watched with apparent casual concern by denim-clad mothers, some with curlers in, or by as many fathers who were out of work. Clifford Harding had three of his kids there; they were aged four, five and six. The fourth who was only six months had been left at home with his mother.

'They look like they're nice kids,' Pyle remarked, standing inside the playground with Harding, but separated from the other parents who were present. Despite the enjoyment he saw, he said, "S not right, this all they have to play in.' He believed that. His own childhood had been spent in the city and he hadn't been able to move out fast enough when he had kids of his own. Green fields and a few trees around to climb, that was what kids needed, or at least some safely constructed apparatus to climb over. It was such environments as this that bred villains; but all the while there were policemen to nick them and prisons to lock them in no one seemed to bother. Probably there wasn't any practical alternative anyway.

'The council keep threatening to put something permanent up,' Harding was saying in a resigned manner. 'They don't do nothing though.'

'They seem happy enough, Clifford.' Pyle looked around the playground then beyond the kids to a young mother who was sitting on a box reading a paperback. She was attractive. Pyle didn't pursue his thoughts. He was there to wind Harding up, not pursue young mothers. 'Yes, they look well happy. You'll miss them. They'll miss you too, I daresay – if I pick you up again.' Harding looked sharply at the DI, who shrugged as if accepting the inevitable. 'It's got to be so. I expected some word on Jack Lynn by now.'

A feeling of unease spread through Harding. 'I have been punting around. I mean, you don't just go up to the man and start asking questions. You have to sus' things out. It takes time, guv, dun' it?'

'I'll have fucking well retired before I hear from you. You haven't got time, son.' The anger that he purposely showed the felon suddenly vanished and he shook his head. 'You've had your chance. You've got to be nicked again.'

This almost caused Harding to panic. His eyes darted nervously around the playground as he teetered on the edge, undecided about breaking and running. But it was his kids who were stopping him, and not just their presence and the prospect of leaving them here – the police would see they got home safely; that was about the only thing the police could be trusted to do. 'What ...?' the question started out of Harding's mouth, taking all the air from his lungs with it. 'What are you talking about? I'm working for you.'

Again Pyle shook his head. Worth all the bumf, hassle and hard work that being a detective entailed was this power it gave him over villains such as Harding. 'There'll be some new

194

charges going up. Involving a security blag out at Harlow.'

There had been a robbery that went off out that way about two months ago, but as far as Pyle knew Harding wasn't involved. 'A lad called Brian Finch put you right in it.'

'Oh yeah?' Harding said, recovering himself slightly. 'Who's he then?'

'"S worth a try, son. 'S worth a try,' Pyle said, uninterested in the denial. 'He's given us enough.'

'Look, you found the shooter at my place. Right, I mean, I'm bang to rights on that. I was silly as a goat keeping it there, but that's all there is. That's straight ...'

'About as straight as a dog's dick. What about Harlow ...? Won't be at all difficult finding someone to stick up to ID you.'

Anxiety gnawed at Harding. He knew the likelihood of that happening, knew it had happened too many times before. 'Leave it out, will you?' he said. He was close to defeat.

'The thing is, Clifford, my governor's making noises about you. I can't justify keeping you clear any longer, not without you give me something ...'

'I will, won't I? I said I'd get it.'

'We're all becoming fucking old men waiting for you, son.'

'Look, I heard he was supposed to be making one,' he tried, but saw the DI wasn't impressed. 'Soon now. I mean, it was what I heard.'

'Tell me something I don't already know, why don't you?' Pyle said sarcastically, not allowing him anything.

The villain considered him for a moment, resisting giving him what he had got so far. In spite of their agreement, to actually go and start grassing was something Harding in some vague, abstracted way thought he would finally be able to avoid. He glanced over at his kids and considered them. The risk in stalling this CID in his endeavour not to become a grass was too great, he decided. Finally he said, 'I heard it was the Tote at Catford.'

Pyle looked at him, his face expressionless.

A muscle around Harding's left eye twitched briefly. 'It's

what I heard. It's straight.'

The DI nodded slowly. This information alone didn't put him ahead of what he had already got from Micky Fielder, but it did indicate that Harding was genuine, and working for him now, albeit reluctantly. 'That's about right,' he said grudgingly. 'What I want from you now is when, and who's involved.'

The villain said he didn't know.

'Well that's what you've got to make it your business to find out, Clifford. Unless of course you want to do it the other way.' Pyle glanced towards the children, leaving him in no doubt about the alternative.

'Might be worth putting a couple of C11 on watch down at Catford, Fred,' DCI Simmons said, turning into his office, followed by Pyle. Both men were still in their overcoats and carried briefcases, having just come on duty. The DCI was pleased about the development with Harding, even though it wasn't a very big step forward.

'We could,' Pyle said sceptically. 'S'pose they might get lucky and see something, guv.'

Simmons removed his coat and hung it up by the door, then proceeded to switch off the desk lamps that were still burning in the deserted office. 'What's the alternative? D'you have something in mind?'

'No. But I didn't particularly want to have to give this one to C11, that was all.' One of the reasons was that he didn't want any other force involved that he might not be able to control; it might have presented a few problems if the need arose to nick Jack Lynn by means of a swift 'un. 'I think it's too close anyway.'

'D'you have anyone to spare on your squad to put down there?'

'That's going to be a problem.' His squad had more than enough going on and were completely stretched. Anyway Pyle didn't think there would be any value in having detectives on watch at the racetrack. There wasn't likely anything to be seen until the blag was going off. Then, if he hadn't got his entire squad down there and a few more besides, there'd be little chance of nicking anyone.

'Well, borrow a couple ...' Simmons suggested, pursuing his tack.

A detective sergeant went past the door, then came back. 'Guv. The super was looking for you earlier ...' Simmons acknowledged the information. 'Did you get to look at that CRO file yet, by the way?'

'No, I didn't. Give me a look back later, will you?' Simmons turned his attention back to the matter in hand. He crossed to the manpower availability board indicator on the wall by the door. The coloured tabs told him at a glance the position of each man on the ten squads. He ran his fingers along the cards for Pyle's squad. 'Is Sampson still off sick?'

'S'posed to be coming back Monday,' Pyle said. It was a sore point. 'I think I'd better have a replacement for him, guv. He ought to go back in division.' Pyle wouldn't have minded seeing him go back into uniform.

'What's the problem?'

'The usual. He's about as wide as narrow tape.' Although by no means an inexperienced detective, Sampson seemed forever in awe of the strokes that were pulled by the Squad. While the DI, like most, would barely tolerate that in a relatively inexperienced CID like Roger Humphries, in the expectation of marking his card, he wouldn't with an older detective more set in his ways. He didn't trust Sampson, who he believed was a potential whistle-blower.

Simmons nodded. The solution was simple. 'Make the recommendation then, Fred. I'll push it through.' He turned back to the board. 'Take Kennedy and Martin from number six. You'll have to juggle a bit though. Most of them are in court all this week, and most of next I shouldn't wonder.'

'I wouldn't mind having someone take seconds out at Lynn's place,' Pyle said. Adding cautiously, 'Might be a bit risky, could go and frighten him off. That'd be handy.'

'You think it's that close to going off, do you, Fred?'

Pyle shrugged. 'According to Harding. And my other snout seemed to think that was about right. I'm waiting to see if he can get anything else.' He had a lot of faith in Micky Fielder.

'I'd like Harding back in just as soon as,' the DCI said.

The DCI was still worrying about Harding and accordingly there was no way he was going to earn his liberty, or none that Fred Pyle immediately foresaw. When he'd done his best he'd be nicked again, Tony Simmons would probably insist on it. If he proved himself, and his best got him a result, then Fred Pyle would do what he could to keep him loose and free from charges resulting out of the firearm found at his place. That was in his own interest rather than solely as a reward to the felon: once a villain was doing a bit that was the best possible lever under him. Villains, especially if they were right good 'uns, lived in terror of ever being marked as a grass. Pyle would see how he shaped up, then maybe have another word with the DCI, try to make him see it his way; he was practical, after all.

'He won't go very far, guv,' Pyle said, reassuring the man.

'What about the Tote?'

'I left them out.' There was a better than even chance that the blaggers would have someone down at Catford on the inside. They had to be getting their information from somewhere, after all. As far as the police operations were concerned there was too much to be said against going to the Tote.

'They ought to be warned,' Simmons said ambiguously, and turned away to answer the telephone that was ringing on DCI Watson's desk.

The disadvantages of warning the people working in the Tote were as obvious to the DCI as they were to Pyle, that was why he had said what he did instead of telling him to warn them. He was simply stating a case and leaving the decision to the DI. However, Pyle wanted to nick Jack Lynn at it, and those going in with him, not have them warned off so they could go and put together another one that the Squad maybe wouldn't get so much as a whisper about.

When he got to his own office the first thing Pyle did even before removing his coat was to check through his messages and this with the vague hope that something urgent would take him out immediately away from the hated paperwork that was piled on his 'posts' tray. He read the scrawl across the pad.

'When did this message from Deptford CID come in, Alan?' he said to DI Welch, who was just concluding a conversation on the phone.

'Last night, I think Frank said,' Welch informed him.

'Fuck! Did it? I wish he'd called me at home.' He picked up the phone and began dialling. 'Fucking grasses, they're more trouble ...'

'One of them been nicked, Fred?' Welch understood the problem.

'Wouldn't you know it ... CID, please,' he said into the mouthpiece. That was the problem with letting grasses have their own little ramps as means of payment for services rendered; they ran the risk of getting their collars felt. When they did, something had to be done to help them. There were no two ways about it, not when they were after information about a robbery which was at such a crucial stage as the one his grass had been punting about on. 'Sergeant Linkup,' Pyle said when he was put through to the CID. After a little while the DS was found. 'Sergeant Linkup? Fred Pyle. You rang me about one of mine ... What d'you pull him for?' The detective down the line explained how he had nicked Micky Fielder in connection with some stolen American Express travellers' cheques.

'Can anything be done?' Pyle wanted to know. Deference to the arresting officer was his reason for asking. It was fairly obvious they could work something out or DS Linkup wouldn't have bothered phoning him. 'I'll come down,' Pyle said when the DS told him he'd help him if he could. 'Won't be before lunchtime though – we've a DIs' meeting here this morning.' That suited Linkup all right. 'Cheers,' Pyle said and replaced the phone. Maybe it was for the best having to give Micky Fielder help like this, he thought, might make him work harder.

During the lunch period the CID office at Deptford nick was deserted, save for the odd DC who wandered through to collect something or look for someone. Such transient visitors didn't disturb DI Pyle and DS Linkup where they sat across from each other at the latter's desk positioned at the top of the room. Dave Linkup was a bulky figure with a lot of dark bushy hair; he was about thirty-five and obviously knew his way about. Pyle wondered briefly what sort of clear-up rate he had – pretty good, he imagined, or he doubtless wouldn't be as amenable as he was.

'I nicked the man your grass knocked out those American X to,' Linkup explained in a casual, friendly way. "Course it didn't take much pressure before he stuck Fielder up. What does he do for you, much?'

'He's been a good 'un,' Pyle said, being purposely vague. 'How d'you come to nick the placer?' Such animals were known to be a cautious breed.

'He's well known here. Used to do a bit for me himself.' Linkup grinned. 'His usefulness is about over. 'He'll have to stay nicked.'

Pyle nodded, understanding the expediency of that. He considered him a moment. 'What about dropping Micky Fielder right out? That going to be much of a problem?'

A telephone started ringing on a side table down by the door; it was one of two lines the CID had in via the switchboard. There was a third direct line on the wall under a canopy. Linkup glanced at the phone, but made no attempt to answer it. 'Wouldn't be too difficult,' the DS said. 'He hasn't been charged. I left him out soon as he told me he was doing a bit for you. Leaves me a bit light though.'

'I daresay it would. I'd appreciate it, Dave . . .' He intimated that he'd find something to help him keep his numbers up. 'Least until he finds out what he's looking for for me, like. I mean, the thing is, then if you need him you can have another look. See how he shapes.'

DS Linkup nodded. 'I'll do you a favour, guv. Help you out.'

'Good luck.' Pyle would remember this amenable DS, and if he could do something for him in the future he would.

The procedure for getting Micky Fielder set free wasn't at all involved. It merely entailed the DS going down to the cells, getting the keys off the gaoler and unlocking the door. There were no other prisoners in the cells to witness this, for those who had been in overnight apart from Fielder had been taken to court. There was no paperwork for the DS to juggle with, for the grass hadn't been charged, and as far as the duty officer had been concerned – and he wasn't and wouldn't be concerned unless some complaint arose – the suspect was merely being held helping the CID with inquiries.

DI Pyle waited outside and when Fielder emerged from the antiquated building and came down the steps he shook his head in mock dismay. Fielder was unshaven and looked crumpled in his soiled brown suede coat. His sculptured hair needed some lacquer.

'Fuck I, Micky,' the DI said. 'I thought you had more sense than to do business with other grasses. I could have put myself in a lot of trouble pulling you out. And for what?'

The grass cringed uncomfortably, but Pyle wasn't about to let him off the hook, not that lightly.

'For what? I'll tell you. Just so you can go and ponce a living. But you're not getting me one any more, are you? I mean, what have you given me? Doesn't amount to a cuntful, does it? A little whisper about something that might or might not even be going off. What else have you got?' Pyle's demand embarrassed Fielder even more. 'Nothing! 'Course you haven't. Been too busy fucking about getting yourself nicked. You've been a right good 'un in the past, Micky. Don't tell me I'm going to have to drop you out.' The DI made it appear as if that was a painful decision for him to arrive at. He paused and measured Fielder before changing tack and adopting a

201

concerned attitude. 'You having some kind of trouble indoors, son? Problems getting your indoor money?'

'No, it's all right, guv,' Fielder said, breathing again, realizing the DI was going to let him live a little longer. 'I was just a bit unlucky, was all. I ought to have known better.'

'How much did that DS nick off you?' Not for a moment did Pyle imagine that Detective Sergeant Linkup was helping out for no other reason than CID comradeship.

'A oner,' Fielder replied sheepishly, as though not too sure he had done right in bunging the DS.

'About right, I suppose,' Pyle nodded, concurring with himself. 'So what's the word on Jack Lynn? Did you hear anything more?'

'No, not yet, I didn't. I was supposed to see a geezer for a drink last night.'

That wasn't a piece of information to please Pyle. 'You're a handy bloke, you are. You'd better look him up, Micky, make yourself busy. I expect to nick Jack Lynn. 'Fact I'm relying on it. I'll be most upset if you don't help me bring that about.' He knew the grass understood. He was into him for a big favour now and had to redeem himself.

It couldn't have worked better for Pyle if he had designed the grass's night in a cell himself.

23

Post-lunch inertia had settled over the Squad office. Detectives went through the motions; it would need a reasonable shout to get them going again, to get them up and away from their desks and the paperwork that had resulted out of so many visits to court that morning.

Eric Lethridge had one in court this morning that resulted in a remand. The DS had just typed the accompanying report. But there were a couple of things related to the defendant that he needed to ch ck out with the DI.

Rising from the desk, Lethridge hitched up his trousers, and slid the report into a pastel-coloured folder. He moved out from the desk and along the office, uninhibitedly scratching his ass as he went. DC Tony Shields, who was at a desk further along the office, was leaning back in his chair watching him.

'What's the matter, skip? Piles?' the DC said as he came past.

'Caught them off your fucking chair if I have, son,' Lethridge said as though it were crabs the younger detective had suggested he had. 'You scratching for work, are you?'

'Not really, skip,' Shields said. 'I got a snout to meet in a minute.' He checked the time.

'Well, make sure you put it in your diary,' Lethridge reminded him and moved on.

'Skip?' DC Humphries said as Lethridge reached the desk he was at. 'What are we doing that placer for after all?'

'Conspiracy to rob. And receiving stolen goods,' Lethridge informed him and moved on. He got inquiries like that from detectives all day long while he was in the office. Assuring them was partly why he was there.

In the corridor Lethridge ran into a DS from C11 called Reg Whitely. He was carrying the standard folder. Anyone who ever moved about the Yard, unless coming in or going out, seemed to be transporting paperwork.

'I was just about to look for your governor,' Whitely said, stopping outside C11's door. 'Weren't you on those Method Index raids for the Walthamstow blag?'

'Along with John Redvers's squad,' Lethridge said cautiously. 'Why, someone making more complaints?'

'Probably, Eric, you've gone a long time now.' He grinned. 'You visited a villain called Harding, didn't you? Clifford Harding. We've picked up a whisper that he's supposed to be making one. He's putting it about that he has some DI straightened.' Whitely shrugged apologetically.

'Maybe he has, Reg. Not too bright though if he's telling people about it. You'd best have a word with the DI.'

Had he in fact been earning off Cliff Harding DI Pyle might have been perturbed by the rumours, if as he suspected they referred to him. He wasn't worried, just annoyed that he had apparently backed a wrong 'un in Harding. The felon's activity in putting one together – presumably the one he had had the gun for – only served to make the DI look a fool, especially when he considered how he was planning to help him stay free. Nothing much was changed by the information DS Whitely gave him, apart from his intentions towards Harding. He would eventually go now, regardless of what he managed to come up with on Jack Lynn.

'What's the strength of your information, Reg?' Pyle asked as though he cared about the current light it showed him in. 'Reliable, would you say?'

'Is it ever that reliable, guv?' Whitely replied. 'But there seems to be something in the wind. Maybe it'll prove to be nothing more than a grudge some grass has.'

'Any chance he might be making one with Lynn?' Lethridge suggested.

'Be ironical, wouldn't it? We might have to have another

look at Harding. Turn him over again, maybe.' That was a certainty to happen, but Pyle wouldn't rush it.

'I'll leave that with you then, Fred, if you like.' Whitely pushed the folder across the desk.

'Yeah, good luck, son. I'll get back to you on any developments.' He sat back in his chair and watched the DS go out. 'What was the word from Bromley, Eric?'

'I talked to that DI there. He reckons they came very close to nicking Gerry Davis. He thought there was enough with his longfirm activities, enough to make it worth taking a chance on doing him over receiving those stolen bonds. But the DPP blanked it, apparently. Sent word back that there wasn't enough to charge him.'

'Ernie Jeymer probably guessed about right then when he said give Davis a miss,' Pyle commented.

'The DI down there sounded well choked. He's sending up all he's got. He reckons that not being able to go after Davis stopped him nicking Jack Lynn. Might be true – but it sounded like a bit of fanny to me,' Lethridge said uncharitably.

'About right. Maybe we'll take another look at Davis,' the DI said. 'But I can't see him coming.' The best he could do was have a word with the Fraud Squad, let them have a look at the financier. Other than that about the only chance he had was to fit him, but to suddenly find Gerry Davis involved in robbery might be stretching credulity a little too far even for the CID.

There was an extra heavy load of work on at the Yard which would keep Fred Pyle hard at it until quite late, or that was what he had told his wife. She did expect him in to dinner at sometime, but not with the rest of the family. In fact, Fred Pyle was seeing Libby Howard on a regular basis. Provided no one came looking for him urgently – grasses and such, that was, and Pyle had left a number where he could be reached with the duty officer in the event of an emergency – there would be no repetition of the problem that had arisen when

Micky Fielder had tried to reach him.

A familiarity had come to their love-making. There was none of the desperation of lovers with the need to perform or impress or prove anything; their acceptance of the inevitable temporariness of the relationship was the cause. Libby didn't for a moment imagine he was going to leave his wife and children for her, nor did she want him to. She found herself caring less and less about him, even though he made love to her adequately. She was acutely aware of how little he actually gave her. She knew next to nothing about him, apart from his being a policeman, married with two children. She felt the whole time that he was on guard with her as though suspecting she was looking for an opportunity to betray him. Because he gave so little of himself, she found herself withdrawing more and more.

For his part Pyle didn't try very hard to impress her, quite simply because she didn't resist him. She was a fuck, a pretty good one, that was all; not someone to trust or an ear he felt any need to whisper into.

They were in bed together in her small bedroom with its lilac coloured walls. Having made love once they were still, though not really relaxed. Libby was thinking about Pyle's predecessor, Brian Finch. She wasn't comparing their sexual abilities; Brian had always ejaculated quickly and hadn't always made her orgasm, but he had been more fun. She didn't feel her sole purpose in the relationship had been for him to make love to, which was what she felt with Fred Pyle; when they stopped doing that there would be nothing at all, she realized. He called round to her place, usually bringing a bottle of something and a takeaway meal, and they went to bed. They didn't talk much, not about important things anyway.

'What's the matter?' Pyle said finally, feeling the oppressive silence but not really concerned about it.

'Oh, nothing,' she said. 'I was just thinking.'

Pyle wasn't sufficiently interested to know what about.

There was another silence. He was thinking it was time to make a move, but he didn't stir himself to check the time.

'Will Brian Finch go to prison?' she asked. The question was an extension of her thoughts.

'You kidding?' Pyle said derisively. He hadn't told her that Finch had been picked up and subsequently released. But he was pleased to think that she had had no contact with him.

'Why do you always answer with a question, Fred? You nearly always do.'

'Do I ...?' He knew he did, but despite the fact said defensively, 'I wouldn't have thought so.' She didn't give him an argument. 'I suppose it draws out the person I'm interrogating ... talking to.' It wasn't a slip of the tongue.

She raised her head off the pillow to look at him. 'I'm not a suspect, am I?'

"Course you are,' he said flippantly. 'Everything you say is being taken down and will be used in evidence against you.' He waited for an amused response. When he didn't get it he realized what she was doing. She was winding him up about Finch, and he had no intention of letting her get away with it. 'Oh, he'll go all right, Brian Finch. He's a villain. Prison's where villains belong.' He paused, but there was no reaction. 'Does it matter to you?'

She shrugged. 'At one time it might have,' she said in spite of herself. It still mattered but she avoided showing her feelings, not wanting to give him the satisfaction.

'Are you sure he was involved?'

'Why wouldn't I be? I nicked him.' He turned to her, reading more from her mask of apparent unconcern that she intended offering. His attitude hardened, and with it his gestures towards her became conversely more intimate. He caressed her breasts, challenging her rather than showing affection. 'Even if that one wasn't down to him there are others that were. What difference does it make what he goes for? He's a professional thief. I'm a professional thiefcatcher. That simple. 'S almost a game, Libby. The idea is to stay out in front. Get a result. You sometimes have to do the job you're given in the only way it can be done. That sometimes means nicking villains for other people's villainy, when they won't come for their own. Even fitting them when you know they're definitely at it.' He paused and looked at her, ceasing in his caresses. He wasn't simply seeking to hurt her, but making a statement of fact about the CID-felonry relationship. 'What member of the general public . . . I mean, all those people who do nothing worse than fiddle their tax or steal from their employers, all those, what one of them wouldn't find that wholly acceptable? After all, we do it in their name, don't we? I mean, it's only because of them that we exist at all. Helps to keep a kind of balance, make a halfway decent sort of place to live in. What d'you imagine it would be like, if all those villains were let have their liberty? Be fucking murder. No one's looking to claim chummy off the street . . . just anyone and fit them. Oh, it's been done, love, don't think it hasn't. But what's the value? A possible conviction entered in the back of your diary, against a lot of aggravation if you come unstuck. And those sort of nickings don't mean fuck all anyway.' He paused briefly, guessing she was close to tears. 'But Brian Finch's going away, that makes a difference. Whatever it's for, that's a result. One to us.' He thought about that for a moment. 'He'll go all right.'

There was a long silence, during which Libby stared at the ceiling. She brought her hands up, placing the back of her wrists against her forehead. She was trying to avoid her tears, afraid to speak in case it opened the floodgate.

'And for a long time,' Pyle said, driving home the last nail.

At last Libby managed to say, 'It's almost nine o'clock.'

'Yes. I suppose I'd better make a move.' But he made no attempt to climb out of bed. He would decide when. 'In a little while.' Instead he reached down and placed his hand between her legs. She resisted his gesture by keeping her legs closed, but he wasn't deterred, and finally she yielded. As he stroked her vagina, a smile wrinkled in Pyle's brain. He intended making love to her once more, regardless of her hostile feelings. He would make her come, cry out in excitement even proclaim her love for him.

24

Lately more and more of his time seemed to be spent in the snooker hall. It was a handy place to arrange meets, and more convenient than pubs where you could only sit around and booze. Paradoxically his old woman was less concerned about him being there than she was when he was pubbing and clubbing, as though his presence at the hall precluded his making one. He guessed it was just the knowledge of where he was that reassured her. He felt no particular stab of conscience over deceiving her; she'd be as sweet as anything when he had it off again and had a nice few quid. Maybe they'd go to Spain for a month out of the way.

Stretching himself almost full length across the table, Jack Lynn played an awkward stroke on the green ball, barely touching it with the white. He eased himself back off the table and watched the ball trickle away into the bottom corner pocket.

Micky Fielder, who he was playing with, banged his cue on the floor in appreciation, even though the shot looked like costing him five pounds.

Lynn chalked his cue, and screwed the brown into a side pocket with a decisive stroke.

'Good hit, Jack.' The man who spoke had approached the table while Lynn was lining up the shot.

This wasn't the man Lynn was waiting for, but his brother-in-law. 'Hello, Tom. How's it going?' Lynn said in a friendly way, then turned to Fielder. 'You want to swallow it, Micky?'

'Do I fuck!' Fielder protested. 'I'd like to see you make those three.' The blue, pink and black balls were left on the table and Lynn was about five points in front.

"Couldn't do us a favour Saturday, Jack, could you?' Tom

asked. 'Do my mini-cabbing for me. I got a wedding to go to – not work like,' he qualified.

'As it happens I can't, Tom,' Lynn said, chalking his cue again. 'I got something planned myself for Saturday.' Having told him that, he immediately wondered if it was wise but decided that his brother-in-law wasn't likely to mention it to Dolly.

Micky Fielder sat against the edge of the adjacent table, kicking the base of his cue with his pointed-toed shoe as if not interested in the conversation, but not missing a word of it.

'Micky'll help you out,' Lynn suggested jokingly. 'He was looking for a bit of work.'

'Not that sort of fucking work,' Fielder interjected. When he had approached Lynn he had implied he was looking for some work, hoping the blagger might put his one up to him. He didn't. 'Anyway, I done my brief, didn't I.'

"S not a problem. I'll get someone.' He waited while Lynn lined his shot. 'Just that Dolly said you was thinking about doing a bit regular like.'

Lynn didn't make the blue, but snookered Fielder behind the black. 'I was thinking about it, Tom, to be perfectly honest. Know what I mean.' He wondered then if he didn't ought to take the cabbing on Saturday and use it as a sort of an alibi. But he didn't pursue the thought.

'I'll have a chat with you later. Gotta shoot now. I got one to pick up.'

'Good luck, Tom,' Lynn said as his brother-in-law left. He saw Bobby Shaw as he moved between the tables with another man.

'No wonder you're such a fucking degenerate,' Shaw said as he and the other man stopped at the table. 'You're always in here,'what I hear.'

'Gotta get my indoor money somehow, son,' Lynn retorted. He glanced at the second man, who was fat and almost soft-looking, and wore tinted glasses. Lynn didn't know him but winked at him as if sharing a joke.

'You fit, are you?' Shaw asked.

'Yeah, just let me nick a jack's here first.'

Shaw stooped to look under the hood at Lynn's opponent. Fielder, having played his stroke, had put Lynn in a snooker on the pink. 'Hello, Micky. Had it off lately?'

'Scratching's all,' Fielder replied disgustedly as he came around the table and joined Shaw. "not much about, is there.'

'Not a lot,' Shaw agreed noncommittally. He didn't introduce his mate.

Playing his shot, Lynn fetched the blue out of snooker and potted it. It was a difficult shot.

'Fuck me!' Fielder exclaimed.

With a triumphant smile, Lynn said, 'Just did. Didn't I just.'

Fielder didn't argue with the result at this point. There was no advantage in doing so. He pulled out the money he was holding, separated a fiver and threw it on the table. 'You did well there, son,' he said grudgingly.

'Good luck, son,' Lynn said in a slightly mocking tone. 'See you around, Micky.'

Fielder watched them start out, knowing instinctively that this was the team Lynn was going blagging with down at Catford dogtrack. He would've liked to have had the front to follow them, but didn't dare to. He would try to get some further information on them by punting around their familiar haunts, talking to faces they knew, buying a few drinks. It wouldn't be difficult, Fielder decided. The proposed blag having advanced as far as it had, there were more than enough rumours flying around.

The first two stops after the hall were pubs where he saw a couple of people he knew. Jack Lynn was doing a bit of work, that was the word. The same word was on other lips when he found his way down to the after-hours drinker in Tottenham Court Road.

Fielder had been at the bar drinking on his own for about ten minutes when a man who had been at the card table previously joined him.

He was in his mid-fifties. He had been a villain in the past and a good 'un, but had more or less retired now, though he liked to keep in touch.

'Getting a living, Micky, are you?' he asked, sliding his well-padded rump onto one of the plastic covered stools at the bar.

'Nothing worth a toss,' Fielder bemoaned – the reply was standard. 'Got hold of a bit the other night, but it didn't come to fuckall. Why, you got something in mind?'

The man shook his head. 'Thought perhaps you could put me into something.' He smiled

'Some chance, m' ol' bruv. Maybe me and you ought to see about making one ourselves. I mean, it's a thought, Ronnie. A little taste for your retirement.'

'Be handy,' Ronnie conceded with apparent interest. 'You got something in mind?'

Neither of these two were blaggers, and each clearly realized that the other was kidding.

'Not really. People whisper in your ear about different things. You know how it is, Ronnie. But it's stuff you've got to have a little firm for.' Fielder emptied his glass and set it back on the bar, but didn't signal the barmaid. 'I heard Jack Lynn was putting one together,' he said casually. 'D'he get all the help he needs?'

'I'd say so. But I wouldn't have thought that was in your line, Micky.' Ronnie commented. 'I heard they were going shootered up.'

"S that right?' The expression contained surprise, as if guns were a daring innovation. 'Fuck I, I wouldn't have none of that. But I gotta get me bit of Christmas money from somewhere. What's that, scotch you're drinking, Ronnie?'

'Cheers.' Ronnie finished his drink.

Fielder motioned to the barmaid now. A couple of drinks with this man and he'd get every bit of information he had about Jack Lynn and his blag. All of which he would duly pass on to DI Pyle.

25

Underground train meets with the grass were far more convenient to him but not as entertaining, Pyle reflected as he watched the leggy fourteen year-old school girls prancing around at netball in the court across from the park seat where he had met Micky Fielder. He assumed the grass couldn't have known the game would be in progress, but perhaps he had, and this was by way of redeeming himself for causing Pyle to drag down to Deptford to spring him the other day. The girls were all in blue shorts and white blouses: one team with green bands, the other red. All gave value for money and even the teacher who charged around the court was worth giving one.

Pale sunlight filtered through the trees, and it was pleasant to be out in the cold park, even without this added attraction. Possibly that was the reasoning of some of the other spectators to the game, Pyle thought, casting his eyes around the benches positioned beyond the perimeter fence. But some of the suspect bastards would have sat there in a galeforce snowstorm with such a spectacle. An active woodentop might have nicked any number of them.

'It's Saturday, guv. Last race, just after the finish,' Micky Fielder said, bringing the DI out of his reverie. Their preliminary banter, discussing the relative merits of those schoolgirls had ended; it was time to talk business. 'That's when it's going off. That's what I heard anyway.' And when the detective looked at him. ''S what I heard.'

'Saturday?' Pyle said. 'That's definite you reckon, Micky, is it?'

'You know me, guv,' Fielder said diffidently. 'I give it as straight as I get it, I don't tart it up at all. You know that. They didn't invite me to make it with them.'

'That's 'cos you're a grass, Micky,' Pyle said lightly. But Fielder didn't get the joke. 'Who's involved apart from Lynn?'

'The only other name I was able to get so far was Bobby Shaw.'

'Shaw?' The name was meaningless to the DI. 'What's he got down to him? Anything worthwhile?'

'A bit of a violence specialist is what I heard. He's done some for GBH.'

Pyle nodded. 'About right.' He preferred thinking the worst of Jack Lynn and his confederates; then putting them away would help justify whatever means he employed.

Fielder hesitated, reluctant to say the next bit. 'I heard they were going in with shooters ... What I heard.' It wasn't very surprising, but still he didn't like having to tell the DI that.

Pyle looked at him as though questioning the validity of that information, then looked away at the girls. One of them leaped up, putting the ball neatly and easily in the net, her blouse parting from her shorts with the jump, showing her bare midriff. The teacher blew the whistle and the two teams came back to the line. A game, well ordered, all the players obeying the rules. Running parallel in his thoughts was the robbery that was planned at Catford. It was likely to be anything but well ordered.

Ignoring the statement about the guns, he said, 'Look at that, will you?' He watched the girl tucking her blouse into her shorts as she walked back to the line. 'It's enough to get you nicked.'

With a glance from the DI to the girls and back, Fielder chuckled. 'I'd take a chance, guv.'

'All the time you've got someone to pull you out of trouble.' There was a pause and the DI turned to the grass with a steady, measured look, pleased with the information he had brought him. 'How you fixed, Micky?'

The question caused the informer some apparent embarrassment. He seemed reluctant to say the words. 'Ain't too clever, guv. That filth who felt m'collar nicked most of what I had – thought I'd be able to borrow some ...'

Pyle simply nodded, understanding the problem. Reaching into his coat pocket he produced five neatly folded five-pound notes, which he gave Fielder. "S only a pony, Micky. If we have it off down at Catford, we should have a nice earner between us from the insurance.'

'Be handy.' The grass didn't object to the notion of having to share his insurance reward.

'Give us a shout if you need another taste.' He could get him another twenty-five or so from the Fund without much trouble. For a moment or two Pyle continued to watch the girls leaping around, then nodded to himself. 'Think you're right, son. Probably would be worth getting nicked for.' He nodded again. 'Definitely going in with shooters, are they?'

"S what I heard. You know' – apologetically.

'Yeah. Don't they all now.' The DI expelled his breath in a dismayed sigh. 'Still, that's the way it goes. You did well, Micky. Just mind how you go, all right?' The detective meant it.

'I'll give you a bell if I hear anything else,' the grass said for the sake of something to say. He rose reluctantly from the bench. 'Don't get your collar felt here, will you?'

'Take care, son.'

Pyle watched the grass as he moved away along the path, nervously adjusting his suede coat off his shoulders.

Ice-cream vending in late autumn wasn't about the best earner Gerry Gibbs could imagine. In fact it was hardly worth anything; a bit moved on Sundays but apart from that it was the summer trade that made the concessions worthwhile. He earned enough then not to have to go out in the winter, but the firm who owned the vans wanted them out on the road. The housing estates of North London where Gibbs had his round weren't all that, especially when the kids were in school. There were one or two schools on his round. He did one regularly of a lunchtime, other firms had the other schools. In the afternoon, if it was dry, he'd slip into the park; kids playing football usually bought a few, or mothers trying to keep their kids quiet.

Stopping his van on the service road across from the tennis and netball courts, Gibbs had shifted his large fleshy weight from the driving seat into the back of the van, as if expecting a rush of business. There wasn't any. Removing his tinted glasses he had polished the lenses on his nylon overall then had settled to watch the game of netball on one of the courts. But that hadn't held his attention, nor would a rush of customers have taken it after he had seen the man going along the path past the van. He had recognized Micky Fielder from the snooker hall last night, when he had been playing with Jack Lynn. He had watched Fielder go on down the path a little way, then cross a strip of grass to a wooden bench and join a man who had been watching the game. Gibbs hadn't paid the man on the bench any attention until then, but had assumed he was another mac man. But there had been something about the way Fielder had avoided the empty benches that had made Gibbs suspect the other man was CID. Gibbs had been close enough to see the animated conversation that had taken place between the two men, but not close enough to hear what was said. He'd have given anything to have been one of those pigeons pecking at crumbs and grit at their feet.

Fifteen minutes had passed as Gerry Gibbs watched what he had finally decided was quite definitely a conversation between a grass and the filth, during which he had sold only one ice-cream. When the detective left a few moments after the grass, Gibbs felt angry, believing that the object of the meeting was directed against him personally. He could just about accept that the filth was only doing the job he was paid to do, but as for that no-good fucking grass, he felt like going after him and running him down in his van. Knowing how grasses worked, it wasn't long before Gibbs was convinced that the purpose of their meeting was to tip Old Bill about the blag. That made him more angry. He wanted some of that down at Catford, but it was odds on they wouldn't be able to have any of it now.

Gibbs shut up shop for the day. His priority now was to see Bobby Shaw and get him to mark Jack Lynn's card.

Sprawling full length on the couch watching racing on the TV was where Bobby Shaw found Lynn after Dolly had let him in. He stood leaning against the back of an armchair in his heavy overcoat, despite the warmth of the centrally heated room, and told all that Gibbs had told him. Little by little Lynn's attention had left the TV and he brought himself up into a sitting position as the words reached into him.

'It was definitely the filth Micky Fielder had a meet with, was it?' Lynn asked at last, the TV having completely lost his attention.

'There wasn't much doubt, Jack,' Shaw said morosely. 'And some heavy filth is what he thought. The Squad probably.'

'That surprises me, it really does.' It dismayed him also, and he was growing angry. He wanted to somehow deny the possibility that this was happening, that the blag was coming on top, but he was too much of a realist.

'Yeah, me an' all. I mean, a right fucking sick'ner, innit.'

'He say whether he thought it might have been a chance meet?' he was still looking for some half plausible reason for not cancelling the blag.

'He wouldn't know, would he. He was doing a bit of ice-cream.' There was a pause, the TV racing commentary filling the silence as each was left with his angry thoughts. 'What d'you think, Jack? About the other thing? I mean, I didn't hear nothing about Micky Fielder before, did you?'

'Still, even if he has gone bent, don't mean he was lollying us, does it.'

Shaw looked at him uncertain. 'Makes it a bit iffy, Jack, dun it.'

Lynn reluctantly conceded the point. 'There's no place he

could have got nothing.'

'I dunno, do I. I wasn't playing snooker with him.'

'Oh fucking good luck!' Lynn said like he was offended.

'I didn't mean nothing like that, Jack. Fuck I! I dunno, I think perhaps we should give it a miss.'

'I gone and got the shooters now, and the cars are laid on,' he said as though this made it impossible for the blag to be stopped. 'I mean, they come to dough, don't they.'

''Course they do.' He paused. 'I don't mind myself, Jack. 'S your decision. But if it means we're going to top up nicked ... know what I mean?'

Lynn turned his attention briefly to the race on the TV, trying to avoid thinking and having to make the decision he knew he must make. 'Maybe we'll give it a miss for a week or two. Be as well.' It might have been a solution. ''S not a problem really. I mean, the money's there every week, twice a week.'

'What about Micky Fielder? I mean, that dirty cunt'll have to have his knees shot or something if he has gone grassing.'

Lynn's attention went back to the TV as the race drew to a close, the commentator's voice rising with excitement. The horse Lynn had backed wasn't placed.

'Fucking thing! Look at that.' He turned back to Shaw. 'Micky Fielder always was a no-good cunt,' he said. 'You might expect him to go the other way. But I don't see where he could have got anything. Still.'

He was outraged at the very idea of being grassed like this, yet at the same time not entirely convinced that they had been; he had a lot of money tied up in this job, so was reluctant to write either off.

26

No further information on the proposed blag was forth-coming from either of Pyle's grasses. No more was really necessary for the Squad to proceed, but it would have been useful to know exactly how many villains were going to be involved and just who they were. Extensive searches and some speculation on the known associates of both Bobby Shaw and Jack Lynn had given the police little more than possibilities.

Detectives from Fred Pyle's squad, and some of those from the current night duty squad, who were lending a hand, mustered in the DCI's room for a briefing. That happened by consensus rather than design; Pyle had been in the office discussing the blag with DCI Simmons, DCI Ronald Linkney, the Squad's third DCI who was now back on duty, and Lethridge, when other CID began drifting in. There was no point in moving the venue next door.

There were sixteen detectives present; all collected arms which DCI Linkney was issuing. Simmons was saying, 'They're planning the blag for after the last race. That means they'll have to wait for the money to be collected from around the track.' That was a reasonable speculation, unless the villains intended to shut the Tote and not pay out on the last race while they scooped up all the money – that would bring too much attention to them. Simmons expanded on the theory that the villains would try and blag all the takings once they had been collected from the numerous Tote offices around the track after the result of the last race, then slip away with the departing crowd. 'As we don't know the entire team this might present a few problems. Chummy doesn't go around with blagger written on his shirt any more,' the DCI said with a grin. 'Fred?'

'Yes. Right.' Pyle was sitting on the edge of Linkney's desk, which was the farthest into the room. He didn't bother to stand. 'Well, as some of you already know, the only two we've marked are Lynn and Bobby Shaw. Their CRO photos are well out of date, and the ones C11 supplied aren't much better. There could be as many as four more in the team, and probably are. My snout didn't know ...'

'They are definitely using shooters, guv?' DC Warren Salter asked.

'I wouldn't like to bet against it.'

When detectives went after villains without prior warning of them being armed they thought little about it, but simply steamed in and made the arrests. Giving them information that the blaggers were armed always dredged up thoughts they'd prefer not to think.

'You've all got guns,' Simmons said. 'Knowing what dog tracks are like on a Saturday night, well, you won't need telling there'll be a lot of people about. A lot of pushing and shoving. Now I warn you, it'll mean no end of paperwork if one of you shoots a bystander. Shoot a villain with a gun in his hand, if you have to shoot anyone.' The DCI meant it. Villains getting shot still meant a lot of paperwork, but nothing like that which would be needed to justify the police accidentally shooting an innocent member of the public. It was something that most armed policemen feared would one day happen.

With a look the DCI passed the briefing back to Pyle.

'Blagging the money from the office here, or from Securicor when it's collected, either event means these exits here are their only way out.' He pointed to marked exits on the blackboard diagram that had been brought from the DIs' office. 'They open these gates here to get the punters away quickly. Securicor comes in the same way with their truck. They go up this ramp and park on the brow. From there two of the guards walk down to the main office. That might be a good place for them to try and have it, as they return.'

'There are a number of windows on the back of that

building, guv,' DC Shields put in. 'What I mean is, they open onto that service road. They could stick the bags through to someone on the outside.'

'Be handy. I hope they do. That would probably mean them sticking their guns out too. That would give you a nice target, Eric, if we get that lucky.'

'Can't see it myself,' Lethridge said.

'Jack. Your team will be in this enclosure here,' Pyle told DS Barcy, indicating on his diagram. 'Ted and Alan, you're here and here,' he told the two DSs from the night duty squad. 'If you spot them, don't challenge them until they've blagged the money, otherwise we're going to wind up with fuck all for our trouble. Let them get what they're there for. Let's nick them bang to rights. Chance them legging it.' He paused and considered the assembly. They didn't look particularly like detectives. They were dressed in a variety of styles that would enable them to blend unobtrusively with Saturday night punters at Catford.

'They're only old mugs,' Pyle said encouragingly. 'Should be a doddle, with a bit of luck.' Pyle glanced first at Simmons then DCI Linkney, expecting one of them to add something. Neither did. 'Any questions?'

The short silence which followed was punctuated by a distant telephone ringing. It was quickly answered. There was tension in the room, a sense of apprehension. Most of the detectives had the same thing in mind at that moment, and all were reluctant to raise the matter, spark off their fears; to do so wouldn't have been acceptable.

Finally DC Jenkins said, 'Eh, yes. All right if I shoot off home now, guv?'

The tension was broken. Relieved titters came from the body of men.

'And I'd better not go, guv,' DC Fenton said. 'I owe the skipper a jack's.'

'Well, I suppose we could send Jack Lynn a note. Asking him to surrender himself here after they've had it off,' Pyle

222

said. The atmosphere was becoming decidedly more relaxed.

'Well, that's it then,' DCI Simmons said. 'Good luck. And remember, try not to shoot any punters.'

The car park at Catford dogtrack quickly filled to capacity, and without being able to exercise their usual peremptory right, no one at the track having been informed they were there, the Squad had to get their cars in position early. They had six cars there in all, including the two that were parked in Adenmore Road, which ran alongside Catford Bridge Station and was the only road exit from the greyhound racetrack. The detectives had a fairly long and tedious wait, one during which thoughts turned to maybe getting shot. It was relieved occasionally by Pyle letting them slip away to the stadium to have a bet or a drink at the bar. He shouldn't have allowed that but decided that relaxed detectives would be more use than if they were tense and looking to shoot someone. And long before the last race they were all back in their correct positions. Not that it mattered much anyway.

The detectives became expectant as the final race on the card approached, as if they had each bet their last ten pence on it. In a matter of minutes it was all over, but nothing was expected to happen immediately so the detectives didn't stir. They were positioned inside and outside the stadium, close enough to both the main exit and the main Tote office to know at once if and when the blag went off.

With the finish of the last race the stadium soon began to empty, along with the car park, where utter confusion seemed to reign, with no one willing to give an inch. Pyle was sitting in his car watching this frenetic movement before his eyes, wondering what was happening in the stadium. They couldn't risk using their radios for contact in case they were seen and alerted the blaggers, but he was impatient to know what the position was.

'Go and see what the fuck's happening in there, Rog', will you?' he told DC Humphries who was in the car with him. He watched him climb out and disappear in the direction of the stadium. 'I think this is probably going to be a rubout,' he commented to his driver without inviting any response. It was a feeling he had.

Detectives in other positions about the dogtrack were coming to the same conclusion; however, their tension didn't slacken.

Minutes ticked away, no faster for Pyle checking his watch as often as he did. It wouldn't be the first time that a blag they had waited for had proved a non-starter, but it was disappointing, none the less. Regardless of what he felt Pyle hadn't written off the blag. In fact the optimum moment for it to go off hadn't arrived, but doubts persisted. It could've been that Micky Fielder had got one or two details wrong; that had been known, grasses weren't infallible. He would wait until there was absolutely no doubt about its not going off before he quit it.

The car park continued emptying. The process grew less tortuous as the cars thinned out. Other punters left on foot, some by bicycle; some with a bounce in their step, others with resignation about their loss. Pyle watched them go, puzzling briefly at the attraction they found here week after week, for most of them were regular punters. He wasn't a gambler himself, not on anything as random as a dog chasing a mechanical hare.

After a while DC Humphries returned to the car.

'There's nothing much going on up there, guv,' the DC said at the open window. 'No one's seen anything yet.'

Pyle accepted this information with a nod. It meant little. The money was up in the office; it had yet to be collected. 'Go and find Sergeant Lethridge, check with him, Rog'.'

All that remained in the car park were fifteen cars, four of them belonging to the Squad. The others probably belonged to people working in the stadium. Possibly some had been put there by blaggers, but it was unlikely. The numbers and descriptions were noted and checked as a matter of routine.

When a Jaguar XJ12 started across the car park and

through the main entrance gates to the stadium, detectives who had started to relax, allow themselves to become distracted, suddenly tensed. This was the first thing to look like anything. Two men climbed out of the vehicle at the brow of the service road.

Pyle reached inside his coat and touched the gun that rested in its holster. He had had a good result in his last gun practice session – the thought sped through his head as though such results had any bearing when confronted with an armed blagger.

The two men from the Jaguar weren't part of Jack Lynn's firm but some kind of factotums to an old infirm punter who they had brought to the car in his wheelchair. One of them lifted the man out and put him in the front seat, while the other folded the chair up and put it in the boot. The car drove off, passing the security truck as it came up into the stadium.

Two guards armed with nightsticks climbed out and disappeared from sight towards the office. They were gone for seven minutes. Those minutes, Pyle found, ticked by very slowly. The two guards reappeared, dropped the money containers into the hatch at the rear of the truck, waited for the third man inside to shut the hatch, then climbed back in the front of the truck and drove away. Nothing happened.

That only left the Squad on watch.

DS Lethridge approached the DI's car and leaned down to the window. 'Fucking waste of time,' Pyle said. 'Unless that was Jack Lynn,' nodding in the direction of the departing truck.

'Think they tumbled us, Fred?'

Pyle shrugged as though unconcerned. 'We didn't advertise ... Fuck it!' The words burst out of him as if he had no control, and his anger vanished with them. 'Fucking sickening, isn't it?' There was no question as far as Pyle was concerned of a crime having been prevented; that wasn't what his being a policeman was about anyway. 'My snout could've got the day wrong. Maybe it'll go next week.' That thought cheered him a little. What rankled was the fact that Jack Lynn, a villain who had been at it too long, one who was well overdue, one to whom Pyle had given a lot of attention, was to keep his liberty. He ought to be behind bars; Pyle knew it, and knew Lynn probably knew it. It was nothing personal as far as the DI was concerned, just a matter of principle; the villain had fallen within his sphere and it was his turn. 'If this doesn't go off, Eric, I think we'll have to look elsewhere for Lynn. Maybe even find something for him.'

The DS looked at his governor, then glanced at the driver, who was staring blankly through the windscreen, purposely not hearing a word. DS Lethridge didn't say anything, he certainly didn't object to the proposed fit up.

'Checks and balances,' Pyle said. 'Checks and balances, son. He's well overdue.' He thought about that for a moment, then nodded to himself. 'Get the lads back, Eric, I'll buy them a drink.' There was an after-hours drinking club he knew on the way back. They could drown their disappointment.

'That's about twenty grand down to nothing then,' Lynn said angrily when he got confirmation from Gerry Gibbs and Billy Braden of the CID at Catford dog-track.

'It would have been down to a right nicking we had steamed in there tonight, Jack,' Billy Braden added, as if to finally try and reassure him that there was no option.

They were in the after-hours club in Tottenham Court Road, tucked away in a quiet corner, keeping a lid on their anger. Bobby Shaw and Gerry Gibbs were with them also.

'We had a right bit of luck there, Jack, I'd say,' Bobby Shaw commented. 'Just you think if Gerry hadn't 'ave seen that no-good slag in the park.'

'Don't bear thinking about, do it,' Gibbs added.

'What sickens me is the thought of that bit of dough down to nothing. I mean just sitting there like that.'

'Still, what chance you got with no-good cunts like that about?' Shaw said. He stared pensively at his glass.

'Everyone's at it nowadays. Can't trust no cunt, can you.'

'He's got to get some stick. Really gotta be hurt, Jack, Micky Fielder. Know what I mean.'

'Oh, he's got some due all right, don't worry about that,' Lynn affirmed. He had been putting the blag together, so it was up to him to say what sort of treatment should be meted out to the grass. 'What fucking good it'll do this one shooting that slag. Still, it's gotta be done.'

'I was counting on this going off,' Braden said. 'Would have been a nice taste.'

'Yeah. I turned down a couple of other tasty things.' They would continue like this for a long while, little considering how lucky they'd been.

'What d'you reckon, Jack?' Shaw wanted to know. 'I mean, how long 'fore we could go after it again, d'you think?'

That was something Lynn hadn't thought about. As far as he was concerned the job was a nonstarter. 'Can't say. I mean, it's gotta be right dodgy now. It goes off, it's down to us, 'innit. We'd be the first to get a pull, wouldn't we. I can do without that sort of aggro myself.'

'Would have been nice though,' Gibbs concluded on a sorrowful note, like he believed some omnipotent power would take pity on him and put him back to the start of the blag without the grass. 'Looked a blinding job.'

Others concurred with solemn nods, and raised their glasses in silent commiseration.

'I gone and laid out good money on cars and shooters,' Lynn said. 'That's the fucking nause. No-good cunt!' he concluded, Micky Fielder in the forefront of his thoughts. Then taking a more cheerful, philosophical outlook, he shrugged off the blag as though unimportant, despite the armoury he had stashed in his lock-up and the cars that had been rung. 'Still, I daresay I can punt around and find something else to go on. There's a supermarket I been plotting up,' you fancy it. We missed a right nicking. Fuck I! Didn't we just!' He emptied his glass, then glanced across the club at the card game that was in progress. That was where his interest now lay. 'I'm gonna see if I can't go and earn my indoor money.'

Lynn got up from the table, leaving the others to drown their sorrows in drink, and think about the bit of work at the supermarket. None of them was unaware of how much some supermarkets took in nowadays. There were more than enough waiting, begging to be tucked up. Jack Lynn was a professional blagger. It was simply work.

27

It was Monday morning and steadily raining, which helped no one's problems, apart from maybe farmers'. Few people chose to be outside on a wet December day and detectives were no exception, even though the alternative was to sit at desks or typewriters and cope with their paperwork.

DCI Simmons was at his desk typing efficiently, ignoring where possible the activity on the fourth floor. He was trying to clear the reports he should have done last Friday, then expected to do Saturday when he came in for the briefing, but didn't get done. He wasn't making much headway what with detectives shuffling in with queries, and phones to answer. DCI Watson was at the next desk, discussing a case with two DIs.

DI Pyle came into the office with the preliminary report he had been given to write on a non-result they had had on a robbery which had taken place out at Harlow. It ran to sixty pages. By the time Simmons rewrote it, adding further negative details from other sources all of which amounted to justifying why they hadn't arrested anyone or recovered the money, the report would probably go to two hundred pages.

'Thanks, Fred,' Simmons said without looking up.

'Full of typing mistakes,' Pyle apologized.

'No problem' – he had to type it all again. Pyle was about to move away, when the DCI said, still without looking up from the keys, 'Think they tumbled you?' He was referring to Saturday night.

'I dunno. Wasn't anything we did, I wouldn't have thought. I had a word with my snout. He reckons he might have got the day mixed up.' He laid his head to one side in a slightly dismissive gesture, implying that grasses weren't reliable. 'You know what they're like.' The viewpoint was convenient for the DI at that moment.

'Be handy.' The DCI stopped typing. 'I'd like to see them come for that. What about Harding?' He knew well enough.

'Didn't weigh in, did he?'

There was a pause. The two detectives looked at one another, each knowing the other's thoughts.

'Have another go at him, why don't you. You can't tell with villains like that. Put some more pressure on. If he's not interested in helping ...' The DCI shrugged. 'It's about time we had him back inside anyway, a villain as active as that. Know what I mean, Fred?'

Pyle knew just what his governor meant. He had the same thing in mind himself and had no need to have it spelt out.

The rain had stopped by the time Pyle had got part of his squad organized to go and look for Clifford Harding. Water lay in oily puddles around the uneven tarmac surface of the battlefield-like community playground. Kids in coloured wellington boots splashed through puddles, risking the wrath of parents who had been dragged there reluctantly on that day. One threw a stone, splashing Fred Pyle as he moved through the gate.

'Don't do that, there's a good girl,' the DI said, and kept walking, watched by the kid who wasn't sure whether to cry or splash him again.

Distress appeared in Harding's face when he saw the detective. His eyes darted about, looking for a way out. There was no way out. Pyle was between him and the gate, and at the hole in the fence there was another detective. Looking around and seeing others now, he realized it was up, that they'd come to nick him.

"S nice, Clifford, isn't it,' Pyle said, sitting on the damp makeshift seat, where Harding was with his second to youngest son. 'Sitting here watching your kids, not a worry in the world other than whether or not it's going to rain again...'

'How d'you know I was here?' Harding wanted to know, as if it made some difference.

'Your old lady grassed you, son.' She had but not in the way the detective implied. He had called at the house and was told Harding was at the playground. 'How old's he?' He indicated the boy.

'Going on four. 'In't you, Russ?' the father said. His son didn't comment but looked at the detective as if knowing why he was there. 'Go and play with Darren, Russ, there's a good boy.'

He was reluctant to go. 'You come, Dad,' he said.

'In a little while. I gotta have a talk. Go on.' He eased the boy away from him and watched as he joined his brother.

Watching also, Pyle said casually, 'Tragic. That's what it is. Fucking tragic, I mean, he's going to be grown up, be a man 'fore he even gets a chance to know you ...'

'What?' Harding was surprised even though he was aware that the DI wasn't there merely to pass the time of day. 'Don't talk like that, for Christsake ...'

Pyle sighed expansively. 'A fact of life. You've got to go away, son. A tasty fifteen years, if I know anything about it.' He thought about that. 'Yeah, about right. You didn't do that business for me.'

Harding glanced about the playground, as he thought of running. He had known from the start what he had been letting himself in for, but had clung to that one vague hope that even if he didn't eventually produce the goods, this moment still wouldn't arrive. He was a fool, he realized, to chance his liberty like that, after all he didn't owe Jack Lynn anything, not a thing. Lynn going away wouldn't make one bit of difference to him, any more than his own nicking would make any difference to Lynn. What a ridiculous situation to have got himself into. What he wished for more than anything then was that he had his chance over again. He wondered about that. 'I'm supposed to be seeing this man tonight,' he tried.

Pyle shook his head both in disbelief and disinterest. 'Sounds like a ramp to me, Clifford. Like you're offering me the prick. I've been silly enough.'

Knowing the trouble he was in, Harding became desperate. 'That's straight, that is. This fella's been putting himself about, getting something for me.' He hadn't any advance on the information about Jack Lynn that he had previously given the DI, nothing to support this claim with.

'What d'you think, I'm fucking silly or something? You've been too busy to get my info'. Putting yourself about and putting one of your own together ...'

'Fuck off, guv. I've been clubbing and pubbing, trying to help you nick Jack Lynn ...'

'A little blag of your own's what I heard. A wages van out at Hounslow.' That was the rumour which Reg Whitely in Criminal Intelligence had passed on, that was what was going to cost Harding his liberty, regardless of whether or not he helped him out. C11 would be looking for the others who were supposed to be involved in that proposed robbery; there was no way it could go off, with or without Harding.

Knowing he was bang to rights, knowing what the procedure was, Harding's eyes flashed around the playground again desperately looking for some way out, as if hoping the other detectives had dematerialized.

Anticipating what the man had in mind, Pyle shook his head again, warning him not to try. 'Let's do it quietly, Cliff, not alarm the kids. We'll have a policewoman down to take them back to their Mum.'

It was those words more than any others the DI said that brought home the tragedy of his situation. The authorities would arrange for his kids to be taken back to his wife: he wouldn't see them for a long time. Harding struggled against tears as he became briefly involved with his son, who had wandered back to join him.

'Come on, Russ, mate. It's time to go home. See Mum. Go and get the others.' He looked up at Pyle who had risen. 'I don't want to go, guv. I really don't.' There was an offer in his tone, an appeal.

Pyle nodded sympathetically. ''Course you don't, son,' he said reasonably. 'And I'd sooner have Jack Lynn.'

'He was well closed up about that blag. You think I didn't try?'

'Wasn't in your interest. You were too busy on that one out at Hounslow.' He paused and looked at the villain for a moment. 'Doesn't matter much anyway. He put one up to you, Cliff, didn't he?' Pyle suggested, laying a new foundation for nicking Jack Lynn.

Harding waited, giving the appearance of being uncertain of the DI's drift. 'What one was that, guv?'

With a faint smile the detective said, 'Don't worry, I'll find something for him. Something that he'll go for with a little help from you. 'S up to you, son. That's what gets you your liberty. All right?'

Harding looked stricken. He hesitated, and considered his children. Finally he nodded, agreeing to what the DI suggested. His liberty was more important to him than Jack Lynn's.

'About right,' Pyle said

Leaving Harding to gather up his children, Pyle moved out of the playground, smiling to himself. He would take Harding in and have him charged with conspiracy to rob, and get him remanded. That would hold him until he found something nice for Lynn which Harding could appear to have put up to him.

Eric Lethridge came round the perimeter fence and waited for Pyle at the car.

'He's not going to be any problem, Eric. Wants his liberty too much.'

The DS looked at him, understanding what he was on about.

'Checks and balances, Eric,' Pyle said as though having some need to justify himself. 'Putting Lynn away will be one to us. Won't it just. He'll be well and truly fitted.' He thought about this, then nodded to himself. 'He'll go all right. Harding as well.' He grinned conspiratorially.

There was no doubt about how the two villains would shape.

28

The CID room on the first floor of Romford police station wasn't very busy at the best of times even though it was divisional HQ. K division wasn't the busiest in the Met; it was even less busy this Thursday morning. Most of the more active detectives were still at court with their previous day's collars. There were three other detectives in the room, which measured some twenty-five feet by fifteen, and was badly in need of repainting where cigarette smoke had turned the standard green and cream to a dirty two-tone brown. Well-worn office furniture had been crowded in without much design. Each of the three detectives gave the appearance of being busy, either typing or writing reports, each hoping the phone would ring and take him out of the office on a worthwhile investigation which would give him a worthwhile result; one that might project him into the sphere of senior officers' awareness.

At the bottom of the CID room the door led onto the narrow corridor which ran through the centre of the building. Opposite it was the door to the DI's office, which was small and untidy and gave the appearance of having even more furniture than the main office. Standing by the side of the scarred desk, Detective Inspector Frank Kenley was talking on the telephone, and showing signs of impatience. His fist, on which he was leaning on the desk top, was tightening and relaxing, the knuckles showing white through the stretched skin. Kenley was forty-four and had got as high as he was going to in the CID, he had peaked and was in decline now. This was reflected in his appearance. He had stopped trying.

'What d'you mean, you can't deliver it before next Thursday?' he was saying. 'That's a week. You have it in the computer, right? And it's paid for. Well, what's the problem then? It doesn't take fifteen minutes in the van to my place, does it …?' He appeared exasperated, knowing he would get nowhere with the petty bureaucracy so frequently encountered in state-owned companies, the Gas Board being no exception. Ordinarily he might not have bothered about pressing for the new stove he had bought, but having been put on a promise by the gas company he had insisted on getting it when promised, even if he had to go and collect it himself. 'Maybe I ought to switch back to electricity,' he threatened, but guessed the woman down the line couldn't have cared less. 'You have actually got it in stock?' he said, and when she confirmed they had: 'All right. Well, I'll get it collected this morning … well, as long as it's ready to collect … That's all right. Good!' He put the phone back angrily. At least it would keep his old lady quiet. Picking up a report from the untidy mess of papers on his desk, he stepped out of his office and across the corridor to the CID room. Standing in the doorway he looked around the office, his eyes settling on a tall, lantern-jawed DC who was working at a desk.

'Simon,' the DI said, as though expecting the younger man to come to him. But he went to the DC. 'What are you doing?'

'The Crime Complaint for that breaking over Heath Park last night, guv,' Simon Brett said, running his fingers through his dark, thinning hair.

'Anyone in sight?'

'A couple of tearaways who might be worthwhile. I think it probably was a couple of kids,' Brett informed him.

'Good.' He was satisfied that the investigation was progressing. He would get all the details from the report and wouldn't need to chase it up personally. 'Well, leave that for now; do me a favour. Get a nondescript and pop over to the Gas Board in Leyton Street and pick up a stove for me, will you?' The DC wasn't really being given the option.

'Where d'you want it taking, guv? Home?'

'Yeah. But be a bit sensible, don't go and log the trip, will you?' The DI returned his look, satisfied he knew the score. It was a disciplinary offence to use police vehicles and policemen for such pursuits, that was why he didn't want them booking on the air, which every police vehicle, unless on some special assignment, was supposed to do, the theory being that they could take a diversionary call. 'Find Peter Footring and get him to give you a hand. Mark his card all right?'

Peter Footring was a temporary detective constable, and as such this was part of his education.

DI Kenley moved away along the CID room with the report for the DS, which he slid onto the corner of the desk. 'A bit more for you. D'you manage to get that legal aid report yet, Tony?'

'Yes. It's in the basket there, guv.'

'Oh' – was how the DI responded; almost disappointed. It meant more work for him.

The lock-up garages in Osborne Road, Forest Gate, weren't particularly busy at that time of the morning. The busiest time was between seven and nine when people collected cars and vans for work. A number of small businesses were run from the lock-ups and some loading up was entailed. People had come and gone without noticing the van parked in Osborne Road across from the garages' service road. Inactivity was boring the detective who was sitting in it and he was struggling against sleep, despite the cold and damp inside the van. He resisted starting the engine for the heater, in case a running engine made people curious.

Detective Constable Matthew Hall worked in C11, and alternated this watching brief with another DC on a twelve-hour shift. That was a long shift, but they were shorthanded in Criminal Intelligence, so it was something he had to put up with. Reaching across to the dashboard shelf, he picked up one of the two stills cameras there and checked it again, making sure it was ready to shoot. He had done that several times since he had come on at six o'clock this morning. The

Canon 500, like the Pentax, was quite ready, all he needed was something to shoot. DC Hall had doubts about anyone showing, having sensed a lack of interest on his governor's part. He suspected that had DI McHale really believed this a prospect, somehow he'd have found the men for a proper observation. He slid the camera back onto the shelf and pulled his anorak closely about himself, paying scant attention to the red Ford Escort that turned into the street and came towards him. The car made a righthand signal, and Hall assumed it was turning onto the service road. Instead it pulled into the kerb and parked. Hall's interest came alive, and he wondered about the two men in the car. They didn't get out, but sat in the car and waited. The DC thought perhaps they were checking the street, but maybe one was simply dropping the other off. Either way they didn't notice him.

Satisfied that they hadn't been followed, Cole Coleman and Philip Hayes climbed out of the Ford Escort and, after carefully locking the doors, started along the service road. As they went DC Hall sat forward and reached for the Canon. Opening the nearside door window, he snapped off a couple of photos of the retreating men and their car. He didn't know that these were the men he was there to observe, having no details other than the information that it would probably be two men as there were two cars in the lock-up, supplied by the ringer. But he found their behaviour curious enough to warrant his attention.

Inside the two garages which had been knocked into one were an Austin 2000 estate car and a Ford Cortina estate, each with a key and a spare hanging from the ignition, the petrol tanks full. When Coleman and Hayes drove the Austin and Cortina out, the garages were left starkly bare; there wasn't so much as a rag or a cigarette packet to subsequently identify anyone by.

Coleman led the way. As he nosed the Austin out of the service road he didn't notice the man in the maroon mini van, or the fact that he was taking photos, any more than Hayes did when he followed. They turned towards Romford Road.

As the estate cars turned off Osborne Road, DC Hall quickly started his car, pulling straight out and almost hitting another car. The DC broke out in a cold sweat as the horn of the other vehicle blared at him, not at the thought of the scrape, but the consequences; he would have lost the two estate cars. Turning towards Romford Road, he unhooked the r/t and threw the switch down.

'MP, MP, from Central 101,' – he said into the handset, trying to raise the Information Room at the Yard. Much to his surprise the robbery seemed to be on and he needed help. 'Assistance urgently required in Romford Road, approaching Little Ilford Lane. Re suspects believed armed robbery soon. Central 101 over.'

There was a lot of static on the air. Minutes seemed to pass before the Information Room responded. 'Unit calling MP, your call sign and signals unreadable. Try again in another position. MP over.'

That was almost inevitable, and Hall might have bet money on it happening. Just at the moment you needed urgent help you ran into a radio blank spot. Fortunately he was moving and there was a chance he would be able to contact the Yard later. He dropped the phone back, without looking at the r/t, his eyes fixed on the two estate cars ahead.

Staying a safe distance behind wasn't easy, especially while trying to keep one vehicle between himself and the rear estate car. There were a lot of traffic lights along Romford Road, and it only needed the villains to go through some and him being stopped. By the time they reached Bell Avenue, Romford, where the villains parked the changeover car, Hall was wet with sweat.

There was a church in Bell Avenue, and Hayes negotiated the yellow Cortina into a gap outside as if he was one of the congregation. Hayes expected Cole Coleman, who was the getaway driver, to say something about the place he had

239

parked the changeover car as he climbed out, locking the door. He walked to the back of the car and put one of the ignition keys in the petrol filler housing as a precaution. Losing the ignition key happened at times during blags.

'All right, Cole?' Hayes said as he climbed into the Austin 2000.

'Yeah, that'll do.'

Coleman glanced in the rear-view mirror, then slipped the car into gear. It glided away as if he had been born at the controls.

Still DC Hall found he was unable to reach the Yard. His signals continued to break up and he began to feel desperate. He knew he daren't dash to phone for fear of losing the car that the two villains had gone off in. If he couldn't raise them soon he'd have to start writing messages and throwing them out of the window. Maybe he'd see a police unit somewhere in the area.

The next stop Coleman and Hayes made was at a scrap yard near Seven Kings railway station, where they collected an old gas-stove that Tully had paid for a few days earlier. The burners were broken and it was caked with grease. The dealer couldn't have cared less why they wanted it. The twenty-five pounds he had taken for it was a lot more than its scrap metal value.

'You'll have a nice cooker there, you clean it up, m'ol bruv,' he commented as they lifted it into the back of the car.

Hayes was about to put up a story about its being for his granny but Coleman simply grunted, and they were off again. Coleman was conscious of the time, said timing was his responsibility; cursed traffic jams and other drivers who delayed them.

Tully and Benny Isaacs were waiting for them at a bus stop on Ilford High Road, the latter with a large gripbag. Both men, like Coleman and Hayes, had on an excess of clothes, overcoats, overalls, hats, none of which looked out of place on this cold, damp morning. The clothes weren't simply to keep

240

them warm, but to effect a disguise, and considerably altered their appearance. Among the hats they had with them was a ski-cap, leather flying helmet, a crash helmet and visor. These were the head pieces they were going to wear with scarves on the actual blag, as they hid their faces without being too obvious.

'All right?' Tully inquired as he climbed into the car.

"S been a doddle so far,' Coleman replied. "In't, Phil?'

'Yeah, no problems, apart from about five pulls for speeding.'

'Leave off!' Tully said.

'How we doing for time?' Coleman said.

'A bit early, I'd say. Take a run up there and park round the corner,' Tully told him. 'We can see it all right as it comes along Bushgrove Road.'

It was lucky that they were early as the security truck arrived seven minutes earlier than its earliest time since Tully had been clocking it. Each of the four men in the Austin estate car thought that boded well as they watched the truck turn at the T-junction into Leyton Street. Even so they couldn't help their tense looks as Coleman started the car. They pulled the headgear down further as if to disguise themselves better, making sure they weren't going to come off as they got stuck in.

Apprehension tugged at Tully as Coleman started the car away faster than he should. He searched the street, an old man turned and looked. Coleman swung the car out into Leyton Street and cruised along to the main entrance of the Gas Board offices, as the security truck was seen turning through the gates to the yard farther along the road.

Inside the building an office worker came through the entrance hall and locked the glass door. Her attention was taken by a man, whom she let out. She didn't notice the pale green Austin with four men in it, even though long ago when she had been given this job each Thursday she had been warned to look out for such things. The Board had never been robbed and she never expected it would be; locking the door was no longer a precaution, but a habit as far as Margaret Ryan was concerned.

The maroon mini van with DC Hall in stopped at a safe distance behind the Austin, and the detective watched through the windscreen as two of the three blaggers who were out of the car offloaded the old stove. He groped for the r/t handset and leaned forward out of sight.

'MP. MP, from Central 101. Urgent message. Central 101, over.' He held his breath.

'Go ahead, Cental 101,' the voice in the Information Room responded.

'MP from central 101. Urgent assistance required at Gas Board, Leyton Street, Romford. Robbery Imminent.' He couldn't keep the excitement or relief from his voice.

'Central 101, message received. You were car to car with local units. Kilo 2, 7, 11 and 12 are on the way.' More would almost certainly turn up, for as soon as an urgent message like that came the Information Room threw down the switches opening all channels so that everyone from detectives en route somewhere to traffic patrol units received the call.

Having reached base, DC Hall wasn't about to tackle the villains single-handed; he had more sense than need of the commendation he might receive in hospital. Anyway, that wasn't what was expected of an officer in C11, he was required to put his face in as little as possible. So he did instead what he was there to do, he began clicking off photographs.

'Fucking stroll on!' Tully said at the weight of the stove as he and Hayes carried it up the steps of the Gas Board offices.

'Bit lumpy, John, 'in't.' Nervousness caused the words to splutter out of Hayes in a giggle.

They couldn't swing the stove freely at the glass door; they simply tipped it into it, smashing out the entire plate. The crash reverberated around the entrance hall and roared back at them. As soon as they had pushed the stove out of the way, Benny Isaacs handed them each a sawn-off shotgun from his gripbag. It was at this point that the two security guards who were in the hall realized that what they had just witnessed wasn't someone protesting about North Sea gas, but a robbery.

At the works end of the Gas Board, Simon Brett and Peter Footring, the two DCs from Romford nick, staggered out of the gates with their governor's new stove in time to see the old stove crash through the door. They froze on the pavement, the weight of the new stove stretching the tendons in their arms.

'I think they're making one,' DC Brett said instinctively, having registered the arrival of the security truck.

'What'll we do?' the less experienced detective asked. He was ready to drop the stove.

'Get this fucking thing into the van, quick!' They rushed the stove into the back of the nondescript police van, heedless of the damage they did to it in the process.

'Hold it or I'll shoot you stone fucking dead!' Isaacs screamed at the two security guards as he ran across the foyer. Both men were on the stairs heading up to the first floor.

The other two blaggers went straight at the guards. Tully, slightly ahead of Hayes, grabbed the first man and dragged him down for Hayes to deal with The second guard, who was further up the stairs, tried to scrabble away, then lashed out blindly with his night-stick. A chance blow almost broke Tully's shoulder. He retaliated angrily, swinging the shotgun by the leather loop he had around his wrist, and striking the guard a blow alongside his neck, just where the protection flap of his helmet finished. The man was unbalanced and fell back towards Tully, dropping his money case as he did. But Tully was still angry and hit him again as he fell.

Margaret Ryan, who had locked the glass door, stood frozen with fear as Isaacs and Hayes set about the second guard, who seemed loath to let go the money container.

'Leggo, you stupid cunt!' Hayes screamed in alarm at him as Isaacs crashed his shotgun down on his shoulders and arms. Eventually he did let go.

Tully, having leaped down the stairs with his case, gave the guard a final kick. He turned suddenly and saw a crowd of office workers on the landing. They were peering down in horror at what was going on, more coming to see what the fuss was about, jostling for a better view.

'Fuck off!' he shouted, and raised his shotgun one-handed. Pointing it in their direction was enough to set them panicking, but he fired one of the barrels. There was a cry of alarm as the spectators fled, each imagining themselves hit. The shortened barrel along with the shortened cartridges caused the shot to fan widely from the muzzle and certainly none of the leads would have hurt anyone at the top of the stairs, even had they hit them.

Outside, the shotgun explosion caused DC Brett to stop in his tracks on the office steps. When he first realized there was a robbery going off he had reacted without thinking what he could best do. Now he was acutely aware of the fact that the robbers were armed and he wasn't, and that there would be little he could do physically to stop them. However, having reached this point, he couldn't turn and run. Swinging round, he shouted to TDC Footring, who was sprinting towards him, 'Get the van – get on the radio for help!'

Footring hesitated on seeing the blaggers emerge from the offices, then ran back to the van.

'Hold it! CID,' Brett shouted. It was worth a try. But it was doubtful whether Isaacs even registered the words as he butted the detective down with his shotgun.

Isaacs stood over the detective, the shotgun inches from his face, while the other two ran with the cases to the car. The short, swarthy blagger in the long white overall and ski-cap watched coolly as the two men scrambled into the car, his eyes flicking between them and the detective. Finally he kicked DC Brett in the face then ran to the Austin 2000, which was now in motion, the back door open for him.

Despite bleeding from the mouth and feeling decidedly groggy, DC Brett stumbled to his feet and gave chase, briefly gaining on the estate car – but without knowing what he'd do if he caught up with it. With a surge of power the car roared along the road towards the mini van which TDC Footring now had in motion, in the opposite direction.

In the police van belonging to C11, DC Hall, who had calmly been photographing the blaggers going in and coming out of the offices, was now issuing details into the r/t.

'... pale-green Austin estate, registration AGY 364T, heading north along Leyton Street. Expected destination is Bell Avenue, where suspects have changeover car, a yellow Cortina estate. Registration ALS 196V.'

Without regard for the other traffic along Leyton Street, the police van with the stove aboard swung out across the road to block the blaggers' getaway, shooting the cooker out of the back. But Cole Coleman anticipated the move as soon as he saw the van start to manoeuvre. He swung the car into the opposite lane, judging the oncoming traffic so finely that it all might have been stationary. He passed behind the police van, which, along with the car that subsequently ran into the new gas stove, achieved nothing but a traffic jam, and that in turn hampered DC Hall's pursuit.

29

Surprise and confusion were prevalent in the blaggers' car over the presence of the CID, but these feelings were tinged with elation at having blagged the wages and got clear. The latter feeling, however, was shortlived, for as they sped away toward Bell Avenue, the sound of police klaxons filled the air.

There were two police cars, in fact, local units Kilo 7 and 12, both coming from the same direction. Kilo 12, which was leading, spotted the Austin 2000 as it made the Bell Avenue turnoff. Kilo 12 was a Rover 3500 and had far more acceleration than the Austin, so closing the gap between them was a simple matter, but one the driver regretted.

Benny Isaacs who was still in the back of the estate car threw up the window and poked the short nose of the shotgun out. It wasn't an idle threat to try and make the police keep their distance. He knew they had to be stopped if they were to get away. He fired without warning, causing the police vehicle to swerve off course and stop. The blaggers' car swept on along Bell Avenue as Kilo 7 drew up alongside the first police vehicle to check that the occupants were unharmed. They were.

The Austin 2000 skidded to a halt alongside the change-over car, even though there would be little point in changing cars as the police being as close as they were would identify the second car. But Coleman was only a good driver, he couldn't think on his feet. He had programmed himself to head for the changeover car and did so unremittingly, despite the loss of time involved now; had they stayed in the first car they might have put extra distance between themselves and the police.

The four men piled out of the Austin with their guns and cases, but minus some of their clothing. Tully and Hayes had removed a coat and the crash helmet and flying hat respectively; Isaacs had removed only his ski-cap, which he replaced with a trilby. Panic touched them briefly over the slight delay which ensued while Coleman was getting the door of the Cortina open. Their sense of panic increased as a third police car nosed out of a side turning.

'Come on, Cole! For fucksake!' Isaacs said and crashed a side window with the butt of his shotgun.

Suddenly the doors were open and the blaggers were bundling in. The engine roared with life. Tully pushed his shotgun through the window to warn off the police, whose car crept steadily towards them. The Cortina accelerated away into Greenborough Road, not stopping at the junction, then shortly made a fast left fork into Park Avenue weaving in and out of traffic. The sound of police klaxons was everywhere.

There were more than the three police cars they had so far seen. Just how many there were the blaggers didn't know, but knew that more and more would pour into the area the longer they stayed around. What their chances were of getting away they didn't know and purposely didn't consider, but none of them would want to give up; each would want to press on relentlessly, be driven into a corner and still not give up without a struggle; that was their instinct for survival, it wasn't at all logical, but it was basic to each of them.

Another police car, answering the original call for assistance from DC Hall, and taking a redirection from the Information Room as the getaway progressed, sped along Southwell Avenue, which was adjacent to Park Avenue. The blaggers' car was ahead of them though, pulling dangerously out of the junction into Southwell Avenue. There was almost a collision between police cars, as others coming up Park Avenue in pursuit tried the same trick and sped out of the junction.

The chase touched speeds of eighty miles an hour along this wide stretch of road, with police cars now vying with each other to be out in front. As one of the police Rovers overtook the less powerful car which was currently leading the pursuit, the policeman next to the driver grinned triumphantly at colleagues in the other car. Getting there first might have earned him a prize rather better than being shot at, going by his gleeful expression.

Judging the traffic to fractions of a second, Coleman braked hard and swung the car dangerously through the oncoming vehicles and into Riding Horse Lane, a turning that ran alongside sports grounds.

'This is fucking murder,' Tully said. He was soaked with sweat and could see himself ending up through the windscreen or concertinaed in a cannon of some kind. He wrenched round to check through the rear window at what progress the police were making. 'We're all gonna wind up nicked!'

'I'll shoot the fuckers first,' Isaacs informed him.

Tension caused the men in the car to teeter on the edge of hysteria. Staying in control wasn't easy.

'We gotta get rid of this car,' Coleman said. 'Every Old Bill in Essex'll have is description.'

The opportunity presented itself almost immediately.

'There!' Tully shouted. 'We'll have that.'

A Jaguar up ahead was just nosing out of a line of parked cars, and stopped to let them pass.

Coleman stood on the brake pedal, at the same time wrenching up the handbrake and locking the back wheels, putting the car into a spin on the damp surface. The Cortina slewed across the road and came neatly to a halt, radiator snug against a parked car and partially blocking the road. The driver of the Jaguar sat and stared at this performance in utter amazement, and was unmoving right up to the point when the villains dragged him out of the driving seat and Coleman took his place.

The entire hijacking took less than a minute but it was long enough for a police car to have come up on them. Isaacs fired his shotgun at the crew from the Jaguar as the car sped away.

Running at random now, the programmed getaway completely out of sync, Cole Coleman was waiting for instructions, while merely keeping the car in forward motion at the greatest possible speed. He had little definite idea where he was going. Repeatedly he glanced at Tully, expecting him to tell him what to do. Finally Tully did.

'Do a left,' Tully shouted above the roar of the car's engine. There was no left turn at that section of the road and the order merely confused Coleman. 'Right, you cunt! I mean right,' he countermanded.

'Fucking well say what you mean, for fucksake,' Coleman screamed angrily back. He swung the car tightly into the turning, cannoning off a parked car as he went.

'You're gonna kill us all, you mad fucker,' Hayes said through the confusion.

Throughout, Benny Isaacs was bracing himself between seats and calmly reloading his gun.

The hijacked Jaguar squealed out of the side turning onto the dual carriageway of Croxted Avenue. The air in its wake was thick with the wail of police klaxons.

Traffic was fairly heavy along Croxted Avenue and, despite his almost tipping over with panic, Coleman once again showed his considerable skill as a driver, weaving in and out of vehicles with every gap that presented itself; even those spaces that only suggested there was room enough to make it he forced his way into, rarely touching the brakes. But all was to no avail, it seemed. There were three police cars close on the blaggers' tail by this time, simply following the swath the hijacked Jaguar cut through the traffic. A fourth police car sped out of the junction of Riding Horse Lane – the blaggers having come round on themselves – and tried to head them off. But the Jaguar jumped the lights at the junction, taking a violent angle to avoid some crossing traffic, mounted the pavement, and finally cut back into the nearside lane of vehicles on Croxted Avenue. Traffic on the junction halted to let the police cars through, and as they closed on the robbers again, so Isaacs let them have both barrels from his shotgun. Lead shot pattered harmlessly against the windscreen, but the suddenness of it caused the driver to brake.

There was a traffic tailback from the roundabout ahead. This was made worse by a police transit van that had come along one of the adjacent roads and gone into the roundabout against the traffic in order to block the villain's car. Coleman had no special driving magic to get them out of the traffic that was locked solid, especially not when he was boxed in on the offside lane. All he could do was mount the kerb of the central island between the roadway and the dividing fence; he drove towards the roundabout that way to the irritation of other drivers who saw the move simply as an impatient driver taking advantage.

'Fuck I! Look,' Hayes said, pointing through the windscreen at the police van ahead. 'We got no chance there.'

'Have it over the fence,' Tully said.

The Jaguar slammed to a halt and the four men quickly abandoned it, taking with them their guns and the two cases. Three of them jumped over the chainlink barrier fence, Isaacs taking it upon himself to cover their retreat from the oncoming policemen, some of whom were out of their cars and running through the stationary traffic. Isaacs fired at them, but still the police hadn't got smart about the distance pellets from a sawn-off shotgun would travel, and they all dived for cover between the vehicles.

On the eastbound carriageway, which was relatively clear, with what traffic there was free moving, the other three men set about hijacking two more vehicles, so they could split up and have a better chance of getting away. The first car they dragged was a Ford Capri over in the farthest lane; it went without a hitch. Tully levelled the shotgun and the driver stopped immediately. Coleman dragged him out and clambered in; Hayes went with him. The thought crossed Tully's mind that maybe he should go too, leaving Isaacs to make out as best he could. But he decided against it. Benny Isaacs was a right good 'un, who deserved better than that.

Tully turned his attention to hijacking another car, but this one refused to stop when he levelled the shotgun. The next he tried, an American Oldsmobile, he gave the driver no opportunity to blank him. He opened fire as the car came towards him. The driver slammed on the brakes. He wrenched open the door; the driver was the height of compliance when staring into the short nose of the shotgun. From the driving seat Tully leaned out of the window with the shotgun to cover Isaacs as he clambered over the fence with the case and the shotgun. The gesture was useless, he realized immediately, as he couldn't have fired without hitting Isaacs.

Back along the road, one of the policemen had climbed the fence also and had flagged down a lorry and had had it slew across the road, to block it. But the lorry wasn't big enough to block all three lanes, and before he could get another vehicle into the gap, PC Vallins anticipated what would happen and threw himself into the breach, trying to plug the hole between the end of the lorry and the barrier fence. He did so not too successfully. Tully was in no mood to stop for an unmoving wolly or anyone else. The policeman bounced off the front of the car as it sped through the gap and away along the eastbound carriage.

The Oldsmobile raced across the junction of Riding Horse Lane with lights in its favour, as two police cars came across the junction in pursuit. Tully made a fast, wide, lefthand turn on to Royal Avenue, his driving skills under pressure were evidently less than Coleman's. Making a right turn to go down by Royal Park, he cannoned off stationary vehicles; making a fast left turn into Woodside Gardens wasn't much better. When he eventually reached Greenborough Road and tried to make a fast right into Bradwell Gardens he misjudged the turn completely and, mounting the kerb, ran smack into a lamp standard. Both men were shaken, but unharmed. The car engine had cut out and Tully didn't even attempt to restart it; all they were aware of then was the approaching wail of police klaxons. They abandoned the car. Isaacs ran off along Bradwell Gardens, discarding yet another layer of clothing as he went and wrapping the shotgun in it. He had left the case of money he was carrying behind.

Taking both his case and shotgun, Tully ran back across Greenborough Road and into the grounds of a Social Services clinic, which was housed in a big, rambling, dirty-brick building. Prams and pushchairs were lined up outside. Policemen from the first two police cars to arrive gave chase on foot. Irrationally Tully felt a gross sense of injustice that he should be the only one being chased – he assumed the others had got clear away. He turned back, firing his shotgun at the nearing policemen, causing them to scatter. The case banged against his side as he ran, but he was loath to simply ditch it. As he turned by some bushes he pushed the case into a pile of leaves that had been swept up, and ran out of another gate, back on to Greenborough Road, where he flagged down a car by standing directly in its path. There was a woman with two small children in the front of the car. Tully wrenched open the back door and clambered in without explanation.

'Drive! Quickly, love, c'mon.' He appealed rather than threatened.

The woman panicked a bit. She let the clutch in unevenly and the car jerked away along the street. Keeping down in the seat Tully peered out of the rear window. There was no sign of the police. He had the woman make a right turn, then another, before having her stop. He climbed out, taking the ignition key. Then wrapping his shotgun in his coat, he walked calmly away, leaving the woman and kids in the car trembling and crying respectively.

Tully disappeared from sight round the first corner.

Gently Jack Lynn stroked his fingers along his wife's crotch; he was comfortable, content, where he lay, his head resting on her arm, his face against her breast. He sensed her anxiety, but didn't want to disturb, not yet. He would have liked to make love to her again, but knew he wouldn't be able to if she kept looking at the clock. There was time enough before the

252

girls came home from school for lunch, but she wouldn't be convinced. She didn't like the girls knowing anything of their sex life, and got quite angry when they said they wanted to get in the shower with him. He would have let them.

Having got the girls off to school that morning, she had gone back to bed with him. Something she enjoyed doing as much as he did. He thought it a point in favour of his keeping the sort of life-style he had as a blagger, the freedom to choose to do whatever, whenever, but didn't put it forward. Since their row about it and his promise to do some mini cabbing, the matter hadn't been raised.

'Come on, lovey. We must move,' she said suddenly.

'Mm, in a minute. This has gotta be better than driving a mini cab.' He slid his finger into her. But she was resisting.

'I've got to get up, Jack. No, stop it. I mean, taking me back to bed this time of morning.' Her resolve became firmer. 'No, come on, stop it. The girls'll be home for their dinner soon.'

'You don't use it, you lose it ...'

'Some chance of that happening to you,' she said. 'You'll wear it out. Come on!' She slapped his chest and pulled away.

'Ah.' He stretched expansively. "S water hot? I'll take a bath.'

'I'll run it for you, if you like.' It was a good excuse to get out of bed. She dived straight into her dressing gown, not wanting him to see her naked.

'Maybe I'll just have a couple more minutes,' he said.

'No. Come on now, Jack,' she said firmly. 'I'm running your bath.' She went out.

Jack Lynn reached over to look at his watch on the night table. It was half past eleven. They would have had loads of time before the girls got back. He stretched again, then rose, glancing down at his erection. It wasn't going to do him any good at all.

30

'They got away? You mean to say they got clean away?' Pyle said with exaggerated surprise. He was in C11's general office of the fourth floor of the Yard, having just been given the news by DI McHale. 'What the fuck were all those wooden tops doing? Playing with each other?'

'They make you tired, don't they,' McHale concurred.

There was a bit of activity going on around the room from other detectives, about six in all, who were mainly involved with paperwork. One detective was trying to raise a unit on C11's own r/t, but wasn't having any luck, the car having gone out of range.

'Still, there shouldn't be too much trouble picking them up,' McHale said by way of consolation. 'They left a great trail of evidence by all accounts.'

'But twelve police cars in the area, and still they were away like birds.'

'It was down to John Tully and his little team,' he informed him. 'Our lad's just developing the photos now. Should be handy.'

'Been handier we'd been there, Graham,' Pyle said.

'Yes,' McHale said curtly. He was evidently embarrassed by the error of judgement on his part, and didn't want to think about either the alternative or the consequences. 'We should have done something more. There're a lot like that, Fred, 'we had more men available.'

'Still, the least said about it the better, I'd have thought.' He wasn't merely consoling a colleague. 'I bet there's a lot of screaming going on over in K division – the blaggers legging it like that.'

''S why I want to keep out of it if I can,' McHale said. 'If that's all right by you?'

'Makes no difference, 'we nick that team a bit lively.' The arrests were for Pyle's squad to make; having supplied the information, C11 wouldn't do any more, certainly they wouldn't attempt any arrests.

'That might embarrass the local CID a bit more, especially if the press gets hold of it. Still, fuck them. I don't owe them any favours.' He turned to DC Hall as the younger detective appeared with his photographs in a folder. 'What they like, Matt? ID them all, can you?'

'Well, they're not too clever really, guv.' The DC proffered the folder reluctantly.

The DI's expression was unyielding as he thumbed through the dozen or so photographic enlargements, passing them on to Pyle as he went. 'Not exactly Lord Snowdon, are you,' he said disappointedly. He paused over a picture. ''S not bad.'

'I couldn't get any closer, guv. Not without them tumbling me.'

Pyle gave him a sharp look. 'I shouldn't say too much about that, son.'

'They show what's going on all right,' McHale commented. 'Be handy if they showed you who.' The photos were short on detail. None of the four blaggers could be positively identified, only what they were doing.

'I don't know, Graham. These'll probably do nicely. I mean, they could be anyone – give us more scope, don't they.' He grinned, like he had something in mind.

'You going to get some raids organized, Fred? Pick up Tully and his mates?'

'Might make a nice show, 'we can,' Pyle said.

There was a need for some concerted police action to redress the balance before the press got hold of what happened out at Romford and started demanding to know just what was going on.

Criminal Intelligence had gathered a fair amount of information on John Tully, and associates of his; more especially people he was likely to work with, and were quickly able to come up with the most likely three candidates on the blag with him.

Four raids were organized simultaneously by Fred Pyle. There was no particular order of merit or preference over who arrested whom. Pyle got Benny Isaacs; DS Lethridge raided Tully's flat; DS Barcy, who was the violence specialist on Pyle's squad, took Cole Coleman and DS Ian Middlewick, who was borrowed along with two DCs from another squad, took the fourth suspect C11 had come up with, a man called Ernie Johnson.

Tully was at home when Lethridge called with three other detectives, all of whom were armed. He wasn't happy about his place being searched, and less happy when told to accompany them.

'I'm not going nowhere till I phone my brief,' Tully said. He knew what it'd be like once they got him to the nick, he'd be told all the phones were continually in use. He could have left it for the woman he lived with to phone, but there was no guarantee they would take him to the police station where they said they would.

DS Lethridge looked around the flat, to see where the telephone junction box was located. He ripped the wire out of the wall. 'Don't talk silly, John. Your phone's out of order. Fucking British Telecom, the cunts. I been waiting a fortnight for them to come and fix mine.'

Tully grimaced, accepting this with a resigned nod.

DS Jack Barcy, who was tall and lean and hungry-looking, with eyes that were large and round and fish-like, was sitting at the kitchen table in Mrs Coleman's council flat, drinking tea while he waited for her favourite son to show up.

Although she bitterly resented the police presence, resented their traipsing through the flat searching, she had made them tea.

'Why don't you rotten sods bugger off and leave him be? He ain't done nothing,' she said, hostilely. 'He's a good boy.'

"Course he is, love,' Barcy replied. 'We only want a word.'

'Yeah, I know how much, you rotten bastards ...'

'Keep it up, love.' There was an air of latent menace about the detective. 'Just keep it up and I won't drink your tea.'

She glanced from him to the other detectives. She knew he wasn't joking.

Unsuspectingly Cole Coleman came along the open walkway of the block and let himself into his mother's flat.

Mrs Coleman tensed on hearing him, as did the detectives. But she responded fast, and shouted a warning to him before the detectives could prevent her. 'Run, Cole – it's the cozos!'

Coleman didn't stop to reason how. He turned and fled. But Barcy and the other detectives weren't far behind him. They came flying out of the flat and along the walkway, catching up with him at the head of the stairs, where Barcy threw a punch which hit the villain squarely in the back, sending him sprawling headlong down the stairs. He sustained a few cuts and bruises. Generally he could count himself lucky; they might simply have shot him.

Main Road police station at Romford was descended upon by the Squad, and even with this relatively small influx of extra men it was ill equipped to cope. DI Pyle arrived with Benny Isaacs at the same time as Ian Middlewick showed up with his suspect; the other two squads weren't far behind.

In the back reception area Pyle caught hold of a uniform who was passing through. 'Where's Inspector Kenley?' he asked, and before the spotty-faced PC could reply: 'Go and tell him Inspector Pyle's here.'

'Yes, sir.' The uniform moved away at a trot.

Pyle turned and looked at his prisoner for a moment, then almost smiled, but shook his head instead. 'What d'you reckon, Benny? Want to put your hands up for it now?' He had no serious expectation of that.

'Leave off, Mr Pyle,' Isaacs said respectfully. 'Not even to help a nice fella like you.'

'About right, I s'pose.' At this point it was little more than a game the detective and the blagger were playing with each other. Later it would almost certainly get heavier.

When Ernie Johnson was interrogated, he was at pains to be as helpful as possible. Though he had previous convictions as a blagger, he now had an alibi, which he insisted was sound. It might well have been, but DS Middlewick wasn't about to give up easily.

'Why don't you do us all a favour,' Middlewick said in the interview room, 'John Tully's dropped you right in it.'

'No, John wouldn't do that, even if it was true,' the suspect said with touching faith. 'Not John. You're pulling my leg.'

'You were the fourth man on that blag yesterday. That's what we got.'

'No. I tol' you where I was, didn't I. With m' old Mum in hospital. The old girl passed away just about the time they was making it. Why don't you check that? You see.'

'Oh, we will do, Ernie. But you're a million. I mean, you go mates with John Tully, don't you.'

'You know I do. I mean, it's on m' sheet, innit. 'S why I got a pull. But you see if my old Mum didn't pop off yesterday. You see if I wasn't at her bedside at the hospital.' He was completely unemotional about this.

'If you were,' Middlewick said, 'then you've no problem, Ernie. We'll see.' He was doubtful.

Embarrassment over what had happened on his manor made DI Kenley very amenable and open to any suggestion by DI Pyle that might get him off the hook. Pyle cheerfully exploited the situation.

'How come your two lads happened to be down at the Gas Board?' Pyle asked in the local DI's office. There was quite a lot of activity going on across the corridor in the CID room, mainly from detectives either chasing up witnesses or taking statements from them. 'D' you hear a whisper?'

'I wish to fuck I had. I'd've had more than a DC and a TDC down there.' He told him what they had been doing there. 'That's just between ourselves of course.'

"Course,' Pyle said collusively. 'So they hadn't booked on the air or nothing?'

'I told them not to,' Kenley explained.

Pyle nodded thoughtfully. 'What are they like? Half-wide?'

'They're all right, Fred. They do what they're told.'

'Their diaries haven't gone upstairs yet, have they?' They hadn't. 'Good. Well, maybe they just ought to stick down that they were on obo – get you out of trouble, won't it?' It appeared that Fred Pyle was being helpful, getting a colleague off the hook; however, it wasn't quite that simple, nothing was quite that simple with Fred Pyle. He anticipated the blank he might draw with Ernie Johnson and was considering the most likely candidate to fill it. With such moves it would be useful to have the local DI obligated to him.

'I don't know as it will,' Kenley said, unknowingly resisting the slot Pyle was trying to fit him into. 'The brasshats are screaming like bastards, the blaggers getting away like that. Been a right upset here there has.'

'Down to the wollies, wasn't it?'

'Mostly. What about C11's lad with the camera? How'd that come about?'

'They had a whisper. Nothing positive. They covered it with one man. How are you saying your two came to be there?' Pyle wanted to know. 'That'll be a disciplinary matter, it gets out about them collecting that stove.'

Kenley thought about this for a moment. 'Yeah,' he said at length. 'Maybe I'd better have them stick down they were on obo.'

'About right. They'll soon forget the fuckup upstairs, now we've nicked them.'

'I hope you're right.'

'Don't you fancy going back in uniform, Frank?' Pyle grinned.

'Not even to take promotion,' Kenley said as though it were a real prospect.

'How you doing with the witnesses?' This he asked in a

peremptory manner. It was his case now, and he made all the running.

'Oh, we've more than enough of those.'

'Not policemen, are they?' Pyle had seen too many cases to court where the only witnesses were policemen and where the villains had got a result almost because of it, it had seemed.

'Some are, of course. But a lot of civilians, too,' he added quickly.

'Good. We'll have to get some ID parades organized. They'll probably get us further at this stage than interrogating this team.'

Identity parades were generally rather formal affairs conducted by the uniform branch; usually it was the station inspector who was in charge. The official idea was to make the parade as fair and unbiased as possible, but there were means of prejudicing witnesses, provided the CID picked the right sort of witness. It was no good choosing one to give a bit of help to, if that witness was likely to turn round and make a complaint about the police. What detectives like Fred Pyle did was simply exploit people's natural prejudices, relying on their basic, emotional right wing leaning. Over seventy-five per cent of the population were that way and it had nothing at all to do with politics: it had everything to do with the maintenance of law and order and, despite their faults, that's what the police were seen to be doing as far as this vast majority were concerned. However, because of the ruling concerning the validity of eyewitness evidence, especially if unsupported by other kinds of evidence, they had to be especially careful at ID parades to let it be seen that they were being fair. Most professional villains employed briefs, and had them within close call in case of a nicking – certainly they made sure they were present at any ID parades they were put on. The police didn't mind too much, even though they sometimes made a nuisance of themselves on their clients' behalf, objecting to participants who weren't similar enough to clients, checking that witnesses had no prior opportunity to see the suspects. The safeguards they were able to get their clients were in fact very limited, despite the overt show that was made, and no one knew this better than the villains in the line-up. If they were wanted badly enough, they knew that the CID wouldn't let a little thing like the uncertainty of a witness stop them.

Having interrogated each of the suspects himself, aside from the arresting officers interrogating them, Pyle had no objection finally to them calling their solicitors, or their solicitors being present at subsequent interrogations; that wasn't how he was going to get these men convicted. None of them were likely to put their hands up.

Tully and Coleman not being too dissimilar in appearance were put in a parade together with ten other men. That was the minimum number required for two suspects going in. Isaacs had to go in on his own among seven other men. The fourth man, Ernie Johnson, wasn't put up; Pyle had finally accepted his alibi. Two nurses and a doctor had spoken to him at his mother's deathbed and the time had been precise, having been noted for the death certificate.

Witnesses came on in chronological order, more or less as they would appear in court. Some of them hadn't been available at the sort of notice the police gave them and would have to attend another parade, some wouldn't be called, for after talking to them the CID discovered they hadn't seen anything at all. The whole process was tedious and time-consuming, and a lot of patience was required by the witnesses, the police and the members of the public in the line-up; the feelings of the suspects simply weren't considered.

Margaret Ryan, who locked the front door of the Gas Board offices was the first in. She was ushered in by a uniformed sergeant, and taken along the line by the uniformed inspector.

'What I want you to do,' the inspector said, 'is walk down the line and see if you can pick out any of the men you saw at the robbery. Just take your time, Miss, we have all day. And don't be afraid.' There was a bored familiarity in his words, having said them hundreds of times before.

The parade was being held in the muster room. Some detectives preferred to have their parades held in light similar to that at the time of the robbery, but it was too cold to be standing around outside today.

Margaret Ryan walked past Coleman who was in second place, hesitated at Tully, who was next to him; went on to the fourth man, then back to Tully and indicated him, though wasn't certain.

The next witness was Peter Mason, who was one of the security guards, the less injured of the two; his colleague James Lawrence was too ill after his beating to attend this parade. Special parades would be held for him at a later date. Mason picked out Tully. 'That's one of the buggers,' the guard said, 'I'm sure of it.' He drew a blank on Coleman, and on Isaacs when he was paraded. Other witnesses, both from the Gas Board and the street, picked out Tully; some of the Gas Board office workers even picked out Coleman, not realizing that he had been left outside in the car.

The very genuine confusion that was apparent from the civilian witnesses was completely absent from the police witnesses. Apart from being trained in observation, they had had the opportunity to corroborate their evidence with each other, see the photos DC Hall had taken, check the existing photographs of the villains the police had on record. They made it look like a swift 'un, Fred Pyle thought, as he stood in the muster room and observed the proceedings, even though he accepted that it wasn't.

'How does it look, Fred?' DCI Simmons asked when Pyle got back to the Yard later that day. Simmons was at his desk going through a large report line by line with a ruler. That close attention meant the report was on a negative result and so couldn't be put in with any kind of mistakes unless it afforded the hierarchy an opportunity to jump on whoever out of pique. 'Get some good IDs?'

'From policemen is about all,' Pyle said wearily. 'Twenty-seven witnesses, and only twelve that I'd call really positive. And they all came from policemen.' Policemen might have had no credibility at all as far as he was concerned.

'Might be a bit of a problem, Fred, if that's how it goes to court.'

'There are a few more to see yet. Some of them might shape up all right,' Pyle said on a more optimistic note. 'I mean they saw them all right, they just seem to get a mental block or something when they walk down that line.'

'I'd like to be sure of them, Fred,' Simmons said in a cautionary tone. 'They'll get some flash brief looking to make a name for himself, he'd probably go and dig something up on a police witness. Won't look too clever at all, will it. In fact it'll start to look a right swift 'un.'

Pyle laughed. 'Some fucking chance, I should think.'

'In the old days,' Simmons went on, 'it only needed a policeman to go into the witness box and say he did it, there was no doubt in anyone's mind. Not the case any more.'

'This little team did that blagging all right. There is no doubt.'

'I believe it, as well as those coppers who ID'd them. But we'll need something else to make sure of a result. Either some forensic evidence to go with their IDs or something more definite from the civilian witnesses.'

'Be handy,' Pyle agreed, 'wouldn't it.'

Spread out over his desk in the DIs' office Pyle had a dozen or so enlargements of the photos taken at the scene of the robbery by DC Hall. He was studying them through a magnifying glass. DS Lethridge was with him, leaning his weight on his forearms as he rested against the desk.

'You know who this fella is in the flying helmet, don't you?' he said deliberately. 'The one who's missing? It's Jack Lynn. That's who it is.'

Without commenting Lethridge took the magnifying glass and looked at a particular photo through it. The face of the person in the picture was obscured beyond recognition by the straps of the flying helmet, but he knew Lynn was due. 'Yes, I suppose that could be him.'

'Could be? Don't talk like a cunt.' Taking the glass back, he studied some more photos through it. 'That's definitely him, Eric. Yes, no doubt about it. We'll give him a pull, turn his place over.'

Lethridge stood off the desk. 'We doing this with a warrant?'

'Might be an idea. What we want at his place is something forensic could use. Like a few hairs from his hairbrush, so they can match them to any in the flying helmet.' He rose, gathering up the photos. 'He'll go this time, I'll make sure of that.' He said this as if he meant it.

31

Jack Lynn slept heavily, and ordinarily nothing woke him before time save the presence of someone coming into the room. If the children woke and cried in the night then it was his wife who got up to them. A squad of detectives simultaneously kicking in both the front and back doors at six o'clock on the cold December morning was unusual enough to awaken Jack Lynn; the noise they made was enough to awaken the dead.

Both Lynn and his wife woke with a start as detectives crashed in and ran up the stairs. They threw open the bedroom door, switching on the light.

'What the fuck's going on?' Lynn demanded, coming painfully into consciousness and flinging the covers back ready to spring out of bed.

'Don't move, Jack,' Pyle ordered.

'Jack!' Dolly said in alarm, as her husband started out of bed like he had neither heard the words nor seen the guns all three detectives who were now in the room were pointing at him. One of the girls in the next room had woken and was crying and calling for her Dad. 'They've woken up Sandra now ...' Dolly went on in a confused, upset manner.

'Just stay where you are, Jack,' Pyle said, 'or we'll shoot you ...'

'M' daughter's crying. You're out of order coming in here upsetting people like this ...'

'Let your wife go to her.'

Dolly looked in an uncertain fashion at her husband. 'What do they want, Jack?' she asked, getting out of bed, wearing a nylon nightdress.

'D'you have to come here like this?'

'You're a dangerous villain, Jack. We had to make certain of you.' There was faint mockery in the detective's tone now that he had the situation in control.

'You rotten bastards,' Dolly screamed at them, the words bursting out angrily. 'I can't help but call you it. He ain't done nothing. Tell them, Jack.'

'Go and see to Sandra, Doll. Go on,' he urged. He knew his wife meant well, but she wouldn't improve the situation by slagging off the filth.

Dolly started out of the bedroom, seemingly placated, but then she suddenly turned back and launched an attack against Pyle. 'You filthy bastard! You're filth, that's all ...'

'Do like you're told,' Pyle said, defending himself. DC Salter aided him, as DS Lethridge and two other DCs, who had come in through the back of the house, crowded onto the landing.

'Leave it out, Dolly – c'mon, 's just a pull. I ain't been at it.'

Eventually she went to her children, both of whom were upset. But she would sooner have stayed and fought for her husband.

'D'you want to put some clothes on?' Pyle said. 'Or are they your going away clothes?' Lynn was in his vest and pants.

'Couldn't this have waited till tomorrow?' Lynn wanted to know, reaching into his trousers. 'I mean, coming here at this time of the morning, worrying the life outta m' family ...'

'Make a start downstairs, Eric, will you.' He turned to DC Salter. 'Have a go up here. Properly.'

'I tell you, I ain't been at it at all,' Lynn protested. 'That's straight.'

'I didn't really expect you to put your hands up to it, Jack.'

'I don't know what the fuck you're talking about.'

'Don't you? You will soon enough, 'we charge you.'

'Leave off, will you. I ain't done nothing.' He paused in dressing and looked at the DI, as if trying to see and identify the workings behind that expressionless face. Finally he said, 'I think I'd better call my brief, hadn't I?'

Pyle slowly shook his head. He wasn't prepared to give him any such advantage. 'I don't think so.'

The other two detectives who had first entered the bedroom with Pyle were busily searching. One had started methodically on the wardrobe, carefully going through the pockets, folds and linings of every item of clothing. The other one was being just as meticulous with the dressing table.

'Someone just stuck my name up, didn't they? That's what this is all about, isn't it. That fucking grass you got working for you ...' Lynn didn't for a moment believe this was a simple routine tug or one that he would easily pull clear of, it was too heavy for that. They had something definite in mind, and whatever it was he knew that their finding the fifteen hundred pounds he had in an envelope taped to the bottom of a dressing table drawer would only help confirm it. He looked at the DI, who smiled mirthlessly at the find.

'A good start, Jack,' Pyle said.

"S only a bit of dough I keep by me. What does it prove?'

'That you had it off the other day. How much here?'

The villain told him. "S mine though, innit.' It wasn't the proceeds of a recent robbery, not one they had called about, he was sure of that.

'You'll get a receipt for it. Along with anything else we find of interest.' Pyle watched as the villain ran a comb through his hair. He decided that was what he wanted. 'You look very nice, Jack. You fit?'

'Ain't you even gonna let me have a look in and see my kids first?' he appealed.

"Course. But you try legging it and we'll shoot you. That's a promise.'

Lynn knew he meant it. Anyway, he wouldn't like to have taken a chance on his not meaning it.

'Go with him, Rog,' Pyle told DC Humphries. As the two men went out Pyle turned to the dressing table and picked up the comb Lynn had used. He glanced round, making sure he wasn't observed, then slipped it into his coat pocket. He wasn't collecting the official hair sample here, he had something else in mind for this.

'What's it all about, Jack?' Dolly Lynn asked her husband as he stooped over the bed in Sandra's room.

'You going with those men, Dad?' asked Carol, who was on the edge of the bed.

'In a little while, I expect love,' he responded to his eldest daughter, wishing he could reassure her. 'I dunno, Dolly. Just a pull.' He had no belief in that.

'Why can't they leave you alone? Rotten sods,' she said, confused and scared.

'I don't want you to go, Dad.' Sandra was still in tears.

'I'll be back in no time. I'll collect you from school, you see.' Sandra wasn't convinced.

'Shall I call a brief or someone?'

'Might be an idea. See how it goes.'

'Where they taking you?'

'I dunno.' He looked round questioningly at DC Humphries.

'Romford, I expect,' the DC said.

'Romford?' Both Lynn and his wife repeated the name like it was unexplored territory.

'Nowhere yet, Jack,' Pyle said appearing in the doorway. 'Let's get started. We've a lot to get through.'

Searching Lynn's house from top to bottom was the starting point for Pyle's squad, and doing the job properly took hours. Lynn was kept there and the search was made in his presence in some rooms, and in the presence of his wife in other rooms. Things weren't taken out and strewn around here as had often been the case in the past. There had been some angry memos about that flying around the Yard after complaints that the Terrorist Squad had proceeded in such a manner. It wasn't concern for suspects' property that had prompted the reaction, rather the fact that stuff strewn had to be subsequently strewn again as the search progressed. Here things were taken down, searched methodically, put back.

There wasn't much of interest, no guns, no further caches of money. There were some interesting receipts in the mountain of paper which Lethridge and DC Fenton sifted through on the dining room table, stuff that Lynn denied knowledge of.

'You're wasting your time,' Lynn would comment whenever they drew a blank, 'there ain't nothing there.'

'We got time to waste,' Pyle would reply, beginning to believe him.

'There's another one of those for that garage, skip,' DC Fenton said, passing the DS a receipt.

'Yeah, that's one of them. Good hit. Keep searching. I'll see what he has to say.' Lethridge went through to the living room where Lynn was with DI Pyle 'D'you get anything?' he inquired.

'No, nothing worth a toss,' Pyle said.

"Course there ain't nothing here,' Lynn repeated. 'This is all just aggravation for us.'

'There was another one of those.' The DS passed his governor the receipt. 'That's five we found.'

'What about this garage, Jack?'

Lynn knew he was in trouble, he knew it when they had found the first receipt. Why he had kept them he didn't know. However, he had to try. 'Don't know nothing about it, do I.'

'No. I guess that's why you got it in a bent name. I don't suppose you have the key either?' The blagger simply offered a hostile stare. 'Makes no difference. Get over there, Eric. Take a look. We'll be down the nick. You want to get your coat, Jack? Those cells get a bit cold.'

At the prospect of her husband being taken away, Mrs Lynn was unable to contain the anger that had been simmering inside her since the police burst into her house three hours before. The narrow entrance hall suddenly seemed very crowded with policemen, it was as though they were trying to oppress her. 'You fucking bastards,' she screamed, startling the CID. 'He's not going anywhere, you

269

filthy bastards – that's all you are filth. You bastards, I hope you rot; I hope you get cancer …'

DS Lethridge caught hold of the woman as she lashed out, and pushed her towards the kitchen. 'Shut up, for fucksake – go and look after your kids.'

Lynn intervened now. 'Don't you start!' he warned him.

'You fancy some?' Lethridge challenged. 'I reckon we could just about manage you, and your old lady.'

'Worrying the life out of innocent people,'s all you sods are good for …'

'You'd better tell her to calm down, or she'll be done for assault …' Pyle advised.

'About your fucking mark,' Dolly screamed. The two girls at the end of the hall were screaming.

Jack Lynn caught hold of his wife and held her. 'Come on, Dolly, be a bit sensible, love. It's all right. 'S misunderstanding, 's all. Come on, be a bit sensible.' Lynn embraced his wife and held her. He glanced along the hallway and saw Sandra and Carol still in their nightdresses, hanging round the kitchen door. Both were in tears. For a fleeting moment Lynn realized how he had failed his family and he regretted the life he led. At that moment he even managed to delude himself into thinking that if he had his time over again he would have had things very different.

The nondescript car that DS Lethridge and DC Humphries were in turned along the service road to the lock-up garage in Shoreditch that Jack Lynn rented in the name of Richard Cook and stopped. Lethridge didn't move from the rear of the car but considered the large Yale padlock on the door.

'You got something to do that lock with, Clive?' he said to the Squad driver.

'Yeah, I should think so, skip.'

All three men climbed out of the car. From among his tools in the boot, the driver removed a pinchbar, which he gave to Lethridge It took the DS only seconds to prise off the

270

padlock and raise the garage door. All three stood for a moment and looked inside, genuinely surprised.

'What a blinding result!' Lethridge said. 'Haven't we had it off. Haven't we just.'

In the garage was an armoury of blaggers' tools neatly laid out, all that Lynn had organized for the Catford blag. There were three sawn-off shotguns, cartridges, a handgun, hammers with handles drilled and looped for easy handling, axes, pinchbars, a bunch of about a hundred assorted car keys, liquid ammonia, teargas canisters, gloves, masks, and rope – for tying up victims.

'Nothing like being prepared, skip, is there,' DC Humphries said as they moved in to inspect the gear.

'Yeah, he must have been a boy scout. Fuck I!' He shook his head in amazement, feeling pleased with their result. 'We'd better have a photographer down here, and C3 – bit of luck there might be a few prints.' However, there wasn't much likelihood that Lynn would even attempt to say they had planted this lot.

True to form Lynn denied all knowledge of the contents of the garage – DS Lethridge went to see the owner of the garages to have him ID Lynn as Richard Cook. Lynn also denied all knowledge of the Gas Board blag. Pyle wasn't allowing either denial any ground.

"S not what we've got, Jack. You were there all right, doing that blagging with John Tully.' DC Jenkins was in the interview room at Romford nick with them.

'Shut up! I told you where I was Friday morning. I was in bed rumping my old lady, that's where I was.'

"S that right?' Pyle was adamant in his disbelief. 'What sort of alibi's that, for fucksake?'

'We could take a swab, guv,' Jenkins interjected drily. 'Check if the semen's three day's old.'

The two detectives were amused. Lynn didn't share their amusement, but had more sense than to retaliate. 'But that was where I was, I tell you.'

'I thought you'd come up with something better than that, Jack. I'm almost disappointed.'

'Sure, I know John Tully. But I ain't seen him in months,' Lynn lied.

'Well, don't worry about that. You're going to be seeing a lot of him over the next few months ...'

'Someone's been getting you right at it, sticking my name up ...'

'You think that's all there is to it, son? If that was the case, a couple of DCs would have popped round at a reasonable hour. You wouldn't have been picked up like this. Be a bit fucking sensible.'

'You definitely got the wrong fella this time,' Lynn said, pitching his words in a low, appealing tone. 'That blag wasn't down to me. I wasn't even near Romford.'

'What about the fifteen hundred sovs we found at your gaff?'

'That? Oh, that was just a bit of dough I had by me. For emergencies, like.' Lynn knew he had to try, but knew he wasn't making much headway when he saw the DI smile.

'Where d'you get it, Jack?'

'How d'you mean? It's mine, innit.'

'You had it tucked away all right,' Pyle allowed. 'So how'd you come by it?'

Feeling himself being driven into a corner, Lynn said. 'Just bits and pieces what get tucked away. 'S all.'

'Fuck I. I wish I could afford to put that sort of money aside. I'd say that came out of that Gas Board payroll. Wasn't a very bright place to hide it, was it. I thought most villains had bank accounts nowadays.'

'He probably wouldn't have had time to put it there, guv,' DC Jenkins pointed out. 'What with giving his old lady a rumping on Friday and the banks being shut on the weekend.'

'No, I s'pose not.' Pyle paused and considered Lynn. 'All right, Jack, stop fucking around now. Put your hands up to it.

Get yourself a bit of help.'

'I tell you, 'f I was involved, the first thing I'd've done was made you an offer.' It seemed like the most logical argument to Lynn.

'Don't prove a thing,' Pyle said emphatically. They went through it again. Finally Pyle said, 'Wasn't that just lucky for you that this celebrated bunk-up coincided with that blag.'

Lynn was getting angry. 'Lucky for you you mean. You got one in hand, and I'm the body – I saw the papers. They made right cunts of Old Bill, that little team, didn't they.'

'Nothing to do with me. We just got word it was down to you – simple as that. The evidence all points that way, Jack. You're going down for this one, son, without a shadow of a doubt. You're well overdue.'

The villain looked hard at the detective, knowing he really meant it. It wasn't often Jack Lynn acknowledged feeling afraid, but he felt a quake of fear deep inside him at that moment.

32

Having decided that Jack Lynn was the fourth man on the Gas
Board blag, DI Pyle intended making quite certain that there
was nothing left to chance on getting him convicted. Too
many villains got a result in court simply because too many
CID took their evidence for granted or were too arrogant
about the process, assuming that because they had nicked
someone the courts would endorse that move with a
conviction. That could no longer be relied on as a matter of
course. Certainly Fred Pyle wouldn't like to rely on it,
especially not with a swift 'un.

In the front office at Romford nick, DI Pyle approached
the duty sergeant's desk. Like most other policemen his basic
workload was paperwork. Other uniforms around the office
were dealing with the resulting paperwork from mainly traffic
offences. One was at the public desk taking details off a
civilian who was reporting his car stolen.

'Where was the clothing put that was recovered from the
Gas Board blag?' Pyle wanted to know. 'Has it gone off for
forensic examination yet?'

'No, sir,' the sergeant said. 'It's waiting to go up now. It's all
in the CID property store.' There would have been little point in
its going up sooner as the forensic labs only operated a nine-
to-five, five-day week.

'Could I have a look, skip?'

'Yes, of course, sir.' He removed from one of his desk
drawers a key with a chain and lead weight attached.

'I won't be walking off with that in my pocket,' Pyle said as
he took the key.

The large-property store was a small, windowless room on
the ground floor. Goods, from lead off church roofs to girlie

274

magazines, were stacked around the place, a bicycle, a lawnmower, some tins of paint, all stuff which had to be held onto by the police until the case in which it was involved had been dealt with by the court and it could finally be returned to its rightful owner.

Unlocking the store, Fred Pyle stepped inside and shut the door. He found the pile of clothing tied in a neat bundle, each item tagged with an exhibit label. The leather flying helmet was the only item he was interested in at this stage. Opening the seal and easing the hat from the bundle, he examined the inside of it; then removing an envelope containing Lynn's comb from his pocket, he pulled some hairs from it and placed them inside the helmet, crumpling the hat to work them into the material. He then stuffed the hat back into the bundle, reset the seal and went out, switching off the light.

'Morning, Frank,' Pyle said to DI Kenley as he stepped into the latter's office on the first floor.

'I hear you nicked the fourth blagger,' Kenley said, evidently impressed. 'How does he look?'

'He don't look bad at all. Could you see your lad downstairs about getting another parade set up?' He could have spoken to the station inspector himself, but it was policy to go through the local DI.

''Course. When were you thinking?'

'This afternoon'll do it – I'm easy.' He had a couple of other things to do before then. One was to get the banknotes found at Lynn's place checked at the security firm's office where the Gas Board payroll was made up – there was just a chance. Also he had to see Clifford Harding who he could now use in helping him convict Lynn.

There probably wasn't anyone anywhere in the entire country working for the banks, security firms or money-in-transit offices who wouldn't co-operate with the police, unless they were investigating ramps by the staff. The reason they were so co-operative was because they knew that without the police they couldn't function as relatively free from worry over potential assault as they did.

The manager of the security office in Romford where the Gas Board payroll was made up was no exception. He was fat-jowled, and flecked with dandruff; he had an obsequious manner and strove to ingratiate himself with Pyle when the latter was shown into his office. Pyle knew he was a million to get a result here, regardless of whether the notes he had taken from Lynn were part of the payroll. The manager said how they'd co-operate in any way they could when the DI stated what he wanted, went on to express what a fine job he thought the police were doing, how splendid it was that they had caught the robbers so quickly. Pyle let him say his piece, he had time for all this if it meant his getting a result; at one point he thought the man must have been at it himself.

'It's a simple matter, what you ask, inspector,' the manager said, glancing through the pile of banknotes Pyle had handed him. 'I'm sure the cashier who made up the payroll will easily be able to identify these.'

The manager accepted that the money was part of the payroll simply because the DI had told him so, and that was how he put it to the cashier when he called her into his office.

'You can identify that they're part of the payroll made up by yourself, Miss Henderson? Can you not?' The manager waited for the young cashier to consider further as she thumbed through the notes. 'They each have their own individual way of marking notes,' he explained to Pyle. 'The same as tellers in banks do.'

Finally the young woman looked up from her task, looked at the manager, then at Pyle and said, 'Yes, I would say these were from that payroll, sir. Several of the notes seem to have my mark on them.'

Pyle nodded. This firm was a million to support the status quo; they didn't want villains at liberty to do blaggings. He would take a short statement, have the cashier sign an exhibits label, then move on to tie up his next witness.

Pyle didn't visit Clifford Harding on his own, but took two

detectives from his squad with him. He wanted the villain in the right frame of mind to co-operate, and Pyle knew this visit would achieve just that.

Pyle waited in the blue Ford Cortina outside Harding's house in Holloway while the two DCs brought him out. One of the detectives opened the door for him and climbed in the back after him. The other went in the front next to the driver. Harding's protests ceased briefly on encountering Pyle. But started again when he got over the surprise.

'What the fuck's going on, guv? I mean, what the fuck's it all about? I mean, I'm getting more pulls than enough.' Harding was visibly distressed. The two detectives claiming him had had the right effect.

'Well, your name keeps coming up, Clifford. Whenever we have a look at anything, there's your name ...'

'Leave it out. I mean, what chance would I have? I keep getting pulled. I thought I was s'posed to have a deal. I give you a bit of help, you give me a bit.'

Pyle nodded slowly. 'That's what I want, son. A bit of help. Frank,' he said to his driver.

The car started away.

The suspect was taken to the local nick, and put in an interview room. Pyle followed him in, shutting the door. Having got Harding to his present agitated state the other two detectives weren't needed.

'Right,' Pyle said decisively, 'What I want from you is a nice statement saying how your pal Jack Lynn put that blag at Romford Gas Board up to you. Okay?'

'Fuck I!' Harding exclaimed, not knowing how else to react. He knew the DI would want something, but he hadn't been prepared for that.

'You want to pull yourself clear of that bit of trouble of your own, don't you? This does it.' Pyle had kept him on the hook for a number of weeks over a firearms charge against him that he had been promising to drop in return for the right sort of help.

Despite the attractiveness of the promise, which he wanted to believe would be fulfilled, Harding hesitated, finding the prospect sickening. The thought of sacrificing another villain's liberty for his own wasn't so bad, but the move would give the filth even greater power over him. 'What have I got to say?'

'Just tell it like it happened,' Pyle explained. 'How he phoned you and you had a meet and he put this blag to you.' Pyle watched him closely. 'Sit down, son. Make yourself comfortable.' He laid a sheaf of statement papers he had fetched in on the small table and uncapped his pen.

Harding remained standing. 'What about that bit of trouble of mine, guv? I mean, is it gonna be dropped out? You know, dropped right out?'

'It will be, Cliff. Like you'd never even seen that gun; like you weren't even thinking of making one with it.' Pyle sounded quite convincing, and he pressed his point. 'I tell you, you give the right sort of statement, help me nick the other fella, it'll be like you never even had any form, son.'

Little by little Harding was reassured. He wanted to believe it. He sat at the table and picked up the pen. 'But the thing is,' he said suddenly, 'What's going to happen if it comes on top. I won't be able to do nothing, will I.'

'How do you mean?' Pyle asked, guessing what he was saying.

'Well, I don't know. I mean, I won't have to go up in court and stick that up? I mean, I can't do that, can I. That'd not only make me a grass – I'm fitting one, in' I?'

'You won't have to go into the box to give evidence,' Pyle smoothly reassured him. 'We're entitled to protect our sources of information – that's standard. Stand on what I tell you.'

Harding looked at the detective, trying to read something to the contrary in his expressionless face. Finally he nodded. 'You'd better tell me what to write.'

'First you want your full name, address and a declaration

that you're making the statement of your own free will without threat or favour.' There wasn't any trace of irony in his words as he watched Harding write.

There was a lot of confusion, and as a result contradiction, from the witnesses who had come in for the first identity parades. Pyle was determined there shouldn't be the same confusion when Lynn was put up. From their statements the DI knew who was likely to prove the most valuable witness, and could see just how clear or confused they might have been; the uncertainty of others he had seen for himself in the muster room during the time he had stayed in as an observer. The security man who had been well enough to attend the earlier parades had meant well but had only thought he had a clear impression in his mind's eye. The other guard, James Lawrence, who had been too badly beaten to attend then, would have been no better, Pyle was sure. However, the DI would make certain of both now.

Avoiding Lynn's solicitor, who was at Romford station reluctantly looking after Lynn's interests – Mrs Lynn had simply got this man out of the phone book – Pyle caught each of the two security guards separately and had a quiet word with them in an interview room.

'You won't have any trouble picking out the fourth man, Mr Mason,' Pyle said to the guard, who was now less bandaged with his injuries than before. 'He was the one in the flying helmet; dark, wavy hair, slightly receding.' Lynn would be seen without a hat on.

'It's surprising how difficult it is, inspector,' Mason said, as though unaware that the DI was helping him. 'Until you walk down that line you think you have a crystal clear picture in your mind.'

'Yes, I know it's difficult. But you won't make any mistake with this one. Remember his slightly crooked nose? He was a bit of a fighter – maybe he got a whack on the last blag before this one.'

The guard looked at the detective for a moment. 'I'll say I

remember him all right.'

Pyle grimaced reassuringly. He knew he could rely on this man.

The DI primed two other witnesses in the same way, deciding not to take a chance on any more. These three would be enough to help get Lynn put away, especially with the supportive evidence he would have. He didn't wait around through the whole of the ID parade, but stayed long enough for his three witnesses to pick Lynn out. He was satisfied.

DCI Simmons seemed satisfied too when he got the reports the following day.

'Those witnesses ID'ing him like that, just about stitches him up,' Pyle said in the DCI's office at the Yard. 'I'd say he was a stoneginger.'

'I'd say so. Especially with what was found in his lock-up. Was the forensic report in yet?'

'Not yet. I'll chase them up. What about the charges for all that stuff in the garage? We putting them all to him?' Pyle wanted to know.

'Why not? It'll look good when it goes up. Conspiracy to rob; possessing prohibited weapons; no firearms certificate. Let's have everything in, Fred. What about those blags at Bromley and Wimbledon that were supposed to have been down to him?'

'I still reckon they were. But there's no evidence,' Pyle said.

'Pity. Nor any for Catford?'

'Only what we found in his lock-up. Unless you want to stick it up on the word of my grass?'

'No, not that much point, is there. We're not desperate. Though it wouldn't be a bad idea to check the possibility of tying him into any unsolved major blags now we've got him. We'll get a warrant and check his bank accounts, see if there are any heavy deposits about the right time.' He saw Pyle's doubtful expression. 'Silly as fucking goats, some of these villains, Fred. 'S worth a try. We'll put up all we can, let the DPP throw it out, 'he wants to.' He turned his attention to two fairly thick pink folders on the desk immediately in front of him. 'There are one or two discrepancies creeping into these statements, aren't there?'

'There won't be any concerning Lynn,' Pyle reassured him.

'No, but these others. Especially those given by the local police. What are they, a lot of fucking idiots over there? Don't they corroborate their evidence before committing it to paper?'

Pyle shrugged dismissively. 'Uniform branch.' he said. He resisted in every way he could the attempts by the hierarchy to integrate the CID and uniform branch. 'Think they'll make any difference, guv?'

'I wouldn't have thought so, Fred.' He gave the DI a knowing look.

Pyle simply nodded, accepting the prospect as fact.

33

They were fitting him and there was not a thing he could do about it, or nothing that seemed to make any difference – for denials were being put forward – and the situation was simultaneously oppressing and depressing and frustrating Jack Lynn. He was getting ready to explode, and someone was going to get hurt when he did. How he had checked his anger for so long he wasn't sure.

As he stood in the dock at Romford magistrates' court and listened to the disconnected, mumbled motions for getting him remanded, he felt sick; it was a despairing kind of nausea. There weren't many in court apart from himself and the magistrate, his clerk, officers of the court, police. DI Pyle was there, and so was Lynn's brief, but as far as the villain was concerned he was about as good as nothing. How had Dolly come to get that useless bastard? There were no reporters there, not even from the local press, or Lynn might have let them have it there and then about his fitting. The press figured they had better things to waste their time on, and one of the officers of the court would collect a few quid for ringing the local paper to tell them how the remand went. There was only one way it could go, Lynn knew that.

'Do you have any legal representation, Lynn?' the magistrate asked, peering over his half-moon glasses.

Lynn's solicitor popped up. 'Yes, your worship. I represent Mr Lynn.'

Popping up at the right time, doing the right thing, upsetting no one, that was all the brief was any good for, Lynn thought.

'How long a remand is being sought?'

DI Pyle stepped briskly into the witness-box. 'One week,

your worship.' That was as long as they could get at a time. 'But this is a matter where the Director of Public Prosecutions will be handling the case. It may be some weeks before he will be ready for committal proceedings. Which it is hoped will be by way of Section 1.' That would save everyone a lot of time.

'I take it there is an objection to bail?'

'Yes, sir.'

Lynn listened as the filth went through his objections: they were standard. Serious nature of charges, fear that he would go on the trot, fear of interfering with witnesses. Having gone through all that, the beak asked his brief if he was asking for bail, like there would be serious consideration given to the application. His brief didn't exactly make an impassioned case for bail, but he did try.

Finally the magistrate said. 'Very well. You're remanded for one week, in custody.'

'To the twelfth of December,' the clerk of the court put in.

Lynn felt like giving them some verbal as he was led out of the dock. He could have slagged them right off, but knew it would do little good, not then anyway. There would be a better opportunity later, when there was a jury to impress.

The remand was to Brixton prison. Lynn vaguely thought it might have been to Romford nick initially, while the filth questioned him about every unsolved blag that had gone off in London over the past two years. But he guessed Brixton was as convenient as Romford almost, if not more convenient to detectives from the Yard. About the only thing that could be said in Brixton's favour was that it was relatively warm in the winter, a fact which had far less to do with the heating system than the body temperatures of the densely packed inmates.

Although while on remand he kept all his options barring his liberty, Lynn was a potential category 'A' prisoner, so he was watched more closely than regular remands. He could have as many visits during the day as he wanted, in theory, but as none of these could be open visits, they had to be restricted, as with other potential category 'A' prisoners, to availability of officers to supervise them.

Dolly came down to see him every day, bringing him a change of clothes, as he was permitted to wear his own clothes; food parcels, as he could have all his own meals sent in, and tobacco to trade or give to others inside, as money wasn't permitted.

His brief, Ronald Watson came down to Brixton to see him. The visit didn't endear the man to Lynn any more; not even out of gratitude for having anyone at all to visit him. Quite the reverse, in fact. It only confirmed him in his opinion that the solicitor was an utter prick.

Since his last stay in Brixton, Lynn found little had changed. The cells were more crowded, everyone was threed up, some even four to a cell. There were odd bits built into and around the wings, mainly for greater security, rather than anyone's comfort. But something that had changed were the visiting rooms for solicitors and police. These were now housed in a relatively new building in the courtyard. There were eight rooms, each measuring some ten feet by eight feet on the first floor of the building, with a couple of rooms for the screws. The prisoners were brought in through a double locking security hatch at one end of the building, visitors, briefs, CID or whoever came in through a similar hatch via the metal stairway to the courtyard at the opposite end.

Ronald Watson sat at the table in number two visiting room with his briefcase open before him. He was a neat, precise member of the legal profession who obsessively avoided infringing the rules. He was in his late forties. He was on edge now, mainly on account of what he considered Lynn's unreasonable demands. His main preoccupation currently was with placing his pen in precise symmetry to his large, unwritten-upon briefpad, while Lynn paced around the room.

With difficulty the solicitor said, 'In view of the vast amount of evidence the police seem to have against you, Mr Lynn, I think your best course might be to plead guilty ...'

Lynn wheeled on him before he had a chance to finish. 'You

got to be fucking kidding, pal, haven't you. What the fuck is all that I been telling you? The cunts are fitting me.'

'We could seek to get the charges reduced for a guilty plea.'

'The cunts are fitting me,' Lynn repeated like he was talking to an imbecile.

'I don't think that attitude is going to help very much,' the solicitor said.

'That attitude, for fucksake! It's getting near Christmas and I'm stuck in this pisshole. How do you expect me to react? I want to be out where I'm entitled to be. I want you to go back to court, get me bail. So I can spend Christmas with m' family. Blank the magistrate, go into a judge.'

'That's absolutely impossible, I can assure you, Mr Lynn. The court wouldn't hear of it.'

'I thought you was s'posed to be working for me, pal.'

'I am trying to advise you what is practical. I've been around courts long enough.'

'I think you must be working for the filth, just 'cos you're getting paid outta Legal Aid ...'

'That's absolute nonsense,' the brief protested.

'About all you've done for me so far is filled out the Legal Aid form, and I could have done that. What about what I told you?' Lynn wanted to know, glaring across the table at the solicitor. 'You going to stick it up in court that I was fitted?'

Watson was decidedly uncertain about this, and avoided the felon's look. He realigned his pen. 'I'll discuss all that you've told me with counsel when I brief him. But I can't say that it's a very sound basis for a defence.'

'Oh, that's fucking t'rific, innit,' Lynn said in dismay. 'So what d'you reckon? I gotta take my fitting? Not only that, I gotta go and fucking well plead to it?'

Reluctantly the solicitor raised his eyes to meet Lynn's. 'If you have some evidence against the arresting officer, then we can make an official complaint against him to CIB2.'

Lynn looked at the brief in amazement. Never in a hundred years would he have any evidence likely to satisfy this man.

'You're about as good as fuckall. You'd better fuck off, you cunt, go on fuck off, 'fore I break your arms – I'll find someone else.'

Anger spread through him rapidly, he only just stopped short of hitting the solicitor, and probably would have done so had the screw not made a timely appearance – so much for the rooms being soundproof.

Other visits for potential category 'A' prisoners weren't so convenient as those for briefs and the police, there was no room for relatively private conversation, no opportunity for physical contact. Jack Lynn ached with the need for it when he saw his wife behind the glass screen in one of the cubicles of the visiting area. She was already seated when they brought him in. The screw who led him in was a reasonable sort of guy, one of those who would do anything for a couple of quid, but as much as he wanted the earner Lynn offered him, there was nothing he could do to get him together with his old lady. Visits were controlled by the gate officers who phoned through and told him where to take the prisoner.

Lynn sat on his side of the glass partition and put his hands on the shelf in front of him. His knuckles showed tense and white. He felt tense. He didn't attempt to speak for a few moments. He wondered what was going through Dolly's mind; she looked tired, he guessed she probably was, but he wouldn't speak about it, he was almost afraid to speak about it in case she came to the conclusion she had had enough, couldn't face the prospect of his going away for another ten or fifteen years. He knew there was a good chance, but he didn't want her arriving at that conclusion.

'How are you, Jack?' she asked, reaching out and putting her hand on the cold glass that separated them. There were microphones in the side panels which made it possible for them to talk to each other without shouting.

'I'm okay.' He sounded far from it. 'How are the girls?' he wanted to know.

'Asking when you're coming home. That Sandra doesn't stop asking. Runs home from school she does, expecting to find you home ...' Her words trailed off. She realized what they were doing to him. There was a silence for a few moments. 'There's some clean clothes and a bit of food in the parcel,' she said. Then unable to stop herself: 'How long's it look like being, Jack?'

'Too fucking long,' he said, with anger rising. He knew it was no good getting angry with Dolly, it would upset her. But he couldn't prevent the words coming out as they did.

'What did that brief say about bail?'

'That cunt! He's been sacked. I had no fucking chance with him. I should think the filth must have straightened him. He reckoned I ought to take my fitting like a man, plead guilty.'

'The rotten bastards,' she said, vehemence spiking her words. 'I mean, you wouldn't mind so much if it was down to you. But when you know you didn't do it. Makes my blood boil – I'd like to see those wicked sods dead. They ought to get cancer, that's what they deserve.'

'Oh, I ought to know better than to waste my time with briefs on Legal Aid. I mean, they're paying him, aren't they; so why shouldn't he tell me just to plead to it.'

'What are you going to do, Jack?' her expression was etched with concern. She felt culpable for having landed her husband with such an indifferent solicitor.

'Find another one. One who's gonna do a bit for me.'

'Why are they doing it, Jack? Why you?' She had been asking herself that ever since her husband's arrest. She knew the answer but needed it putting into words.

'It's my turn. That's what the filth said when I tried to have a deal with him. I was well overdue's what he said. What chance?' he concluded in disgust.

'Jack?' Dolly said in a calmer tone. 'You didn't do nothing, did you? You weren't at it?' He had told her he wasn't and she believed him, but she had to be absolutely sure. It wouldn't have mattered if he had been – even though he had assured her he was going to quit – just so long as she knew.

"Course I wasn't. You know where I was, don't you.'

'They won't put you away. They can't.' She said this with quiet confidence, as though having, despite herself, some implicit belief in justice and truth winning out simply because it was just and true.

'There'll be a lot of aggro 'they do. I tell you, I'll wind up topping someone ...'

'They won't, Jack,' she said trying to calm him. 'What'll I tell the girls?'

'I dunno. Tell 'em ... tell 'em I send my love. I'll see 'em soon.' He rubbed his forehead in an agitated fashion, as if going through the process of thinking. 'I'm gonna have to get myself another brief, if I'm gonna have any chance. I gotta get one working for me. How much you got tucked away in the post office, Dolly?'

'I don't know. About two thousand I think. Very near, anyway.'

'A fella in here told me about a brief, a right good 'un. Gladwell. Go and see him. Alex Gladwell. Got a firm over King's Cross way. Go and see him, see if he'll do a bit for me – he's s'posed to be a bit near the mark.'

'What if he can't take your case ...?'

'Well, I don't fucking know,' he snapped, not having considered the possibility. He studied his wife for a moment, realizing she was getting upset, knowing she was having as hard a time as him. It was always the wives who did the time, the husbands were merely locked up. 'I'm sorry, love,' he said calmly. 'What a way to top up just before Christmas, I don't know. Go and see Gladwell, love. See if he'll have some of it. I don't know if what you've got tucked away is enough. But Tommy's holding a few quid for me, so there shouldn't be no problem. Tell him that it won't be down to Legal Aid. It should be all right, Dolly. You see.'

There was an awkward pause. Dolly wasn't entirely reassured. She wanted to believe it would be all right.

'I could use a little taste in here, Doll,' he said with a faint smile now.

His wife didn't know how to respond. 'Jack,' she said. It was almost censuring.

'Yeah, they'd probably rush in and fit me while I was at it.' He brushed his index finger against the glass like he was brushing her cheek. 'I was told this guy Gladwell is well bent. He might even be able to go and arrange bail for me so I'm out for Christmas. Tell the girls – it'll be all right, you see.'

Lynn was becoming decidedly more cheerful, almost like he believed it was possible.

However, he knew he shouldn't rely entirely on his brief, he would have to try and do a bit himself, about getting a result. That meant having another go at Tully and his mates, see if he couldn't persuade them to give him an out.

'How come they fitted you like they did, Jack?' Tully asked, as though the right answer would free him entirely of any responsibility in the matter.

Lynn had gone visiting within the prison and was in the cell in which Tully was threed up with two other potential category 'A' prisoners. Neither were present. The cell held all the home comforts that he could afford, all of which helped cushion the impact of what could be the start of a long prison sentence. However, none of those comforts could make them forget where they were, what the prospects were. Noises echoed through the labyrinth of cells and corridors of Brixton with a curious sense of unreality for most of the inmates, mainly because they were on remand. Cell doors and gates banged; prisoners called to one another; the prison officers' protests were feeble, for too many of them were taking too many earners off prisoners for them to conduct themselves as effectively and uncompromisingly as warders in other prisons tended to.

Lynn considered Tully where he lay on his bunk and wondered if he was having a go at him. 'I dunno. They've gone and booked me for the fourth man on that little team.' As a matter of prudence he wouldn't mention whose team it was in case someone was listening. Even though John Tully wasn't leaping to help him, he wouldn't actively seek to put Tully in trouble. 'Maybe someone just stuck me up.'

"S not just that, though, is it?' Tully said, still trying to mitigate his own part. 'Look at all the other stuff they done you for.'

'They want me put away, 's what it's all about. The thing is, they ain't got fuck all without that one at Romford.' Lynn believed that was an accurate assessment of the case.

'A right get up,' Tully conceded.

'I mean, I know who that was down to, John. And you definitely know it wasn't down to me, right?'

'Oh, no doubt about that at all.'

'Well, the thing is, if they nick the fourth man on that little team, then they ain't got no case, have they?'

'I wouldn't have thought so,' Tully said obligingly. 'But I don't suppose they're even trying now.'

'No, 'course they ain't. But what's the chances, d'you think, John?'

'I dunno. I mean, I wish I could help you out, but I can't, can I. I mean, there's no way I can help you out without putting myself in it. I mean, I'm not pleading to it. Nor are the other two. And I don't suppose the other fella's gonna put himself on offer, not with his old lady being pregnant an' all.' He didn't know if Philip Hayes's wife was pregnant, but it seemed not an unreasonable line to take. 'I'm sorry, Jack. I'd like to help you out, but I can't, can I. Sorry,' he concluded.

Lynn remained standing by the closed cell door for a long while. Finally he nodded. He was sorry too, very sorry.

34

The sense of purpose and positiveness that Alex Gladwell gave off in the legal visiting room restored some confidence to Lynn and made him think he was going to get a result, and not only that, but one that would exact a high toll on those fitting him.

Alex Gladwell was a neat, round figure in his chalk-stripe suit, and to his way of thinking every inch a member of the legal profession. He was only in his late twenties and wore a wispy moustache as if trying to disguise the fact. His apparent youth surprised Lynn, even though his wife had told him he was young. The villain hadn't expected him to be this young. He had the appearance of being efficient, not missing a single point in Lynn's story. He looked slowly over the notes he had taken, while Lynn waited a little anxiously. The reason for his unease was the possibility that this solicitor might not believe him.

Looking up suddenly, Gladwell said, 'It's all very interesting what you've told me, Jack, and, as far as I'm concerned, all within the realms of possibility. But do you honestly expect to go up with that story, and not only have the court believe it, but actively support you by acquitting you? Is that what you expect?'

'But it's the truth what I told you,' Lynn said urgently, like he believed Gladwell was his last hope. 'I am being fitted by the filth.'

'But do you expect to go to the Old Bailey and have the court support you in that contention? That's what I'm asking.'

Although uncertain what he was driving at, Lynn said, 'Well, 'course not. I mean, that's part of the fucking system, innit. It's always favoured them. They don't wanna believe for a moment that Old Bill's at it or fitting people. Or if they know it they never fucking well admit to it, do they.'

Gladwell nodded. 'What we have to do, Jack, is make them accept that fact. Make them acknowledge that the police are as corrupt as you and I know them to be. That they do fit people up, that they are fitting you. Easier said than done, especially as we don't have much going for us. Your record for one; and the other three defendants. None of them is prepared to help put you in the clear.'

'They won't do that,' Lynn confirmed. 'Means sticking up the other man, dun' it.'

'Then we need someone to put your case in court. Someone who knows what he's about, and is prepared to accept that the police get up to the sort of things we know they get up to. Someone who isn't simply going to support the status quo.' He hesitated and looked at the prisoner. 'The only thing is, Jack, the man I have in mind won't come cheap. In fact he won't take the brief on Legal Aid alone. But he would be worth every penny he gets, I'm sure.'

'Well, the thing is my liberty's at stake.'

'Your wife said she had about two thousand pounds when she came to see me. She also told me you had access to some other money, though.'

'M' brother-in-law's holding a few quid for me.'

'We might need it. What I'll do is offer counsel two thousand pounds the other way to take the brief. I'm sure we can find an area for talking around that price.'

The solicitor explained how bunging top class QCs, who wouldn't normally take cases on Legal Aid, unless likely to prove very spectacular or newsworthy, was regular practice. It sounded reasonable to Lynn, who had no faith in the Legal Aid system, and he had heard before of briefs taking earners, that was why he had told his wife to mention the fact that he had money available to Gladwell. All such payments were tax free so doubled or trebled their value to the barristers.

'Is it stolen money?' Gladwell asked casually. Lynn didn't

reply. 'If you expect me to act for you to your best advantage, then you have to be straight with me. I don't really care very much one way or the other. I get a living by not passing moral judgement on my clients.'

'Well, the thing is, Mr Gladwell, I been getting a living from villainy for a long time.'

'That's all right, provided we don't allow the court to get that impression. What about the fifteen hundred the police found at your place?'

'It didn't come from where they said it came from.'

'You're certain of that, are you?'

'I told you, didn't I. I wasn't on that blag.'

'If you're sure that's fine. But the police are certain to claim that's where it came from. They might even come up with some evidence to support that claim.'

'There's nothing I can do about that, is there?'

'No way you can show a legitimate source of income?' He watched Lynn think about the question, then shake his head. 'Pity.'

'I s'pose I could stick down mini-cabbing.'

'Do you actually do any?' Gladwell wanted to know.

'Now and again, for m' brother-in-law, Tommy Jones.'

'Would he go into the witness-box and say that, do you think? Perjure himself if necessary?'

'Tommy? He's as good as gold.'

Gladwell made a note of the name. 'Has your wife any criminal record?'

'Leave off! Dolly? 'Course she ain't. What d'you think she is?'

'It's very important to establish that fact, especially as she's your only alibi for the time of the robbery. Did she know how you got your living?'

Lynn shrugged. 'She was always rucking me to quit.'

'She knew then.' He made a note. 'What about those other charges, Jack?' He referred to the sheaf of white copies of the written charges. 'Conspiracy to rob Catford Tote? Any foundation at all?'

Again Lynn hesitated.

'What's the problem, Jack? Don't you trust me?'

Lynn shrugged, embarrassed about answering. 'I mean, I ain't had no dealings with you before, have I.'

'Equally, I don't know you. That's what the purpose of this is. If you don't trust me I can't do my best for you. Not if I'm only half informed, and almost certain I'm going to make a fool of myself when briefing counsel.' He waited, shrewdly regarding the villain.

With a reluctant nod, Lynn told him about Catford and how they believed they were grassed. The solicitor leaped on that, saw the likely prospect of the police trying to protect their informer as a useful lever. He wanted to know also about the raids at Bromley and Wimbledon that Lynn had been charged with. Again reluctantly Lynn told him they were down to him, but that he had been well clear.

'So unless the police have suddenly come up with some dramatic new evidence, which I doubt, it looks like they've simply thrown these things in for good measure. The idea probably being to overwhelm the court with your apparent criminality. That's good,' he said to himself, and laid his two index fingers together across his cupid lips in a thoughtful pose. 'If we could get those charges dropped out, or at least have the police soft pedal them ... I'll arrange for a meeting with the CID and see if we can't do some business for you.'

'Do business with them?' Lynn said, slightly outraged. 'The cunts are fitting me!'

'A fact of life, Jack,' the young brief calmly informed him. 'They might give you a cheap rate as a result. But possibly they want you away more.'

'That's what they fucking said – I was well overdue.'

Gladwell nodded. 'I know Inspector Pyle. He's accessible, to say the least. Though from what you tell me I doubt that he'll do you too many favours. Are you prepared to spend, what, say a thousand pounds?'

The thought of having to go into the filth was never of any concern to Lynn, but in these circumstances it irked him. 'Is that what bunging him comes to?' he said grudgingly.

'It could well do.'

'What if he ain't having any of it?' Lynn asked.

'Then we'll have to try for another tactical advantage. We'll make a formal complaint against him to CIB2 for conspiracy to pervert the course of justice. In fact, I think we'll make a complaint anyway. And see what we can dig up on his confederates. They find that shoe pinches rather painfully on their feet.'

A vein of excitement started through Lynn by the close of their meeting, whereas before he saw little hope. It was the best day's work he ever did getting this brief to act for him, he concluded.

'While you're going into the filth,' he said, watching the young man collect up his notes. 'What's the chance of getting me bail over Christmas. I mean, I could bung him a few quid. What d'you think, Mr Gladwell?'

'Not good, I'd say. I'll certainly put it to him. What's it worth to you? Five hundred?'

'I think so. Yeah, that'd be all right.'

'I'll see him. But don't count on it, Jack. He's almost certain to want to keep hold of you now he has you.'

Lynn nodded, accepting that from this solicitor.

'It would be nice to have Christmas with m' family. Know what I mean.'

Gladwell considered the man before him. 'I'll see what he says.'

The Feathers in the Broadway, just along the street from the back entrance of the Yard, was as convenient for Gladwell as it was for DI Pyle. That was where they agreed to meet when the solicitor phoned him.

Gladwell bought two large scotches and took them to the table where Pyle was sitting, tucked away in a recess. There was no one in the bar who either felt they needed to avoid. The brief sat and watched the older man as he raised his glass.

'Good health, Alex.' Pyle was friendly enough. There was no reason for him not to be, knowing there was no way he could lose by this meeting.

Gladwell continued to look at him. 'What are the chances of our getting together on this, Fred? Any chance, is there?'

'I wouldn't have thought so – I'd like to have helped you out . . .' He hesitated, as though he was in a position to help and needed the right inducement.

'He wasn't looking for all the charges dropped. Just some of them. So he goes up with no lesser advantage than his three co-defendants.'

"S not up to me any more, Alex, is it' He sipped his scotch. 'You representing the other three?'

'Just Lynn. You're not expecting a conviction on the conspiracy and bank robbery charges.'

"S not a problem. The evidence is all there.'

'Is it?' Gladwell said with interest.

Pyle smiled. 'You're a cunning bastard. Aren't you just.'

He was neither expecting nor trying to dupe Pyle like that. He said, 'It's worth a thousand pounds to you, if you could help.'

'I'd like to, I really would. That sort of dough would come in handy. I promised to take the wife and kids on a winter holiday after Christmas.'

'It would be perfectly safe, Fred. I'd make sure of that,' the solicitor assured him.

'I wouldn't be worried on that account. It just can't be done the way you want it. It's down to the DPP.' He drank some scotch and thought about the problem. 'Why don't you go into the DPP's office? 'Spect they could use a nice few quid same as anyone else. There's a deputy there called Rawlings. Well bent he is.' He set his glass on the table and slowly twisted it round by the base. 'Alternatively I tell you what I might be able to do. I could have a word about getting those other charges dropped out if he'll plead to the Romford blag.'

Gladwell shook his head. 'He's claiming he's being fitted. He's not taking it kindly.'

'It happens, Alex,' Pyle said, as if the matter was of little consequence. He saw the question posed in Gladwell's face. 'Not this time. There was no need. I've too much evidence to fuck around like that. About a dozen eyewitnesses for a start.'

'Police ...?'

'Some,' Pyle said. 'Nice bit of forensic, too. He'll go all right, even with you as his brief. Tell him to do himself a favour, plead to it, get himself a reasonable sentence.'

'That would make it too easy for you, Fred.' Gladwell smiled confidently, even though the meeting wasn't going as he hoped it would. 'I briefed Horace Macmillan as counsel today.'

Pyle allowed himself to be impressed. 'Nice to know Lynn's got that sort of dough.'

'There's no sort of problem in that area,' Gladwell said, still hoping to do business.

Pyle shook his head conclusively. 'The wife and kids'll probably have to make do with Butlin's.' There was nothing to stop him taking their money for a promise, as he had done with other villains in other circumstances, but he decided it was too risky here.

They talked generally about the case through another drink; then discussed the possibility of bail for over Christmas, but this the DI thought a nonstarter. Finally Gladwell told him about the complaint they were making to CIB2.

Pyle considered that for a moment. Such moves were almost standard and never surprising. 'I won't lose sleep over that, Alex. Good luck, anyway.' He finished his drink in one swallow.

35

Because the investigation wasn't his, DI Kenley hadn't been privy to all the information and all that had gone on in the case. But he knew enough to know that the evidence that had just been brought up to the CID would possibly cause a few problems, if not some serious doubts as to the involvement of one of the Gas Board blaggers. What had been handed to him was the second case that had gone missing with half the Gas Board's payroll after the chase. One of the uniform branch on patrol in the area had had a wander around the group of Welfare buildings in Greenborough Road when he had come across the case in a pile of leaves. Kenley suspected that the uniform had gone in for a leak or a smoke, rather than any sort of follow-up to the investigation. That would mean another ballocking from the brass if they weren't careful, Kenley reflected, as that whole area was supposed to have been thoroughly searched. However, that was nothing to the problem the find would present Fred Pyle, for Kenley knew the Squad DI had supposedly recovered part of the missing half of the payroll from another source, from one of the suspects.

He dialled DI Pyle's number at the Yard, but it wasn't Pyle that answered. He asked for Pyle and gave his own name. While he waited for the DI to come to the phone, he looked out of his office, across to the CID room. There were a couple of detectives down that end of the room, both within earshot; Kenley stepped around his desk and closed the door.

'Fred …' he said into the phone. 'Yeah. Oh, not so bad. Yourself?' The prelusive niceties over, Kenley said, 'Bit of a problem's come up, I think. Well, I dunno, maybe it's a problem.' He told him about the policeman finding the case.

'Is it all there, Frank?' Pyle asked calmly, not a bit surprised.

'Every penny of it. All the wage envelopes intact.' He hesitated. 'Puts you in the shit with that other bit you found at his place, doesn't it?'

'It could do, son. But I'd say that money we found at his place was part of it all right.'

'How could it be ...?' Kenley began, but stopped abruptly, realizing what he was being told.

'The wages clerk at the security office ID'd it. No problem.'

'Well, what d'you think about this? I mean, what d'you want doing about it?'

Fred Pyle didn't need to think about that. 'Stick it down in the rear of the Charge Book and lock it away for now, I should,' he told him. 'I'll have a word with my governor, see what he thinks.'

Before going along to see the DCI, Pyle could have almost guaranteed what his reaction would be. He was no more interested in the find than he was himself. It wasn't really significant, not now they had the money found in Lynn's possession ID'd as part of the payroll. DCI Simmons's main interest in this find was how it added up with other things they now had in hand.

'There are various pieces of contradictory evidence still coming to light, Fred,' Simmons said, leaning back from his desk. 'The forensic report on the blood samples wasn't very helpful.' Although the report didn't rule out the possibility of the four suspects, the sample found in two of the stolen cars from cuts received from the jumping in and out of cars during the chase matched the blood of two of the villains, who were in the most common group, but they had no cuts on them that the police had found.

Pyle shrugged. "'S not that important. Just leave it out at their trial. There's plenty of other stuff.' Although some of the witnesses' testimony was confused and contradictory, Pyle knew that if you had enough not-sures the jury tended to come to the conclusion that it was a yes. 'What about this money thing? Will you put it up to the DPP?'

'I s'pose I'd better, just to cover ourselves. But I don't think they'll be too interested, Fred. They're keen down there to go ahead and get convictions for all four. Especially now they're all committed for trial. You start having second thoughts about one, begins to make the others look iffy. Whatever way you book it, that money you found at Lynn's place has to be bent. We'll get a result all right, Fred. Don't worry about it.'

Pyle was far from worried about the prospect.

However, that wasn't the case with DS Lethridge.

"S all right for Tony Simmons to say that, Fred,' DS Lethridge moaned, standing supporting a large scotch in the corner of the Tank on the ground floor of the Yard. 'He ain't putting himself on offer, or the one with a fucking complaint against him, is he.' Lethridge had also been named in the complaint that arose out of Lynn's arrest.

'I should worry about that,' Pyle said reassuringly. 'You'll have a lot more of those before you draw your pension, Eric.' He finished his drink.

'This fucking rate I can't see me drawing it. It's beginning to look like a right swift 'un.'

'I wouldn't have thought so. The DPP's office wouldn't fancy it so much, 'it did. There won't be any problems, we get it on in front of the right judge. Someone like Quigley'll be handy. He won't tolerate any suggestions of a fit up, no matter how swift it looks. He knows the police don't do those sort of things.' No suggestion of a smile touched Pyle's face as he said this. 'The chief's having a word with someone in the DPP's office, see if they can't have a word with the Clerk of the Lists, make sure the case gets in front of Quigley. 'S as easy as that, Eric.'

It was. Sometimes judges themselves made sure they tried certain cases; it was even easier for them. But however a defendant came to appear before a certain judge, one thing was certain, if it was arrived at by design, the chances were that it would in no way benefit the defendant.

36

Since finally parting with three and a half grand to bung Horace Macmillan for taking his case, Jack Lynn had seen the silk only twice in the seven months he had been on remand. He had seen the QC's pupil a few times and the solicitor any number of times. But he couldn't say it all added up to any great surge of confidence that their infrequent attendance gave him. He even wondered if the advice they had given him over the committal proceedings hadn't been wrong. Whenever he had gone for trial before it was always after full committal proceedings, when everything Old Bill had was put up and challenged, and a chuck was looked for at the end. Now, having been committed by means of a Section 1, nothing was challenged. Both defence and prosecution were like old school chums meeting up together for no purpose other than to have a chat. The truncated process didn't even get him up the steps any quicker as he imagined it would.

Lynn was in one of the cells below the Old Bailey courts on his own. Normally you waited in a cell with all the other defendants you were going up with, but Mr Gladwell had arranged for him to be on his own as the silk wanted a word with him before he went into court. Jack Lynn, dressed in a dark, conservative suit, collar and tie sat waiting on the single bench bed in the cell. His expression was thoughtful, his mood reflective as he considered the past seven months, the holidays and birthdays he had missed with his family. The girls knew where he was, having been to see him in Brixton, but he wasn't sure if they understood. Lynn's reflective mood was broken by the sound of the lock turning.

The door of the small white-tiled cell, with its graffiti-scarred walls, opened and Horace Macmillan stooped through the low doorway, followed by Gladwell. The silk was tall, strutting, arrogant; he had a polished pink face and loud-voiced confidence. His manner was expansive and he seemed to dwarf his instructing solicitor.

'Morning,' he said, adjusting his gown. 'How are you feeling? Did you get a good breakfast?'

'Right fucking slop, innit,' Lynn put in quickly.

The barrister wasn't really interested in his opinion of the culinary expertise of the prison service, or in having his questions answered for that matter. 'We've some good news and some bad news I'm afraid, Mr Lynn. The good news is that we've managed to get some dirt on the police involved in the case, quite a bit. Or rather Mr Gladwell has. The sort of stuff that if we get away with bringing it up will tend to damn them in the jury's eyes. Certainly it will go a long way to diminishing their credibility.' He paused briefly. 'However, the bad news is that the case is set down on the list before Mr Justice Quigley.'

'Fucking hell!' Lynn exclaimed, 'That wicked bastard.' The prospect filled him with genuine fear. Too many villains had been sent down for too many years by that judge for Lynn to be anything but dismayed.

'Precisely,' the silk said, as though they were his feelings too. 'However, all is not lost. I'll endeavour, even at this late stage, to get it put out of the list and on before another judge.'

'Can you do that?' Lynn asked. 'That bastard'll weigh us off with about thirty for fuckall.'

'We can try. We'll certainly do that.'

Macmillan's reassuring smile didn't reassure Lynn one bit.

With John Tully, Benny Isaacs and Cole Coleman Lynn went in to the dock at the Old Bailey's number two court, which was the second largest. They were jointly charged with attempted murder, robbery, robbing cars, possessing firearms, no firearms certificate, and conspiracy to rob. Alex Gladwell had found the deputy at the DPP's office and made a deal with him for his client, so that Lynn went up with no additional charges. It had cost twelve hundred pounds.

Before the business of selecting a jury got underway, Horace Macmillan rose to his feet to make his pitch.

'If I could crave the court's indulgence, My Lord,' Macmillan said, 'and ask for the case in respect of Jack Lynn to be put out of the list. My instructing solicitor is anticipating some new evidence which has been delayed. Evidence which could prove vital to my client's defence.'

The star of this court, and indeed any he appeared in, was Robert Quigley, who was quick to see this defence counsel trying to upstage him. Mr Justice Quigley was the law, he lived for the law, its rule being upheld. He was classically austere-looking, in his early seventies, with close-shorn white hair, and spiky white eyebrows above his dark, thick-rimmed glasses. His nose was slightly beaked over his thin, pale lips; the ample flesh on his face, like that of his body, was weakening and beginning to sag. He had been known to smile, but rare was the occasion he smiled in court; this happened more often at the Garrick Club where he exercised his slightly mordant wit. He regarded Horace Macmillan somewhat deprecatingly. This wasn't the first time they had met, and on the occasions before when they had done so they had clashed.

'I am sure you will find this court very indulgent as this trial progresses, Mr Macmillan,' Justice Quigley said. 'But don't start out by trying its patience. Unnecessary delays in criminal trials are costing the tax-payer a good deal of money. Something each of you might bear in mind with your usual unnecessary lengthy exposition into the doubtless virtues of your respective clients,' he went on, including the other three defence barristers in the warning. Justice Quigley was without doubt always heavily prejudiced against the defendant, but he was a judge who rarely said a word out of place, a word that couldn't be interpreted as taking the fair, middle ground on subsequently being read back in transcript, for the written word showed no emphasis or favour when read back in the appeal court. However, the words were overtly biased the way the judge spoke them. 'Perhaps in the event of this vital evidence not being forthcoming when the time is relevant,' the judge said, almost mockingly, 'you might make a further application. But it's now seven months since committal – I would have thought that ample time to prepare a defence.'

'With respect, My Lord,' Macmillan said, having no intention of letting the judge get away with that, 'perhaps you'd care to listen to my argument.'

'No, I wouldn't,' Justice Quigley said emphatically. 'I'd much prefer to proceed with the selection of the jury.'

It was an indication of the way the trial was likely to proceed.

Most of the morning was taken up with the selection of the jury. Horace Macmillan made five objections. One had no opportunity to cross-examine potential jurors to find out their views, profession, or the way they spoke; no reason had to be offered for the objection, but it could only be appearance. From their body-language and attire Macmillan could shrewdly assess at a glance the sort of background people came from. Those he weeded out were doubtless middle-class professional people who believed they had the most to lose from the breakdown of law and order, and who saw anyone in the dock of the Old Bailey, charged with what Jack Lynn was charged with, as a threat to well-ordered society. As Lynn's defence consisted mainly of undermining that order by attacking the police, they were the last people he wanted on the jury. He left the two black men just on the chance that either one or both might have had some brush with the law and as a result prove not too unsympathetic to Lynn. Each of the other defence barristers made token objections. But at last there was a jury.

The opening address by the prosecution was long and detailed despite his remarks about it being a relatively straightforward case.

As the prosecutor, Gordon Harpenden-Smith QC, stated

what Jack Lynn was supposed to have done, in company with the other three defendants, Lynn could feel himself getting angry and wanted to shout out his denial. Several times the words were on the tip of his tongue, and he knew he wasn't going to be able to stay quiet for the full course of the trial. Harpenden-Smith was stout, middle-aged, and had three chins; he also had a habit of removing his eye glasses when talking and waggling them up and down in his hand, rather as if he was suffering from Parkinson's disease. After about an hour of it, Lynn was thoroughly irritated by the habit, and felt like telling him to keep his fucking hands still. Had the man not been slagging him off he doubted he would even have noticed the gesture.

Witnesses for the prosecution came on in chronological order, after statements from the police plan drawer and official photographer had been read; street plans and photographs had gone in as exhibits at committal. Each witness seemed to take about a day in the witness-box giving evidence, which the prosecution seemed to draw from them with great skill, greater skill than that which each of the four defence counsellors displayed in cross-examination, so it seemed to each of the four defendants. Then, that was merely a subjective viewpoint. The cumulative effect of the various defence attacks was, in fact, a considerable impression of vagueness among the witnesses, who variously shifted ground from: Quite definitely it was one or other of the defendants, to: It might have been him, or, Not sure; or It was someone like him! Tully, Coleman and Isaacs sat quietly through the evidence, no matter what witnesses said they had done. Lynn frequently sprang to his feet to protest, scream his denial, call witnesses liars; they were never merely mistaken, but were part of the police conspiracy to fit him. He knew that, knew how the filth operated. The judge warned him about his outbursts, told him he would be removed to the cells if they persisted; his counsel cautioned him to try and keep a check on his emotions also. But it was easy for that little team on the defence bench to say such things, they weren't in the dock listening to all those lies, which finally made little difference to them anyway. Some days Lynn felt worse than others about his prospects.

It wasn't merely coincidental or ironical that by the eleventh day, when the last civilian witness appeared for the Crown, more of them had positively identified Jack Lynn than any of the other defendants. He knew how and why and felt a sick-making, sinking feeling in his stomach. Travelling back to Brixton that evening in the prison transporter, which was an enclosed truck divided into twenty cubicles off a central aisle, Lynn felt depressed and defeated. He knew for certain that he was going to end up with a heavy prison sentence and was feeling sorry for himself. His thoughts were worrying over the evidence that his silk had countered with, why the man hadn't brought out such and such a point. He was hardly aware of the animated chatter that was coming from various cubicles – the van was full, taking prisoners from other courts at the Old Bailey back to Brixton – until John Tully spoke to him. They had hardly spoken in the past eleven days; each of the other three blaggers were afraid of upsetting him in case he set about them.

'They're well fitting you, Jack,' Tully said from the cubicle immediately in front of Lynn. 'And that fucking judge, he's bending over backwards to help them.'

'What a no-good wicked bastard, him,' Isaacs added from across the aisle.

'But you cunts are helping him do it,' Lynn said angrily. That was all he said, but it silenced the entire truckload of men. They were grateful Lynn was locked in, confined within two square feet, his knees tucked under the seat of the back of the forward cubicle.

Lynn let his gaze go out of the tiny horizontal window, as he wistfully considered his lost liberty and how that was likely to be his future for a long while.

The first of the police witnesses was DC Matthew Hall, who

was lucid, to the point, professional. Lynn felt even more depressed as he listened to him tell how supposedly he and Coleman had collected rung cars from lock-ups in Forest Gate; parked the changeover car, collected the stove to crash the door with, picked up the other two bjaggers and made the blag. So positive did the filth seem that even for a moment Lynn believed he might have done this one, and wondered what chance the jury would have of not believing it. This was the detective who had taken the photographs that were there in court; these didn't add doubt, which any reasonable person might have taken from those pictures, but rather they seemed to prove conclusively that Lynn was there.

'They're exhibit 17, My Lord,' Gordon Harpenden-Smith QC put in helpfully. 'The jury have copies in Bundle 2.' He waggled his glasses as the paper was shuffled and everybody found the relevant copies of the photographs showing the robbery in action.

Harpenden-Smith need not have done anything further to score points at this stage, the judge did it all for him. He said, 'These are quite the most remarkable photos I have seen.' Justice Quigley's comment together with his glance across the court to the four men in the dock left no doubt that he believed that these men and those in the photographs were the same. 'You are to be congratulated on both your steady hand and a steady nerve. Especially in view of a beating you had to watch a colleague taking.' He considered the photos again then glanced across once more at the defendants and nodded. 'Quite remarkable.'

The confidence DC Hall displayed while giving evidence wasn't quite so apparent under cross-examination by Horace Macmillan, but his professionalism was only slightly diminished by the force of the defence counsel, who proceeded as if his case was already made and won.

'Wasn't this procedure rather unusual, constable?' Macmillan asked, requiring the man to explain how he came to be tailing the robbers.

'No, sir. I don't think so.'

'Presumably you've had lots of cases where you have been conveniently armed with a loaded camera, instead of what might have been more appropriate, a loaded pistol, have you?' The implication was that the detective was conducting himself in an underhand manner.

'It was the first I've been on, sir,' DC Hall said.

'I am sure it was. Did it not strike you as odd that you should be asked to pursue a gang of robbers singlehanded, and armed with only a camera?'

'It was an observation detail . . .'

'One that was, by the merest coincidence, set up only a day before the robbery. Doesn't that suggest prior knowledge of the robbery?' Horace Macmillan said, apparently innocuously.

'I don't think we're interested in that kind of conjecture, Mr Macmillan,' Justice Quigley put in, perceiving the QC's direction. 'The witness has stated how he came to be where he was at the time.'

'With respect, My Lord. It's my contention that the photographs offered in evidence, remarkable as they might be in content,' – sarcasm dripping off his words – 'in no way identify the defendant Jack Lynn.'

'Then what is the point you are seeking to make?' the judge asked testily.

'That the police had, in fact, prior knowledge of the robbery, but chose not to prevent it or send a squad of armed detectives to apprehend the robbers as that would have left them little scope for their indictment of Jack Lynn. These quite remarkable photos offered in evidence do that extremely well, if only in their inadequacy.'

'In order for that to be acceptable you would need to establish a *prima facie* case against the police. This I feel you won't do by pure conjecture,' the judge said. 'But you're welcome to try.'

The points his silk was scoring against the police were all lost again in that one gesture of the judge's, Lynn felt. The old bastard had the upper hand the whole time.

The cross-examination of the detective was making little impression on the jury, even though his brief made a number of points about the fit-up conspiracy: leading the DC to admit he was a keen photographer, then demanding to know why the photos were so out of focus; wanting to know how many other people he had photographed who had showed an interest in going to the garages in Osborne Road, Forest Gate – there were none; how he managed to tail these two cars as he did on his own, when normally about six police cars would be employed for such a detail; how remarkably lucky he was to get so close to the robbers in Leyton Street, and undetected. The obvious conclusion was that he wasn't this good or lucky but had, with prior knowledge, been able to position himself outside the Gas Board and wait for the robbery to go off so he could take his fit-up photos. The silk knew his stuff all right, Lynn didn't doubt that for a moment, and up before any other judge would have been well ahead.

DC Simon Brett was very effective in the witness-box, mainly due to the fact that he had tried to prevent the robbery and had taken a beating in the process. Even the most liberal-minded juror responded to those sort of heroics, which had no bearing on the four men in the dock necessarily; someone had been commissioning an armed robbery, and this detective, singlehanded and unarmed, had tried to prevent it and had taken a beating.

He was examining one of the sawn-off shotguns that had been taken from Lynn's garage.

'Are you able to say whether that was one of the guns used in the raid on the Gas Board?' Harpenden-Smith asked.

'It is exactly similar, sir,' DC Brett said. 'I recognize the same plaster binding round the stock. Also the same sort of leather loop through the handle.'

'Exhibit 27, My Lord,' the prosecution said.

As he watched the usher take the exhibit from the witness, Lynn felt like calling him a prick, saying that every sawn-off shotgun ever used to make one had plaster around the sawn stock and a loop for holding it.

'It looks a singularly offensive instrument,' the judge said, waving it away.

Lynn got a mildly pleasant surprise as Harpenden-Smith proceeded with his witness. The DC went on to ID Benny Isaacs as the man who knocked him to the ground. Lynn had believed he would have been a million. The witness did however state how Lynn had been there and that he had subsequently ID'd him when paraded. With great effort Lynn restrained himself from calling out.

Stanley Eaton QC was a willowy figure in his fifties, and had skin tightly drawn across his face as though having undergone plastic surgery. It was easy to imagine that the result made it difficult for him to smile, for he never did, not even when he made a particularly favourable point in Tully's defence.

'How long were the robbers in the office building?' Eaton wanted to know.

In the witness-box now was DC Peter Footring, who had been made up from temporary detective constable. He was less sure of himself than his colleague. He hadn't corroborated every aspect of his evidence. 'About a minute,' he replied. The previous witness had said about two minutes. Possibly a not very important point other than the general confusion it added to.

'Long enough for you and your colleague to get the gas stove loaded onto your van and run those sixty yards or so to the scene?'

'Yes. That's as it happened.'

'Why didn't you go to assist DC Brett? Surely with two of you you'd have had a better chance?'

'He told me to go back and radio for assistance.'

'Even though the detective from Scotland Yard, Hall, was doing just that?'

'We didn't know he was present, sir.'

It was a point Horace Macmillan pursued.

'How did you happen to be where you were at the time of the robbery?' the QC asked.

The detective constable was expecting the question. 'We were watching for the robbers.'

'If that was the case, you seemed curiously unprepared.'

'We weren't sure when the robbery was going to happen. If it was even.'

'So there were two of you there in case it did, ready to call others to your aid, just as DC Hall was supposedly doing?' DC Footring agreed. Macmillan reiterated the point, then said, 'Was it not true, in fact, that you weren't there because you had heard a rumour of a robbery, but contrary to police regulations you were collecting a stove for a senior officer to deliver to his home?'

'No, sir,' Footring said emphatically, like the emphasis would carry the argument. 'We were using the stove as cover to watch for the robbers.'

'I suggest that that isn't true at all. That you were there by the merest chance. Do you wish for an opportunity to change your mind about that? To avoid perjuring yourself.' Macmillan suggested, opening a folder as if about to pull out a deposition of some kind to contradict the constable's evidence. It was a ploy frequently used by the CID during interrogation, but this young detective constable might have been forgiven for not being so familiar with it.

Footring hesitated, but before he could answer the judge intervened.

'Mr Macmillan, I fail to see the purpose of this tangent, or what possible difference it could make how the police came to be there. The important point is surely the fact that they were present, and witnessed all that occurred.'

'I am returning to the matter of police conspiracy, My Lord,' Macmillan informed him matter-of-factly. 'I am suggesting that the police conspired not only before the crime was committed, but afterwards also, to make certain that their evidence was corroborative, and in so doing masked their own malpractices.'

'If that is the case then I'm sure the Director of Public Prosecutions will take the appropriate steps,' Justice Quigley said in a dismissive tone. 'Meanwhile, perhaps we could take a more direct path through the facts of the case and so assist this court.'

'But almost the entire defence of my client, My Lord, rests in the sincere belief that the police conspired against him.'

'Very well, Mr Macmillan,' the judge conceded with apparent graciousness. 'We will hear your argument.'

The statement by the judge, the tone in which it was said, seriously undermined any argument that would subsequently be put.

Lynn had promised his silk that he would stay calm, stay silent; had promised the court, and he had promised Dolly. But he didn't know how much longer he could stand the prick.

37

A dozen or so policemen passed through the witness-box, all of them involved in the chase that took place after the Gas Board robbery. Once the prosecution had elicited all its evidence from them, each of the four defence barristers took the evidence apart piece by piece. All were relying on diminishing the credibility of the police to some degree in their defences, though none as much as Macmillan was. There were any number of contradictions in the evidence, and while these worked generally for Tully, Isaacs and Coleman, they tended to work against Macmillan's defence for Lynn in as much as active police conspiracy would have tidied the loose ends up more.

PC Vallins, who had tried to organize the roadblock during the chase, got quite a lot of sympathy as he told of the injuries he had received when run down by the fleeing robbers. And Harpenden-Smith made much of it. He had positively identified Isaacs and Tully. But Michael Newall QC, counsel for Isaacs, reduced the credibility of that identification somewhat when he produced the test acceleration capability of that model of Oldsmobile car, and on going through the evidence point by point, found that the policeman got to see the two suspects for only one or two seconds through the reflecting windscreen of a car travelling at seventy miles an hour.

DI Pyle, as the officer in charge of the case, was the last policeman to give evidence. This was taken from his first knowledge of Lynn's involvement, through his arrest, searching his property, finding the contents of his garage, his interrogation and identification. He was more professional than any who had gone in before him, had probably been in the witness-box more times, certainly under more pressure. Harpenden-Smith couldn't want for a better witness. Pyle went through all that he had as facts in the case without interruption, the prosecution didn't need to prompt him. Afterwards there were other points he wanted to raise or emphasize, so he went back to them.

'How far in advance did you know about the robbery, inspector?' Harpenden-Smith asked.

'It was first brought up about a fortnight before by a colleague in C11. Though we weren't able to do anything about it at the time through insufficient information.'

'From your subsequent inquiries you found out who was going to be involved?'

'Two of them, was all.'

'Putting a detective on watch with a camera, is that a usual procedure, inspector?'

'It's one we're having to employ more and more, in order to cover as many investigations as possible.'

'You try and stretch your very limited resources over as wide a field in order to give the public the best service possible?' Harpenden-Smith said.

'That is correct,' Pyle said.

'I would like to go back for a moment if I may to consider your earlier evidence about the contents of the lock-up garage. To refresh the jurors' memory, this contained a veritable arsenal, marked exhibits 37 to 82, photographs of which are in Bundle 2. Perhaps you would just remind the court what explanation the defendant Jack Lynn gave about the contents of this garage.'

Pyle flipped back through the notes he had with him in the witness-box. 'When I questioned him about the contents of the garage, he replied, "Don't know nothing about them. I let the garage to a fella I met in a pub, a man called Richard Cook." Lynn had in his possession receipts made out to Richard Cook.'

'For money paid to him?'

'No, for rental to the owner of the garages, one James Fowlie,' Pyle replied.

'We heard earlier in this trial from James Fowlie who identified Jack Lynn as being Richard Cook, the man who rented his garage. But prior to that, had you made any inquiries or tried to establish the existence of Richard Cook as a third party renting the garage not from Fowlie but Lynn?'

'We did. We made extensive inquiries, but the result was negative. Our conclusion was that Lynn and Cook were one and the same.'

'That the sub-lessee didn't exist, that the garage and its nefarious contents were the responsibility of Jack Lynn entirely?' Harpenden-Smith concluded.

'Yes, sir.'

When Macmillan took the floor to cross-examine the DI his offensive tack was full of ploys to try and distract the witness. 'How long have you been a policeman, inspector?' the QC asked, glancing over his notes as though ready to contradict him if he gave the wrong answer.

'Twenty years, just on,' Pyle replied, not allowing himself to be even slightly puzzled by the question.

'And during that period how many complaints have been made against you?'

This was an area Jack Lynn was most happy for the defence to get into, but he wondered whether Macmillan would have any more success than he had had with his earlier attacks on the credibility, the truthfulness, the honesty of the policemen who had been into the witness-box. The judge would find some way of diminishing the attack, rendering it less effective, not directly, but with all the cunning the old bastard usually used.

'Is this pertinent, Mr Macmillan?' Justice Quigley asked right on cue, his tone very reasonable. 'Or are you merely pursuing the theme of police corruption you have been doggedly persisting with?'

'I think it very pertinent, My Lord. If you will bear with me for a while.' His implication was that he wasn't being given a chance.

'I would like you to come swiftly to the point,' the judge said, allowing the tack.

Macmillan bowed his head to the judge with excessive courtesy. 'How many complaints, Inspector Pyle?'

'About eleven, I think – they were all unsubstantiated.'

'Having been investigated by your colleagues,' Macmillan paused, making it appear like a conclusion, 'you were cleared of the charges eleven members of the public saw fit to bring against you? Is it true that you have a complaint currently outstanding against you? For conspiring to pervert the course of justice?'

'I have,' Pyle said. 'But only from one of the prisoners in the dock. Lynn.'

'Is that to infer that he no longer has any rights, inspector?' the QC asked sharply.

'No, sir.' Pyle was slightly defensive now.

'So his còmplaint *per se* is no less valid than anyone else's?'

'He has the same rights as anyone to complain about the police.'

'Would you tell us the specific nature of this complaint?'

'Lynn is claiming that I manufactured evidence against him to get him convicted.'

'Isn't that precisely what you're doing, inspector?' Macmillan made the prospect sound like an everyday occurrence.

'No, sir. As far as I've been able to ascertain, Lynn was very much involved.'

Justice Quigley was unable to allow this attack upon the police to go on without interruption. 'Do you believe this to be a malicious complaint against you, inspector?' the judge asked, as if there was no doubt.

'Yes, My Lord, I do,' Pyle said.

'A device all too familiar to criminals nowadays,' the judge commented, cutting the ground from under the defence. 'Proceed.'

'When arresting Jack Lynn, did you not say: "It's your turn, son. You're well overdue." Meaning he should have been put away a long time ago?'

'No, I didn't.'

'You're quite sure?'

'Quite sure.'

Macmillan glanced over his notes, as if they contained the unremitting truth. 'When did you decide Lynn was involved in the Gas Board robbery?'

'Approximately two days after the robbery took place,' Pyle replied.

'After you had, in fact, arrested and subsequently released a fourth man?'

'Happens all the time.'

'The police arresting the wrong people?'

'Eliminating suspects,' Pyle countered.

'So having eliminated this man, you had a vacancy and Lynn was the most likely candidate. How did you discover he was involved, as you claim, in this crime?'

'Through an informer, sir.'

Lynn, who had been following the cross-examination closely, became alert with anticipation now.

'A source you believed to be reliable?'

'Very reliable.'

'A member of the criminal fraternity?'

'He was,' Pyle said.

'And still you consider him reliable and truthful,' Macmillan said dismissively. 'Why did he give you this information?'

'I'm not sure I know, sir.' The real reason would be the last thing Pyle would want out, especially not in court.

'Was it out of duress? Did you have some sort of lever on him?'

'No, sir.'

'Then revenge? That's a common motive among informers. Could that be why this criminal chose to come to you with his information?'

'I can't think that was his motive. I went to him.'

'Does this man, this criminal informer, have any convictions for his own crimes?'

'Yes, he does.'

'And you believe the word of a convicted criminal was enough to arrest Jack Lynn?'

'It proved so, sir. Having arrested him we found other evidence,' Pyle said evenly.

'Let us examine some of this evidence. We have less than satisfactory eyewitness testimony, apart from twelve police witnesses – all of whom, incidentally, are quite certain they didn't discuss the case or corroborate what each saw. A more disinterested bunch of policemen one could not wish to meet. We have a flying helmet which the police say Lynn wore for the robbery, only it's two sizes too small; the hair sample found inside, on which there is a forensic report, not only matches Lynn's hair, but approximately thirty-two per cent of the population of this country. Then we have the find at the garage, a garage which Jack Lynn sub-let. But no extensive search was made to find the sub-lessee because the police were convinced they had the right man. And they came to their swift conclusion on the word of a convicted criminal ...'

Lynn glanced apprehensively at the judge who was growing impatient as this defence silk summarized the fit-up evidence – he didn't think he'd allow him to go on much longer. But Lynn thought the silk made some worthwhile points, which the jury appreciated.

'Mr Macmillan,' the judge interjected finally. 'Perhaps you would conclude this rambling surmise, and restrict yourself to cross-examination.' He wasn't in fact offering him a choice.

'My Lord,' Macmillan said, acknowledging the point. Then to Pyle, 'Was this reliable informer named Michael Fielder?'

Pyle hesitated. He was surprised that the QC had this information.

Recognizing the detective's dilemma, the judge said, 'If you feel a need to protect the identity of your informer, inspector, then you may refrain from answering.'

'Revealing the man might endanger him, My Lord,' Pyle said.

'Very well.' It was standard practice that the police weren't required to name names.

'This unnamed informer,' Macmillan persisted, 'is he an active criminal?'

'I wouldn't think so. Merely an associate of criminals.'

'Is it not true that you have a *quid pro quo* arrangement with criminal informers, allowing them to commit minor crimes, provided that they supply you with information on other bigger crimes?'

'No, sir,' Pyle said emphatically.

Pyle remained in the witness-box for three days, being cross-examined by each of the other defence barristers who tried to open further the gap in the credibility of the police that Macmillan made, which the judge subsequently tried repairing. Lynn was confused and demoralized by the time the DI stepped out of the witness-box. He thought his cause was no further forward, while, ironically, he also thought the three men in the dock with him might get a result. They had every reason at this rate to take it all as calmly as they were; he had only barely managed to keep his presence in court, having called Pyle a fucking liar at one point. The judge had given him his final warning; it might as well have been his sentence.

38

Although he wasn't unhappy about the way things were going in court, DI Pyle wasn't absolutely convinced they were going to get a result. One couldn't guarantee anything nowadays, and that was about all that could be guaranteed in court. One could coast along comfortably throughout the trial in the firm belief that the jury were eating up every word the prosecution was feeding them, then suddenly they could go right the other way. If that was how it came out it might leave him with a lot of problems, Pyle thought, especially with the complaint Lynn had in about how he was supposedly perverting the course of justice. A result for Lynn would endorse that, and it was odds on that the blagger would proceed with the complaint, the mood he was in, rather than drop it as most villains did once they had their result. However, he didn't allow the prospect to worry him. For one thing that the prosecution had going for it which was certain to knock the defence sideways, particularly now all the evidence from police witnesses was concluded, was their additional-evidence witness who was being introduced at the last moment. He had just left Clifford Harding in the cells below court, having kept him well clear of Lynn and the others. Harding was far from happy about the position he was being forced into by the DI; it would possibly endanger him, maybe cost him most of his friends, but the alternative would cost him more, Pyle had made that quite clear. The alternative meant Pyle pressing ahead with the possession-of-firearms charge which he had hanging over Harding. That would mean the loss of his liberty for an absolute certainty. With his record as a blagger there was no way he could not go down on that, and the villain knew it. The possibility that once he got into the witness-box Harding would renege on their deal and become a hostile witness was something Pyle had considered – that had happened to him before with witnesses – but he didn't think it likely here. Anyway, he had the statement that Harding had written and signed, and he had warned him of the likely consequences if he did go back on their deal: not only would he lose his liberty but he would do so in addition to being booked for a grass as his statement would simply be read in court.

Heading along the corridor for the police room, wearing his mac, which was still damp from the wet summer morning, Pyle encountered Harpenden-Smith with one of his juniors. They exchanged a few pleasantries. The QC wanted to know about the witness. Pyle told him he was in the cells.

'Is he going to co-operate, inspector?' he asked.

'Well, he's not exactly happy about it,' Pyle informed him. 'But he's here.'

'Excellent. It's important we have his evidence. Juries are getting somewhat leary of unidentified informers these days. His appearance should set their minds at rest. Excellent. See you in court.'

Surprise hit Jack Lynn with the force of a hammer blow when the prosecution rose and said he would like at this late stage to introduce some additional evidence, then called Clifford Harding. He sat and watched the man slither through the court and into the witness-box where he took the oath, all the while avoiding looking across at the dock. The thought running through Lynn's head wasn't about what Harding knew, but what he would say. For it was fairly obvious that he was part of the fit-up, that Pyle had primed him, put him on a promise. The dirty no-good cunt! Anger was racing through him. He would never have suspected him of going the other way: Fielder was the grass, he had been convinced of that, not Harding. But then Harding had been bang in trouble; surviving, keeping their liberty was all that mattered to some. Keeping his liberty was all Harding might do.

'Jack told me he had this one going off at the Gas Board at Romford, worth about seven or eight grand,' Harding was saying from the witness-box. 'He said he was a bit short-handed, like, and asked me if I wanted to make it with him...'

Anger exploded out of Lynn like water from a burst main. 'You liar!' he screamed. 'You dirty, no-good fucking liar. I'll top you! You lying cunt, I'll fucking slaughter you ...' Lynn started to climb out of the dock to go after the witness, all reasoning gone now. He was dragged back by two warders who were in the dock also.

Confusion and a babble of interest followed the scuffle in the dock. Silence was called for, but there was no immediate response.

'Remove that prisoner,' Justice Quigley said firmly. 'He will be held in the cells for the duration of this trial.'

Lynn didn't want to go, and put up a fight. His very life might have depended on him getting to Harding and doing him some damage. Other uniforms came to the assistance, and with kicks and punches both given and received, they got him down the steps from the dock. In the area below there was more room to manoeuvre, so Lynn had less chance with five against one, but still he didn't give up. It was a full five minutes before they were able to subdue him sufficiently to get him into a cell and lock the door.

It took a long time for Lynn to stop resisting, but still his thoughts churned angrily, and all he would've needed was a glimpse of Harding to get him going again, or better still an opportunity to have a go at him, do him some real damage. He had nothing to lose now, he was convinced of that. Harding's appearance in the witness-box had really finished any chances he had of getting a result. The thought depressed him as he sat on the bench bed. His jacket was torn and the sleeve was coming out of the shoulder. Buttons had gone from his shirt, and there was blood on him from a nose bleed one of the uniforms had got. A couple of ribs ached, and his left cheek was painful, but other than that he wasn't hurt physically.

After about an hour the screw looked in on him, but didn't speak. Then again just before lunch. This time he asked him if he wanted some food. Lynn didn't feel like eating particularly, and the food hadn't improved over the four weeks at court, but he accepted the offer.

Shortly after he started his lunch, Tully, Coleman and Isaacs trooped into the cell for their food.

'That was a right fucking upset up in court, Jack,' Tully said. 'Should think that fucking judge'll give us all about an extra ten for that.'

Lynn didn't say anything. There were a lot of questions he wanted to ask, but if he started here these three men would bear the brunt of the anger he felt towards Harding. It wasn't that they didn't deserve it, but more that they were useful, especially three-handed.

'That silk of yourn, Jack,' Tully went on. 'Absolutely ruined that no-good slag, he did.'

'Won't be worth a toss, his evidence,' Isaacs added as if trying to please him. 'He's a bit of a brief, Jack, in' he.'

'Did all right, did he?' Lynn was unable to avoid that.

'Fucking slaughtered him. Reckoned how him and Pyle had a deal, Pyle had put him on a promise. He did terrific.' Tully left Lynn feeling a little better about his prospects. Turning to the door, he pursued the warder. 'Oh, Charlie! Where's our grub?' That was more important.

Just before the court resumed Horace Macmillan came down to see Lynn. They were left alone in the cell, the other three prisoners having been taken back to court.

'The prosecution has concluded its case,' he told Lynn. All of his arrogance remained as he stood, legs braced apart, his hands clasped behind his back, pushing out his gown. 'Superficially, the evidence is very damaging. But I think the jury are sufficiently confused and plagued with doubts by this time for us not to worry too much.'

'Can I go back in court now?' Lynn asked. Somehow he felt he would have some small control over things if he was present. But Macmillan shook his head.

'Mr Justice Quigley is nothing if not consistent. I'm afraid you're going to have to sit it out. I'm not even going to call you.'

That surprised Lynn. 'Why not? Someone's gotta say they're lying.'

'You'll have to trust me. You go into the witness-box, the first question the prosecution is going to ask is how you get your income. Can you tell them? The second question, how did you pay for your house? Currently valued at, what, twenty, thirty thousand?'

'But I got it when property was down. For five grand, was all,' Lynn protested as if making a valid point.

'Most of the jury will still be paying for their houses on a mortgage. I'll say all that you wish to say, and without allowing them any advantage. Just be patient.'

Lynn gave the barrister a peculiar look, like he suddenly thought him an idiot, and was unable to relate to him at all. He was just some strange animal in a wig and gown, a type he met periodically in his life and now entrusted his entire future to. He realized with a degree of perception, which he hadn't quite grasped before, just how precarious his future was.

'Is there anything you want now?' Macmillan asked.

'My bit of liberty,' Lynn replied automatically.

'That I will endeavour to secure for you.'

Each looked at the other, both doubting the feasibility of that. The doubt stayed with Lynn long after the barrister had departed. Lynn was alone then, and had never felt more lonely in his life. His future was being talked over some twenty feet above his head, though he suspected it had been decided long before. At that moment he couldn't grasp the reality of the situation. It was as if he had started to float and had subsequently lost all contact with life around him. Occasionally people passed along the corridor outside his cell, nameless, faceless, voiceless people, shuffling along in his miniature limbo-world like the one which might confine him

324

for the next fifteen years or so. Alone as he awaited the conclusion of the case for the defence – which could only be brief – all he had for comfort were his thoughts, a copy of the *Daily Mirror* loaned him by one of the warders, and the graffiti scratched into the walls. One legend read: 'Fifteen for armed robbery – I'll do it on my prick. A. Duncan.' It was dated two weeks ago. Lynn wasn't reassured at all. The thought of A. Duncan, whoever he was, starting a fifteen was more depressing for some reason than the prospect of himself being weighed off. He wasn't sure why: probably because that villain was done, while there was still some hope that he might get a result himself.

The defence cases for each of the four defendants were over a good deal quicker than that for the prosecution. The shortest was for Lynn, his main witness being his wife, who offered his alibi and couldn't be shaken from it.

The prosecution took the whole of one day delivering his closing address. Harpenden-Smith was eloquent if not very passionate. Horace Macmillan was both eloquent and passionate in closing: his client was innocent, the victim of a police conspiracy; he gave the jury no alternative but to find Jack Lynn not guilty. The speech might have been more effective had not the other three defence barristers taken a similar line.

The jury listened with studious attention while the judge summed up, adopting thoughtful poses, hanging on his every word in order to fill the gaps left by their inattention, lack of concentration, and failing memory over the past five weeks. What the judge said at the end was all that really mattered, every juror past, present or potential knew that.

'The vast array of evidence presented here over the past weeks would appear overwhelming in its indication of the guilt of the four men who appeared in the dock.' There were only three there now, Lynn was still being kept below. 'Witness after witness has testified as to their presence at the scene of the crime, and the subsequent crimes in aiding their getaway.' The judge removed his thick glasses, his tone becoming dismissive as he indicated the alternative. 'But you must consider the elements of conflict and confusion apparent in this testimony, and ask yourselves whether this amounts to a reasonable doubt. Were the witnesses simply confused in this emotion-charged situation, as people sometimes are, or was the confusion purposely designed by the robbers who, with criminal foresight, had on a lot of extra clothes to first disguise themselves, then subsequently discard when effecting their escape? You must consider those points carefully, but remember these robbers had their faces uncovered, and they were seen. If you find the eyewitness testimony too confusing and unreliable, as it is sometimes proving nowadays, when unsupported, then you must give weight to the remaining evidence. First there is the garage which contained the most base instruments of mayhem one could encounter. A man found with a sawn-off shotgun in his possession must be condemned for what he is, a robber prepared to do violence as a means to his end; for there is no possible legal pursuit in which such a weapon could be employed. There was a lot of money found in Jack Lynn's possession, a great deal of money for which he was unable or unwilling to account. Having such an amount of money isn't a crime in itself, but honest men can adequately give account of such sums, and Lynn could give no account of it, for he had pursued no legitimate occupation other than casual taxi driving. Then one must consider the testimony of the security company's employee who identified some of the banknotes as part of the money she made up for wage packets in the payroll. But as counsel for the defence pointed out, wages clerks, along with bank tellers mark thousands of notes during the course of a year, some of which coincidentally could have arrived in those in Lynn's possession.' His tone gave the coincidence no credence at all. 'Also there are those remarkable photographs of the robbery actually taking place. If, however, you wish to dismiss both the eyewitnesses' testimony and evidence presented in court, then you must accept the supposition, which seems to constitute the entire basis for the defence, that there was a huge police conspiracy afoot here. A conspiracy involving not one or two police officers, but all sixteen who were actively involved in the case, and many more besides, including both the prosecution and the office of the Director of Public Prosecutions. If that is the case you will doubtless find the defendants not guilty, and a new form of police institution will be urgently required. However, should you dismiss the defence hypothesis that there was a vast police conspiracy in operation, then you should find the defendants guilty.' Justice Quigley paused briefly. 'The defence made much of the fact that eyewitness testimony was totally invalid. Not merely in this particular case, but in general. When you retire shortly to consider your verdict, I want you further to consider the implication of this also, for the implication reaches far beyond this single case. If such testimony is in future to be held up as being totally invalid, then it leaves the armoury of the police in their fight against crime sadly depleted. It leaves them without that invaluable support of honest members of the public, who are prepared to step forward and assist when their assistance is required.' He removed his glasses again and tapped the heavy frame against one neatly manicured thumb while he regarded the jury for a moment. 'I want you to go away now and carefully consider your verdict.'

Pyle, who was sitting in court with DS Lethridge, looked like he knew what the result would be. There could be little doubt after that summing up. Not that he had much faith in juries.

39

The faces of the four defendants turned expectantly and full of apprehension to the tiny cell door as it was unlocked. The door swung outwards and the warder looked in. The jury had been out for over four hours. They were long, uncomfortable hours for each of the blaggers. That was the longest part of the trial, waiting for the jury to return with their verdict.

'Come on, lads,' the warder said cheerfully. 'The jury's coming back in.' Tully, Isaacs and Coleman shuffled reluctantly to their feet. Lynn remained seated. 'You too, Jack.'

None of the four prisoners said anything as the warder stepped aside to allow them out of the cell. Isaacs came first, followed by Tully, then Cole Coleman, and finally Lynn, no less reluctant to go up the steps than any of the others. Their faces were set with a slightly haunted look, each showing traces of fear, apprehension; some carrying it better than others. But none cracked as some of the hardest villains did at such times, in need of a stiff brandy which the gaoler had been known to oblige with.

The four men went up the steps in silence.

With everyone back in their positions in court, the jury were called and filed awkwardly into their places, some feeling very self-conscious with the weight of their verdicts and all eyes in court on them. Some glanced across at the prisoners standing in the dock, others avoided looking at them. When the jury was seated the clerk rose.

'Who is the foreman of the jury?' the clerk asked.

'I am,' a woman said.

'Have you reached a verdict in respect of each of the prisoners?'

'With the exception of Coleman,' the woman informed the court.

The exception meant further delay. Justice Quigley wasn't pleased. 'Then I may tell you at this point,' he said testily, almost warning them, 'that you may return to the jury room and arrive at a majority verdict, of ten to two.' The judge dismissed them with a terse hand gesture.

The jury were out for an hour and returned no further advanced.

'Is there any likelihood of your reaching a ten to two majority if you were given further time?' the judge wanted to know.

'No, sir,' the woman said, quite definitely.

The judge's humour wasn't improved by this. 'Very well. Let us hear the remaining verdicts.'

'May I make an application for bail at this stage, My Lord?' Peter Robbins QC, for Coleman, said, bobbing up.

'You may not!' The judge was plainly irritated.

Robbins resumed his seat, sorry he had spoken. The move wouldn't advance his client's chances when he made a later application for bail.

'Count one charges John Francis Tully with attempted murder,' the clerk said. 'How do you find him? Guilty or not guilty?'

'Not guilty ...'

'Oh, t'rific. That's bloody t'rific ...' the words simply bubbled out of Tully in nervous excitement at his result.

Pyle and the policemen with him in court were surprised, as were a lot of people in the court, not least the defence. That wasn't the only surprise as the clerk went through the various counts seeking the jury's verdicts.

'Count three charges Benjamin Michael Isaacs with illegally possessing firearms,' the clerk continued in the formal, ritualized manner. 'How do you find him? Guilty or not guilty?'

'Not guilty!'

Isaacs merely giggled with delight now, having had a nice result on the two previous counts and silence being called for at his excited response. Like Tully he got a result right the way through the card.

The results were like some bad joke against themselves, the CID thought as they sat in court listening. It didn't make any sense at all.

'Count one charges John Albert Lynn with attempted murder,' the clerk went on with familiar monotony. 'How do you find him? Guilty or not guilty?'

'Guilty.'

The response suddenly brought the entire court up sharply.

'What ...? Leave off!' Lynn said in a low, stunned manner. He had felt certain he would get a result as well.

The verdict of guilty on every count against Lynn caused a hubbub of comment around the court. Silence was called for. Lynn stood stock-still in the dock, angry, but stunned with disbelief. What followed immediately afterwards he had little awareness of. But finally awareness of the bitter irony in the result did poke through his numbness: the one person who was actually innocent of that blag being convicted, while those who were involved got a result, was really ironical.

It struck Fred Pyle the same way. Only he learned more of a lesson from it than Lynn would. It would teach him not to be so arrogant in respect of villains' actual guilt, nor to rely on that fact coming out just because it was a fact. That sort of evidence ought to have been worked on as closely as that which was manufactured. Still, it was done now, and there was no second bite.

'I can't offer you this court's thanks,' the judge told the jury. 'You have by your verdicts shown how fallible juries are.' He turned to the dock and said grudgingly, 'Release John Tully and Benjamin Isaacs. Coleman will be taken back to prison to await further trial. I will hear your application for bail afterwards, Mr Robbins.'

The three blaggers shuffled out of the dock quickly, not

330

wanting to get involved with Lynn in any way, especially not Tully or Isaacs.

'Tell them,' Lynn appealed, as if realizing for the first time what was happening. Then more desperately as they went: 'Tell 'em, you slags!'

The clerk ordered silence.

Justice Quigley looked at Pyle as he stepped into the witness-box and opened the folder he had brought with him.

'The prisoner has seven previous convictions, My Lord,' Pyle informed the court. Had they had had some kind of deal he might have left out most of the poison, which in turn might have saved him a few years. Usually the consideration was either for a guilty plea or an earner.

'I will hear the last three,' the judge said.

Pyle went through the details of each which amounted to eight years for robbery, which had been his last conviction; three for conspiracy and two for stealing a motor vehicle.

'Thank you, inspector. Are there any special circumstances surrounding the prisoner which this court should be made aware of before passing sentence.'

Again there was no deal between CID and villain. 'No, My Lord,' he said.

'What about the fitting, you filthy bastard?' Dolly Lynn shouted from the public gallery, where she stood gripping the rail. She was in tears. 'You bastard! You rotten, filthy bastards!'

The clerk called for silence through the disturbance which followed Dolly's removal.

'John Lynn,' the judge began when order was restored. 'You have been found guilty of attempted murder, robbery, conspiracy to rob, possessing firearms. All base crimes of a man out to further his own wicked ends. In these crimes, which I believe you were the instigator of, you alone must bear the consequences, for by your silence two of your confederates have gone scot free. You are a man who has lived his life by crime, and one who, if free, might reasonably be expected to do so for the rest of his active life; therefore I must curtail that activity. For the attempted murder of two police officers, you will go to prison for fifteen years. On each of the other three charges you will go to prison for a total of five years; the sentences to run concurrently. Take the prisoner below.' The judge paused while Lynn was led warily away by the two warders, who had two colleagues close at hand as if expecting trouble from Lynn. He went down quietly, in fact.

'Throughout this somewhat protracted trial,' Justice Quigley said, 'there have been a number of allegations against the police. Allegations which, I am pleased to say, the jury appear to consider unsubstantiated. By this one verdict the actions of the police officers have been completely vindicated. Indeed, throughout this trial, under constant attack as they have been, I have found the conduct of the police exemplary. It would be a truly sad day for the police institution if such cavalier accusations were proven. For if the police are dishonest, then there would be no security for the citizens of this country. I commend Inspector Pyle and his colleagues for their integrity, their diligence and the scrupulous manner in which they have conducted themselves.

Pyle sat accepting the commendation without so much as a blush.

It was done, they had got a result; not quite the result they had expected, but as the judge had said, the verdict vindicated their actions. The end always justified the means, Fred Pyle believed. Getting villains locked away was an important achievement, however it was effected.

'We got a bit of a result there, Fred,' Lethridge said, as the two detectives emerged from the main entrance of the Old Bailey into the warm evening sunshine.

'Didn't we just.' He was feeling pleased with himself. 'Be a long time before he does any more villainy.' There was no sense of guilt or remorse over the way they had sent him down. He was a villain after all. 'Still, it does make you wonder, Eric. Those others getting a result.'

"S not enough any more, is it. Being bang to rights.'

It wasn't. In future they'd look extra hard, no matter how good the evidence seemed to be.

They turned up the road towards the Magpie and Stump at the top of the street.

'They can't do it, Jack,' Dolly Lynn said angrily through her tears. 'The rotten bastards can't do it. You weren't there. You was with me ...'

'They wanted me bad enough ... We'll see what happens on appeal,' Lynn said. That was the next step. He wasn't going to take his fitting lightly, there'd be murders inside; yet paradoxically he was almost resigned to his future.

'I won't stop screaming it's a fit-up, Jack ... I won't ...' Dolly was in the corridor outside Lynn's cell speaking to him through the grille. The warder wasn't obliged to allow the meeting, but he had done so while Lynn was waiting to be collected and carted off to prison. He would go to the Scrubs initially then down to the Island, probably.

'It's time to go, love,' the warder said, appearing quietly at the woman's side. He understood the problem it was for wives at this time. Occasionally there were very bad scenes in the corridor here.

'Jack?' Alarm came into her voice. She had a million things she wanted to say to him. She didn't want to leave him. She couldn't; she loved him; she needed him; their children needed him. Their fingers touched at the grille. She wanted him to hold her so much.

'Give the girls my love ...' It was all he could think of; he wanted to tell Dolly how much he loved her, but didn't, and later regretted not doing so.

'Jack ...' She went away with the uniform.

Lynn pressed his face to the grille, desperate for one last glimpse of his wife.

'You lousy bastards!' Dolly screamed along the corridor. 'You lying sods. He didn't do nothing!'

Her voice was finally lost with the slamming of a heavy door, when she was shut on the far side.

Lynn was aware at that moment of the steel bars against his face. He felt desolate, trapped.

40

The dark green Ford Transit headed along the motorway at a steady fifty-five miles an hour. The midday road was fairly uncongested, but the driver was in no particular hurry. And he was even more certain that his principal passenger was in even less of a hurry to get to his destination. The driver saw the police motorcyclist ahead make a lefthand signal for the slip road, the police behind would do the same, as they had reached the county border. There a new police escort of two motorcyclists was waiting to take over. Jack Lynn was a category 'A' prisoner and little expense was spared getting him there safely.

The minibus with its horizontal barred windows tended to invite stares from people who then averted their eyes, possibly out of guilt or a there-but-for-the-grace-of-God sense of relief, especially if encountering a prisoner looking out of a window. Only one of the four occupants of the van was looking out of the window. Jack Lynn was sitting on his own, staring morosely at passing scenery, his thoughts churning as he reflected on the freedom of choice people beyond the bus still had. That freedom was now denied him. He suspected that most of the people out there were no less prisoners. The four screws escorting him were certainly prisoners themselves, only they did have room to manoeuvre, had some chance of getting themselves a result. The philosophical point didn't sustain him. He had been weighed off with twenty years at the Old Bailey four very long days ago, twenty years, the result of a fitting from the filth. He had spent three nights in Wormwood Scrubs, sitting or pacing the whole time, thinking about his sentence, not believing it, feeling numb with disbelief; he was still barely able to grasp the fact even though the initial shock had worn off, leaving tiredness. Thoughts rolled through his head as if on a loop. They started with Detective Inspector Pyle, who had fitted him, having informed him he was well overdue; went on to the three slags he had stood in the dock with, whom he knew had been involved in that particular blag, and who, ironically, had got a result themselves but hadn't offered him an out; they went on to Justice Quigley weighing off with twenty after the jury had returned a guilty verdict on all the counts against him. His wife's protest as she had been led away after seeing him in the cells below the court was the point at which he stopped thinking.

A family travelling along the motorway to their holiday, with their car overloaded, stared at the prison truck as it overtook them. The kids' excited expressions changed to bewilderment as their father explained about the van. The picture brought Lynn on to his own kids, Carol and Sandra. He had seen little of them during the nine months of his remand and trial, and still hadn't got used to being without them. He thought the world of those girls, and because of them could willingly have topped the Old Bill who had put him away. They were aged twelve and nine, and would both be grown women by the time he got out, unless he got a result on appeal. He was hopeful, but even so this forced separation was a wedge driven between them.

'You sure you don't want a few hands, Jack?' said one of the screws, who paused from dealing cards.

'Come on, deal the cards!' one of the others said testily.

'Oh, what, you losing a few bob, Ernie?'

'C'mon. You got more fucking rabbit than my old woman.'

Distracted for a moment, Lynn looked across at them but didn't comment. He had no desire to join the game. He was forced too close to the screws as it was. He watched the cards slide clumsily out of the dealer's hands, and thought vaguely about the waste of money sending him down the road on his own with four screws and a police escort. Two other cons at the Scrubs were due for the same prison. One a Scots-

Cockney called Billy Hamilton, the other a Welshman called David Morris, both had been category 'A', like him, would go down with a similar escort. Lynn turned away to gaze out of the window again, his agitated, angry thoughts quickly absorbing him.

Jack Lynn was forty-one years old and all his working life had got his living from villainy, apart from a few brief periods when he had had jobs or had been doing time. He was well built, and although he had been slightly over weight when he was arrested he no longer was. His dark curly hair had grown longer than he normally wore it. His clothes which were now fairly loose on him had a crumpled, slept-in appearance, even though he changed frequently during his remand period. He had retained his own clothes, not having gone through reception at Wormwood Scrubs, nor having been assessed because of a prison officers' dispute.

There was little in Lynn's appearance that immediately identified him as a villain; however, his contradictory, slightly didactic querulous nature did, and he often argued with all the conviction of the uninformed. As a criminal, and one who had never denied his criminality, Lynn had always accepted the odds in favour of his being arrested sometime. He knew you had a run, and depending on how lucky rather than clever you were, you earned a nice few quid, then when trouble came you tried to have a deal with Old Bill, get a result; if you couldn't then you did your time. If you couldn't do your time, as a CID had once said to Lynn, then you shouldn't do the crime. He understood that. There had been no problem when he had been arrested before. But over the last few years he had had a good run, been involved in one or two nice blags. Old Bill had wanted him for the one he had plotted up at Catford, but couldn't nick him for that so they had fitted him for something else. It had been a diabolical conspiracy on the part of the police, the prosecution, the judge; they were all actively involved, Lynn believed. He would have taken his nicking had he been involved on that blag, but couldn't believe he had drawn twenty years for the Romford Gas Board which he most definitely hadn't been on. The most he had ever known about it was that John Tully had been plotting something up. Jack Lynn felt very aggrieved over his current predicament; his feelings of anger and hostility towards authority were firming into a hard determination to do something about his sentence. He would resist it for all he was worth.

There were two meal stops en route to the prison and for neither of them was Lynn allowed to get out, other than to go to the lavatory in handcuffs when accompanied by two screws. Food was brought out to him and eaten in the van.

The crenellated gatehouse of the prison was an anachronism; the square battlements rose like an early Victorian folly that someone had built on a whim, and bore little relation to the rest of the building other than in the material used. Even more incongruous, perched high on the battlements, were the two closed circuit TV cameras which swung in alternate arcs across the road in front of the huge, studded gates, picking up any movement and showing it on the consoles in the gate-room. The prison van was identified as soon as it turned onto the drive, but even so one of the screws was still obliged to get out and ring the gate bell. The wicket gate opened and Lynn's papers were passed in. The wicket gate closed and shortly afterwards the double gates juddered slightly and rolled open on well-oiled runners. The truck moved into the gate area.

Jack Lynn watched from the minibus as the huge gates closed slowly in the wake of the vehicle as though aware for the first time that their intention was to incarcerate him for the next twenty years. There was a growing sense of panic in him. This was it, he thought. Now he was actually inside the prison, it was as though that very move stripped away any last vestige of hope. While he was outside anything might have happened, the minibus might have crashed along the road, giving him an opportunity to get away – he'd have taken it. While he was outside those gates, even though he was under escort, he hadn't quite lost all sense of freedom.

'One on!' a gate warder shouted, informing the rest of the gate staff, like they were blind and couldn't see the single prisoner in the van or weren't expecting him.

The screw who had taken the driver's papers reappeared and handed him back two of the dockets. The main gate having been safely closed and locked, the warder went forward and unlocked the heavy ironwork gates at the opposite end of the security area. He swung them open one at a time, then waved the truck on.

The Ford Transit moved slowly out of the gate security and across the yard towards reception. The gates were slammed in its wake. Jack Lynn looked back as the noise echoed about him. He shuddered. It was noises such as gates and doors being banged that he remembered most vividly from his previous stays in prison.

Followed by two of the screws from the minibus, the new arrival shuffled through the double security gates and into the reception wing. In the main hall where all the prisoners arriving were processed, a screw waited behind a metal table which for safety was bolted to the floor. A trusty was close at hand to assist the reception screw, whose general demeanour was unwelcoming.

The room was twenty feet by thirty, with a line of six holding cells along one side; they were windowless cubicles which were smaller than ordinary cells. Prisoners were shut in those for the night after completing reception. Ranged behind the table was a block of Dexicon shelving that reached to the ceiling. On the shelves were hundreds of cardboard boxes containing prisoners' effects. On one end of the table were empty boxes, one for each prisoner, and a box of mothballs for storing in with their clothes. There was the prisoners' personal property book, into which the reception screw entered every kept item. Usually the reception screw sold on through the trusty any cigarettes, tobacco, sweets that were confiscated; it was one of the perks. At the end of the room was a corridor which led to the bathroom, also the room where the medical officer examined reception prisoners, and the room where prisoners were finger-printed and photographed. Every surface was shiny cream and green stippled paint, that was apart from the white lines on the floors were prisoners were required to stand the prescribed distance from the officer receiving them as though they were contagious.

'Stand on the line,' the escort said. There was a line on the floor three feet in front of the table. Lynn toed it.

'One on,' the second warder informed the reception warder, and handed him the second and third copies of his committal papers, which he glanced over.

Putting the papers on the table, he pulled his clipboard with reception forms on it towards him. 'Full name.' Warders never said please or thank you to cons, nor to fellow officers, but did to the chief officer, deputy governor and the governor. All the brutalizing aspects of prison affected the screws no less than the prisoners. Any vestige of sensitivity they may have entered the service with quickly became buried and lost, like those good intentions which perished on the rocks of perversity.

'John Albert Lynn.'

All they needed was his surname to identify him, Lynn knew; they had endless details on record about him, but wherever he went they were all taken again as if the sole purpose was to keep someone in work.

The reception warder looked slowly up at him. 'You've forgotten something.'

Lynn simply looked back, knowing what he wanted.

'You'd better understand something right from the off. When you address any member of the staff, no matter what their rank, you call them sir. Understood?'

It was a try on. Some prisoners could be intimidated, but Lynn had no intention of even starting out that way.

'You got some chance, pal,' Lynn replied.

There was a tense pause as each looked at the other, the reception screw trying to decide his next move.

In a tone heavy with menace, the reception warder said, 'Looks to me like you're going to make a lot of trouble for yourself, John Albert Lynn.' He shook his head. 'In future you're a number. You're now prisoner 469783. That's what you'll be for the next twenty years. Don't you forget it. When required to do so you'll identify yourself by that number, then if further required, and only then, by your name. Understood?'

Again Lynn hesitated. Despite himself he knew he had to go through the process. Trying to prevent it at this stage was pointless.

They ran through his particulars; after stating his occupation the warder asked about his insurance card and P45. He hadn't got either.

With a deprecating nod as though expecting nothing else, the screw said, "Course you haven't. I daresay the state'll be obliged to keep your wife and kids for the next twenty years, even though you've contributed fuckall.'

Lynn tensed. He felt an inclination to spring the screw and kneedrop him in the groin. This was only the start of the abuse he would get; probably most of the time they didn't realize they were abusing people. 'Old Bill fitted me,' Lynn said, his hands at his side flexing into tight fists. 'The state's fucking well entitled to support my family.'

'Don't answer back,' the escort warder said.

The reception warder was unimpressed by Lynn's argument. He rose from behind the table as if to emphasize a point. 'I'll give you a piece of advice,' he said, stabbing the air with a thick middle finger, 'and you'd better fucking well heed it 'cos we got the means in this nick of dealing with hard cases like you. Stay in line or you'll be on report faster than you know.' He glanced at the other two warders present, as if reassuring himself.

Having screws pressure you on reception, trying to establish beyond doubt their authority, was standard practice. But Lynn was determined not to take too much of it.

The way he felt to begin with, plus the pressure he now sensed building up inside him, suggested there was going to be some kind of straightener before much longer, he knew it had to come.

Bathing was an essential part of a prisoner's reception, though because of numbers, lack of staff and inadequate facilities, bathing wasn't a too frequent part of the prison routine. It was usually nothing better than a weekly occurrence, and some of the prisoners even avoided it then. The idea of a bath on reception was to check the possibility of bringing contagious diseases or infections into the close prison community, though the six inches of water a prisoner was allowed was barely more than a nod towards cleanliness.

The bathroom in the reception wing was like something out of a museum. It had six antiquated baths set in the stone floor, each with huge, worn taps and scoured-off enamel. As Lynn came in naked past the white-coated warder at the door a prison trusty who moved a mop listlessly between the baths watched him with uncommon interest.

'Get a towel and soap there,' the warder said, indicating some small oblongs of folded towelling on a metal table, then turned away out of the bathroom.

'The water's nice and hot,' the trusty said encouragingly to Lynn as he approached the bath.

Lynn didn't say anything, but felt instant hostility towards this man. He thought prison homosexuals were part of the mockery of prison celibacy, and meeting this one in his present mood was about the final insult. By having him there for new arrivals to encounter on reception, it seemed the prison administration were trying to precipitate trouble. However, Lynn was still sufficiently in control to know that it wasn't worth getting himself nicked just for the satisfaction of whacking him.

As he sat in the water and began washing himself Lynn noticed the trusty first check that the warder hadn't returned, then edge closer. He stopped and looked at him, with his reddened lips and darkened eyes – dyes from the hardcovers of library books were used – then glanced down at his crotch. 'I'm getting a blue veiner here, Ginge,' he said invitingly.

The trusty glanced round again to check that the screw hadn't returned, then edged over to the bath, his mop still in his hands. He leaned forward as though he was going to oblige Jack Lynn. But without warning Lynn grabbed hold of his thinning hair and yanked his head down, forcing his face into the water; the trusty let out an hysterical shriek as he went under. Lynn wasn't really interested in drowning him, but rose out of the bath, avoiding stepping on him. The screw reappeared at a run.

'What's going on?' he wanted to know.

'That soapy bastard needs a bath,' Lynn said, picking up his towel.

'What happened?' the screw said to the trusty who was on his knees at the side of the bath, spluttering and coughing.

'I slipped, Mr Gregory. I slipped, sir,' he managed, panic still in his voice.

The screw didn't believe him. 'Get yourself dried,' he said curtly to Lynn, 'and get over and get yourself some clothes.' He turned his attention back to the prison queen; probably the prison officer used his services from time to time. Lynn didn't respond to the screw's reaction that typified the injustice that seemed ever present. Instead he moved out, drawing the sparse towel round himself.

As a general rule prisons were relaxing over the wearing of prison clothes. At one time every prisoner was compelled to dress in similar outfits, including the ties that were issued. Nowadays, although the clothing was issued to every prisoner, it could be worn or left off, the decision was for the prisoner. Prison authorities didn't learn much from experience, but were slowly coming to understand that there was little advantage in trying to force a man to wear a tie or shoes, especially if he had little or nothing to lose if he chose not to.

The clothing store which was part of reception was run by a trusty, supervised by a screw. The trusty sized Lynn up with a glance where he stood in front of the table, the sparse towel round his waist. 'What are you? 'Bout forty-four chest?' he asked.

'Forty-two,' Lynn replied. 'Thirty-four waist. Something that fits a bit near the mark would be handy.'

The trusty considered the request. 'Get any snout in?' he asked. That would determine how new or well fitting the clothes Lynn was issued with would be.

Lynn knew the rules – probably the warder responsible for the store would cop half of what the trusty got – but wasn't going to play. It was bad enough having screws pull those strokes without having what was after all supposed to be one of your own doing it. 'Yeah, I got about three ounces jammed up m' daily.'

'Ah, you flash cunt,' the trusty said in a dismissive manner, changing his mind about the clothes he was about to give Lynn. Instead he quickly collected up an ill assortment of clothes, some of which weren't even clean, and set them on the table.

Lynn picked up the vest. It was several sizes too big, but he would have put up with that had it been clean. It was stained down the front. He threw it back at the trusty, who, although big, didn't put Lynn off at all. 'Change it,' he said.

'You gotta take it as it comes, pal.'

Lynn pointed with his index finger, emphasizing his warning. 'I won't tell you again.'

The trusty had been doing this job long enough to recognize when he'd got trouble on his hands, but he didn't want to be seen to back down too easily. He got Lynn another baggy vest, while Lynn stepped into the pants. They hung down his legs like a curtain, but he let them go; not so with the trousers that he stepped into. He removed them patiently.

'I told you thirty-four waist,' he said, throwing them at the trusty, whose attention was momentarily distracted by the warder who had stepped through the door.

'What the fuck d'you think this is,' the screw demanded, 'Savile Row? Pick those clothes up and get them on, 'fore I get the principal officer to you.'

'You tell this cunt to get me down something that fits.'

That wasn't the answer he was expecting. 'Right!' he said, panicking slightly as though Lynn had threatened him. 'You stay where you are, don't move.' The uniform backed away, then suddenly wheeled out of the store.

'You picked a wrong 'un, upsetting that screw, pal,' the trusty said, trying to mitigate his own position.

The prison officer shortly returned with the principal officer who was in charge of the reception wing. He was Gordon Walters, who was older, heavier, measurably shorter than his colleague. He had been in the service a long while and knew most of the dodges and fiddles and was more sure of himself.

'This officer has reported you for using threatening behaviour,' Walters said.

'I just asked for some reasonable clothes ...' Lynn said reasonably.

PO Walters said, 'This is not a West End tailors.'

'It's not even clean,' Lynn was digging in.

'We make the rules,' the PO said. 'Rule twenty states: A convicted prisoner shall be provided with clothing adequate for warmth and health in accordance with a scale approved by the Secretary of State.' Most prison officers could quote verbatim from the rule book. 'It doesn't say anything about it having to fit or be clean. It's adequate for your needs. If you want to wear fancy clothes you should have thought of that before getting yourself convicted ...'

'I was fitted by the fucking CID,' the prisoner protested.

'Save it. We've heard it all before,' the PO told him. 'You're doing time, and you'll do it our way.'

'Fuck it! You give me clean clothes, or bang me up like this.' Having made his stand, Lynn wasn't about to retreat.

'You're going to come to a lot of grief here, you persist in this attitude,' the PO said. 'A lot of grief.' Then for some reason Lynn couldn't fathom, the uniform capitulated and turned on the trusty. 'Why haven't these clothes been laundered?' he demanded, turning them over. 'They're disgusting. Get them down to the laundry, and give the prisoner some decent clothes.'

With that he departed, leaving the warder as disappointed as the trusty.

'You pulled a right stroke there,' one of the warders said as he took Lynn along to the MO's office.

Lynn didn't bother to reply. His navy blue battledress type uniform fitted him well enough, so did his striped shirt. His shoes were new. It was a minor victory.

A medical examination was considered an essential part of reception, but it was so perfunctory that it could easily have been dispensed with. The MO's office was sparsely furnished; a desk, a chair, a cupboard and an examination couch were the only items of furniture. The seedy-looking Dr Eynshaw, the MO, had heavily nicotine-stained fingers and dandruff across his shoulders. He was in his late forties, but looked older. He was sitting at his desk reading a newspaper and ignored Lynn who stripped and dropped his trousers and pants at the line before the desk. Marking some horses on the racing guide, the MO put the paper to one side and found a reception medical form.

'Your number, name and initial,' he said, without looking up.

'Lynn, Jack Lynn.'

The MO stopped writing and looked up at Lynn for the first time. 'Don't you understand plain fucking English?'

'469783,' Lynn said grudgingly.

'Raise your arms.' He shone his torch on Lynn's armpits, without getting out of his chair. Then on his pubic hair. The examination was briefly interrupted by a coughing fit. A blob of phlegm shot from his mouth and landed on the form; he casually wiped it away with the back of his hand. He had Lynn turn and bend over, then shone the torch on his anus. 'Any VD crabs or lice?' he asked uninterestedly. Then went on: 'Any illness? Visited a doctor or hospital recently?' He was satisifed to accept Lynn's negative answers. 'Ever been a homosexual?'

'Leave off.'

The doctor went on writing. 'You're fit to work.' That was the end of the examination.

Lynn remained as he was, trousers around his ankles. He felt angry and frustrated. This was part of the humiliating process all cons were put through. Those who perpetuated the system treated the men they incarcerated like dogshit, but they were worse than that themselves, Lynn knew. They allowed prisoners no dignity or respect, and so deserved none in return. As though fulfilling some role expected of him, Lynn finally raised his prick and pissed against the side of the desk.

'What are you doing?' alarm rose in the doctor's question. 'What are you doing that for, you fucking maniac?'

'This is a pisshole, innit?' Lynn said as if surprised. 'You look like a pisshole attendant.'

'You're on report!' the warder bellowed at him.

The prospect caused Lynn no concern at all. He merely finished urinating.

41

Lynn didn't complete reception, which would have meant being interviewed by the chaplain, the chief officer and a welfare worker. Instead he was escorted to the punishment block and placed in a cell, and the following morning taken before the governor to answer the charge.

Immediately prior to going before the governor Lynn was put in a cell adjacent to the adjudication room, which was on the block. There he was given a copy of the charges, on the back of which form he could answer them in writing if he wished to. Lynn didn't, for he knew it would make no difference one way or the other; he was dismissive of the whole procedure. Next he was searched, then told to remove his shoes and was given a pair of carpet slippers several sizes too big; they were to prevent him kicking the governor.

Two warders marched Lynn into the adjudication room. There the prison governor, a picture of self-righteousness, sat behind the small desk, which was bare, apart from the records of prisoners on report that morning. Also present was the Chief Officer, Robert Carne, who was tall and overweight. He not only had a moderate nature but surprisingly liberal views for the position he held. The same couldn't be said for the officer in charge of the punishment block, PO Alec McClean, who was also present. He was a thin, gaunt-faced Ulsterman who was well-suited to his position. Also the warders from the MO's office were there. Lynn had no one on his side. The room was drab, painted familiar institutional colours, and free of furniture or adornment; there was a line painted on the floor six feet from the desk.

'On the line,' the chief officer barked. 'Toes touching it.'

Lynn toed the line, the escort warders positioning

themselves either side of him, just in front of his shoulders, both facing inwards; the idea was to prevent the prisoner springing the governor.

The governor, Archibald Maudling, was the best fed man in the prison, and looked the most indulged. He was heavy and gross-looking, with large jowls; his face was large and oval and he wore glasses which he had a habit of removing and waggling. His dark hair was swept straight back, accentuating his disdainful expression.

'Not a favourable start,' he said after the prisoner had been identified. 'It doesn't bode well that you couldn't even get through reception.' He wasn't interested in any response from Lynn, but glanced towards the chief officer. He shook his head. 'Mr Maitland?' he said, looking at the warder who had charged Lynn.

'469783, sir. Charged under the rule 47, sections, 13, 14 and 20 in that he treated with disrespect the medical officer who was examining him during reception; used abusive and improper language to the medical officer; offended against good order and discipline in that he urinated on the floor of the MO's office.'

'How did this urinating come about?' the governor asked. 'Through incontinence?'

'No, sir,' the warder responded. 'He raised his member, sir, and directed it.' The uniformed man seemed embarrassed. 'When the MO asked what he thought he was doing, he replied: This-is-a-fucking-pisshole. You-are-a-fucking-pisshole-attendant.'

'You'd better think again ...!' Lynn interjected. He knew the entire adjudication was a charade, and it was pointless offering any kind of defence. Governors like Maudling always accepted the word of screws; prisoners weren't allowed to be represented by solicitors or call independent witnesses, and the governor's word was final. That didn't matter so much on the relatively minor offences heard by the governor, but the procedure was no different for the graver of the offences heard by the Visiting Committee.

Lynn was ordered to be quiet, and the screw continued giving his evidence, at the conclusion of which the governor nodded. He always backed his men.

'What have you to say in your defence?' Maudling asked.

'Nothing. I was fitted by the filth,' Lynn stated categorically. 'I've no intention of doing my bird ...'

'I'm not interested in that.' The governor was plainly irritated by what was likely to prove a troublesome inmate. It didn't matter to him how Lynn had arrived here, the fact that he was there was all that mattered. And now that he was he would abide by the rules. 'If you're issuing warnings or statements of intent, let me advise you for your own good. You'll break before we do.'

The governor and the prisoner looked hard at each other, each despising the other.

'Why did you urinate in Dr Eynshaw's office?'

'Looked like a pisshole to me ...' Lynn began.

'Outside!' the governor ordered.

Before the governor had completed his order the escort about faced Lynn and marched him out. In the shiny green and cream corridor, the older of the two warders, Reg Allison, shook his head in dismay. 'Jesus wept,' he said. 'You're not asking for trouble, son, are you?'

In the adjudication room the governor deliberated on Lynn's immediate punishment. Maudling paid lip-service to the opinions of his staff, but could adequately decide such things himself.

'I think we're going to have a lot of trouble with that one, sir,' PO McClean said. 'Troublemaker's written all over him, sir.'

'You think he should be referred?' the governor said. The charge was serious enough to be referred to the Visiting Committee.

The chief officer didn't agree. 'He's a grievance, sir. He could become the disturbing influence Mr McClean suggests.

But we've had other prisoners arrive with a grievance. A few days behind their door, they've settled down. We might do his cause more harm than good 'we refer him.'

'Has he got a cause, chief?' Maudling said.

'He seems to think so, sir.'

'I won't have him disrupting the smooth running of my prison. I'd prefer to have him transferred to Broadmoor.'

The chief officer knew he meant it. The riots they had had at the prison last summer were still a bitter memory for the governor. Not simply because of the damages to both property and prison staff; the governor saw it as a personal affront to his efficiency and the effectiveness of his rule. He had sought and got a number of prisoners transferred to Broadmoor after that little upset. For his part Chief Officer Carne was coming to understand that a hard line wasn't necessarily the best way to treat hard-liners. But the more enlightened he became, the more deeply the governor entrenched and he unfortunately had the last word.

'There's no mental history, sir,' the chief ventured.

'Pity.' Maudling thought about that. 'All right, I'll deal with him. Have him back in.'

When Lynn was back in the adjudication room, the governor said, 'You have been found guilty as charged. Although this case is sufficiently grave to warrant its being referred to the Visiting Committee, I have decided to deal with it. You will be held in solitary confinement for three days, and lose fourteen days' remission.' He removed his glasses and waggled them pointedly. 'You must understand that I won't allow you to become a disruptive influence. Further offences of this nature will be dealt with most severely by the Committee ...'

'I don't intend serving my sentence,' Lynn stated.

'Address prison officers respectfully!' the chief snapped.

The governor's lips tightened. 'You're going to make life very uncomfortable for yourself.'

'That's ballocks. The filth fitted me up,' Lynn said, ignoring the warnings.

'Sir. I think the prisoner should be further charged under Rule 47,' PO McClean said. 'Treating an officer with disrespect. Namely yourself, sir.'

Maudling appreciated that. 'Very well, Mr McClean. You are so charged,' he said to Lynn. Then announced, as though after weighty deliberation, 'I find the prisoner guilty as charged. A further fourteen days' loss of remission. Take him away.' He might have been a medieval king.

'It's all ballocks. This is just a kangaroo court,' Lynn protested as he was taken out.

That was the whole procedure of adjudication from start to finish. The prisoner was guilty even before he got to say his piece. The fact that a prison officer said he did it made that so. Rarely did a prisoner on report get a result. Lynn accepted that all screws were liars and were compelled to lie when going before the governor, as to tell the truth would show them up for the petty bastards they were.

The cell in the punishment block where Lynn was escorted to was larger than a normal cell, being about eight feet by fourteen. When the door was banged after him he stood against the wall for a moment and took stock of his situation. Jack Lynn was a man who could take solitary confinement; it wasn't something he'd ask for as a preference, but felt he was no worse off for being on chokey. It was imprisonment itself he found so difficult to reconcile, not its various degrees.

In the end wall of the cell there was a barred window that was too high to see out of, and there was no furniture to drag over and stand on. The cell contained only a low fixed cot bed with its thin mattress and the statutory duck cotton sheets and three blankets. The plastic pot for pissing in stood in the corner by the door. The green and cream walls were without adornment apart from the occasional pieces of graffiti. Like all the cells on the high security wing, they were stipple painted so that any attempts to remove the mortar from between bricks would be immediately apparent.

Alone now to consider his prospects, Lynn felt a sense of dismay. It rose up almost to overwhelm him. The only way he could prevent it doing so was by not thinking about his future. He was distracted by muffled sounds beyond the cell. He stood off the wall and listened but was unable to identify them. The noise worried him, but proved a distraction from his own problems.

Boredom was the rock on which so many prisoners perished; in solitary everything that was boring was accentuated, while Lynn was no better than the average prisoner at coping with boredom. He lay on the bed, but knew if he slept he wouldn't sleep at night; but by turns his thoughts closed in on him or he became aware of a screw watching him through the grille in the door. Physical exercise was what most prisoners in solitary finally resorted to, and Lynn was no exception. It was then he discovered just how unfit he was. He managed to do only eighteen press-ups before his arms gave out and he crashed to the stone floor, where he lay heaving.

The punishment block, unlike the wings, was a single storey building with a central thoroughfare, intersected from the entrance by inner barred gates. There were cells along either side of the corridor, an office for the PO and one that the warders used. A cupboard called the library held about half a dozen books for the use of those who hadn't lost all privileges.

Brian Lang, a trusty, pushed a trolley through the central thoroughfare, bringing the supper trays to the four men in chokey. The warder checked through the grille of a cell outside which Lang had stopped, then unlocked the door. The trusty was about to take the tray to the door when the warder, Cyril Jordan, stopped him. He took the tray and pointed along the corridor to Lynn's cell, then pulled open the door and stepped into the cell. There a prisoner, Bob Mark, was cowering on his bed. He appeared to have recently been beaten up.

'Come on, Bobby,' the warder said in a friendly manner. 'A

nice bit of grub for you.' He set the tray down, not taking his eyes off Mark. He paused, then scooped some grit and fluff off the floor and sprinkled it over the food. He smiled at the prisoner as he backed out of the cell, shutting the door.

Jordan opened Lynn's cell, and leaving Lang there, moved back to Mark's cell.

'Hello, Jack,' Lang whispered across the threshold. 'Heard you'd arrived.'

'Not for fucking long, Bri!' Lynn responded, but recognized immediately what a senseless statement it was.

'Mind how you go.' Lang spoke quickly, a habit from many such snatched conversations. 'They got a special punishment routine here, 's murder.' He checked along the corridor to where the screw was peering into Mark's cell. 'Fucking slaughtering that poor bastard, they are.'

'What's that?'

'In the next cell but one ...' He saw the warder turn in his direction and ended abruptly.

'C'mon, what you after, a fucking tip?' Jordan said.

'Just taking his wine order, Mr Jordan,' Lang said cringingly, as if mocking Lynn for the warder's benefit. That was essential for survival as a trusty.

After the door was slammed locked, Lynn considered the tray, which had on it a pint mug of tea, four slices of white bread, a small pat of marge, and a dollop of what appeared to be lumpy catshit but was in fact stew. The potatoes and carrots had lost any resemblance to vegetables. The cutlery was plastic. Lynn raised the plate and smelled the main dish. Despite what it both looked and smelled like, he knew he'd eat it. The same with the tea, the first mouthful of which he spat into the pisspot – there was extra bromide in that sent down to the block, he was sure.

Lynn's meal was interrupted by shouts from Bob Mark and a muffled crash of the tray. 'I'm not fucking eating it,' came the distorted shout. Lynn pressed his ear to the door, trying to

354

make out what was going on. 'Keep it up you silly bastard, you'll get some more,' he heard Jordan say. Though maybe he said silly boy. Lynn wasn't sure. There were further shouts to be let out from Mark; then silence. Lynn listened throughout his meal and the rest of the evening, but heard nothing more from Mark.

The only reading material in the cell was a mutilated Gideon Bible. Lynn wasn't that desperate to read something but used it in the same way most prisoners used those bibles, for toilet paper – there was rarely any supplied in prison. His pot had to serve him throughout the night; there was no way the screws were going to let him out for a pony.

Lynn was suddenly awakened from a shallow sleep in his lighted cell by a cry. Hearing prisoners cry out at night wasn't unusual; some did so through fear, others conscience, yet more because of an unexpected visit. It took Lynn a few moments to identify where the noise came from. It sounded like the lad along the corridor being beaten again. He was making a disconcerting wail. Lynn got out of bed and sprang up to the window and hung there as that was the best place for listening – illegal conversations were often held that way. Finally his arms gave out and he dropped down and went to the bell push; he couldn't avoid getting involved, even though he didn't know Mark. He was responding to the sense of injustice, which related to himself. Someone had to try and do something; maybe someone would do the same for him in there if he got some aggro' from the screws.

There was no answer to the bell, nor any immediate indication that a bell somewhere was summoning a warder. Lynn didn't attempt to go back to bed, but sat listening. After a while Bob Mark fell silent; then a while after that Lynn's door was unlocked and Jordan appeared.

"You ring your bell?' he said.

'Half an hour ago.' Lynn measured him with a look.

'What d'you want, a sleeping pill?' There was a mocking smile on his face. Jordan was six feet, with blond hair and a rigidly straight back and neck, which was essential to enable him to see from under the acute angle of the slashed peak of his cap. He had a youngish, fleshy face and thick lips. He was a Geordie; the prison service seemed full of them.

'What's wrong with that lad? Screaming like that?'

'Like what?' Jordan listened pointedly. 'I don't hear no screaming. You must've had a bad dream. Get back to bed and don't ring that bell any more.' He waited for a moment, challenging Lynn to make a comeback. He didn't. The uniform stepped out, slamming the door.

With perseverance the press-ups came easier for Lynn. He exercised in that way in his cell both before and after breakfast. The time would come, he guessed, when he would do fifty with ease, probably one hundred. But for now twenty left him breathless and sweating.

He was that way on the floor recovering when Reg Allison unlocked the cell and bent through the low doorway. He was a tall man with a pronounced stoop, possibly from bending for too many low doorways. Allison was a long-serving officer who hadn't long to go before retirement; despite all the time he had put in, some grains of compassion had stayed with him, or had been rediscovered. Possibly he felt he had nothing to lose by yielding a little now that he was at the end of his career, or maybe he was trying to redeem himself for what he had been a party to over the years.

'Time for a bit of outdoor exercise, son,' Allison said as Lynn rolled over and looked at him.

'They letting me out?' Lynn reached for his towel.

'You'll do all right,' you can keep a sense of humour.' That might have been the easiest thing in the world while banged up. He winked, then checked outside in the corridor, making sure his colleagues weren't in earshot. Turning back, he said, 'I'll give you a piece of advice for what it's worth. Watch your step. They're looking for an excuse with you now. Any excuse'll do.' He winked again. 'Come on!' he said, changing his tone, 'Outside.' He stooped back through the doorway.

Lynn watched him, his expression thoughtful. He suspected the advice was a ploy to get him to toe the line; it would only make him dig his heels in more.

The exercise yard was oblong, enclosed by a sixteen-foot chain link fence which was topped by rolls of barbed wire set in 'Y' brackets; this was itself enclosed within a wire-topped walled compound, which was finally enclosed by a perimeter wall; topping that were spikes. It was a maximum security prison. A warder with a dog was on duty outside the wire compound; another, without a dog, was in the exercise yard. Four prisoners were led directly into the yard by a door from the wing it abutted – that was the only way in or out – and with them was Reg Allison, who locked the door after them. Included were Jack Lynn and Bob Mark. The latter shuffled and stumbled, sobbing to himself as the four moved around the yard in single file, six paces between them. Mark, who was immediately in front of Lynn, worried him.

'What's the problem, pal?' Lynn asked quietly as they moved farther away from the warders. There was no response. He glanced around, checking where the warders were, then lengthened his stride to get closer to Mark. 'What is it, bad news from home?' That was the single biggest cause of distress in prisoners, exacerbated by the fact that they were helpless to do anything. They couldn't meet privately or for any length of time with their wives and families, nor were they able to write to them without having the prison censor reading the letters.

Still there was no response from Mark. He was a big man in his late twenties, thickset, but his height was disguised by the fact that he was hunched over and hiding his face as he shuffled along. He was in a world of his own.

Lynn dropped back to the con behind as they went round. 'What's wrong with him in front?' he asked. Then immediately lengthened his stride as they came past the nearest point to the warders.

'You Jack Lynn?' the con said when they closed the gap again.

'Who are you?' Lynn asked cautiously.

'Frank Timper. Heard you was down. How long d'you get?'

'Three days, 's all. What about him?'

'Poor bastard,' Timper said. ''S bit simple.'

''S that all?'

'Naw. He's not that simple.'

'Oi! No talking there, or you'll be on report,' the warder with Allison said. 'Space yourselves out. Come on.'

As they continued round in silence Bob Mark tripped and fell to the ground without trying to prevent himself. He lay there sobbing. Lynn went forward to help him, and saw at close quarter now just how badly marked his face was. Lynn had been in enough fights to know that the scabs and bruises were caused by fists. What he saw disturbed him. He had seen other prisoners beaten up during his last taste, and that had disturbed him no less then.

'All right, leave him,' the warder said.

Lynn withdrew, feeling helpless. He knew he ought to do something but didn't know what.

Lying on his bed after Lights Out Lynn listened for any sound from Bob Mark, and responded to the first scream he heard. It was followed by muffled shouting to be left alone. Lynn sprang off the bed in his vest and pants and rang the bell. There was no response. He searched round the cell for something to bang the wall with. There was only his shoe.

'Bob! Bob Mark? You all right?'

He waited. There was no response, other than Bob Mark's stopping crying. Lynn dropped his shoe and listened. There was total silence in the punishment block. This was suddenly broken by further cries from Bob Mark like he was getting a beating. Angrily Lynn stabbed at the bell push, and held his finger against it.

'Take your finger off that fucking bell!' a screw ordered.

Lynn ignored the order until the shutter in the door flew open, revealing Jordan's face.

'What's your fucking problem?' he demanded.

'What's wrong with that lad along there?'

'What's it gotta do with you? Just mind your own fucking business . . .'

'I broke the simple fucker's glasses . . .' Another warder, the fat Oliver Dorman, said as though it was a great achievement.

The shutter slammed, shutting Lynn off from this conversation.

Something had to be done about Robert Mark, Lynn decided, speculating that he was getting more stick than he deserved. He didn't appear for exercise the following day. Lynn tried a couple of times during the day to get some information but without success.

'Cook's run off with the gardener again, Jack,' Lang, the block trusty said cheerfully as he brought the familiar tea, bread and marge, meat stew and pudding to the cell door.

'Fuck it, I'm thinking of finding another hotel, Bri.'

Catching Lynn's eye, the trusty winked. 'Don't make a pig of yourself.'

Lynn thought little of the gesture, being preoccupied with Bob Mark. As the warder went to close the door, he stepped forward and stopped him. 'Mr Allison?' he said civilly. The warder stooped at the door and waited. 'What happened to Bob Mark last night?'

Allison hesitated. 'I don't know. I wasn't on duty.'

'They beat him so fucking badly they kill him . . .?' Lynn asked angrily.

'Just watch it, son. That'll get you in trouble.'

'All right,' he retorted, 'put me on report. See if silly ballocks wants to know about it.'

The warder shook his head, then stepped into the cell. Lynn sized him up, deciding he'd have no trouble with this screw if he tried to put one on him.

'What good will it do you?' Allison said in a friendly sort of way. 'They'll charge you with groundless complaints. You'll wind up doing a month or more down here.'

'What about Bob Mark?' Lynn demanded. He was committed now.

'He had a fit. 'S what I heard. He has 'em all the time. He shouldn't be here really. Look, leave it with me, I'll find out how he is, let you know ...'

Reluctant to give ground, Lynn said, 'He didn't look like he got that from a fit.'

'He had to be restrained,' PO McClean announced from the doorway. Neither had heard his approach. 'He was doing gross personal violence to an officer.'

Lynn looked at this man with the contempt he deserved for his statement. 'I heard it.'

'Did you now?' he said confidently. 'Then you'd better take it up with the governor. I'll put you down on application to see him tomorrow.' He glanced at his subordinate. 'Mr Allison.'

When they had gone Lynn realized the significance of what he had done. But getting involved in Mark's fight did help to stop thinking too much about his own problems. He turned his attention to his supper and lifted a piece of bread. As he did so he saw something beneath it that shouldn't have been there, and remembered Brian Lang's wink. Replacing the bread he checked round, making sure he hadn't been watched. Then, sitting masking the tray, he cautiously lifted the bread and found half a bar of chocolate. He smiled, cheered by this. He would remember the gesture that could've got Lang nicked, and repay it some way if he got the opportunity.

Applications to see the governor were taken in the adjudication room during the morning, along with the charges. Lynn was escorted in and stood before Maudling in the same manner as though on report.

'469783, on application, sir, to make a complaint against an officer,' Chief Officer Carne announced.

'Is the officer who the complaint's against present?' the governor wanted to know. Prison officers were given every possible opportunity to defend themselves.

'I took the application, sir,' PO McClean informed him. 'He refused to name the officer.'

'Well?' the governor said, his gaze falling upon Lynn.

Lynn hesitated. He had had all night to think about what he was being drawn into, and he remembered Mr Allison's advice. His being nicked again wouldn't do much for Bob Mark. And in the unlikely event of his getting a result they would have it in for both him and Mark.

'What is the complaint?'

Still Lynn remained silent.

'Answer, man, or you'll be charged with insolence,' the governor said testily.

'I made a mistake, sir,' Lynn said finally. 'I apologize for wasting your time, sir.'

The governor and the chief officer exchanged looks, satisfied that Lynn was settling down now, toeing the line.

'Very well,' the governor said. 'I accept your apology. I think you'll find this change of attitude will make your stay here far easier for you.' He nodded, concurring with himself.

That easy.

42

In the wings of prison the resounding clanging and slamming of doors and gates seemed ever present. No one ever closed a door quietly. It was for reasons of security that doors were slammed. It got so that, after a few weeks on the wings, prisoners, like the warders, ceased to even notice the doors being banged.

Once through the locked outside door to the wing, entrance to the wing proper was barred by a heavy section gate that formed a security reception area. Allison and another warder who escorted Lynn from the punishment block waited while a wing warder came forward and unlocked the inner door.

As Lynn stood on the threshold and looked over his new environment he didn't overflow with joy. The wing was old, overcrowded; it had afterthoughts bricked-on. The centre of the three storey was clear through to the skylights in the wooden-trussed roof. The only thing impeding this space was anti-suicide chainlink netting that stretched horizontally at each floor. Apart from stopping anyone jumping to his death, the chainlink had an oppressive effect. On each of the stone landings around the well of the wing, cell doors were set back in the brickwork, the entrances low and restricted; the doors opened outwards and had a two-inch Judas hole in the centre which was designed to give a view of every part of the cell. To the right of each door, fixed to the shiny-painted green and cream wall, was a cardholder with the cell card of each prisoner giving his number, name, sentence, the colour of his card denoting his religion. Most prisoners put one of the denominations down, some adopted those that afforded the most privileges – Catholics got fish on Friday; Buddhists got vegetarian diets – and putting down no religion meant a prisoner was banged up during chapel times. The wing on which Lynn was put held both special and category 'A' prisoners, and as they were considered the most dangerous in the entire maximum security prison they had special exercise and recreation facilities. These for the most part were training weigh's and table tennis, both on the ground floor; on each of the landings there was an association room where prisoners could eat their evening meal and watch TV. The main office used by the warders was on the ground floor, so was the PO's office. There was a green baize notice board fixed to the wall. A heated trolley for meals was against the wall beneath the notice board, idle now that the wing was deserted. Lights burned on the ground floor where daylight didn't penetrate. Fixed to the wall at the end of the wing was a worn iron staircase that pierced the chainlink safety nets.

'One on!' Allison called to the warder who unlocked the section gate. '469783, Lynn.' He passed over Lynn's movement book. This went with Lynn everywhere he went in the prison and had to be signed by the officer into whose charge he was given. After locking the gate the young wing warder glanced at the photo in the book then at Lynn before going away for the PO, who would sign the book.

Allison raised his eyes, as though cheesed off with the procedure, like it wasn't fundamental to his existence. Lynn didn't respond; his eyes met those of a trusty, who had stopped polishing the floor and was leaning on his mop, interested in the new arrival. He immediately looked away and resumed his work.

'I expect you'll be behind your door for a couple of weeks,' Allison commented. 'While they assess you.' He knew he would, it was standard. Lynn knew also.

The young wing warder, who was called Powell, returned with the principal officer who compared Lynn against his photo before signing the book.

Allison looked at the con as if about to say something, but finally didn't. He returned to the gate to wait for the warder in the entrance to let him out, while Warder Powell ordered Lynn to move off. The PO took the movements book to his office.

'Hello, Jack,' a con greeted Lynn as he came round the first floor landing with Warder Powell. 'Heard you was down here.' He seemed genuinely pleased about the fact.

Lynn for his part was surprised. 'I thought you was on the 'Moor.'

The con, Alan Thompson, who was descending the stairs, was about forty-five. He had all his front teeth missing from fights he had had in the prison; the front part of his hair was missing also. Thompson had that greyish-yellow pallor of the long-termers, caused in part by the psychological as well as the physical effect of prison, and one which took a long while to shed even after release.

'Fucking murder down there. I'd sooner be in this pisshole with these cunts,' Thompson said. He was quite used to stir, and was a man with little to lose, which was reflected in his attitude towards authority. However, he would only carry his anarchy so far, for he knew that they could give him more treatment than he could dish out to them.

Powell looked at the con as if to warn him about his abuse, but didn't. 'Move on,' he said to Lynn.

'Don't take no nonsense from Enoch there,' Thompson advised. It was Powell's nickname. 'If you need anything while you're banged up, just give me the word,' he offered and went on down.

On the top landing, Powell checked off cells until they reached one with an empty cardholder. He popped Lynn's card into it. 'Your new home,' he said.

Lynn looked at him, but squashed the inclination to tell him not for long.

As Powell pulled open the door, a prisoner inside jumped off the bed in abject alarm. 'What the fuck are you doing in here?' Powell demanded.

'I was just lying down, sir. I wasn't feeling well, sir.' The prisoner, Simon Menzies, was unduly nervous, and sidled round the wall of the narrow cell as the warder stepped inside. He was tall, slim, fine-boned, and looked younger than his thirty-odd years. But fear had etched itself deeply into his face.

'Out!' Powell snapped. 'Back where you're supposed to be, 'fore you get my toe up your ass.' Not untypically Powell tended to bully the weaker elements of the prison; he wouldn't have tried that on the likes of Lynn or Thompson, but suspected that they would have approved of this particular action.

Menzies cowered away from Lynn as he emerged from the cell, and hurried towards the stairs, his head going from side to side, as though he was expecting to be attacked. Lynn watched him clatter down the stairs.

'Killed a little girl, that one.' Powell explained as Lynn came in.

'Yeah. And he's been sleeping on my fucking bed?' He was suddenly incensed; the offence might have been contagious.

'There's been worse in here at times, I know.'

'I think I'd better have another cell. Smells a bit iffy in here.' The prospect of Menzies having been in the cell both disgusted and angered Lynn.

Powell considered him, deciding whether or not to go along with this. Finally he stepped out of the cell, taking the cell card along to the next cell and changing it with the card there, which was Bob Mark's.

'Here you are. Mark won't care where he's put when he gets out of hospital.'

Lynn was uncertain about nicking this cell. Mark had enough problems without his adding to them. But when he saw it was as bare as the one he had been offered, he didn't feel so bad. The cell was six by twelve, with a tiled floor and shiny cream walls – they must have run out of green paint. The furniture consisted of a washstand in the corner, a small table and chair and a narrow, low cot bed with three blankets and ducksheets piled at the top end. There was a heavily barred window high in the end wall. The cell contained nothing else, apart from Mark's meagre personal effects stacked on the table. Seeing those, even without knowing how long Mark had done, moved Lynn to greater compassion for the man.

'This is it. There's nowhere else.'

'What about those?' he said, indicating Mark's possessions.

The warder collected them up. 'You'll have the chaplain and the social worker round to see you soon.'

'Oh terrific,' Lynn said sarcastically.

Lynn was exactly two weeks behind his door and got a lot more than one visit from the chaplain and the welfare officer. He was less than friendly towards them, making similar statements to those he had made to the governor, that he had been fitted and didn't intend doing his bird. These formed part of his assessment and went on his record. Anything that was ever said to prison staff went on a con's record, and then on to the Home Office computer, despite what might otherwise have been implied.

He was given a pile of mail bags to sew behind his door; he sat on them instead. He didn't smoke so had no desperate need of pocket money, and there were enough books to read which he found preferable to sewing mailbags. Even so, he was glad when at last they opened his door.

On this wing Lynn was ranked among a cadre of hard men, an élite who had done worthwhile villainy and had wound up with long sentences: there were about fifteen of them. There were others on the wing who had done less worthwhile villainy and had wound up with equally long sentences, usually because of the damage they had done to property. Lynn's acceptance by the cadre was reflected in the respect readily accorded him. The other thirty or so prisoners on the wing were made up of murderers, rapists, hangers-on and the nonces. The latter were the child molesters who had to be kept separated the whole time under Rule 43, locked behind their doors, let out only with an escort.

At dinner time, which was five-thirty, food was served from the trolley on the ground floor, and prisoners collected their own food served by a trusty. There was a definite pecking order. A hanger-on wouldn't dream of getting his food before a right villain, but would come before the nonces.

'Get your supper,' a warder told Lynn, unlocking his door.

Lynn sauntered out onto the landing. The warder pointed down the stairs to where the food was, then moved away to unlock the next cell.

On the stairs Lynn ran into Alan Thompson. This time the latter was about to turn along the second landing with his food.

'Jack. All right, son?' he inquired. 'Get your bit of grub and fetch it up here in the TV room. All right?'

'Yeah. 'S that where you eat?' Lynn was unfamiliar with the wing's routine.

'There, or behind your door, just as you fancy. Go on, 'fore those fucking nonces get their'n.'

On the ground floor there were a lot of prisoners milling around the trolley waiting their turn. Also present were two warders keeping an eye on things.

Stephen Collins, a major villain and one who was always served among the first, saw Lynn as he was moving out with his supper. 'Hello, son,' he said expansively, causing heads to turn. Collins giving a con such obvious respect made the newcomer someone special. 'Al told me you was here. A fucking turn up.'

'In't just,' Lynn responded.

'Get stuck in 'ere,' he said, then turning back to the trolley, 'Who's that for?'

'It's Lentin's,' replied the trusty.

'I should fucking think so. What, before Jack gets his?' He simply took the tray and gave it to Lynn.

'Jack.' He offered him the tray. 'You'd better put a bit more on that as well.'

Only so much food came over from the kitchen, and

because the catering officers had their fiddle, it was only ever barely enough, which was why there were two screws by the trolley, to make sure what there was went around. But they didn't do anything to prevent the extra share that was heaped on to Lynn's plate.

On reaching the second level, Lynn turned along the landing. 'I'm gonna have my bit of grub in the TV room here,' Lynn explained.

'You don't want to go with them mugs,' Collins ventured. 'Come up to the threes,' – there Collins held sway.

'I just told Al I'd see him.'

Collins waited, a little put out. He liked having people respond to him. But then, as though Lynn were some kind of celebrity who he had discovered and didn't want to let go of, 'All right. I'll come there.'

The TV room was the size of a double cell. It had a central table where Lynn and Collins joined Thompson and two other prisoners who were eating. Three more were sitting watching 'Nationwide' on a black-and-white TV tucked away in the corner.

'They're no-good fucking ponces,' Alan Thompson was saying angrily. 'Them three what got done with you, Jack.' It might have been himself involved and wronged. How they were fitted or unjustly weighed off; what their chances were on appeal; who was the governor; who was fucking who, was more or less the staple conversation of cons.

'What the fuck can you do?' Lynn responded. 'The filth decided they wanted me long before Tully's little firm showed.' He was almost philosophical about this, though wasn't accepting that he had had a good run and it was now his turn. Had he been weighed off with about a five he might have done, or if he had actually been nicked for one he was involved in.

'John Tully always was a no-good cunt,' Collins said. In another context at a later date he was as likely as not to say what a nice fella he was.

'They was definitely entitled to give you an out,' Thompson said.

'You stuck in your appeal, Jack?' one of the other cons at the table asked. He was Micky Dunkerton, who was in his late thirties. He was neatly dressed compared to the others, who didn't bother with ties or coats. Some prisoners would even wander around in their vests. Dunkerton wore a collar and tie, and his jacket and trousers were neatly pressed. He worked in the prison laundry.

'My brief done it right off.'

'I don't want to depress you, son,' Collins said – in fact there was nothing he'd like to do more. 'But you know yourself the way that is, either you've done half your bird before you ever get to appeal, or same as those slags in the lower courts, they always favour the judge what put you down.'

'You are depressing me, Steve. I know all that, dun I.' He didn't take kindly to being reminded of the immediate prospects for his appeal. But despite them he would still press ahead, and at the risk of losing the time he had already served.

'Just marking your card,' Collins said, as though that was all he intended. He was a bit older than Lynn, a bit fatter, with a babyish complexion. He had a querulous nature, and didn't like to see anyone get something he hadn't, whether it was an extra letter or a result on appeal. He liked to be Jack the Lad and dominate people, and frequently did, especially weaker elements; basically he was cowardly, a fact that was revealed in the firm he had once run. Unlike Jack Lynn, Collins would back down from a confrontation if he could do so with his reputation intact; and his reputation was formidable. He was doing thirty for various assaults, robberies and murders.

'The thing is,' Thompson said, eating the last of his pudding, 'they keep you hanging round hoping you'll swallow it, rather than risk the time you already done.' The sentence going back to start from day one after an unsuccessful appeal, which the prisoner might have been waiting two years for, was a very sore point.

'Got some new evidence against the filth, Jack?' Collins inquired. 'That's what you need.'

'My brief's working on it.' Lynn believed the young solicitor he had was doing nothing else. 'He's a bit near the mark.'

'You ought to talk to Tony Scuffham down on the ones,' Micky Dunkerton said. 'He's doing twenty-five with a recommendation. He handled his own appeal.'

'How'd he go?' Lynn asked with interest.

'Oh, it went against him, Jack.'

''S fucking handy,' Lynn retorted. He looked at the faces around the table, as though assessing them. They each had to be all right or Alan Thompson wouldn't be sitting with them. ''It does go the other way, I tell you, I'll have to plot one up, 's all.'

'Out of here? You got to be joking,' Collins said. 'What d'you reckon I been thinking about for the past seven? Get one going, Jack, me and Bri'll make it with you.'

The fifth man at the table, who hadn't said a word through his meal, glanced over at Lynn with interest now. He was Brian Smith, who was in his late twenties. He was the odd man out at the table, and it wasn't simply his markedly different social background. He wasn't a villain, but had been adopted by Steve Collins so was readily accepted.

'I'd've thought you'd have had something by now,' Lynn said. He couldn't understand that attitude with a long one to do. He would never settle down to his twenty years.

'Ain't even been attempted. Too many fucking grasses. You can't even have a shit round here without you're grassed.'

'Something's got to be tried.'

'You wait and see,' Collins said, a little embarrassed at this apparent failing on his part. 'There's one or two grasses I'll mark your card about later, Jack. Though you'll smell most of them iffy cunts.' He winked at Lynn.

Lynn recognized right off what this con was doing. Collins was trying to bring him into line, to give the impression that he was part of the little team he had dancing to his tune. It wasn't on, Lynn decided. Glancing round the table, he looked for any food that was left. Dunkerton hadn't finished his pudding. 'Don't you want that, Mickey?'

'No. You wan' it?' He pushed the unfinished food towards Lynn.

'It ain't that good, is it,' Collins said.

'I'm a growing lad,' he said, surprised how quickly he had adjusted to the low quality of food.

'You look like you could do with putting on a bit,' Collins said and pushed his chair back. 'You need any snout, son?'

'No, I don't use it.' Lynn said.

'Most in here let you brown 'em for a bit. Gonna watch telly.' He rose and moved across to the TV, where, with some peremptory right, he changed channels, even though he didn't normally spend his association time on the twos. 'Watching that rubbish,' he chided. 'This side's better.'

The protests from the three cons in front of the TV were muted as Collins settled in one of the chairs.

'You gonna do a bit of work, Jack?' Thompson said, taking out his tobacco. There was no real option other than a protest after the doctor had pronounced a prisoner fit to work. Most preferred to work, for although it was dull, repetitious labour like making soft toys, it did help to alleviate the boredom, especially if they were in a shop working in a group rather than behind their doors.

'To be honest, Al, I've been sitting on a pile of bags behind my door.'

During reception a prisoner was sometimes allocated work to suit his particular talents. Lynn had missed out on that, but had no qualifications anyway that would get him a job in the library or administration where there was some fiddle.

'Brian's in the machine shop. 'S all right, you can get on that.'

'I'd just as soon stay behind m' door to be honest, working for these cunts.' He pushed his empty plate away and leaned back in his chair.

'Yeah. Ain't all that,' Thompson confirmed. 'Eighty-four pence was all I went and earnt last week. Stupid, in'it.'

'But that's rehabilitation,' Brian Smith remarked drily. It was the first time he had spoken since Lynn had sat down. His accent, despite his attempt to disguise it, was different from the others'.

'Be very handy, I get out in about twelve,' Thompson said cheerfully. 'Be no end of openings stitching mailbags. They could fucking well machine in a day what it takes us all year to sew. Sure you don't want none of this, Jack?' – putting his tobacco on offer.

Lynn shook his head. 'What's your chances of parole, Al?'

'I put in to go before the Board. I ain't got much chance. What do they do, look at your record, see what you done, how you shaped. I was well involved in that ruck we had last summer. Don't give you a lot of chance, do it.' He sat silent.

'What about Roger Busby?' Collins said from across the room. He had expected the group at the table to break up when he left, and when it didn't he continued to give it his attention, certainly more than he gave to the TV. 'They turned him out, didn't they. A right nutter, him. Put a screw in hospital.'

'Yeah, didn't make much sense.'

'What happened to that big fella in chokey?' Lynn inquired. 'Bob Mark. D'you hear?'

Thompson glanced towards the door, making sure there wasn't a warder around. 'Put him in the hospital, the fuckers did.'

'I heard the whacking they give him.'

'He's as simple as soap,' Collins interjected again.

'He's a nice lad, 'you talk to him sensibly,' Dunkerton said. 'Quiet as anything.'

'He was involved in a motorbike crash,' Thompson explained. 'His mate on the back was killed, it tipped him over. He ought to be up the road somewhere. He gets violent now and again.'

'That why they whack him?' Lynn asked. Mark interested him, and he began to feel a curious sense of responsibility for him for some reason. Possibly he should have protested more when he heard him being beaten, pressed on with his complaint in front of the governor.

'No-good fucking screws. They pick on him, they know he can't do fuckall. You run across Jordan on the punishment block? Tall blond-haired screw? Definitely a maniac that one.'

'The PO down there, McClean, he's a bit suspect an' all,' Lynn said.

'Cor, what a no-good cunt. He's on holiday from Ulster. Couple on this wing are all right. What it is, they're scared, know we ain't got fuckall to lose. They don't get too flash. Discipline and security's all the rest care about. I tell you, you'd be as well off trying to get moved to Broadmoor. But don't try violence to get yourself there. Know what I mean.' Thompson winked.

The news did little to encourage Lynn. He knew a lad who had done some at Broadmoor. He was a right good villain and there hadn't been anything wrong with him until sent to the high-security psychiatric hospital for attacking a couple of screws. There was a lot about the sort of bird he was doing now that was going to discourage Lynn and depress him, and although the seven months he had done on remand in Brixton while awaiting trial had cushioned the impact of this, a lot of adjustment was still needed. All that remand had acclimatized him to was his loss of liberty, for ahead of him had still been hope that he would get a result in court. Here there was lesser hope of getting a result on appeal for him to cling to, but it did help him to cope. What life would be like if he didn't get his appeal he didn't even dare think about.

Although he had spent time on his own in prison, mainly enforced, and was therefore grateful to free association, he was more grateful for the fact that it gave him the opportunity to exercise the one thing that all prisons stripped all prisoners of, that was freedom of choice. He enjoyed being with the other prisoners, talking to them, listening to their stories, but choosing to leave their company and be on his own in his cell was a luxury Lynn had too long been without.

Lynn was lying on his bed when Brian Smith appeared in the doorway. He had brought two mugs of cocoa and buns.

'May I come in?' he asked. Another con would've wandered in and waited to be told that he wasn't wanted. 'Cocoa. It's not very good.'

Lynn didn't say anything, but leaned on his elbow and watched the younger man. He could see how uncertain he was.

'It's just about drinkable,' Smith went on, 'after you get used to it, that is. It's taken a couple of years.' He chuckled nervously as he set down the mugs. 'I wanted to talk to you about what you said at dinner.' He looked at Lynn, then checked the landing before pulling the door to. 'Were you serious about making one out if your appeal's turned down?'

The question surprised Lynn. He hadn't expected this sort of approach from him. 'I think I'll get a result all right,' he said noncommittally, trying to decide how serious Smith was.

'What if you don't? Could you stick this for twenty years? Even for the seven years you'd need for parole eligibility?'

'What d'you have in mind, Brian?'

'I have one I've been working on for about a year.'

Lynn was suspicious. 'I thought you and Steve went mates?'

His expression was dejected. 'You heard how he reacted. Most are like that. They're all getting used to their bird, they even depend on it. It tells them when to get up, what to eat, when to sleep. By going to prison men forfeit the right to make their own decisions. That's what being sent here is supposed to be about really. But once here, if they're here any length of time, they forget how to make choices for themselves, or get so that they're afraid to. Finally about the only decision you can make yourself is whether you use your pot or piss your pants. Then that's exactly what the system wants, Jack.' He spoke with a sense of conviction that suggested that he knew what he was talking about. 'It isn't interested in rehabilitating you, it can't, it hasn't the facilities. And what would it rehabilitate you for. Unemployment? This is where they work on you,' he jabbed his forefinger against his head. 'They want to deaden that, turn you into a well-responding, well-behaved vegetable. They don't need to operate on people to quieten them down. They're achieving the same effect in a much more morally acceptable way. Look at some of them here, for Christsake, they're no more responsible for their actions than Bob Mark is, only they no longer even break the rules as he does.'

'I don't know,' Lynn said without thinking, resisting what he instinctively knew was the truth. Openly acknowledging it would put more pressure on him, challenge him to do something about it. 'Steve said he would make one.'

Brian Smith shook his head emphatically. 'It's what he likes to believe.'

Lynn sat on the edge of the bed and sipped his cocoa. ''S not all that, is it,' he said, wrinkling his nose in disgust, solely for Smith's benefit. 'The thing is, I got m' appeal.'

'I hope it goes well for you, I mean that,' he said. But it was what he left unsaid that impressed Lynn most.

He considered the man. 'What d'you get nicked for, Brian?'

'Destroying property,' he responded defiantly, but didn't elaborate or lionize his deeds.

'How come you sorted me out?'

'I heard about your reception, thought you'd be likely to take a chance. At least I was sure you weren't a grass,' he said confidently.

'Yeah, enough of those about,' Lynn reflected bitterly. One had helped put him here. Lynn wanted to be part of any plan anyone half-reliable had for making one out in the event of his appeal going the other way; but what he didn't want to think about at this stage was that disastrous possibility. 'Keep me in mind, Brian, will you?'

Smith agreed with alacrity. 'Of course. Who else is there?'

43

Day began in prison just like the day before, and the day before that. Prisoners could and did rely on it from the time they were unlocked, the procedure they went through, the reactions of screws and inmates alike. The waking up bell rang throughout the wing at seven a.m., a strident, discordant noise that prisoners failed to notice other than as that which started their daily routine; it was simply part of the general noise pattern, as were the groans and coughs that followed, along with the familiar shouts of protest. 'What was your old woman doing while you was on last night?' was a favourite one for winding the screws up – they were very minor ways of getting back at the people who kept them locked up twenty-four hours a day, seven days a week.

Lynn rose easily with the bell, his bladder bursting; he relieved himself in his pot which was three-quarters full. He shaved in cold water in the small bowl on the washstand in the corner.

At eight o'clock warders moved along the landings unlocking the cells for prisoners to slop out. With familiar regularity prisoners filed out with their pisspots, some to the brim, others shat in during the night – strictly pots weren't for prisoners to evacuate in but the chances of getting out to use the recess after being banged up were nonexistent, ringing the bell for that purpose pointless. A queue began to form at the recess on the end of each landing.

'About time,' prisoners said as they were unlocked, their tone depended upon who the warder was.

Other prisoners still to be unlocked rang their bells, which only brought shouts for them to stop from the warders.

'M' pot's overflowing, Mr Westbury,' a con said from

behind his door.

'Then fucking well tread it down,' Westbury, an over-weight warder with a large head made larger by mutton chop sideburns, shouted back.

There was a smell of stale urine and excrement rising up through the wing. It never really disappeared, being only masked with disinfectant. After about three or four prisoners had been in the recesses of a morning the smell was vile, but like everything else, it was something prisoners had to get used to. It was only their own smell, they were told if they ever complained. Smells in prison were something that were ever present: predominant were urine and the peculiar smell of damp metal, and at meal times it was boiled cabbage, regardless of what the meal was.

'Quiet there!' the principal officer on the wing shouted as he came on to the landing. 'This is not association.'

'Ballocks,' was the reply from an unidentified prisoner. There was laughter from the recess queue.

'Who said that?' the PO screamed. His name was Allen, and he liked discipline, would have preferred more of it from the rabble, along with more respect for both himself and his officers. But he was smart enough to know that if you pushed these men too hard, backed them into a corner, then all you'd get was a confrontation, and a total breakdown like the riot they had last year. That would have been a bad reflection on himself. He knew when to let a con have a small victory. 'Come on, who said that?' There was a stony silence from the queue now; only the sluice flush was heard. PO Allen yielded. 'Another fucking word 'I'll have you behind your doors.'

Breakfast, collected from the trolley on the ground floor, was eaten in the cells. It consisted of tea, which was served with every meal, porridge, which was in fact Grade A Canadian pigmeal, one dried, shrivelled rasher of streaky bacon and four slices of bread. Despite it's all being singularly unappetizing, Lynn ate heartily – and could have eaten it again when he was done.

At nine o'clock, with breakfast finished prisoners were slopped out again, then set to work. Lynn was lying on his bed reading when Warder Westbury opened the door.

'Work detail,' Westbury announced. 'Mailbag shop, you.' He moved on, expecting Lynn to rise and go to it, then came back immediately, mildly surprised that the prisoner hadn't moved. 'Oi! Get your-fucking-self onto the mailbag shop detail.'

'No fucking chance,' Lynn said. He didn't care for any of the jobs prisoners were put to, especially not for the rates of pay offered. He fancied mailbags least of all.

The warder was thrown by the unexpected response. 'What did you say?' he asked, giving himself time to think.

'I ain't working.'

'We'll fucking well see about that!' he said menacingly, then wheeled out, slamming the cell door.

Brian Smith, who had been along the landing, had paused, approving of the protest on Lynn's part. He thought it was fantastic that someone like Jack Lynn had arrived there; he was like a breath of fresh air. With luck they might even have another riot.

'What the fuck are you doing?' Westbury demanded, venting his anger on Smith, who he knew he'd get no comeback from. 'Get to work, 'fore I have you on report.'

Brian Smith smiled to himself as he moved off in the direction the warder had taken. Jack Lynn was going to put this lot on their toes, he was sure of it, and the prospect delighted him.

When Warder Westbury returned with the PO and opened Lynn's cell door, Lynn was standing pissing in his pot. He ignored them for a moment as they stepped into his cell.

'All that tea for breakfast,' he said finally.

'Mailbag sewing detail,' PO Allen said in a tone that suggested he wouldn't stand for any argument. 'Get to it.'

'Not while I'm appealing against sentence,' Lynn said simply, and sat back on his bed in defiance.

'Get off that bed, 'fore I drag you off it.'

Lynn didn't stir, but gave him a measured look. 'You'd regret it, 'you tried,' he said evenly.

'You're on report,' the principal officer said, recognizing immediately that he was neither to be reasoned with nor threatened. He turned on his heels and went out.

On report, was the screws' favourite expression. Lynn perfectly understood what it meant, what the consequences were likely to be. He'd have the usual brief hearing in front of the governor, who would back the charging officer then summarily dismiss him with the appropriate amount of chokey. He didn't regret his action, whatever the likely consequences. He would have preferred not to have been banged up behind the door, in the same way he would have preferred not to have been in prison. However, he felt an instinctive need to protest lest he might slip into the routine of the prison that Brian Smith had described and become like all the other cons who mostly simply tried to do their time and keep their noses clean. Lynn wouldn't allow himself to get like that. It was a firm promise he had made himself. He had been fitted: he wasn't going to do his bird – and if he did he would offer whatever protest to it that he could. The alternative was ending up like the prisoner he had seen in the Scrubs, Billy Hamilton. Brian Smith was right, Lynn thought, about cons getting to rely on their bird. It was frightening.

The MO was the next to visit Lynn. He was still on his bed reading when a screw unlocked the door and the scruffy-looking doctor stepped inside. Lynn gave him a cursory glance, then went back to his book.

'How are you feeling?' the doctor asked.

'I'm all right,' Lynn replied uninterestedly. He knew what the form was in giving that reply.

'Good. You're fit.' With the pronouncement that he was fit in fact for punishment, the doctor turned and shuffled out.

The required medical examination of anyone on report – to ascertain that they were fit enough to be punished – made the subsequent adjudication by the governor a foregone conclusion. Lynn wondered, as the doctor departed, leaving behind the early morning smell of booze on his breath, when last he had made a proper medical examination, whether he was in fact capable any more. The prison authorities were no different in their attitude over medical attention for inmates than most people, himself included, were over the treatment of animals: as long as the person had some qualification, it didn't really matter that he was incompetent. Having been pronounced fit for punishment by the prison's doctor, that was all anyone in the service was currently concerned about.

'Responding to Officer Westbury's request,' PO Allen said, giving evidence to the governor in the adjudication room, 'I went to the prisoner's cell and ordered him to join the work detail for the mailbag shop. Again he refused to work, without giving any reason. His tone was disrespectful; I told him to address me as 'sir' and ordered him to get off his bed. To which he replied, "You'd fucking well regret trying to make me." I saw there was no point arguing as the prisoner was becoming very hostile. I informed him that I was putting him on report, sir.'

Frustration was causing Lynn to ball his fists as he stood on the line in the adjudication room, listening both to the lies and the instinctive bias of the screws' evidence. It was so obvious that he wanted to scream at them. But he resisted.

'Well?' the governor said, turning his attention to Lynn. 'What have you to say?' His disapproving tone clearly suggested that whatever Lynn had to say would be dismissed out of hand.

'No point saying anything to that rubbish, is there.'

'Address the governor respectfully,' the chief officer ordered.

Lynn scowled. 'I was fitted up by the police; I am waiting for my appeal to be heard ...' He doubted that his words were even heard.

'You will conform with the rules and regulations governing

the good order of my prison. This includes working when ordered to do so. If you are determined to make a habit of wilful resistance, I warn you it's a habit we will certainly break you of.' Maudling removed his glasses and glared at the prisoner, trying to intimidate him. 'Outside,' he ordered.

'About turn!' the chief officer rapped. 'Move yourself.'

The uniform on either side of Lynn escorted him out, leaving the governor, the chief officer, and PO Allen and McClean to decide his fate – his guilt was never in question.

'I think a psychiatric report might be useful here, you know,' the governor said, flicking through the leaves of Lynn's report as if discovering for the first time that there wasn't one. 'Any suggestions?' He paid lip service to the democratic process of justice, but was quite clear in his mind about these things.

After a deferential glance at the chief officer, solely on account of his senior rank, PO McClean said, 'I think he's trying it on, sir. Testing us out.'

'What's the answer then? He knows he'll be punished.'

'Possibly he feels he has nothing to lose, sir,' the chief officer suggested. 'Three days' solitary confinement is meaningless in the context of twenty years. The same as any loss of remission at this stage.'

'He's likely to become very disruptive if allowed to dictate the terms,' Maudling said matter-of-factly. 'He can't go unpunished. You're not suggesting that, chief?'

'No, sir,' the chief said, despite himself. He didn't want to see their inflexible attitude turn the prisoner into a martyr. Sometimes it was better to be cunning than strong.

'I think this one's a candidate for special isolation, sir,' PO McClean offered, pandering to Maudling's viewpoint.

'Break him before he establishes a pattern of anarchy?'

'What about his appeal, sir?' Carne interjected. 'It's that which might be unsettling him.'

'Possibly, chief. His appeal will doubtless take its course.' He paused, tapping his thumb with his glasses. 'I'll bear in

381

mind your suggestion, Mr McClean.' He thrust his glasses back on his nose. 'I will make this man toe the line, knuckle down.' He meant it.

The result was Lynn getting seven days behind his door, with a supply of mailbags to sew there, plus fourteen days' loss of remission. Also he received a visit from the psychiatrist. The procedure was that the prisoner had to agree to see this doctor; Lynn simply didn't refuse to see him.

The psychiatrist wasn't exactly a leading light in his field, or if he was he disguised the fact reasonably well. Unlike the MO who was permanently at the prison, the psychiatrist only visited, but was no less seedy. He wore a small-checked suit, that Lynn guessed was bought at Burton's ten years or more ago and had been slept in ever since; his shirt was crumpled and his tie had gravy and custard stains down the front. Lynn, who was continuing his protest and had four days' beard growth, and was unwashed, was nothing like the mess the psychiatrist was in. They weren't getting along very well; had this doctor been a bit near the mark then Lynn might have welcomed talking to him, even though he knew all he said would go down on his record.

'Why on earth did you agree to see me if you weren't going to co-operate?' the psychiatrist asked, exasperated.

'Relieves the boredom behind your door, dun'it. What else are you any good for?' He had no end of insults for the man.

'Don't you want to be helped?'

'Some fucking chance of that, I should think. You gonna recommend they let me out?' Lynn asked.

'That's not what I'm here for.'

'Isn't that supposed to be the whole idea, get people rehabilitated?'

'One of the functions of prison is to keep wrongdoers locked away from society.'

'That's the only fucking answer any of you cunts have got. Bang them away. You're one of them, ain't you. I mean, you don't even want to try. You might as well fuck off – pulling my prick's more value than talking to you.'

'Have you always had this resentment for authority?'

"Talk silly for fucksake. How would you feel, them cunts fitted you and banged you up for twenty?'

'Is that why you're determined to break the rules? Get back at those who put you here?'

"'S only one thing I'm determined about, not doing my time.'

'At any cost?' the psychiatrist asked.

Lynn looked at him, clearly recognizing what he was trying to establish in his questions, that he was a wrong 'un. He felt curiously reassured that this doctor was simply a part of the system that was trying to hold him down, keep him locked away. It was all like a house of cards, and once that bottom layer had been set, all the others had to hold to their position, take the line that was required of them or the whole structure might collapse. He said as much to the psychiatrist, who didn't seem to listen, being more interested in the surface anger. That made Lynn more angry. Then immediately recognizing what this man was doing, he let his feelings slide away from him as easily as they flowed.

'Why do you get angry like that?' the psychiatrist wanted to know. 'Don't you think it's right that a criminal should be punished?'

'I wasn't angry,' Lynn said perfectly calmly. 'Of course it's right, otherwise we'd have fucking nonces on the loose.'

'But it's not right for you to be punished?'

Lynn shrugged. 'One thing's for fucking sure, 's no good relying on anyone on your side of the system to be anything like fair. All you're doing is trying to ease them cunts' consciences who put me here. Well, you can go and fuck yourselves,' Lynn said. He laughed, feeling in control now. 'You probably all do.'

The psychiatrist snapped his notepad shut, concluding the interview. He saw no point in continuing it. The prisoner was psychopathically overbearing, arrogant; it would take many sessions and a lot of good intentions on his part to break down the barriers he had erected. Unfortunately there wasn't the time or inclination for such an involvement. From their short session he had, however, noted enough about Lynn to make a report, give an expert opinion.

Before the seven days behind his door were up, Lynn received a visit from his solicitor, Alex Gladwell. The prospect filled him with excitement and expectation. For a while he expected that they would blank the visit on account of his being behind his door, but then silly ballocks had said nothing about loss of privileges, and a visit from a brief didn't really come under that heading anyway.

'You're supposed to sew those sacks, not sit on them,' Powell said when he unlocked Lynn for his visit.

'Oh, I will, Enoch, I will,' Lynn said. 'Just as soon as the needles come back from being sharpened.' Similar comments were made by the screws whenever they opened the cell door. He thought about giving them a surprise one of these times by actually sewing one of the bags.

Less and less the screws reacted to his insolence, knowing there was no point. Lynn saw it as a trial – one that he was winning, and those little victories pleased him.

Alex Gladwell got a very good living as a solicitor; most of his business was criminal law, and most of that was from criminals of Jack Lynn's calibre, men who got their living from serious crime and rationalized the nickings they got. Whatever Gladwell's ability as a solicitor, and it wasn't inconsiderable, his greatest asset was in the relationship he had with the CID, and the deals he was able to make on behalf of his clients. Almost all such deals were illegal, and necessitated the passing of money from the villain to the detective involved on the case, with the result more often than not that the villain didn't go into the dock or if he did, then with the CID's help in getting a result. Not a single detective who Gladwell had approached had gone wrong on him; the

384

discretion with which he proceeded precluded that. If the business his client wanted doing could be done, then the rest was mere detail to be worked out, and the price negotiated; if it wasn't possible for the CID to do any business for some reason, then they simply said so. There were never any comebacks. Gladwell had tried to do some business on Jack Lynn's behalf but had been unsuccessful, which had been both an indication to him of how much the CID wanted him put away and how much work they had done on him. But just because Detective Inspector Pyle hadn't done any business didn't mean that the police could be of no assistance. Putting the right price into the right policeman still could get him a lot of valuable information that would help with the appeal, especially about the police involvement in the case, details of which hadn't come out in court. But that all cost money, which was one of the things he had to talk to Lynn about. Censorship in prison being such it wasn't something he could write to him about. In fact as far as his clients were concerned he rarely wrote letters.

As with all visits the prisoner was put in first and waited with a screw while a second warder brought Alex Gladwell over from the gate waiting room. He showed him into the small room used exclusively for legal visits, and stayed also, locking the door behind them. The two screws tried to be as unobtrusive as possible, which wasn't easy in that twelve-feet-square room.

'How are you?' Gladwell said, shaking Lynn's hand.

'Oh, I'm t'rific,' Lynn said, his tone full of sarcasm. 'Just t'rific.'

Undeterred, Gladwell said: 'Can't say you look it. In fact, you look fucking awful.' He never let anyone have a conversational advantage, though he sometimes allowed people to believe they had. 'How are they treating you?'

"S not exactly Butlin's, is it. Though I heard it's as hard to get out of there.' He was becoming slightly more cheerful in the presence of his solicitor.

'Sit down, Jack,' Gladwell told him, taking a seat at the table and opening his briefcase.

Looking over at the screws, Lynn said pointedly, 'You can't even fart in private around here.'

'Don't worry, we'll write each other notes then eat them.' He grinned. 'You're behind your door?'

'I'm gonna stay there if necessary, till I get my appeal,' he said defiantly. 'How's it going, Alex?'

Gladwell arched his eyebrows. 'To be perfectly honest, our first priority is money. The second priority, though very important, is new evidence. We can't proceed very far without either.'

There was a pause. The small round eyes of the solicitor watched Lynn closely. Some clients when things had gone against them reacted emotionally and questioned what they had got for the money already parted with. He decided Lynn was more practical.

More dismayed than disappointed, Lynn said, 'Well, I ain't got either, have I. I mean, how the fuck could I, stuck down here? Can't you get nothing off Legal Aid?'

'For the sort of digging we're doing?' he said. He knew his client wasn't thinking logically, but was amused by the idea of getting a Legal Aid certificate in order to go into the police for bent information. He had explained to this client before the position about Legal Aid, telling him that no solicitor or barrister worth his salt accepted those briefs unless the case was particularly interesting, or notorious. The only way to persuade them to do so was with ex gratia payments. 'If you had some new evidence to put before the court, your appeal would be a simple open and shut case.' It would amount to a misdirection by the judge as a result of the new evidence that hadn't been available at the time.

'Well I fucking well ain't got none, have I!' Lynn said angrily. 'I dunno who the fourth blagger involved on that one was.'

'Don't worry about it, Jack. Your appeal's been lodged,

and what we have at the moment gives us a better than good chance.'

Lynn silently considered the problem, his anger yielding when he began to see a way out. At first he avoided it, but there was no alternative. He needed Alex Gladwell, who wasn't going to go on working for nothing. 'I'll have to sell m' house,' he said reluctantly. 'Get Dolly to. That'll solve the money problem. Where'll she go with the kids, though? Her mother's, I s'pose.' He looked at the solicitor, as if expecting some understanding of these domestic problems. 'Should be worth about twenty-five or thirty grand, 'bit of luck, 'time she pays off a couple of debts.'

'Sorry to have to be that way, Jack,' the solicitor said quietly. 'But it comes to dough going into different people.'

Lynn nodded, reluctantly accepting the situation. Dolly would understand, and do what he asked about the house; though she liked that place, it was the first proper home they had had. The kids were settled there too. It was a shame it had to go. But that was the way things went, he reflected philosophically, you never got too far ahead before you got a knockback.

'Our strongest ground lies in the charges against the detectives involved in the case,' Gladwell said. 'But we can't expect too much from the inquiries CIB2 are making; they'll simply do their usual number. They don't really want to nick their own, especially if they can give them an out. They might have to, though. DI Pyle is being investigated as a result of Countryman. We get something substantial on him, that way we can show a miscarriage of justice through the judge's direction. I'll delve as deep as I can. The more dirt we can get on that little firm the better. It'll all help.'

'What do you think, Alex? Seriously?'

'I'm a realist, Jack. I told you before that I'm not concerned how you got your living. But I sincerely believe that in this case you were fitted. No matter how many other robberies you may have had lined up, I accept that you didn't rob the

Romford Gas Board. Unfortunately we weren't able to convince the court. Whether the appeal court judges are convinced depends on what we come up with. If the fourth man who the police put you up instead of were to be arrested and confess ...' He shrugged. 'Life is rarely that easy. As things stand your chances are pretty good, I mean that sincerely. But by the time I finish they're going to be ninety-nine per cent good. There's nothing in it for me telling you that if I didn't believe it. We'll get you a result all right.' The solicitor measured him with a look, then said, 'I won't stop working on your behalf, Jack, I promise you that. I'll do everything I can to get your release.' He nodded, as if confirming this. Then dropped his voice to a whisper. 'If all else fails I'll send my managing clerk into you with some hacksaw blades.' He winked. But it wasn't such a ridiculous proposition. His managing clerk had been used before to liaise with cons on the inside over escape details. Gladwell spread his pudgy hands over the papers that he had removed from his briefcase. 'We've a lot of details to get through here. You feel fit?'

'I got time,' Lynn replied. He was feeling a lot more cheerful now.

44

A cheerful feeling spread through Brian Smith as he waited on the third floor landing outside Jack Lynn's cell. He had collected his supper tray for him and was waiting for the warder to unlock his cell. He was due out from behind his door, and the way Brian Smith felt it might have been him who had been banged up and was being let out. Other prisoners shuffled about either collecting their food or on their way to their cells or the TV rooms; the only difference this evening was that Brian Smith wasn't aware of them. As he watched the screw slowly select the key he began to feel a sense of impatience, and felt like telling him to hurry up.

The warder swung the door open and said, 'Come on, time to join the other animals.'

Lynn looked at the uniform when he stepped out through the doorway. Brian Smith held his breath, in case Lynn said something or did something and got himself banged up again. He didn't, the warder didn't even notice the look.

'Haven't you sewn those mailbags yet?' Smith said, imitating a warder. He wouldn't have tried a joke like that on anyone but Lynn. Jack Lynn had a quality of defiance which Brian Smith openly admired. He smiled. 'If I had a trumpet, Jack, I'd blow it.'

'Why's that, Bri?' Lynn said flatly. He had quickly sussed out this lad. He knew from previous prison experience how people sometimes latched onto you, they wanted you to fight their battles, especially younger prisoners. Sometimes it was all right, he found, other times it was embarrassing. Instinctively he knew the attraction was partly sexual, but he wasn't able to articulate this. He didn't object to Brian Smith latching on to him as he did, especially as he had an escape of some kind plotted up; in some ways he rather enjoyed the attention.

'You're from behind your door,' he said, slightly deflated now. 'I collected your dinner.' He extended the tray.

'To be honest, I was looking forward to getting it myself. It's the little highlights what make your day, 'you been behind your door.' He watched Brian Smith's disappointment, his own face expressionless, but then suddenly winked. 'Good luck, Bri.' He took the tray from the younger man, and they went towards the TV room together.

Bob Mark came up the stairs with his evening meal. Since his accident his powers of concentration were severely impaired and he had to work towards single and simple objectives. His current objective was reaching the threes' TV room with his dinner. He neither wanted nor could he cope with the distractions that Westbury, the landing screw, offered him.

'Oi!' Westbury said, catching him as he turned along the landing. 'He's the lad what nicked your cell.' He nodded after Jack Lynn.

Bob Mark, whose face had healed but was still shaded with bruises, looked along the landing, then at the screw. He tried to hold on to his objective, watching TV, but it was being pushed out. He had preferred the cell he had been in previously, he wasn't quite sure why.

'He took a right fucking liberty with you. You ought to go and sort him out.' The warder winked conspiratorially, then moved away down the stairs, leaving Mark a picture of confusion.

There were six prisoners in the TV room, which was no different from the one on the lower floor. The faces were different, that was all. Most of them turned from the TV and greeted Lynn when he came in. Collins was at the table with a prisoner who was doing life for stabbing a policeman. Collins paused from his food and watched Lynn as he and Brian Smith sat at the table, their backs to the door.

'Steve,' Lynn said, greeting him. 'All right?'

Collins offered a disapproving look. 'We do like to observe a bit of decorum here, son. Like shaving.'

'Oh yes,' Lynn said without giving anything. 'The trouble is you lose touch with the niceties, banged up. There was nights I weren't even bothering to dress for dinner.' He sat.

'Down the slippery slope you go,' Collins commiserated. ''Fore you know it you've forgotten which knife to eat your peas with.' He shook his head in apparent dismay. 'So what's the outcome of this little ruck? You gonna do a bit of work after all?'

'Hadn't thought about it,' Lynn said. ''S not much point, is there.' It was an unintentional slight against all those who worked, one that forced Collins to justify his position.

''S up to yourself. Providing silly ballocks don't get the hump with everyone else,' Collins said.

'Why should he?'

Parkshot, the fourth con at the table, felt compelled to align himself with Collins, who was currently sharing his favour. 'Well, you know what he's fucking well like, 'he's upset.'

The same compulsion came over Brian Smith in siding with Lynn. 'Fuck it! Maybe we should all refuse to work.'

Collins gave him a condescending look. 'I'll tell you what, son. I'll take your job in the machine shop, 'you go and refuse to sew mailbags. How's that?'

'I made m' point, Steve,' Lynn said reasonably, attempting to defuse the situation. 'I might do a bit now.'

They ate in silence for a while.

Bob Mark appeared in the doorway. He paused and looked round, trying to identify the man who had taken his cell. He saw the TV and was distracted momentarily. Collins, who was facing the door, saw him and glanced at Lynn, but didn't warn him as the big man came across to him.

'You got my cell,' Mark said, stopping behind Lynn. 'You got my cell.'

Lynn turned and looked up at the man, judging his chances if it came to a fight. 'That's all right,' he said reasonably. 'You can have it back.'

The offer immediately confused Mark. He hesitated, then said, 'No, that's all right. I don't mind. Mr Allison tol' me you was asking after me in hospital.'

'How are you now?' Lynn felt slightly relieved that he didn't have a fight on his hands. He didn't doubt he could have put Mark away, but guessed he had enough problems as it was.

'I'm all right now, I think. They give me some stuff over in the hospital. Calms me down like.'

'Well, why don't you sit down and have your dinner, 'fore it gets cold?'

Bob Mark hesitated, the television was in the forefront of his thoughts now. 'I'm gonna watch telly,' he said.

'That's all right then. Go on, we'll have a chat later.' He watched Bob Mark go over to the TV and sit down.

Collins grinned. 'Thought you was in trouble there for a moment.'

Lynn nodded. 'Steamed in and given us a hand, Steve, would you?'

'He's a strong lad. Seen him put four screws away, I have. You gotta be simple, pulling strokes like that.'

'He seems all right to me,' Lynn said.

The feeling of excitement Brian Smith had felt at the start of the free association period on account of Lynn coming out had vanished. He sat at the table resenting the attention Lynn was giving Bob Mark, and he was having difficulty keeping the emotion off his face.

Steve Collins noticed the young man's reaction, but didn't comment. It simply became one of those pieces of information he stored away for future use, when he would wind Brian Smith up.

'What'd your brief have to say, Jack?' Collins asked casually.

'Oh, he reckons there's a blinding chance of me getting a result,' Lynn lied. He didn't want anyone to know his problems, that way no one would derive satisfaction from any misfortune of his.

'Pleased to hear it,' Collins said, and glanced at Brian Smith again. 'All you gotta do is get it on then.'

'That's all,' Lynn replied. It might have been the easiest thing in the world.

Jack Lynn spent a bit of time with Bob Mark trying to help him sort himself out. It wasn't just that he felt sorry for him, but knew he got a shitty deal from everyone; he was dismissed by most of the cons as simple, and picked on by most of the warders, who knew they were certain to get a reaction from him, because he was easiest to wind up.

'How long are you down for, Bob?' he asked as they shuffled around the exercise yard together. He had read his cell card, but was trying to draw him out by getting him to talk. He didn't talk much to anyone, and only answered direct questions if he felt like doing so.

'I dunno, Jack, do I,' he replied slowly. 'That's what gets my goat. They won't gimme no release date, will they.' He sounded aggrieved.

'Didn't the judge say how long when he sent you down?'

Mark shook his head. 'He said I had to be locked away for the safety of society.' Lynn looked at him as if doubting that. ''S what he said, Jack, he did. If they'd only say when I could go out, I think I'd be all right. Know what I mean? It'd give me something to concentrate on.'

'Maybe we ought to try and do something about trying to get you a release date.'

'You think it could be done? That'd be t'rific.' He smacked his hands together excitedly, as though he had already achieved his goal.

It was a quarter past eleven and Lynn's entire wing, apart from the nonces, was out in the exercise yard, forty-two men moving around in a circle in pairs, the mandatory six paces apart. Talking was permitted between each pair but not with the pair in front or behind. Brian Smith wanted to walk with

Lynn, and felt as aggrieved as an estranged wife when Mark took what he considered was his rightful place. Prisoners weren't allowed to walk in threes or he would have stepped right alongside. Instead he found himself walking with Steve Collins as he had done on several occasions recently. Observing what was going on, Collins didn't miss his opportunity, didn't miss pointing out to Brian Smith how close he thought Lynn and Mark were getting.

'It's really nice the way old Jack is taking an interest in him. Got the simple fucker eating out of the palm of his hand. You'd think he was his Dad, you would.'

Brian Smith glowered, but didn't comment. Being brighter than the average con it didn't take him long to realize what Collins was up to, though for what reason other than to relieve the boredom or out of jealousy he couldn't say; however, despite the logical process that brought him to such a conclusion, there was nothing he could do to prevent himself reacting emotionally.

Collins sought him out during association that evening, finding him on his own sitting in front of the blank TV screen in the threes' TV room. The television had broken down, which was why the place was deserted.

'Tucked up in Jack's cell like a couple of birds they are,' Collins said, winding him up. 'You'd think they were giving each other one, you would.'

Feeling himself reacting Brian Smith said, through tight lips, 'You ought to watch what you say, Steve. Either one of them could put you away.'

A smile started across Collins's face. He knew he had gone too far and knew he had to retrieve the situation. 'You got no sense of humour, Bri, 's your trouble. You got to let go a bit, learn to recognize a joke otherwise they'll cart you off in a strait jacket.' He watched the young man, then sat and took out his tobacco. 'Anyway, an educated lad like you ought to be writing that petition to the Home Secretary for him, not Jack.'

'What a waste of time,' Smith said dismissively. 'There's only one way that loony will get out. The same way I plan to. That won't be by waiting till they say when.'

Pretending he didn't know what Smith was talking about, Collins said, 'Yeah, you ain't got a release date either, have you.'

'Sooner than anyone thinks,' Brian Smith said. 'I'm not going to sit in here and rot until they decide it's safe to let me back into society. I'm going to do something about it. You see if I don't. 'Normally closed mouthed, it was repressed jealousy that was causing him to be so informative.

'Put us in, 'you got one plotted up,' Collins said casually. He waited, but Brian Smith didn't respond. How serious his proposition to escape might have been Collins wasn't sure, but he was a man who didn't want to miss out on anything that was going on around the wing. 'The thing is, Brian, I got dough on the outside, a lot of it. And I've still got a lot of worthwhile contacts. I weren't no old mug, you know; some silly fucking cowboy who couldn't do nothing but stick a shotgun over a post office counter. I could arrange to have a boat to take us off the island, across to France or Morocco, anywhere you want.' He waited watchfully.

Brian Smith considered what he had said. Maybe he was genuine, but still he hesitated.

'The thing is, you're relying on Jack,' Collins said, allowing himself to appear hurt at Smith's indecision, 'I tell you, he's no value, no value at all. I'll tell you why. He'll get his appeal, get a result, he's a stone ginger. He won't want to make one, I guarantee it.' He paused. 'Think about it, Bri. Do yourself a favour, son. Put me in.'

Brian Smith committed himself no further than to say he would think about it. Despite anything Collins said he preferred to pin his hopes on Jack Lynn.

Unaware that he was the centre of this attention Jack Lynn was along the landing in his cell, having finished writing the petition to the Home Secretary about getting some indication of a release date for Bob Mark. The chances of getting a result were slim, he guessed, but it was worth a try, as it encouraged Bob Mark. There were a lot in prison like him, and they probably had no more success with their petitions. He was doubtful the Home Secretary even saw them; probably the prison censor referred them to the governor, who blanked them out of hand.

'You gotta sign this now, Bob,' he said, pushing the letter form towards Mark.

A worried expression came over Mark's face. 'Can you put down about them breaking m' bins? Makes m' headaches worse without 'em, it do.'

'Well, I could put it down. But we'd be better off not stronging it. I mean, otherwise silly ballocks'll just end up backing it. Here, stick your signature on that. We'll pull the MO about your glasses. All right?'

He trusted Jack Lynn's advice. He signed the petition.

Alan Thompson appeared in the door, looking flushed with excitement. 'Jack, there's a couple of nonces out on the twos, watching telly.' He sounded outraged.

'What, on their own?' Lynn was no less outraged.

'No, with two screws, 'S all part of silly ballocks' normalization plan. He's trying to integrate the nonces.'

'Fucking liberty! We can't have that.'

'Too fucking right. He'll have us twoed up with the dirty cunts next.' Thompson's indignation increased the more he thought about the situation the governor was trying to put over on them. 'I told a few of the others to have a wander down there.'

'Have some of them get some boiling water from the urn, Al,' Lynn suggested. 'We'll scald the cunts.' Just to think about what some of the nonces on their wing had done sickened him, and when he thought about it he wanted to hurt them so badly that they would die a painfully lingering death. Jack Lynn had no notion that this tremendous anger related to the fear deep inside him that he might be no different

396

basically from the sex offender, or child molester.

'There's a few already getting some,' Thompson told him.

'Let's see to the monsters, then.' He started out after Thompson. Bob Mark went with them, forgetting about his petition.

In the TV room on the second landing, Menzies, the fine-boned child-murderer was sitting with another killer of children, the eggheaded Donald Ludlow, who was in his mid-fifties, but looked older. The fact that he was a broken, shambling man who had no expectation of ever getting out of prison or even leading any sort of existence there other than one under constant escort and observation didn't engender any compassion in other prisoners. If the opportunity presented itself someone would put the nonsense cases away; most prisoners were unswervingly dedicated to that cause. Even if it meant being charged again, they would still take a chance.

The two child-murderers were sitting between two warders watching Coronation Street, but both lost their concentration as other prisoners started to arrive in the TV room. The two regular prisoners who had been there had left when the screws had brought these two in. They hadn't minded that, but the arrival of these other cons like this was very worrying. They could easily overpower the two guards, and murder them. The prospect made the nonces quake. Their eyes flitted nervously around as more prisoners arrived, none of whom was interested in the TV. They sat in chairs or leaned against the wall or sat on the edge of the table and stared at them. Lynn arrived with Bob Mark. One of the warders who looked after the second landing, Joe Marshall, glanced up, but took little notice of the prisoners. It was the TV room after all, and this was association period.

Alarm continued to rise through Menzies and Ludlow, climbing towards a screaming pitch. Sweat broke out along their foreheads as they waited for the attack they knew was coming; they alone among the Rule 43s on the wing had agreed to go out during association to try and gain acceptance by the other prisoners. How they regretted that decision now, how empty were the promises of the warders to keep them safe. They were ready to run.

Collins came in, followed by Brian Smith. That made fifteen ordinary prisoners in the room and the atmosphere was electric with tension. No one was aware of the TV, but waited instead for that one spark to start things off. Steve Collins provided it as he stepped over to the TV.

'What's this rubbish you're watching?' he said. 'The other side's much better.' He immediately switched channels; then, without even bothering to identify the programme, 'Ah, that's a load of ballocks.' He switched the set off.

There was no disguising then that the nonces were the centre of attention.

But as though unaware of what was going on, Warder Marshall said, 'We were watching that.'

He was another Geordie, in his mid-thirties, and wore a clipped moustache. He also slashed the peak on his cap so that it hung almost vertically down his forehead and over his eyes, forcing him to carry his head very erect in order for him to see. A lot of the younger warders slashed the peaks in that way, especially the more arrogant ones; the older screws rarely did. In some prisons the governors disapproved of their officers wearing their hats in that way; Governor Maudling approved of it. Of all the warders in the prison Marshall's claim to fame was that he had achieved the most overtime in a single week, doing ninety-eight hours actual; he did so much overtime that he would often bang prisoners up at night, and unlock them in the morning. He was certainly as much a prisoner as any con, if serving his time less reluctantly. Jackson, the second warder, was a curious mixture of dedicated company man and entrenched union man. Along with his colleagues he ran the prison service; it was no longer the prison governors or P1 Division at the Home Office, both of those bodies were terrified in case there was another strike or work to rule. The prison officers ordinarily avoided industrial action but controlled things instead by precipitating the tension around the prisoners; if putting in for a pay rise then they would pressure the prisoners to such degree that there would be a minor riot, which would get maximum publicity for their dangerous and troublesome job; the same happened when overtime was cut back – Joe Marshall and many like him couldn't survive on the basic wage. When it came to questions of discipline and adjudication, the governor knew that if he didn't back his men they could make more trouble than the prisoners. Marshall and his colleagues knew that also.

'No one else was watching it, Mr Marshall,' Collins said civilly. 'Anyway, it'll corrupt these two, won't it?'

Marshall's eyes quickly circled the room, assessing the gathering. 'All right, what the fuck's going on?'

'Going on?' Dunkerton said in apparent surprise. 'We just come for a bit of association. You know, a chat and a smoke with the chaps. What do we find? Fucking monsters forced on us.'

'You got kids, Micky, haven't you?' Lynn said conversationally.

'Yeah, I got five boys. Think the world of me, they do. Come down and see me regular and everything.'

'I got kids too,' Collins commented. 'Nothing I wouldn't do for them, you know. Breaks your fucking heart when you think what some wicked bastards done to kids ...'

'How'd you like these animals getting hold of yourn?' Lynn asked generally. His voice trembled with emotion and he could barely get the words out evenly. It was as much as he could do to stay in control and keep from rushing them. 'Trying to make them go down on them like one of them done, listening to their cries, pleading with them not to, then strangling them when they wouldn't – 's what we gotta associate with ...'

These words caused all the hatred and revulsion that had been building up to explode like an expulsion of breath from restrained lungs. It was equalled by fear from the two nonces. The two screws were also very afraid, for although neither had any sympathy for the two nonces, they were supposed to look after them.

'Back to your cells,' Marshall barked harshly at Menzies and Ludlow. 'Fuck off, quickly!'

They didn't need telling twice. They went like two rabbits suddenly breaking out of a blinding spell created by motorcar headlights.

Alan Thompson came along the landing towards the TV room with Frank Timper and two other cons, each with a pint of boiling water from the tea urn that was on the ground floor during association. As the two nonces ran from the TV room in panic, they ran straight into the shower of scalding water, Ludlow getting slightly more of it than Menzies, though the latter let out the loudest scream. In pain and confusion they hurled themselves along the landing.

Cons forcing their way out of the TV room to pursue the nonces drove the two screws out ahead of them. Marshall and his colleague struggled to get some control, but the anger and fear and loathing of the prisoners was beyond the immediate control of these two warders.

'All right! Everyone back to your cells. Go on!' Marshall screamed, panic apparent in his voice. 'Back to your fucking cells!' There was no response from the cons who pressed on along the landing. Both Marshall and his colleague dived through the rabble of men for the alarm buttons which were strategically placed throughout the prison. Which of them hit a button first wasn't important. The alarm bell that started up drowned out all other noise.

45

The news of a disturbance wasn't something Archibald Maudling enjoyed receiving at the start of his day. It made him angry. He demanded to know why he hadn't been telephoned at his home last night; in fact the deputy governor who had been informed had decided that there had been no need to disturb the governor. But Maudling hadn't been placated with that. The disturbance having been nipped in the bud meant little; he knew the signs, he told Chief Officer Carne and PO Allen who followed him as he strode angrily into his office. There was unrest, discontent fermenting, he was sure of it. Born out of just such an incident were last year's riots, he reminded them, as though he alone was the only member of staff to recognize this.

'How are Menzies and Ludlow this morning?' he finally got around to asking. He had little more sympathy for the child-murderers than the prisoners; however, they were in his charge, he had a responsibility towards them.

'The MO treated them for superficial scalds,' the chief informed him. 'It shook them up more than anything. They'll be all right, a couple of days behind their doors.' Chief Officer Carne would have preferred that they were left behind their doors for the rest of their natural lives, never being let out, never seeing the light of day, having their food pushed through their slots. Reading in the files of those prisoners some of the things they had done to their victims had made him feel sick; he had three children of his own and found it impossible to keep them out of his mind's eye as he had gone through those details. Robert Carne prided himself on being fair-minded and moderate in his reactions, but he wouldn't hurry to prevent any of those nonces from getting a beating.

To see one of them suffering physically reduced his deep fear and loathing. He didn't doubt how they must have suffered mentally, but that knowledge didn't satisfy him, any more than it did ordinary prisoners.

'Was it a premeditated attack?' the governor asked, sitting heavily behind his large, orderly desk. His office by contrast to the adjudication room was spacious and well appointed, it had a carpet on the floor, and curtains; there were paintings and photos on the wall, and a cabinet containing cups and shields.

'There were no witnesses, sir,' PO Allen answered, embarrassed at the admission. 'The prisoners claim they were taking the hot water to the TV room on the twos for their coffee when Menzies and Ludlow rushed out and crashed into them. Mr Marshall confirmed that, sir.'

'Animals,' he said unthinkingly, 'that's all they are. Not an ounce of decency in any of them. What hope is there of ever rehabilitating this particular collection of animals, even if one had the inclination.' He wouldn't give any of them house room if he had his way. Passing the more violent specimens on to Broadmoor was something he would readily do, but unfortunately there was a limit to the numbers Broadmoor could take. 'Keep them locked up after breakfast, Mr Allen. I'll see them in their cells, all of them.' He thought about that for a moment, then added, 'I only wish I could keep them there the whole time.'

On the landing of Lynn's wing there was a lot of noise, prisoners were protesting about being kept banged up without being allowed to slop out after breakfast. Men regimented day after day as prisoners were, forced to evacuate their bowels at a set time, got into firm habits with such bodily functions. In the normal course of events they got to slop out some three-quarters of an hour after breakfast; a quarter of an hour past usual slopout time, cons had a genuine need. Some prisoners were banging on their doors with tin ashtrays, others ringing their bells, others calling out. Screws moved agitatedly along the landings, shouting through the doors for them to be quiet, telling them the governor was coming over.

'... I'm breaking my neck for a pony,' Micky Dunkerton shouted, hammering the door.

'Then use your pot, or hold it till the governor's been round,' Warder Westbury said as he went along the landing. He swung his keys against the door of the next cell. 'Stop ringing that fucking bell!'

'I wanna use the recess,' came the response.

'You can't!' He moved along to the cell where Bob Mark was banging his door. He looked through the Judas hole, then turned the key and wrenched the door open, startling Mark. 'What's this fucking noise? You want to be put back in hospital?' he threatened.

Recovering himself, Mark said, "M' pot's full.'

Westbury glanced down at the pot. It wasn't full, which he suspected was the case with most of the other pots; they were just having a little ruck over being banged up. He grinned and said, 'Why don't you try eating some of it?'

The governor could hear the noise from across the prison and was irritated by it. His one fear was that such a protest would start off something with the other prisoners, which was to be avoided at all costs. Demonstrations of this sort had the habit of spreading like a fire through a tenement.

The noise struck Maudling forcefully when the chief opened the main entrance to the wing. As he stood in the security vestibule and waited while PO Allen unlocked the inner gate, he bristled angrily. Someone would be on the punishment block for it, he decided.

'What's all this fucking noise, Mr Allen?' the governor demanded, as though he was incapable of identifying the protests for himself.

'They're complaining about not being allowed out to the recesses, sir,' PO Allen snapped.

This only added to Maudling's displeasure. 'We'll see about that,' he said. Bodily functions might have been an unreasonable demand. 'I'll show them they can't carry on like this. We'll start at the top, chief.'

The governor strode away towards the metal staircase, causing the two uniformed officers with him to put in a quick step to catch up.

'Open it up,' Maudling ordered Westbury. The four of them were outside the second cell from the end of the landing, which was Steve Collins's cell. No one had checked through the Judas hole; ordinarily Westbury would have done so before unlocking the door, but the governor's mood wasn't such that he wanted to get on the wrong side of him by not doing as he was told instantly.

There was no immediate sign of Collins when the warder swung the door open. They found him when Maudling, the chief and the PO stepped into the cell. Collins was in the corner, his trousers down, sitting astride his pot.

'Sorry, guv, I was took short,' he said in mock apology.

Although a man sitting astride a pot, his trousers down his legs, had a considerable physical disadvantage, in this situation he had a genuine psychological advantage. Collins having engineered the situation wasn't at all embarrassed; while Maudling flushed and didn't know what to do or say. He knew it was his fault that the man was forced to this. He muttered something incomprehensible and turned out. He would have to come back to question the man about his part in the disturbance last night, for he certainly wasn't going to while he sat on his pot. PO Allen looked suspiciously at Collins, then followed the other two out, slamming the door.

The next cell was Micky Dunkerton's, and the door was opened with the same lack of caution. They found this prisoner with his trousers down also sitting on his pot, which had been placed for convenience on his chair. His apology was no more sincere than Collins's had been. 'A bit of diarrhoea, sir.'

'See the MO,' Maudling shouted and spun out of the cell, more angry than embarrassed now.

His anger increased when the next cell revealed Frank Timper on his pot, straining something as if in labour. Maudling knew then what was going on. It was certainly more than coincidence that three men in succession should be doing the same thing. They checked through the Judas hole of the next cell and found Lynn in the same position. Bob Mark doing the same number infuriated Maudling. He turned away, trembling with anger.

'They won't get away with this, chief. I want every rule enforced to a letter on this wing. I want the ringleaders of this little charade. We'll see who has the last laugh. They'll laugh on the other side of their faces.' He strode off along the landing and went down the stairs. He didn't wish to see any more prisoners.

Enforcing the rules and regulations to the letter was perhaps the simplest way of hitting back at the prisoners, for the officers had the satisfaction of knowing they were behaving perfectly legally. One of the best or worst rules, according to the side one was on, was in unlocking men three at a time for their meals, and making sure they were locked back in their cells with their food before the next three were let out. It guaranteed that everyone but the first three got cold food, and food that wasn't very appetizing hot, was even less appetizing cold. The whole process took well over an hour, when normally it would have taken no more than fifteen minutes; the same rule applied when slopping out, the process was painfully slow. Privileges were severely curtailed; the no-talking rule on moving from one place to another was enforced. Offences against discipline were frequent, resulting in many prisoners on governor's report. The screws were in their element: suddenly all their power had been returned to them, besides which they had enormous opportunity for overtime.

To begin with frequent references were made to the nonce incident that had started the rule enforcement as they sought the ringleaders. Then when they got nowhere they asked less and less, but the strict enforcement of the rules stayed, even though everyone seemed to forget why they were being enforced. Eventually they would be relaxed again, but meanwhile some of the prisoners were getting angry with the regime. However, all refrained from taking action. It was as if they all instinctively realized that if any one prisoner protested, then he would be put down the block as the ringleader.

More warders than usual watched the forty-two prisoners as they exercised around the yard in pairs, even though the rule enforcement had relaxed slightly.

As Jack Lynn walked around with Mark, Steve Collins, who was six paces behind with David Morris, said, 'That was a result, Jack, doing them fucking nonces, whatever way you book it. No one was nicked, was they. Everyone's behind his door working.'

'What did it achieve, though?' Lynn wanted to know. 'Apart from all this aggravation.'

'Well,' said Collins, a little surprised. 'We showed silly ballocks that he can't normalize the monsters. They didn't give us much for it. We ain't worse off for it.'

'We're no better off either, are we.' It wasn't a question.

'No talking, you two,' a warder yelled and ran down the yard towards them. 'You're on report.'

They had finally found the ringleaders.

46

Time didn't exactly slip lightly away for Jack Lynn, but it passed; he counted the minutes and the hours as they stretched into days. Time passed quicker when he was out from behind his door, and allowed to associate with other prisoners, but not much quicker. He was counting off the days and weeks to his appeal; he hadn't yet been given a date, and he didn't know how long it would be before it got on. That in-between time was his actual sentence, notwithstanding the result he might or might not get, it was time that couldn't be returned to him. The prospect of his not getting his conviction turned over and his having to do the remainder of his sentence was something he couldn't even think about.

He was due his first visit from his wife since being away, and the prospect excited him. He would have liked Dolly to have brought his daughters down to see him, but as much as he had wanted to see Carol and Sandra he had resisted, for there was too much to talk about with his wife, so many adjustments to try and make. He only got a visit for an hour every three weeks and it wasn't enough. The letters didn't help either. Deeply disturbing personal problems that a man and a woman had when forced into a separation of this kind couldn't be gone into in a letter that you knew a screw was going to read. The thought of that inhibited every word he ever set down on the page. He would like to have told her about his sexual needs, told her how much he wanted to make love to her, and have her write some of those things to him; however, they would only be gloated over by the screws, their intimacies dipped into and shared among the staff. They couldn't even write about money and how their problems might be resolved; she wouldn't write to him in detail about the aggravation she was getting from the Social Security for the fear of worrying him, knowing he couldn't do anything about it.

The letter he was writing in his cell during association was taking him a long time; the exercise caused him to think concentratedly about his wife and family, which in turn caused him a dull feeling of frustration.

He looked up, welcoming the distraction as Brian Smith appeared in the doorway. He carried a paperback book.

'Oh, you busy, Jack,' he said uncertainly, wondering if perhaps Lynn had no time for him on account of his background. He tried to control the resentment he felt over the amount of time and attention this man gave Bob Mark.

'Writing the Missus, 's all,' he said, and turned the standard letter sheet face down – not that there was much in it or that Brian Smith was likely to try and read it. 'I'll see her before I finish this.'

'Due for a visit, are you?' It was something to say.

'Tomorrow. 'S not before fucking time.' He watched the younger man, waiting to see what he had in mind.

"S that book on the Bermuda Triangle I was telling you about.' It was an excuse and he was acutely aware of this. There was another pause. He slid the book onto the narrow shelf over the bed.

'You got a family who visit you, have you, Bri?'

Brian Smith said, 'I have a family, but they wouldn't even visit Cowes now. It was one of their properties I destroyed.' He smiled and fell silent. 'Did you think any more about what I mentioned?'

'About the other thing?' Lynn said cautiously.

Brian Smith turned and checked along the immediate landing, which was clear. Although unlike most villains, he hadn't been born knowing these cautionary moves, he had soon learned them inside. 'The thing is, Jack, Steve Collins approached me. He wants to be put in.' He was trying to twist Lynn's arm and get him to commit, but didn't have the courage to go too far.

'He might be very useful to you,' Lynn said generously. Both knew in fact what value he'd likely be.

'Possibly,' Brian Smith replied, slightly thrown by the response. Then, revealing his hand, 'He possibly wouldn't prove terribly reliable.'

'I do fancy some of it, Bri.' He was thinking about his wife and family, and how long it could be before he got his appeal on. 'Let me think about it some more, can I?'

Brian Smith was delighted with even this small commitment. His smile almost split his face in two. 'Yes of course. 'Course you can.'

Ordinarily Lynn would have formed his own opinion about a con, and formed it quickly, knowing whether he was a wrong 'un or not, whether he could trust him or not. Brian Smith didn't fit into the pattern of most cons, most of whom would have gained acceptance to the élite by virtue of the villainy they did and the sentence they drew. Brian Smith's unspecified sentence alone couldn't have got him in any more than the nonces' long sentences would; the fact that he had been accepted in the first place was due to Collins who had befriended him. Collins doubtless saw him as raw, pliable material to be moulded into the shape which most suited his own purpose. How Collins felt now that this would-be pupil had moved out of his immediate sphere of influence was evident in the way he reacted to him from time to time. But it wasn't enough. Jack Lynn wanted to be sure in his own mind that he wasn't still doing Collins's bidding.

In the mailbag shop, which was about eighteen feet by twenty and contained three benches at which some twelve top security prisoners worked, Jack Lynn was at one of the benches with Alan Thompson and Bobby Mark. Conversation, though not officially permitted, was sometimes condoned by the screws, and at other times snatched behind a raised hand; far up in a glass booth at the end of the shop was a discipline screw; the other three who supervised in the shop were distinguished by their white coats.

409

'What d'you think about Brian, Al?' Lynn said, glancing towards the warder, who wasn't looking in his direction but at Steve Collins who was wandering around. 'Think he's a serious prospect to make one with?' Of necessity he talked quickly, his voice barely above a whisper.

'Serious as any, I s'pose,' he replied, his hand in front of his mouth. 'He keeps well closed up.'

'That's what I thought.'

'He'd be safe enough, Jack. The thing is, he ain't got nothing to lose, has he.' It wasn't an argument against getting involved with him as far as Lynn was concerned.

'I ain't exactly got a lot to lose, have I,' Lynn said matter-of-factly.

Alan Thompson arched his eyebrows and tightened his lips, acknowledging the point.

Their attention went to a uniformed warder who was admitted to the shop. After a few words with a white-coated screw, the latter came along to Lynn and told him to leave his work. He had a visitor. Lynn didn't need telling twice.

The movements book that went with Lynn was something he came to resent more than any other single object. For that more than anything made him feel more like a numbered parcel than a person. It went across to the visiting block with him.

The visiting arrangements at this prison were quite tolerable, or comparatively so. In the visiting block there was a large room in which there were eighteen tables in a line. On one side of the tables there was a single chair, on the other side, there were two, sometimes three, prisoners being allowed up to three visitors. Those visiting facilities were for prisoners who were halfway trusted as there would only be six warders watching three times as many cons and at least that many again of relatives or friends. Such visits weren't for Jack Lynn.

Category 'A' prisoners saw their visitors separated from the others. Across the corridor from the main visiting room was a series of small, secure rooms. They were one of the bricked-on additions to the prison; these weren't cells but cubicles that held anyone as fast. Lynn was escorted into one of these rooms and told to sit at the table which, apart from the two chairs, was the only piece of furniture. One concession to progress was that these cubicles had no bars at the windows, nor wire mesh, what they had instead were glass window bricks, the same as most modern police cells now had, and which would have been even harder to break through.

Lynn was kept waiting for a few moments, and convinced himself that it had been done purposely to wind him up. His wife had to have arrived or they wouldn't have called him down. He tried to stay calm, but found it increasingly difficult. When the door was unlocked from the outside he jumped, genuinely startled. He stood as his wife was brought in. He expected the screw who was in with them to tell him to sit, but he didn't. Nor did the uniform who showed Dolly in.

She was wearing a summer frock and looked terrific, Lynn thought. She looked as good as he could ever remember seeing her, despite the anxiety etched in her face, and the fatigue which he tried to deny to himself was there.

One of the screws spoke a few words to his colleague. What he said Lynn wasn't sure, and was only vaguely aware that the uniform who had showed Dolly in went out again. The other one was locked in the room with them. Lynn was very conscious of that man, who inhibited his response towards his wife. They embraced and kissed self-consciously. Lynn wanted to press himself against her, press himself into her, feel her body against his, reassure himself. The memories and images of his wife were still sharp in his mind; it was Dolly he thought about when he masturbated.

'How are you, love?' he said quietly, his voice quaking with emotion.

She tried to speak, but couldn't get beyond her greeting, and that was barely audible. Her face crumpled as though no longer able to take the strain, she turned her head to hide her tears.

The warder directed Lynn into his chair; apart from greeting and departing, physical contact wasn't permitted.

'Ah, Doll,' Lynn said after a moment, uncertain how to react. 'Come on, love, sit down. Don't upset yourself.' He looked confused, instinctively knowing he had nothing to offer her. He bent over to physically comfort her.

'Sit back there now,' the warder said to him.

Lynn looked at the man in uniform, having absolutely no understanding of him or what made him do what he was doing. He considered protesting, but didn't.

'I'm sorry, Jack,' Dolly mumbled through her tears. 'It's just, I dunno ... I dunno, lovey.' At one time she had been able to cope; she had got through his previous prison sentences all right, she hadn't enjoyed it for a moment, but she had survived. She didn't know if she could this time. Twenty years was longer than anything before, too long for the mind to grasp. On those occasions before there had always been the knowledge that he had actually done the crime he had been doing time for; this time he hadn't, he had been fitted up and that was tearing her apart.

'Yeah, 's murder,' Lynn said, more crushed by his wife's reaction like this than anything else. 'C'mon, Dolly, don't upset yourself, love. Don't give these cunts the satisfaction. They nicked enough off us as it is; the no-good slags, they have. C'mon.' He watched her as she tried to check herself. He searched for something to say that might deflect her, but couldn't think of anything. Everything he wanted to say was either directly related to their present position or would simply serve as a reminder of it. Finally he asked, 'How are the girls?' It was the wrong question, of course; but then, almost any question would be.

She caught her breath again. 'They're missing you, Jack ...'

That prospect coming out in the open like that caused Lynn a lot of pain. He arched his eyebrows to try and ease the

412

pressure at the back of his eyes. 'Both all right, are they?' It took a lot of effort.

Dolly nodded. 'They wanted to come down and visit ...' She had a vague feeling he knew all that; they had been into it in their letters, deciding it would be better to leave it for a few visits. She moved quickly on: 'They wanted me to give you their best love ... Sandra won't settle to nothing, keeps asking about when you're coming home ... Christ, when I think about what them rotten slags done to you ...' Anger came bubbling through. 'Them girls'll be grown up 'fore you're out ...' She sobbed again.

'No they won't, love ... they won't,' he insisted, 'I promise it won't be like that.' He could see that she wasn't wholly convinced and reached across to reassure her. Then, glancing at the uniform, he hesitated, withdrew his hand and looked helplessly at his wife.

'I'm sorry, Jack,' she said, taking her handkerchief from her dress pocket and pushing it against her nose and eyes. 'Coming here, upset like this ... sorry, love. It's just ... just ...' She searched helplessly for the words to express all that she felt, all the love she had for this man, all her sense of frustration, all her hate for those who had put him here, all her need; the words failed her. And if she had found them it was doubtful she could have said them with that warder present. Her thoughts jumped. 'Only one visit every three weeks, it's hard to cope ... no, I'm sorry, Jack,' she found herself saying again.

"S all right, love.' He nodded wearily. 'They wind you up so much you can't think of nothing to say hardly till the time's all gone. Does you up in the head, it do.'

'Tommy ran me down in his cab,' she said, wiping her eyes again and smudging her mascara slightly. 'Been a tower of strength he has, and your Mum. She sends her love.'

'How is she?'

'She's all right, Jack, you know how she copes.' She felt the urge to reach over and touch him, but was familiar with the rules and knew the visit would be shortened as readily for her breaking them as him. The prospect put her on edge. 'Tom said if there's anything he can do for you or us. Let him know.'

Lynn nodded gratefully. He had always liked his brother-in-law, and it was offers like the one he had made to his wife that reassured Lynn in his assessment of the man. 'He's a diamond, your Tommy, he really is ...' He paused and considered her, wondering how he could reassure her. 'Dolly,' he said in a whisper. 'I won't do the twenty, nothing like, that's a promise. We'll have some sort of life, the girls and us, we will.'

She was bewildered, wanting to believe his words, but afraid to. "S all I keep thinking about, Jack. That somehow they're gonna release you, and I don't know ...'

'I'll get a nice result, you see,' he said firmly. 'The brief was well confident when I saw him. D'he say anything to you?'

'Just stuff about selling the house, 's all. Told me not to worry about nothing. I had some estate agents do the house. There's been a couple of offers right off. One for thirty-two thousand, another for thirty. If the first man can get a mortgage, he'll have it.'

'That won't be hard, will it?' Lynn said, seeking reassurance.

"S what the agents said.'

Lynn was thinking about the sale price, how much his brief would need to do what he planned to do, and what there would be left for Dolly and the kids to live on. Whatever the amount, the one thing he could guarantee was that it wouldn't be enough, any more than it was enough to show for all the villainy he had done in his time.

'Where you and the girls gonna go?' Lynn asked.

'We can move int m' Mum's, till we get another place,' she said very practically. 'I put m'name down for a council house, but I dunno ... there's about a three-year waiting list. I expect we'll get one of them high rise flats. We'll be all right at Mum's, though; the girls, they want to go there, don't they.

414

They don't mind. Their friends won't be too far ... they make friends all right, kids always do ...'

'Dolly,' Lynn said, interrupting her slightly manic conversation. 'I'll make it up to you, losing your home like that, I promise. I will.' He knew how much that had all meant to her. 'After the appeal we'll get somewhere in the country maybe ...' Their eyes met momentarily, then were quickly averted, neither wanting the other to read the doubt there. 'What about the Social Security? What did they say?' She had written to him she was having problems getting money from them.

'I had a right ruck down there. They reckon m' money'd been stopped because of the house, till it's sold. 'Cos we own it, that is. Stupid, innit.'

'They can't do that,' Lynn retorted. He had no control over his frustrations as the words burst out of him. The warder stood off the wall in anticipation of trouble. Lynn glanced at him and quietened. 'It might be fucking months before it goes,' he said practically.

"S what I told 'em. But they don't listen half the time. They don't wanna know, do they. They wouldn't give me m' fare down here neither ...' She didn't want to add to her husband's troubles with these problems.

'The liberty-taking bastards!'

"S all right, Jack, we're managing,' she said, trying to offer him some comfort. If there had been the opportunity she would have spilled everything out to him. 'I'll be down those offices first thing tomorrow. They got to give us something. The way they carry on you'd think it was their own money they was giving you.'

'I'll see if I can get the welfare in here to do something. I don't s'pose they'll do fuckall though, be like the rest of them.'

'It wouldn't matter, Jack, we wouldn't starve. There's been a lot of offers from your friends and different people. A lot of neighbours have stopped and asked if they can help. They've given a few quid an' all, 's amazing. Remember that old Edna

Roberts round the corner, she sends her best. She give the girls a pound each out of her pension the other day. She ain't got nothing herself.'

'She's a goodhearted girl.' He thought about the offers, touched by the generosity. But he knew they weren't saying the things to each other they ought to be saying. He glanced at the warder, and still resisted reaching over and touching his wife. 'If only you got a bit of privacy here. You can't say fuckall, not how you feel or nothing without those slags listening ...' He paused, thinking about how they might overcome the problem, but ran against a brick wall. 'How's it been, Doll?' he said very quietly. 'You look terrific.'

'Don't, Jack.' She closed her eyes, as if trying to close off her needs. 'I can't tell you how much I miss you.' It did her no more good than it did him, but the words just slipped out.

'I'll make it up to you, Dolly, I promise, love. Somehow I'll make everything up to you and the girls. Tell them that. We'll have our own Christmas, and all the birthdays what got missed, and the holidays. We'll do 'em all when I get out, you see.' The words had a hollow ring. He saw the disbelief in her tear-clouded eyes and he had to look away.

A dull ache of frustration and confusion sat at the back of his head and neck as he moved along the echoing thoroughfare on escort back to the workshop. He was pensive, distracted, thinking about his wife and his daughters. The prospect of not seeing Dolly for another three weeks depressed him; the thought of the Social Security making them struggle for what they were entitled to angered him.

'Oi! Where the fuck d'you think you're going? Home?' The warder said as Lynn went on past the mailbag shop.

Lynn spun round, as if to challenge the warder, who simply stood at the door and pointed into the shop. The prisoner had no choice; he stepped inside the shop and resumed his place at the bench.

Alan Thompson watched him for a moment, but seeing he was upset, declined to say anything. Sometimes he wondered

416

if it was worth having visitors, despite how nice you sometimes felt when they were there, if there weren't too many problems to be chewed over; afterwards, almost to a man, prisoners felt bad, angry, frustrated, disappointed. He felt sorry for Jack Lynn right then, for he looked as though he had taken this one particularly badly.

Not all prisoners displayed the same sensitivity or sense of awareness of distress. Some, if they were aware of it, chose to ignore it, while others used it to wind them up. Steve Collins was the latter kind. It was like a scab he would pick at until fresh spots of blood appeared.

Stopping by Lynn's bench with a pile of canvas cut for mailbags, Collins said cheerfully, 'Good visit, Jack?'

'Yeah, terrific,' Lynn responded automatically, hardly aware that he had been spoken to.

'Yeah, always nice seeing the old lady. Let me know the next time she's coming down,' he offered. 'I can put you in touch with a screw over there, 's well bent.' He glanced round checking that the warders in the shop weren't too close. 'Could make life really nice for you down there. Know what I mean?' He winked.

Lynn paused from his work and glanced at Collins. 'That's handy,' he said flatly.

'Even let you give her one, the price is right,' Collins said.

'Leave it out, Steve, for fucksake,' Thompson said. He knew what the man was doing; he was probably bored with the routine of the shop and was looking for a bit of sport, looking to get someone at it.

"S only trying to do him a favour, 's all,' Collins said, as though taking exception. He moved away to his own place at the bench in front.

'He's a no-good slag at times,' Thompson said quietly, but whether Lynn heard him or not, he didn't respond.

Thoughts troubled Jack Lynn as his fingers worked stitching the thick seams of the canvas sacks; there was no solution at all as far as he could see. His troubles were reflected in his face, and he paid no attention at all to his work. There was no need, it was mindless repetition.

'What the fuck's this?' A whitecoated warder said, suddenly looming before him. He produced a metal tape from his pocket, ran a length out and put it against some of the stitches Lynn had sewn. 'Letters'll fall through those. The Post Office want eight stitches to the inch, no more or no less. That's eight, for your information,' he said, holding up eight fingers. He then indicated an inch on the tape. 'There's an inch. Can you grasp that? Eight stitches to the inch. Get and unpick them.' He checked a finished sack. 'And that one.'

From the moment he became aware of what the screw was saying Lynn had difficulty staying in control. There before him was a hole in the face of a uniform, and it was pouring abuse at him, only at that moment he wasn't in a sufficiently stable condition to take it. The rejection of his work, at which he earned less than a pittance, seemed to epitomize his problems in relation to his family's struggle for money with the Social Security. Frustration caused tears to cloud his eyes and his mind; anger burst out of him like water from a broken main, and wouldn't stop now until the pressure was gone. He hurled the work he had before him on the floor. 'This is fucking silly,' he screamed, hardly able to get the words out. 'It's silly. I got a wife out there and two kids trying to live on Social Security and I'm sewing silly fucking mailbags for twopence an hour and you cunts tell me they're no good. Why'nt you cunts give us some proper work so's we can go and earn a living for our families, you cunts. You cunts, sewing silly fucking mailbags, you cunts!' He was screaming at the top of his voice now, trembling with rage, hurling materials, mailbags, anything to hand about the room.

The two other warders in white coats ran forward to assist the third. As they tried to take hold of him, he hit one of them, Warder Evans, splitting his nose, causing a fountain of blood. The first sign of the disturbance getting out of hand was enough for the watchful discipline warder in the glass booth to

418

hit the alarm button. The clanging bell that started up immediately drowned out the noise of the protest, but didn't deter Lynn, nor Bob Mark, who jumped in to help immediately he saw his friend set about by the three screws. It took only about a minute for twenty warders armed with heavy batons to come charging through the door in answer to the bell; it took them less than that to sort out the two troublemakers.

47

Sitting behind the small bare desk in the adjudication room, Governor Maudling was a picture of self-righteousness. Also present were PO Allen, PO McClean and three of the four warders from the mailbag shop. Warder Evans was in no fit state to appear, having had his nose broken by Lynn. Finally there were two warders either side of Jack Lynn, who was toeing the line in the too large carpet slippers he had been made to put on. The two escort warders were pressed closely in on Lynn, and had got him to the line only after one or two sharp digs; they watched him closely, even though he was in no sort of condition to cause trouble for anyone here.

Jack Lynn was barely recognizable through the cuts and bruises on his face. The flesh over his lips and around his eyes was very puffy. It wasn't something those screws in the mailbag shop had done to him, nor would have attempted in front of other prisoners, all of whom would almost certainly have stepped in and done a bit. Instead Lynn had been carted off to cells down in the block, where eight screws had set about both him and Mark. All Lynn had tried to do was defend himself; there had been no point trying to put himself about and do more damage, which in turn would only have made things worse for him. He had briefly lost consciousness twice during that beating, but on neither occasion did the screws stop; one of their own kind had been hurt so they had no intention of stopping until all their anger and hostility towards those two prisoners in particular, and all prisoners in general, had been momentarily assuaged. Lynn hadn't seen Bobby Mark since they had been removed from the mailbag shop yesterday, but Lynn hoped he had fared better than himself, though doubted somehow that he had.

Just what sort of a mess he looked, Lynn had no means of knowing, but from the way he felt he could guess what he was like. However, the governor didn't bat an eyelid at his condition when he was brought in before him, but then he mostly avoided looking at him.

'It's beyond my scope to hear this case,' the governor informed him, having heard evidence from the three warders, all of which was corroborative. 'Regrettably I lack the authority to punish you sufficiently.' Guilt was already decided upon. 'I am going to refer your case to the Visiting Committee to deal with, though I doubt even they have sufficient authority to punish you as you deserve. Personally I should like to see you flogged; it's the only punishment animals like you seem to understand. However, the Home Office in its wisdom has ruled against such practice.' That was something Archibald Maudling deeply regretted. He sighed through his nose, making the sigh more like an angry snort. 'You will be confined to a cell in the punishment block pending your hearing. Take him away.' He made a dismissive gesture with his hand, without looking further at Lynn.

'About turn,' the chief ordered. 'Outside!'

Lynn was marched briskly out, despite the pain such movement caused, helped along by a couple of smart blows in the ribs by the escort. There was no protest or appeal now; he had after all put a screw in the hospital.

'Keep him away from other prisoners, Mr McClean,' the governor said after Lynn had been taken away. 'I want him to have no contact at all with other prisoners until he goes before the Committee.'

'Yes, sir,' McClean said. He understood the governor's reason, and would have anticipated it even if he had neglected to tell him. Seeing a prisoner in the state Lynn was in, especially one who was fairly popular, was likely as not to have caused unrest.

Out of the adjudication room, Lynn was returned to the

holding cell where his shoes were returned to him, but he didn't get to put them on. Instead he was taken away in his socks.

The escort marched him along the block to the section gate. Beyond it stood Warder Jordan in that familiar stance screws adopted, legs apart, arms folded across their chests. He made no attempt to unlock the gate, but simply grinned at Lynn – this was the first he had seen of him, having been off duty when he had been brought down yesterday.

'The man who tries to beat up warders,' Jordan said mockingly. 'Looks like you didn't make much of a job of it, doesn't it. Doesn't it just.'

Lynn simply looked through the bars at the man, knowing he daren't say a word; knowing this uniform would be looking for an excuse.

'We got your mate down here. He didn't do any better than yourself. Simple fucker.' He waited for Lynn to respond and when he didn't, he unlocked the gate and curled his index finger at him, then headed off along the corridor.

Lynn was escorted to the cell door which Jordan pulled open. There he was stopped.

'Try it on with me,' the blond screw in the cut peak warned, 'you'll look like a beauty contestant now compared to how you will look. Understand?' He didn't expect a response. 'Inside.'

Without a word or a sign of any kind Lynn stepped into the cell; he stopped with his back to the door and waited. The door slammed, then he heard the grille shutter open, and close a short while afterwards. Finally when he was alone he let go, letting the pain wash over him; he felt even more pain as he lowered himself to the bed. But he had been determined not to give those bastards the satisfaction of seeing the pain he was in. He guessed he ought to have reported sick, but didn't for the same reason; anyway, the MO being what he was, there would be no point in seeing him.

Lynn eased himself down on the bed, he was bone-weary

from both the punishment he had taken and the fact that he had been unable to sleep last night because of the pain. He was still unable to lie in one position because of the pressure the weight of his body caused. His back and ribs had taken a lot of stick. Fleetingly he wondered how Bob Mark was and felt a pull of affection for him for steaming in to help as he had.

Two days and nights crawled away with Lynn in this tender state, not fully aware of anything other than his pain. Tiredness forced him to sleep, then he would wake suddenly in a paroxysm of pain and soaked with sweat at the prospect of another beating. He missed the meals that were put in his cell, didn't exercise or slop out; then the pain started to ease and become more tolerable. The more he moved the easier movement became.

The third night he was able to sleep without too many problems. But he was awoken suddenly by cries from the next cell but one. It was Bob Mark. The brief freedom he had had from pain in sleep caused him to momentarily forget. He sat up too quickly for his own good, and winced. He expected to receive the same as Mark was getting and was disconcerted when it didn't happen. He watched his door, but there was no one outside as far as he could tell. He waited and listened.

'Bob?' he called through the silence of the block. 'Bob? You all right, son?' There was no response. He launched himself cautiously off the edge of the bed, and pressed his finger against the bell. He wondered as he did so what the outcome might be. He'd have preferred not to remind the screws that he was still around; he didn't want to take any more stick from them. But he wanted to find out about Bob Mark, to know if he was getting another beating, even though he could do nothing about it.

There was no response to the bell, and there was no further sound from Bob Mark. He thought about springing up to the window and calling along the block, but knew that even if he had the energy to spring up to the bars, he wouldn't have the strength to hang there long enough to make contact. He reluctantly pressed the bell again and waited. There was still no response. Eventually he went back to bed; back to sleep, hoping that it was nothing more than a nightmare Bob Mark had had.

While on the block prisoners were supposed to have an hour's exercise in the yard each day. If they got twenty minutes they were doing well. It wasn't convenient for staff to exercise prisoners as they should have been exercised; there were too many prisoners and too few staff. There was the additional problem with Lynn in that the governor wanted him completely isolated.

When he was escorted through the block and out by the block gate into the yard Lynn was surprised to find he was the only one there, apart from a warder outside the wire with an Alsatian on a lead. There was no reason why others weren't out, none that Lynn could see. It wasn't raining, and there certainly were others on the block.

'Where the others?' he asked through his still slightly puffy lips.

'No talking', the warder responded, 'or you're back inside. Just walk like you're s'posed to.'

Lynn looked puzzled, even a little disturbed. Something was up, he didn't know what. But he wasn't about to answer back, not while he was feeling as tender as he did.

In the early days of this current stretch of solitary, Lynn didn't get to see the trusty, Brian Lang, who brought the food trolley, so had no contact to find out what was going on or how Bob Mark was. Instead food was handed to him on his tray by a screw. He hadn't long been eating his evening meal when there came the sound of crashing from another cell. A tray was flung against the wall, and Lynn knew immediately that it was Bob Mark. His muffled shout, 'I'm not eating that filth,' confirmed it. A scuffle ensued; a cell door was slammed; then there was silence. Lynn waited a few moments, then rose to the bell, but hesitated as he reached for it. He thought about the stick he might get if he got involved. He questioned whether he could actually do Bob Mark any good by getting involved, and finally deciding that he couldn't, he turned away without ringing the bell.

After he had eaten his food, Lynn sat at the end of the bed his back against the wall, his legs drawn against his chest feeling defensive, imagining screws were going to come in and stop him thinking about Bob Mark. He felt guilty over Mark's trouble, for hesitating as he had. After all Bob Mark hadn't held back for a moment when he had been in trouble in the mailbag shop. Though probably he should have done, Lynn argued to himself, as you had no chance steaming in against warders; they'd get back at you some way, they would await their opportunity. But he decided he ought to try and find out how the man was at least.

He rose decisively and went to the bellpush and stabbed his finger against it. He'd have no problem if old Reg Allison answered it, but he didn't think there'd be any response at all. He was startled when the shutter on the grille flew open. The fleshy face of Oliver Dorman was on the other side.

'What are you ringing your bell for now?' Dorman demanded.

Lynn hesitated. This was one of the screws who had worked him over when he had first been brought down to the block. 'I want to go the library,' Lynn said.

'That any way to ask?' said the fat Oliver Dorman in a reasonable tone. 'Well, say it properly, then.'

'I'd really like to go the library please, Mr Dorman,' Lynn said, and only then saw the mocking smile the other side of the door.

'The library's closed.' He slammed the shutter.

Anger burst out of Lynn. 'You no-good bastard!' he shouted, heedless of the consequences.

The shutter in the door immediately opened again. 'What did you say?' the warder asked, his tone still reasonable.

It seduced Lynn sufficiently to say, 'Bob Mark? Is he all right?'

A thoughtful expression came over the fat face. 'What, you mean the big fella? Good as gold. Released this morning, he was. I expect he's home by now. Wouldn't be surprised he's not giving his old lady one.'

Lynn watched the Warder, while with difficulty he checked the rage that was rising through him.

'Anything else?' the warder asked, smiling.

'Yeah. Get cancer, you slag.'

It might have been a particularly sensitive point. If it was then Lynn knew he would suffer later for the remark. But for now the warder simply slammed the shutter.

As he found he hurt less and less, so Lynn began exercising, and increasing the amount he was doing. It helped to move the stiffness that lingered from the bruising he had got. He could feel himself getting fit again, and found it a good feeling compared to how he had been a week ago.

'Keeping in shape?' Warder Allison had opened the cell up for Lynn to slop out after his last meal of the day. 'That's the idea,' he said encouragingly. He didn't like to see prisoners moping around, getting depressed with their lot. He watched Lynn rise and wipe the sweat off his face with his towel. 'Put your slops out.'

'What's the chances of going to the library, Mr Allison?' Lynn asked. He had had nothing to read apart from the Gideon's Bible since landing in solitary.

'You're s'posed to be denied all privileges,' Allison said, slightly embarrassed about the fact that he had yet to be found guilty. 'What sort of books d'you read? I'll see what I can do.'

'Anything'd be handy. That bible's getting a bit thin.' He went out to the recess with his pisspot.

Lynn was a little surprised when Reg Allison opened his cell a little later that evening and gave him a book to read. He decided the screw was a diamond after that. Until Warder Jordan opened his cell door later that night, that was. Oliver Dorman stood in the doorway behind him, his arms folded across his chest.

'Where did you get that?' Jordan demanded. 'Give it here.'

'I brought it in with me,' Lynn said, handing the uniform the book. Instinctively he protected the man who had given him the book, but wondered immediately if it hadn't been a get up on Allison's part to give these two bastards an opportunity to come into him.

'Stand up when you address an officer,' Dorman ordered.

Lynn complied. He didn't want to have a fight with these two.

'All right, where d'you get this book?' And when Lynn didn't answer, 'You're on report.' They took the book.

They proceeded with the charge to Lynn's surprise. In the morning he was taken down for adjudication, given his form on which to answer the charge if he so chose, made to change into slippers and taken before the governor, who found him guilty and gave him three days' solitary as if that was something different to what he was already doing. The only difference it made was that it was one more black mark on his prison record should the need ever arise for him to go up in front of the Parole Board.

As his bruises and cuts diminished so the screws relaxed the instruction about keeping Lynn isolated. Brian Lang, the block trusty, was the first to make contact when he brought Lynn's food. Though there was little chance of their seeking or passing on information, for a warder stood at the door while the food was handed over.

'Forgotten the condiments, Bri',' Lynn said cheerfully one evening. The uniform took no exception to such exchanges.

Both men checked in the direction of the warder who had moved along the block. 'What d'you hear about Bob?' Lynn whispered, leaning close to the trusty.

'Give him a right good spanking last night, they did,' Lang informed him.

Lynn had heard something of it and had hurled himself up to the window and had called along to Bob Mark, but hadn't got any reply. 'What was the upset over?'

'That no-good cunt put dirt on his grub again –' Lang stopped abruptly at the warder's approach.

'What's this, a love affair?' Dorman said, filling the doorway.

'Don't make a pig of yourself, son,' Lang said, and laughed, as though taking the piss out of Lynn.

Later that night when most of the other prisoners were in bed asleep, their lights out, Lynn was sitting on the floor reading the few pages that were left in the bible. He looked up suddenly, hearing two people out in the corridor. For a moment he thought perhaps one of the screws was checking through the Judas hole; there was something going on out there. What it was he didn't know and couldn't speculate; it was just a feeling he had. Cautiously he rose to the door and listened.

In the corridor Warders Jordan and Dorman stopped outside Bob Mark's cell. Jordan checked through the Judas hole, and seeing Mark at the back of the cell crouched on his bed, he unlocked the door carefully. Easing it open to disengage the latchlock, he left the door without opening it further.

Inside the cell Bob Mark, whose face was red and blue and yellow from a beating more recent than that he had taken for helping Lynn out, watched puzzled. He waited, expecting the door to open wide, and became upset when it didn't. 'Fuck off, you bastards,' he shouted. 'Leave me alone.'

Still nothing happened, and Bob Mark became more afraid. He didn't know what to do.

Putting the light off by the switch outside Mark's cell, Jordan and Dorman crept back to their office along the corridor. There one watched from the doorway, while the other put the corridor lights out.

In his cell Bob Mark was confused even more by the darkness. It wasn't something he was used to, having spent his entire sentence to date with the lights on. He had a fear of the dark from when he was a lad. He had slept nights with the light on and had sometimes wet the bed with it out. Fear of the dark had got worse since his accident. He didn't know what was going on and could feel panic creeping over him. He tried to hold it in check, but couldn't. His breathing quickened, he could hear the blood pounding against his eardrums and that frightened him even more. Images sprang at him out of the darkness. He didn't know what they were, but was powerless to do anything, anything but run, that was. He ran at the door and shoved it open, but stopped on reaching the darkened corridor; he was uncertain here, scared, like a captive animal that suddenly finds freedom and doesn't know what to do with it. At least he had known where he was in his cell.

A flashlight clicked on, catching Bob Mark in its beam. 'Where d'you think you're going?' Dorman asked.

Lynn, with his ear pressed hard to the door, heard him say, 'You trying to escape, you cunt?'

There was a sound of running feet, followed by some swift blows. From the cries of protest it was evident to Lynn who was getting the worst of it. The scuffle went on for a few moments, then there was silence. Maybe they had knocked him unconscious, or perhaps he had crept quietly away back to his cell. Whatever the outcome, Lynn knew that somehow he had to do something for Bob Mark, get him a result or he'd wind up topping one of those screws, if not both of them.

48

Jack Lynn had spent fifteen days in solitary confinement before he got to go in front of the Visiting Committee. The procedure was the same as for Governor's adjudication. First he was taken along the block where his shoes were removed and he was given a pair of slippers; then he was given the charge sheet on the back of which he could write his reply to the charge if he so chose. The charges amounted to gross personal assault on a prison officer, namely Officer Evans; Lynn chose to make no reply.

The Visiting Committee comprised two male JPs and a woman of no lesser standing. Sometimes there were five members of the Committee present; three was the minimum. The chairman, Edward Wykes, a lean bespectacled, starched-collar pillar of the establishment, one to whom convicted men could in no way relate, was behind the small desk in the adjudication room. The other two members were either side of him, as though appearing on the magistrates' bench. Governor Maudling was also sitting, just off to the side a little way, as if to suggest that he wasn't influencing any decisions by the Committee. Also present when Lynn was escorted in were Chief Officer Carne, PO McLean, the two assisting warders from the mailbag shop and Officer Evans, who still had a huge plaster across his busted nose; certainly the dressing was larger than it needed to be, and wasn't really necessary at all at this late date. But what it did was add credence to the evidence about the assault put forward by him and his colleagues.

The entire procedure as far as Lynn was concerned was no less a farce for having this supposedly independent committee to hear the case. Everything about the hearing favoured the screws. Lynn had no representation, and no right to call witnesses. It was a trial at which he could be confined to a cell for a couple of months or could have extra time tacked onto his sentence, but one which from the start he had no chance of winning. He stated to the Committee what had happened, told how he was upset after a visit from his wife and left it at that. He had no real justification for having assaulted the screw after all. He hadn't been attacking the screw personally, rather the system which he was part of.

Lynn was taken out of the adjudication room while they decided what to do with him. He didn't for a moment think that they were considering any option other than finding him guilty, it was a foregone conclusion. They needed less than five minutes to decide what was to be done, and then he was wheeled back in, made to toe the line.

'Having deliberated at length on the evidence against you,' the chairman said formally, 'and taking into consideration your doubtless emotional state at the time, this Committee finds the offence proven. But however distressing a visit from your wife might be it does not mitigate assault, much less gross personal assault to Officer Evans. This sort of behaviour is outrageous, barbaric. If you were outside the confines of this prison, appearing before my bench, I wouldn't hesitate in giving you the maximum sentence within my power.'

Lynn caught a glimpse of PO McClean who was across the room. The prospect seemed to please him. For his own part Lynn was neither surprised nor disappointed, it was the reaction he had come to expect.

'Prison officers have emotional problems also. At times these can be as acute as any prisoner's. But they don't relieve their frustrations by assaulting prisoners,' he said without irony.

Words of protest almost burst from Lynn. Only by biting down on the soft flesh inside his lip did he prevent himself saying some of the stuff he knew went on, cases like Bob

Mark's. Screws always relieved their frustrations on the inmates, and the weaker the prisoner the more he got from a screw who had taken some stick from his old lady.

'What a sorry state our penal system would be in if they did,' Wykes continued, as though he seriously believed it left little to be desired. He epitomized for Lynn the general lack of information the public at large had about what went on in prisons up and down the country. 'This sort of behaviour simply cannot be tolerated.' He paused as though expecting Lynn to interrupt. And when he didn't, 'Do you have anything further to add before we pass sentence?'

Lynn hesitated, there was a lot he had to say, the words were struggling to get out, and resistance more difficult the longer he was with these people. 'No, sir.'

'Very well. Sentence is one hundred and eighty days' loss of remission; stoppage of earnings for a period of twenty-eight days; cellular confinement for a period of twenty-eight days.'

It was a result. Lynn could hardly believe it. His eyes flitted across to PO McClean, who looked disappointed. Lynn had expected to cop at least an extra year, and that was the PO's expectation.

The magistrate considered the man before him. 'Do you wish to say something to this Committee?'

Lynn hesitated and glanced at the governor.

'You need have no fear of being victimized, if that's what inhibits you,' Wykes said as though he personally was able to guarantee that. 'Governor Maudling?'

Maudling cleared his throat. 'If a prisoner has a valid complaint and makes it through the correct channels we will do all in our power to remedy it. Provided it's found to be valid.'

The chairman was satisfied. 'That's fair enough,' he said to Lynn.

There was a pause. Lynn was conscious of everyone's eyes on him. He wondered where he should start. There was so much wrong with the system that he would like to include everything. 'Well, sir,' he began cautiously. 'I mean, I knew I was well out of order whacking Mr Evans like that –' contrition was a good start, he thought, it would lull them. 'I'm sorry I done it. But the thing is, things build up for a man when he's inside. You gotta have some of it yourself to know like, you can't tell just coming in for a visit. It ain't the same. You gotta have a taste, and I realize that just ain't practical. But you gotta be here and experience that the system's unjust, it frustrates you the whole time, stops you thinking and acting like a man, makes you like a restrained child who ain't allowed to do nothing off his own bat, and those short visits from your wife, they only make it worse. 'Cos all the time you're banged up you can't do nothing for your family, and you wonder what's hapening to them the whole time, if they're all right; then your Missus comes down to see you and tells you the problems, or you see it in her face if she don't crack, and there's fuckall you can do. You don't even have time to sit down with her and sort it all out. I mean, so much has built up you can't think of nothing you got to say you're so anxious. The thing is, if they'd find us some proper work so's we could go and earn a wage to send home and support our families, half them problems would vanish, sure they would. It really ruins you, does you right up in the head, knowing your family's out there struggling and you're just rotting in here, either sewing a few mailbags or making a few toys sitting in your peter. I mean, prison's only s'posed to restrict your liberty, to stop wrong 'uns getting their living. But it does worse than that, it punishes his family, and does him up in the head 'cos he knows it's happening. You can't wonder at villains getting released and going straight back to work, prison don't exactly rehabilitate them; you're fit for nothing when you get out. Unless you're allowed to make one or two decisions for yourself you forget how to; it's demoralizing, it strips away all you need to survive on the outside. 'S hard for ordinary people to see what sort of conflict is going on inside. I mean, I know most cons ain't exactly lovable, you got the worst of 'em down here; but all this place is, it's a dumping ground for the dregs, the problems society can't cope with, 's all. And everyone gets treated the same, diabolically. I dunno, the system is all wrong, it's unjust, it treats you like some low form of animal life; dogs in Battersea get better treatment, they do. I mean, this little lot takes all your self-respect, takes all your dignity. What are geezers in here after all, I mean, they're only the villains what got caught, 's all. They're entitled to something, well some of 'em. But this lot, it wants everything, dun it. We got nothing left.' The words were finally bubbling out of Lynn as though he had no control over them, and when he stopped he felt exposed, vulnerable.

There was a pause, Chairman Wykes seemed slightly embarrassed, and cleared his throat. 'That was quite a speech. You've obviously given matters a great deal of thought.'

'It's what builds up inside, sir,' Lynn said humbly.

The starched-collar heading the Committee didn't know quite how to proceed, he was slightly confounded by the prisoner's emotional outpouring. Although he sympathized with his lot to some extent, he knew he mustn't forget why they were there; he couldn't be seen to condone what he had done.

'I'm sure where your points have any validity, the Home Office has them under constant review.' He glanced towards the governor, who concurred with a nod. This encouraged him. 'No one wishes to have men stagnate when they could otherwise be turned into useful, productive members of society, believe me.'

'Tell me, Lynn,' Mrs Marlow, the only woman member of the Committee, said deprecatingly. 'What dignity or self-respect did you leave those guards when you smashed them to the ground with your shotguns?'

'I didn't, did I. Didn't smash no one with no shotgun. Leave off. I was fitted by the filth. They just decided it was my turn, that's all!' Anger appeared like shards of glass. The two escort warders pressed a little tighter, as if anticipating his springing forward to attack the Committee.

Interjecting through Lynn's denial, Mrs Marlow said, 'A jury of twelve men and women thought differently.'

'Yeah, only the judge was bent, wan' he. All the Old Bill what got up in court perjured themselves. It was a right get up, I mean, what fucking chance you got ...'

'Watch your language,' the chief warned.

Beyond caring, Lynn said, 'Well, go on then, nick another hundred and eighty days off me. What's the fucking dif'? Bang me behind m' door for as long as you like, don't alter the facts one bit, does it.'

The odds were decidedly against the prisoner, Wykes reflected briefly, but there was little to be done, as order had to rule over chaos, and chaos would most assuredly rule if the likes of Lynn had his way. However, he couldn't deny the grains of compassion he felt for him. He said, 'You're appealing against sentence?'

'Yes, sir. Just waiting for it to go on.'

'Well, good luck.' It seemed an inadequate remark to make. He hesitated again, feeling further embarrassed, not quite knowing how to dismiss this man. 'Was there anything else?'

Lynn glanced over at PO McClean, hating the Ulsterman, probably more than the two IRA men behind their doors on the wing would've hated him, if for different reasons. 'Well ... I'd like to make a complaint on behalf of another prisoner, Robert Mark. He's being held in solitary and getting a regular beating from the screws. The dirty slags steam into him for no reason at all.'

'That's a very serious allegation,' Chairman Wykes said formally. 'Have you followed the proper complaint procedure, taken it to the governor?'

'No, sir. Wouldn't do any good, would it.'

Governor Maudling sat bristling at this, but declined to comment, as though to do so was beneath his dignity. In fact to have done so might have resulted in a slanging match with the prisoner.

'Do you wish to name the officers you believe are involved

in this mistreatment of a prisoner?' Wykes asked.

Again Lynn hesitated, wondering if this was a very smart move. They might try some kind of retaliation against him, or if they didn't they almost certainly would against Bob. 'No, sir.'

The accusation would be taken less seriously now. It was more or less a standard complaint against officers; prisoners did quite naturally resent them.

'Very well,' the chairman said. 'This Committee takes note of your complaint, and will inquire fully into it. That's all,' he concluded brusquely.

Lynn was escorted out. He had a sentence on chokey to start.

There weren't many cases for the Committee to adjudicate on – Lynn's certainly being the most serious – which was a reflection on the efficiency of Governor Maudling's policy of discipline and security. There were few complaints also; and their inspection of the prison was confined to one wing and the kitchens, and most of the complaints concerned the food. The lunch that was being prepared looked wholesome, appetizing and plentiful. Certainly it looked nice enough for the Committee to eat it had they been so obliged. Then the catering offices were given plenty of notice of the visit, so an extra effort was made. Not only did they not make a profit in the fiddle they had on the food they bought for meals, they actually lost money on those days when the meals were inspected – fortunately inspections weren't that frequent!

Their tasks done, and nothing more than that, the Visiting Committee were back in the governor's office to have coffee and biscuits – their lunchtime not being the same early hour prisoners got theirs.

It was over this that Edward Wykes announced to the prison governor that he was resigning from his social work. Maudling made polite noises of disappointment.

'You'll be missed here, Edward, I can assure you.' He sipped his coffee. 'You're quite adamant about resigning all your

Committee work?' – as though it was his job to dissuade him.

'I'm resigning from the bench also, Archie. Finally it all came to be too, too depressing. All we're doing is tackling the effect, it seems. Nobody appears to want to, or knows how to, tackle the cause of the problems.'

'One simply has to shut off. Try to avoid conclusions,' Maudling counselled. It was his recipe for getting from day to day. 'I'm not sure that there is an answer, Edward.'

'Maybe not,' Wykes said ponderously. He sipped his coffee. He was thinking about some appointments he had in the City this afternoon, that was partly why they had gone around the prison so quickly. The prisoner Lynn had complained on behalf of popped into his head. 'What about this chap Mark? Any substance to that fellow's allegation?'

The governor smiled. 'Not a hope. Friend Lynn seems to have set himself up as a prison ombudsman. He's getting to be a persistent troublemaker.' Neither the deputy governor nor Chief Officer Carne, who were present, said anything to the contrary. The deputy governor wouldn't know anyway, dealing mainly with administration as he did. 'Mark is a category F prisoner. He's liable to do himself an injury, as well as others. He has to be restrained for his own good from time to time. It's a sad case really, Edward,' he said as though especially concerned about Mark. 'He shouldn't really be here with us. But what can one do? One can't simply go on passing the buck with these no-hopers. That's what I personally find depressing, Edward. The fact some of them can't be helped.' He paused briefly. 'Would you care to see him?'

'No,' he said. 'I ought to get moving if I'm to catch my train.' He was satisfied that there was nothing amiss. The report he would make after their visit would be favourable; everything was and would go on running as it should at the prison.

49

Prison staff usually comprised quite a few of life's failures; although a few saw the job as a vocation and joined solely for that reason, most had tried somewhere else and failed. Failed to get into the police force – usually the examination was too stiff there; failed the fire service, even people who failed to make it as traffic wardens often wound up in the prison service. It was the easiest of all civil service entrance exams, the easiest medical, and you only needed to be five feet six inches in your socks. A number of people retiring from the armed forces and who were lost without that regimentation found their way into the prison service. Everything that attracted failure was to be had in abundance in the service: secure employment, overtime, automatic power over a less fortunate section of society, strict regimentation. However, few recognized or accepted the fact that they became prison officers because they had failed at something else; most deluded themselves that they were doing a worthwhile job, that it was their choice, in no way influenced by external considerations. Some were even happy in their belief.

Equal failures were to be found among those people who formed the professional body of the prison service, the doctors, welfare officers, clerics, only they usually had a greater awareness of their failings which they tried to blot out – some with drink – or tried to deny, holding rigidly to that position, allowing no possible challenge to their authority.

Reverend Paul Hardiman, the prison chaplain, was no exception among these ranks. Not only was he a failure, he looked it also. He had a seedy, crumpled appearance which inspired confidence in no one. His fingers were heavily stained with nicotine where he chain-smoked; dandruff lay thickly across his shoulders and cigarette ash was almost as thick down the front of his jacket. He had only once had a parish, from which he was moved when the parishioners stopped going to church altogether; his bishop had recommended him to the prison service, and it suited Hardiman perfectly; here there was never any need to measure oneself, for there was no standard, with abundant opportunity to condemn others as worse failures if need be.

'Evening, Oliver,' Hardiman said as he shuffled up to the section gate in the punishment block. Dorman returned his greeting and unlocked the gate for him. 'All seems very quiet,' he observed, and drew on his cigarette, which was now no more than a stub, burning his fingers.

'All gone down the pub, Rev,' the fat uniformed man joked, and relocked the gate. 'Who d'you want to see?' he asked as he moved along the corridor. He guessed correctly that it was Lynn.

As he shuffled after the uniform Hardiman stepped into the warders' office to dispose of his cigarette stub.

Lynn was face-down on the cell floor doing press-ups. He was up to the forties and going with ease, so chose to ignore the two men who stepped into his cell.

'You got a visitor!' Dorman informed him.

The chaplain waited, a little embarrassed that he was being ignored. He looked at Lynn, then at the uniform, then finally inclined his head towards the door, indicating that it was all right for him to leave. The warder looked down at Lynn, feeling the inclination to lift his toe into his ribs, but let it pass. He went out slamming the door. Still Hardiman waited without speaking. He took out his cigarettes and lit one, not for a moment considering that this prisoner might find it objectionable. There was no ashtray, so finally he threw the spent match in the pisspot in the corner.

'Fifty,' Lynn said, more for his own benefit than Hardiman's. He was sweating, but felt little strain. He sat round and looked at the chaplain, wondering what he wanted.

Lynn didn't say anything.

'Keeping fit. Healthy body, healthy mind.' There was a pause during which Hardiman became even more embarrassed. 'Would you care for a cigarette?'

'Don't smoke,' Lynn said. He almost told this man not to, but guessed he might have left. Although he didn't invite him and didn't particularly want to talk to him, his visit broke the monotony of the evening.

Hardiman nodded. 'Very wise, especially here. Half the time that's all prisoners ask to see me for, to cadge cigarettes. Yes, you're very wise.' There was another pause. Hardiman didn't know how to talk to people, he was awkward, couldn't broach a subject or come to a point or put anyone at their ease. 'I came to see if I could assist you, with your problems that is.'

The statement took Lynn slightly by surprise. 'You? What the fuck d'you think you can do?' He rose off the floor and got his towel to mop the sweat off.

Hardiman was uncertain. It wasn't the reaction he was expecting. 'Perhaps if I knew the problem?'

There was no empathy with or feeling that he would like to talk to this man. Lynn said, 'I never had any religion. To be honest I've only ever been to church when friends got married, 's about all.'

'Your cell card says you're C of E,' the chaplain said lamely.

'If it had been down to me I'd've stuck down Jewish for the different food you can have sent in.' Lynn didn't bother to explain how C of E was inevitably on cell cards. 'You stick down nothing you're banged up while the others go to chapel.'

'Is that all the service means to you, a trip out of your cell?' He had the best attendance at his services ever in prison and didn't want to consider why it was that prisoners went.

'Well, you ain't exactly Billy Graham, are you?'

This was another scab that had been picked off, exposing his inadequacies. Hardiman quickly sought a salve. 'Does God not address himself to you in any way?' Ash fell down his coat. He brushed at it vaguely, then flicked his cigarette in the direction of the pisspot.

'Yeah. I'm stuck in here, down to fuckall. T'rific.'

'The apostle Paul was imprisoned, and endured great hardship.'

''Talk like a cunt! What about that no-good slag who put me away? Be fair! What about him? You lot make me fucking die, you really do; you're all in league with each other. Coming here and telling me Paul was imprisoned.'

'You sound very bitter, James,' Hardiman said, getting Lynn's first name wrong.

'Wouldn't you be? Wouldn't anyone?' Lynn demanded.

'There are no easy answers why these things happen,' the clergyman said. He had no answers at all, other than the most obvious and the most apt: men went to prison for committing crimes. He had no belief in this man's innocence.

'I know why,' Lynn retorted. 'That no-good cunting detective wanted me put away.'

'Cast your burden on the Lord. He will sustain you. He may not offer immediate solutions, but it does help to tell Him your troubles.'

'Shut up! – how's He helped you?' Lynn was feeling hurt and uncharitable. 'I mean, you're doing time here just like anyone else. You have to wait for the screws to unlock the doors just like me.'

'Maybe this is a penance.' Mostly Hardiman avoided thinking about such things.

'I tell you what, pal, you couldn't get a living outside. Prison's as much a dumping ground for those on your side of the system. I mean, where else could you fucking lot of rubbish go? Look at some of them screws, the fucking dregs they are.'

This was another truth for the padre, one he had no wish to face up to. 'If you wish, James,' he said, focusing his attention along familiar channels, 'I'll pray with you.'

'What for?' Lynn wanted to know. 'Me getting a result on appeal?'

'That's a start. God will listen.'

'Well, if it's all the same to you, I'll put my bit of faith in m' brief. I mean, I always believed in things I could see and touch. They open the gate and hand me a travel pass back to London, I'll believe that.'

'Let me help you some way. Trust me, James. Trust me, please. Anything you tell me will be in the strictest confidence.' He seemed desperate, as though this was his last chance, and believed for his own sake that he mustn't be denied it.

Lynn wasn't about to reach out to this soapy old bastard. He was part of the system which he instinctively mistrusted and he knew that anything he might have said to him would go right back to the governor, go on record. There was no such thing as the respect of the confessional in prison, despite the assurances given by the men of the cloth serving prisons. He watched him draw on his cigarette, the smoke as essential to his lungs as air, then again flick the ash casually at the pisspot and miss it as he had before.

'Can I offer you no comfort?' Reverend Hardiman asked.

'Tell you what, you could do one thing for me,' Lynn said, giving rise to expectancy in the chaplain. "S a lad down here called Bob Mark. You could try an' do something to stop these dirty fuckers picking on him, 'f you're man enough. They keep it up, I'll top one of those bastards.'

'You're mistaken, Lynn,' the chaplain said firmly. He wasn't about to listen to such accusations. 'These are decent chaps doing a very difficult and unpleasant job. You're mistaken, surely.'

Lynn looked at him, realizing how well he had understood what he was. "Course I am,' he said, apparently yielding. Then, 'Go on, fuck off, you wanker. Go back and let the governor brown you.'

Reverend Hardiman couldn't get out of the cell fast enough when the prisoner started making insulting remarks of that nature.

He wrote a report for the record on the meeting he had had with Lynn, putting in everything of their conversation that he could remember, the bias favouring himself in a similar way the warders related details of charges they brought against prisoners. Added to this was the padre's opinion of his mental state, this was even more damning.

This opinion Hardiman offered the governor the following morning en route to chapel. Hardiman was dressed in a surplice and carried a bible, the familiar cigarette hanging from his mouth. The governor walked with his hands in front of him, firmly clasping his own bible.

'I'm not a qualified psychiatric worker, governor,' Hardiman was saying in a slightly obsequious manner, 'but I have seen enough psychopaths in my time to recognize one in Lynn.'

'I would have thought you eminently qualified,' the governor interjected, to the evident delight of the chaplain.

'He persists in this belief that he's persecuted. That he's innocent.'

Maudling said, 'I feel sure it will be a long time before he gives that one up.'

'Maybe. Maybe. The man's an incorrigible liar. He has no belief in anything but himself. That degree of self-centredness I found very disturbing. I would venture the opinion that he's the type of habitual criminal who learns absolutely nothing, either from experience or punishment.' He puffed quickly on his cigarette, automatically brushing the ash off his surplice. 'His "nothing to lose" attitude can only work against ordered society, especially in here.'

'You think he would prove disruptive if put back on the wing?' Maudling suggested.

'Most assuredly!' Hardiman felt his own sense of power now. 'He'll always find morons in here whom he can impress with his destructiveness. Really he's the type of prisoner who should serve his entire sentence in isolation.' He knew the governor's views on that. 'Yes, that's what he needs.'

With a sage nod, Maudling said, 'Unfortunately the Home Office hasn't come round to that one yet.' There was a note of regret in his voice. However, he wasn't without hope for the future. Some more morally acceptable version of the now disbanded sensory-deprivation special control units were what was needed. He wouldn't demur at keeping the likes of Lynn locked in such a unit for as long as was needed. That was the way to deal with resistance by prisoners, the most satisfactory and economic means.

It would come, it had to.

50

'Leave it!' Jack Lynn told a prisoner who came towards the dinner trolley on the ground floor where the trusty was waiting to serve out the food. 'We gotta do something about Bob Mark. Get him some proper medical attention.'

'Leave off, Jack, I'm starving,' the prisoner protested. The protest was feeble; he could see Lynn meant business.

'And Bob's up there dying by the sound of it. Pass the word. Alf.' Lynn stopped another prisoner as he came down the stairs. One or two were getting through despite his organizing the protests. A few of them wanted to get their food regardless of Bob Mark, who didn't mean anything to them, but what they didn't want to do was go against Jack Lynn or get out of step with everyone else on the wing.

Mark had got off the block a few days after Lynn, his cuts and bruises all healed. He had settled back into the routine of the wing, but had then complained about pains in his stomach which had got worse; and he had vomited a couple of times. The MO had been unimpressed when Mark had reported sick, and declared him fit for work. The following day he had been equally unimpressed when Mark couldn't rise. He had diagnosed indigestion, and still declared him fit for work. It was then that Jack Lynn decided they'd have to have a protest.

Despite the word going round as it had, one or two still slipped out when the screws unlocked them, that was why Alan Thompson went along the second floor landing telling cons about the hunger strike after the warder went along unlocking them. The threes they were solid to a man; Frank Timper stopped anyone on the first landing. It all looked solid enough to Lynn. He went up the stairs and returned to his cell; he was as hungry as any but more determined than most.

Apart from the warders creeping uneasily about, the wing was silent, and the slightest noise echoed up to the wooden trussed roof. On the ground floor there was no activity at all around the trolley; the trusty, who knew what was going on, waited, slightly embarrassed. The two warders who were close at hand watched apprehensively as though expecting this to prove a lull before the storm.

The quiet in the wing eventually reached PO Allen in his office on the ground floor, and he was puzzled by it. Usually he was put out by the noise at meal times and invariably considered going out and telling them to be quiet. He emerged from his office to be confronted by the deserted wing. He marched along to where the trolley stood as if that was where all the answers lay.

'Are they all fed, Mr Rogers?' he asked one of the uniforms.

'Just coming for you, sir,' Rogers explained. 'They've all stayed in their cells, refusing their food.'

'Why? What's the problem?' The PO snatched the lid off one of the containers to inspect the food. The reason for their refusing might have lain there.

'They're protesting over Mark,' Rogers replied.

'Right,' the PO said, like he was determined not to let this go any further. 'Feed the nonces first.' There was no way that they were going to refuse their food. He marched off back to his office and straightaway phoned the chief officer to have him sort it out. Carne said he would be across directly, and told him to call the MO over.

The position hadn't changed by the time the chief got across to the wing and was admitted. He was met by PO Allen and two warders.

'All still refusing, Mr Allen?' Carne asked. He could tell from the quiet that they were.

'Yes, sir,' Allen snapped. 'Still refusing.' He believed the hunger strike reflected personally on him and that his subsequent brusqueness might redeem the situation.

'Who got it started, d'you know?'

'Lynn did, sir.' That was only a whisper, but he had turned it into a hard fact.

Chief Officer Carne nodded knowingly – there might have been no possible alternative. 'Have any demands been made?' There hadn't. 'Is everyone involved?' He was informed that all were, barring those Rule 43 prisoners such as the nonces. They stopped at the trolley, where Carne lifted one of the lids and sniffed; he nodded, satisfied that there was no reason for refusing the food in the manner it had been prepared.

'What does the MO say?'

'He's up there now, sir.'

Carne moved away up the stairs, the other three uniforms close on his heels.

When the chief got to the cell the MO was examining Mark in an uncertain fashion which brought him out in a sweat.

'What's the word?' Carne asked.

'Same as it was this morning, I'd say. A touch of indigestion. I've given him something.' The doctor was afraid to change his earlier diagnosis.

The chief's medical knowledge didn't extend beyond first aid, but he was doubtful as he looked down at the writhing figure on the bed.

'Stand up!' PO Allen ordered as he stepped into Lynn's cell ahead of the chief officer.

Lynn rose nonchalantly off the bed, as if neither knowing nor caring why they were there.

'You haven't collected your dinner,' Carne said. 'Do so.'

Shaking his head slowly, Lynn said, 'When something's done about Bob Mark's getting ...'

'The MO's just seen him.'

'A proper doctor, not that fucking piss-artist.'

There he had it; there was no argument. 'Refusing to obey a lawful order. You're on governor's,' Carne informed him. He wheeled out; the others followed.

'Collect your dinner,' Carne ordered when they opened Brian Smith's cell.

'If someone medically qualified cares to look at Mark, Chief,' Brian Smith said courteously. 'Then I will.'

'Refusing to obey a lawful order? Come on, lad.' He waited, expecting Brian Smith to respond. 'All right, who put you up to it? Lynn?'

'Chief?' Brian Smith was bemused.

He was another who went on report. The uniforms wheeled out, slamming the door.

'... As a man of some sensibility, one who has seen a lot of suffering in his time,' Collins said, making a little speech when confronted in his cell by the chief and his gang, 'I can't stand idly by, knowing that a fellow prisoner is suffering in need of proper medical attention ...'

'Ballocks!' Carne interrupted. 'You're the man who crucified rivals through the kneecaps if I remember correctly. So don't give me that old rubbish.'

'Everyone's entitled to change, Mr Carne, mend his ways,' Collins said defensively.

'Get your food, I won't tell you again.'

'Do something about Bob Mark then I'll eat.'

Carne looked at him calculatingly, wondering what chance he had of winning an argument with this man. All he could do finally was put him on report, which he did.

He saw enough prisoners to know that the protest was solid; there was no way they were going to take the food that was offered them. Instead it went back to the kitchen.

Governor Maudling was angry over the protest he had on his hands when the chief informed him of the situation. In theory the entire wing was on report. But Maudling wasn't interested.

'I don't want to see any of them, Chief. Just leave them locked up. They're all as guilty as each other.'

'What about Lynn, sir?' the chief officer said tentatively. He was a case for special treatment, he felt.

'I'm growing heartily sick of hearing that name.' Fleetingly he considered the prospect of having him transferred.

'Perhaps if we were to make representations to the Home Office, try and get them to hasten his appeal, sir.' It seemed the logical solution to the man in uniform. He had thought of taking the proposal to the deputy governor, but he was so ineffectual that he might as well not have been there. He doubted the man had any influence at all on Maudling. At the prison he had previously been stationed at the deputy had run it completely.

'You believe he'll settle down, even if his appeal goes against him, chief, as I suspect it will?'

Carne wasn't sure. 'We've nothing to lose. Certainly it will put Lynn out of his misery.'

'Maybe,' said the large, heavy jowled man from behind the desk. He saw the move as a possible sign of weakness on his part; it would appear the prisoner had put one over on him. 'I don't really like giving one of these animals the satisfaction, Chief. What's the position with Mark?'

'I had a quiet word with the MO. He's been transferred to hospital, with a suspected ruptured ulcer.'

'A simple enough mistake,' Maudling said. 'Well, keep a tight grip, Chief. I don't want a repetition of last summer's riots. In the meanwhile I'll consider your suggestion about Lynn.'

When the ambulance came and took Bob Mark out to the local hospital, escorted by two screws, the prisoners on Lynn's wing felt a sense of elation at their triumph. It had cost them a meal, but that was little enough; they could feed off their victory for a long while.

'What the fuck are they doing? Washing the blood off?' the man in the gate waiting room said impatiently, pointedly looking at his watch when one of the screws opened the door.

A couple of women who were waiting with their kids for their visits were encouraged by this protest.

The warder was slightly nonplussed. Neither solicitors nor their managing clerks usually reacted like this man. 'Ready for you now, sir.'

'About fucking time,' the man said rising and grinding his cigarette into the floor. He was taken across to the legal visiting room where Jack Lynn was waiting for him in the company of a warder. The man visiting Lynn was Trevor Reid, Alex Gladwell's managing clerk. He was in his early thirties, older than his boss in fact, and certainly looked more like a villain. He wore his hair longer than his fashionable clothes said he should, and he had the contemptuous manner of villains with authority. He glanced round when the warder stepped inside the room with them and locked the door. 'Fucking liberty,' he said, before turning to Lynn.

'Mr Lynn,' he said civilly. 'I'm Trevor Reid, Mr Gladwell's managing clerk. We met at your trial, I don't know if you remember me.'

'Yeah, of course I do,' Lynn said, pleased to see a friendly face. 'How's it going, then?'

He glanced round at the two screws again. 'Be nice if we could conduct this meeting in a bit of privacy.'

'It is, sir,' one of the warders replied. 'In sight of but out of hearing of an officer.' He was quoting the text.

'I s'pose you're both fucking deaf.' He sat opposite Lynn, ignoring the two uniforms. 'Alex asked me to pop down and see you,' he whispered. 'Got some right good news, we have. Your appeal's been set for two weeks tomorrow. But that's not all, Jack. Your chances look very good now, they do. We did a busy out at Romford nick, got some info' out of there. The second half of the proceeds from that robbery you were supposed to have had, it turned up intact. What's more, it turned up well before you went to trial.'

'The dirty no-good cunts!' The words burst out of Lynn; he couldn't keep them in. 'That proves it then, dun it.'

'It goes a long way. What it suggests is there was a conspiracy against you from the off; that the fifteen hundred pounds found in your possession couldn't have come from the robbery as Old Bill claimed; that the evidence from the cashier at the security firm was a get up.'

'What does it amount to, Trev?' Lynn asked, a vein of excitement running through him. 'Will it do it?'

'There's no doubt. It gives a lot of weight to the grounds for your appeal: the misdirection of the jury by the judge.'

'But is it gonna come to a nice result? That's the thing.'

'There's no way it can't, not now.'

'Fuck I,' Lynn said, greatly relieved. 'That is good news.'

Excitement went back to his cell with him, it caused him to laugh to himself, it caused little shudders to rock his body; he thought about freedom, walking about on the outside; he thought about his family, about Dolly, how all throughout the months he had been locked away she had kept hoping, kept faith. She was a diamond. His excitement about his future prospects aroused him sexually as he continued thinking about his wife. He found himself getting a hard-on; he closed his eyes and imagined himself alone with Dolly, in their bedroom; how it would be when he got out; how it had been in the past; it had been good, very good. The image stayed sharp and clear on the back of his eyelids. He ran his hand up her strong, well-shaped legs, under her skirt; he felt her moist crotch as he reached into his own flies, she hadn't any pants on and he eased her legs apart, letting him enter her with his finger; he stroked her a few times keeping the rhythm he was making with himself now; she liked that and was making that low pleasant moaning sound she always made. I love you, Dolly, he told her over and over and his breath came faster as his excitement rose; he sensed her excitement increase; she was very wet, her need was as great as his. She pulled her skirt up her thighs and he slid on top of her; he didn't fumble despite his lack of practice; her hand found him and helped guide him into her; his penis was hard and reaching; he could feel her arms clasped around his back, like they were never going to be apart again, her soft lips on his. Suddenly he ejaculated, his body going rigid with the intense, transient pleasure, and when it was over, he kept his eyes closed, not wanting to return to the harsh reality of that cell.

51

Faced with the prospect of his appeal coming on soon and the almost certainty of getting a result, the time Lynn had left became relatively easy for him, he even enjoyed it in a curious way, the company at least, and being able now to laugh quietly at the screws who would serve their time until they retired. One thing that slightly worried him was Bob Mark and Brian Smith having to remain behind. Both had come to rely on him and expected something from him, his attitude had pumped up that expectation; now he would be leaving them with theirs to do and little prospect of getting out. He didn't quite know what he should do about them, if indeed he could do anything. He could have a ruck at the Home Office, especially about Bobby Mark, but that was about all; prolonging his own stay inside wouldn't help either of them.

Where he sat at the table in the threes' TV room, Lynn's gaze fell on Bob Mark who, fully recovered from his stomach operation, was across the room watching TV his eyes glued to the screen, entranced by a stunt motorcyclist. Lynn brought his attention back to what was being said at the table. It had started off as an intelligent discussion about police corruption, but had eventually come round to story-telling. Every one of the prisoners at the table had a story to tell about how they were fitted by the police, or how Old Bill had earned off them; probably every con in the prison, in every prison, had a similar story to tell.

'I did some business with the filth on the Squad,' Micky Dunkerton was saying. 'Me and a pal of mine had some gear plotted up that some other villains had had off. It was about twenty grand's worth of leather coats. Well, we steamed in and done the business all right, nicked all the gear off them, had a placer all lined up, everything. Then about ten CID jumped us, right boary geezers, all tooled up with pickaxe handles. "You fucking move, you cunts, and we'll split your heads right open." They meant it an' all – they had hold of us. Well, first we thought that they were these villains we'd turned, I mean we didn't know. Then they told us like. That was your pal, Steve,' he said, glancing over the table at Collins, 'Alan Greene, one of the DIs down there. He took about two grand off us, pumped us right up about some help.'

'Well, how bad's that?' Collins saw his being associated with a sensible CID as a compliment.

'Terrific,' Dunkerton responded flatly, 'till he sent another squad out the next day and nicked us again along with the placer.'

'He always was a snaky cunt, that one,' he said, suddenly disassociating himself from the DI. There was a silence at the table. Collins was the focus of critical attention. He needed a weaker element to shift the focus onto. Brian Smith was the obvious choice. 'How come a bright boy like you ever got sent away, Brian?' he asked. 'I'd've thought a psychiatrist could have got up in court and got you a nice result, especially with your background.'

"Talk fucking silly, Steve,' Brian Smith responded, as if purposely trying to disguise his antecedents. 'My old lady took me to all sorts of trickcyclists when I was a kid. We seemed to camp in Harley Street. What she was doing was looking for the right one; the one who'd confirm what she wanted to hear. Finally she found him, he was in a class of his own this one. He said to her, "Mrs Smith, I'll tell you why your unfortunate son burns things." "Yes, yes," my old lady replied, hanging on his every word. "He's an arsonist, madam."'

There was laughter around the table which seemed to be at Collins's expense. It was interrupted by a shout from Bob Mark across the room.

'Here, why'd he do that?' Bob Mark said, reacting violently to the TV. 'That's fucking stupid.' He was leaning forward as if about to attack the TV.

'To think we starved ourselves for that,' Collins said uncharitably.

'What's the problem, Bobby?' Lynn wanted to know.

'He jumped the river on his motorbike,' he explained, confusion bringing him close to tears. 'It's stupid, he could've gone on the bridge. I'll smash that fucking set, I'll smash it!'

'Leave off, for fucksake,' one of the prisoners watching TV said warily, not wanting him to smash the set but not wishing to have to fight him about it.

'They'll bang him up again, 'he starts,' Collins cautioned, turning to Lynn.

'Bob, Bobby? Don't worry about it, son,' Lynn said firmly. His words seemed to have a calming effect. He turned towards Lynn, waiting for some direction. 'Come on, we'll do another petition to the Home Secretary about some release date. They must've tore your other one up.'

Mark hesitated, he was aware everyone was watching him. He glanced toward the TV. The motorcyclist had gone. 'Can I bring m' pudding?' he asked.

Lynn winked at him and rose from the table, feeling the danger pass.

They didn't get as far as Lynn's cell much less writing the petition. As they emerged from the TV room, David Morris came hurrying along the landing.

'Jack,' he said breathlessly. 'We got that new molester trapped down on the twos.' Judging from the level of excitement running through the man it might have been an escape route they had.

'Where're the screws?' Lynn asked, immediately getting caught up in what was about to happen.

'They're all down below. Al's getting hold of Bayliss to brown him.'

'Get the others, Davy,' Lynn said, jerking his thumb

454

towards the TV room. He inclined his head at Mark indicating for him to follow as he started down the stairs.

In his cell on the second floor, cons had trapped the newest nonce, whose door had been left unlocked during association, almost certainly on purpose. Mervyn Latimer was an articulate, owl-like man in his mid-twenties. He was very scared and was becoming more tearful as more cons crowded into his cell. Veins bulged on his wide, thin-skinned forehead; his terrified eyes darted over the implacable faces before him, faces filled with hatred such as he had never before encountered, not even from the police who had arrested him. They seemed to be waiting for something to happen, he knew not what, but found the uncertainty painfully unnerving. The thought that they might be waiting for him to attack them and so give them an excuse for physical violence flashed through his head. He didn't want to disappoint them. He gestured wildly at the hard, gross, criminal faces, inviting the attack, wanting to get it over and done with.

'... I didn't molest young boys!' The words blurted out. He knew what they were thinking. He thought perhaps he could explain, make them understand. 'I didn't, you must believe... I had a one to one relationship with a friend, who I loved. I loved him very much.' The words didn't seem to be reaching them, but he persevered. 'It was no different from loving a woman, just as meaningful. No different. We loved each other.' The words were falling against a stone wall; these men seemed incapable of understanding that kind of love. He tried another tack. 'How can you condemn me? How can you attack me for what I did, it's no worse than some here, some of you attacking old women and robbing them, or murdering people ...'

'Not children, you filthy cunt,' a con said angrily.

Suddenly he was getting a response. By provoking them he would get it over and done with. 'I loved him. He was sixteen almost. You can't attack me for it, it's not fair. I'm no different from you. Some of you have done far worse ...'

'Don't say we're the same, you dirty fucker,' another prisoner said, lunging at the young man. 'I never done no boy in, you fucking animal ...'

'I loved him, you morons don't you understand ...' Latimer's words were lost in the hostility he invited. Other prisoners landed punches and kicks in a buzz of hatred.

Suddenly the attack ceased, and they folded back, leaving Latimer on his cell floor whimpering and bleeding. The reason wasn't that they thought he had had enough punishment. Alan Thompson had arrived with Bayliss, a middle-aged homosexual who both through his needs and syphilis had degenerated to a point beyond hope, a point at which no one really wanted contact with him, not even the screws in the hospital where Bayliss had to continually go for treatment.

'There you are, Bayliss,' Alan Thompson said, indicating the young man on the floor. 'Didn't I promise you something a bit tasty?'

At the sight of Latimer the ageing queen's matted eyes positively sparkled, his sore-encrusted lips parted in a smile. He didn't for a moment consider that he might be passing on his infection, or further endangering himself through sexual contact, he had but a single thought, and that was to answer his own needs that were beyond physical sex. This was about the only real contact he had lately, when straight prisoners called upon him to give a trapped nonce some stick. But even the connotations of that, he found, were better than complete isolation.

'What, are you all gonna watch?' Bayliss said. He knew they were.

There was both a revulsion and a fascination in seeing the performance as it started, also a sense of satisfaction in knowing that the nonce was being hurt where it would hurt him most. There was no doubt that Latimer was being hurt from his cry of pain as Bayliss anally raped him, while two cons twisted his arms and held him. Bayliss probably had the biggest penis in the prison, certainly too big for Latimer, who bled profusely. Bayliss didn't care, he chortled with excitement and pain, which increased with the other man's suffering.

None of the prisoners were sure which of the two men cried the loudest when Bayliss achieved orgasm, at which point he must have been in at least as much pain as his victim, though beyond caring – but weren't very interested. They felt relieved emotionally. Some of the deep sense of disgust, loathing, hatred, even the shame that was reflected in their faces was placated, believing that the nonce had got a little of what he deserved. Part of their revulsion was for that which they most feared in themselves. One by one they turned out of the cell, Lynn included, and went back to their own cells.

They had had a result, having weighed off a nonce without anyone being nicked, without any of the screws even showing up to investigate the noise that they couldn't have avoided hearing. But none felt particularly good about it.

There were no reprisals over what had happened to Mervyn Latimer, no one went on governor's report, no one was charged or even questioned about the incident. The truth was that the warders were pleased that one more nonsense case had got a little of what he deserved. There was no way they could not have known about the incident, if not from Latimer then from one of the grasses on the wing. They knew he had to have his rectum stitched, and that he had probably contracted syphilis, but that would take a few weeks to manifest. Such things were dismissed by the MO with a simple entry on the man's record to the effect that he indulged in homosexual practices. That was easier than having to admit that the warders on the wing had failed in their duty, had compounded the attack.

Prisoners didn't discuss or dwell on the incident, which was unusual. None of them regretted it happening, Lynn was sure of that. He didn't regret it, it was something that had to be done, and would be done again if they got the opportunity.

457

Nevertheless it had a disturbing effect on Lynn. He wasn't sure why, having seen such things before. Maybe he was changing, maybe he knew instinctively that that wasn't the answer, any more than banging him or any of the other prisoners up was the answer to their problems. It was but a short-term answer that satisfied a need to punish rather than understand.

'You know,' Lynn began ponderously, 'that nonce the other night, you think that was about right, Al?' They were in the mailbag shop, Lynn talking behind his hand and giving an eye to the discipline screw.

''Talk silly, Jack,' Alan Thompson replied as if never more sure of anything. 'Look what he done to that young boy he was s'posed to have thought so much of. You wouldn't think. He's got a lot more coming, that cunt.'

Lynn still wasn't sure. Something made him uneasy. 'I dunno,' he said, and stopped on catching a glimpse of the screw in the booth as he looked up from his newspaper. He was merely admitting another screw to the workshop. 'Look at the wicked strokes Steve's pulled. I mean, I done people with axe handles; he done an Old Bill,' – indicating Bob Mark. 'You done security guards ...'

'But they're fair game,' Thompson said. 'I mean, they expect that, don't they.'

'They're still people, Al.'

'Most of 'em ain't, not once they put that uniform on. And they didn't do what that wicked fucker did. You think about your own kiddies, Jack, think about that animal getting hold of one of them. It don't bear thinking about, does it.'

It didn't. Lynn knew he was right, but still he was left feeling ambivalent about the whole incident. He remained thoughtfully silent, stitching his eight to the inch.

One of the white-coated warders approached the bench. 'There are some police officers to see you,' he said.

'Oh yeah? What do they want?' Lynn replied. For a moment he thought it might be DI Pyle calling about something else in the frame to charge him with should his appeal go well. Alarm crept through him. Alan Thompson echoed his doubts.

'S'pect there's another fitting, Jack, 'you get a result,' he said.

'Fuck 'em. Tell the cunts there's nothing I want to see them about.' It was his prerogative.

'Watch your language,' the screw admonished, 'or you'll be on governor's. You'd be advised to see these. They're from CIB2.'

'Oh, that's different. Why'nt you say so in the first place. Yeah, I'll see those filth all right.' There was only one thing CIB2 could be coming to interview him about, that was the complaint he had in against the CID arising out of the fitting he had taken.

The two plain clothes police officers were sitting at the table in the legal visiting room when Lynn was escorted in, their black standard issue briefcases on the table before them, along with a folder of papers. One was a detective chief inspector, a thin-lipped, thin-faced man with a blond moustache and thinning hair. The other, a sergeant, was even thinner, and had round shoulders. Lynn didn't care for either and instinctively felt hostile towards them, anticipating that he wasn't going to get any sort of result with them.

'Come in, sit down, Lynn,' the sergeant said, his brusque manner suggesting that the interview was a foregone conclusion.

Lynn didn't move from where he stood just inside the door. 'You want my co-operation, pal, try being a bit civil.'

Taking immediate control of the situation, the chief inspector said, 'Don't let's be difficult, Mr Lynn.' His tone was civil. 'You made the complaint against the police. We'd just as soon go back to the Yard if you don't wish to proceed with the complaint.'

That was fairly obvious to Lynn as he stood looking at the man. Finally he sat opposite the policemen.

'I'll be outside if you need me, sir,' the warder who had

escorted Lynn said.

His departure wasn't lost on Lynn. Anyone visiting from his side and the screws always stayed to listen. It didn't exactly make him more responsive.

'Care for a cigarette?' the chief inspector asked, removing a packet from his pocket.

'What's that s'posed to be, an inducement to have me go easy on your side?'

'Now look, old son,' the chief inspector said in a man-to-man tone. 'This is no easier for us ...'

A note of laughter from Lynn interrupted. "Talk like a cunt for fucksake!' Lynn retorted, the statement not pleasing either of these men. 'I'm doing twenty years; you're outside. Talk about it being no easier for you! What d'you take me for, a cunt? 'S that cunting Inspector Pyle, the dirty no-good cunt, fitting me. He ought to be in here.'

'The complaint against him has to be proven. That's what this interview is about, to try and establish the truth.'

'He fitted me all right. Told me himself, said I was overdue. That's what he said. Without any conscience at all that wicked bastard nicked twenty years off me, just so he keeps his numbers up, has a nice result, 's all. Fucking murder, in' it. 'S robbing my children of their father, 's what he's done. Ruined my family. I've had to sell m' house and everything; they're on Social Security. I dunno, what a no-good cunt, him. Manufactured all the evidence, he did, and what he didn't fit me up with, he went and left out in court so it wouldn't support my story.' Lynn stopped abruptly, having the impression that he was talking too much, and that what he was saying was making no impression on these two.

There was a pause. Then the chief inspector said, 'We would like a full statement, Mr Lynn. Whatever details you can give us, however apparently trivial they might seem.'

Lynn wondered if he should say anything. These men were after all policemen, colleagues of the man he was trying to nick. Why would they want to see one of their own nicked?

'Oh yeah, I got details, if your lot takes any notice, that is.' He intended stating no more than that, but having started, the grievances poured out. 'Where was I at the time that robbery took place. I'll tell you, I was in bed with my old woman, that's where. But she's the wife of a villain so why would anyone believe her. Pyle didn't arrange that, but what he did arrange was a villain called Cliff Harding who he got to lolly me right up. He had previously nicked him with a shooter and held that over him. You see if he went and nicked Harding with that shooter, 'course he didn't – no-good cunts had a deal. But the best of it is my bit of dough that was s'posed to have come out of the Gas Board – fifteen hundred quid, right? That's what Pyle put up in court. Only what he didn't put up was that the missing part of the money had already been recovered by Old Bill out at Romford all intact, all in the wage packets still. It's down in black and white proving that my dough didn't come from the Gas Board, that I wasn't involved. See if you can wash over that little lot.' Having made the statement, Lynn immediately wondered if he hadn't revealed too much of his hand, whether they wouldn't simply slip out to Romford and now remove that evidence.

The two policemen were substantially unimpressed.

'We'll need all the particulars, Mr Lynn,' the detective chief inspector said, like the prisoner hadn't told them anything worthy of note yet. 'Perhaps you'd like to take it all down, Tom,' he said to his colleague. It was routine for them; they had heard it all before; well, most of it.

52

The date of his appeal approached for Lynn like Christmas for a child, never seeming to arrive; when suddenly it did – it was held at the Appeal Court in the Strand – it seemed like it would never be concluded as if he would never hear the result. He was distracted while waiting for word, and convinced at times that he had had a result but it was being kept from him by the screws. A sense of impatience was building up in him, and he was beginning to feel frustrated again. Christmas had arrived but he hadn't got his presents.

Coming down for his midday meal after being unlocked, Lynn was a little late, others were before him waiting to get their food; automatically he went to the head of the queue. No one protested about the move which Lynn accepted as his natural right.

'What's the word, Jack?' a prisoner who was waiting for his food asked ingratiatingly. 'D'you hear how it's s'posed to be going?'

'No, not a word,' Lynn said despondently, taking his food away on a tray.

On the first floor landing Lynn met PO Allen, who was on his way down. 'D'you hear anything yet, Mr Allen?' he said civilly.

'The governor'll call you down when he hears the result. Put you out of your misery.' He went down.

Lynn paused and watched the warder go, knowing he didn't care one way or the other. He felt like throwing his food over him, knowing as he did that PO Allen was part of the conspiracy. But he also knew they would make him serve his chokey before giving him his result. That would delay his reunion with Dolly and the girls. The slopout bell sounded and Lynn responded automatically, dully rising with his pot when Warder Westbury unlocked his cell door. The gross mutton-chop face seemed to be grinning at Lynn like it had a secret he wasn't about to share.

'No word yet, Jack?' Brian Smith asked solicitously as he came along the landing with his pot.

'Those bastards're probably just keeping me on the hook, 'give me aggravation.'

'Yes, I wouldn't be surprised,' the younger man replied. It wasn't an experience he had been through himself, not having bothered with an appeal, but he could guess from Lynn's appearance what it was doing to him. For his own part his feelings about Lynn's appeal were very confused. As a friend he wanted him to get his result and win his freedom, but as a prisoner who had to endure an indeterminate sentence himself he saw Jack Lynn as a light at the end of a very long and dark tunnel, and he didn't want to lose contact with it.

Just before stopping work at four-fifteen the warders came and collected Lynn to see the governor. There was his usual escort, and his movement book went with him, properly signed. Lynn was taken to the governor's office, not the adjudication room, though marched in by his escort in just the same manner. They stood close alongside him should he not get his result and try and take it out on the governor. Their presence like that didn't bode well, Lynn thought fleetingly. He tried to shut the thought out. Apart from the governor, Carne was the only other officer present.

'You know why you're here,' the governor said, glancing at his papers as if to remind himself.

Instinctively Lynn knew what the result was, but tried to resist acknowledging it. Pressure was descending on him, causing him a lot of pain behind his eyes and in his shoulders and neck; his breathing was becoming shorter and he felt slightly sick.

'We've had notice of your result at appeal,' Maudling stated ponderously. 'And there's some good news for you, I'm

463

pleased to say.'

Hope flickered momentarily through Lynn.

'In the light of new evidence put before the court, the appeal judges have reduced your sentence by three years to seventeen years. However, they could find insufficient grounds to justify reversing the decision of the lower court; therefore the original conviction stands. Further, you have been denied leave to appeal to the House of Lords.'

'They can't do that, they can't!' Words burst out as emotion welled through him. 'Those cunts,' – referring to the appeal judges. 'Those other dirty cunts fitted me up ...' referring to the CID.

'Watch your language!' the chief officer warned him. The escort tensed themselves in anticipation.

'Seventeen years. I can't believe it ...' The magnitude of it stunned him, having expected a result.

'I realize this must be a disappointment,' the governor said, carefully squaring the papers on his desk as if to avoid his embarrassment. 'The appeal court's decision is final, so I want you to settle down now, accept it. A simple adjustment is all that's required. Behave yourself, don't lose any more remission, you can be out in twelve years' time, still a relatively young man,' – Maudling, like most of the advocates for the penal system, had absolutely no notion of what it did to a man, having gained all his experience from the wrong side of the wire. 'However, make life difficult for us,' he warned, 'and we will respond by making life very difficult for you. So keep your nose clean, earn your maximum remission; serve your sentence the easy way. Time will soon pass, you'll find, provided you settle down to it.'

The words were absolute mockery Lynn found. He was having great difficulty staying in control. Thoughts and images of his wife and children passed rapidly through his head. It would break their hearts. He could barely grasp the significance of that length of separation; the girls would forget him; Dolly would have to take up with someone else, while he would rot away. The prospects were sickening. He couldn't do it, couldn't sit here and do his time. Too many people would get hurt.

'That's all,' Governor Maudling said, dismissing him.

'About turn! Move out,' Chief Officer Carne ordered.

Lynn turned and marched out automatically, hardly noticing the firm grip the two screws at his side had. They didn't realize it but their grip had a steadying effect. He was teetering on the edge of total chaos, unable at that moment to separate the chaos outside from the inner chaos he felt.

Emotion churned through Lynn as he was escorted across to the wing. He was angry, hurt; held in a state of disbelief; he was ready to strike out and hurt somebody just as he was hurting at that moment, had been hurt over these past months. Seventeen years! The thought was causing his head to pound. Again he thought about his children, also about his wife. Dolly would be fifty-five by the time he got out – how could he expect her to wait seventeen years for him? Carol, his eldest daughter, would be thirty, and Sandra would be twenty-seven, both grown women who would have made lives of their own, and would have forgotten him. The nausea he felt had no connection with eating or with the contents of his stomach, it was a feeling that no amount of vomiting would alleviate: he was sick at heart. In order for him to find any relief someone would have to receive some pain from him, someone who was responsible for his position or was contributing to it. Inevitably it would be one of the screws. DI Pyle was the bastard who had fitted him, and it was him who he would really like to have hurt, but the man had proved he couldn't be hurt, and Lynn didn't imagine for a moment that the complaint against him that was currently being investigated by CIB2 would do it.

As he was put into his cell on the threes, Lynn turned with a cry of anguish that reached out from the deep within him and he launched himself at the two escort screws. The move was a reaction that was left too late. As if anticipating what was about to happen they quickly slammed the cell door, and Lynn hit solid steel with the full force of his charge, his fists pounding the door as though it were a uniform and would yield to punishment. The flesh on his knuckles tore open, letting blood spurt, but at that moment Lynn wasn't aware of any pain; the suffering inside was greater. 'You dirty cunts! You no-good fucking cunts! I was fitted by that dirty cunt!' he screamed over and over until he was hoarse from shouting and exhausted from pounding the door. Tears streamed down his face, but right then he wasn't aware of those either. Finally he was silent and still, and he felt physical pain as it began to dominate his emotional pain. He wrapped his towel around his knuckles, uncertain how he had come by the injury, and lay down on the bed and quietly reflected on his situation. But as soon as he began thinking about his predicament he immediately began dredging up all the hostility, the hurt, the anger, the anguish. Someone was going to suffer besides himself, someone who was part of the system, someone who was either directly or indirectly responsible: they would share his pain, he assured himself over and over again.

The warders didn't unlock him for supper or association that evening, not even to slop out; they were too wary for that, guessing how Lynn might behave. He was best left alone to come to terms with the fact that he was in for the seventeen years, and the only way he was going to get out before that time was by toeing the line in the required manner.

However, Jack Lynn had other ideas. After debating with himself for two days he believed himself incapable of actually serving his time. He considered the fact that he was a villain, that he had been active at the time of his arrest, that he had made other blags that he hadn't been captured for, even that he had sold a body to the filth – as long as they had someone for a blag, as far as the CID were concerned that was a result. Maybe it was his turn and the fact that he had been weighed off, even in the fashion that he had, was right; maybe he should accept it, serve his time. Jack Lynn only saw his imprisonment as being unjust. He'd been fitted and loathed the double standards that had landed him where he was.

By the end of the second day Lynn was sufficiently calm, had sufficiently adjusted to his situation for him to start thinking logically. He realized that attacking screws and hurting them would in the long run hurt no one but himself. He knew he had to use cunning instead of anger if he was going to do anything for himself, all the cunning he could muster. He thought about Brian Smith and that immediate alternative which he offered to his seventeen years inside.

Brian Smith was lying on his bed reading a newspaper when Lynn went along the landing during association on the third evening after the result of his appeal.

There was silence as they looked at each other, both knowing what the other had to offer, but both a little embarrassed about broaching it.

'Sorry to hear about the result you got, Jack,' Brian Smith said at last.

Lynn had received such expressions of sorrow from prisoners he had encountered throughout the day. Some of them had even meant what they said. 'Weren't it a turnup, knocked me sideways, it did.'

There was another pause. 'I see Old Bill got a result at the Bailey, Jack,' the younger man ventured, referring to the newspaper. It was the first results of a massive investigation into police corruption during which a number of detectives, some of them quite senior officers, had been suspended. 'All chucked.'

'What else d'you expect?' he said dismissively. It was a fact of life. Putting his head out of the door he checked along the landing, making sure there was no one about. 'You all set on that one you was plotting up, Bri, are you?'

'No. Not at all,' Brian Smith said, sitting around on the bed. 'I was more or less waiting for you. To see what happened with your appeal.' He was slightly embarrassed, as it seemed he had been willing the rejection.

Lynn didn't even notice that apparent interpretation. 'I'll have some of it with you,' you like.'

'That's fantastic,' Brian Smith said excitedly, like there could now be no possibility of their not making it out.

'What's the chances of putting one more in, Bri?' Lynn asked.

'Who? Not Steve Collins?'

Lynn shook his head. 'Leave off.' Collins was about the last person he'd want to take those sort of chances with. 'I was thinking about Bob. I mean, there's no other way that poor sod's gonna get out, is there.' He hadn't yet put the prospect to Mark, but felt sure he'd want some of it. Certainly Lynn wouldn't want to leave him behind without putting the offer to him.

Brian Smith hesitated. He would have liked a valid reason for not taking Mark along. 'Well, I hadn't thought about three. Is he well enough, do you think, after his operation?'

'I'd say he was,' he said. 'He'll be all right, I reckon.' He checked the landing again.

'Wouldn't you go without him?' Brian Smith said cautiously. That wasn't something he really wanted to test.

'I want to make one as bad as you do, Bri. I wouldn't put a gun to your head like that.'

Reluctantly Brian Smith agreed. 'Well, if you think he'll be okay.'

'Good as gold. You see. What d'you have in mind?'

'I have some keys which I made. They'll get us out of the wing, I'm sure. What it means is knocking out the landing screws.' He waited apprehensively for Lynn's assent.

'That's all right, that shouldn't be too much trouble. What about outside?'

'Well, I haven't worked it out. Any suggestions you have would be useful. We have the dog patrols to cope with and both the fence and the wall.'

'Yeah, they want some thinking about.' He glanced at the younger man, seeing the anxiety in his face. 'They're problems what can be overcome.'

'Look ... is it all right there?' Smith nodded at the landing. 'They're all watching telly.'

From inside his mattress Brian Smith produced two sets of keys and a large knife.

'Fucking stroll on!' Lynn exclaimed. He had seen prison chivs before, but nothing like that. 'Where the fuck d'you get that from?' he asked, taking the weapon.

'I made it. It'll do, Jack, won't it, if we take a hostage?'

'I'd say so. 'S hope you don't have to stab no one.' He handed the knife back.

'What about the keys? Any chance you can look after them? They're a bit of a problem. I can't leave them here during the day, and they run the metal detector over us as we leave the metal shop. I don't really know why I made two sets,' he said apologetically, as Lynn took the bulky keys.

'Yeah, I'll have them, 'course I will. I'll give Bob a set to mind ...shush!' Lynn cautioned suddenly, hearing someone on the landing. Brian Smith thrust the knife back into his mattress.

Collins appeared in the doorway. 'What you skivers up to?' he asked suspiciously.

'Leave off, Steve,' Lynn said. 'Thought you was a screw for a moment. Bri was just about to go down on me, weren't you?' He winked at Smith.

'You cunts've got one plotted up, not putting me in,' Collins said intuitively.

'Shut up, Steve, for fucksake, you'll get us all nicked.' He checked the landing and found it clear. The situation left him with a bit of a problem, whether or not to bring Collins in on the breakout. Neither of them wanted him but he was smart enough to work it out for himself. He had an idea to allay the man's suspicions. 'Steve, come here. I wanna talk to you.' He signalled Briam Smith with his hand as he led Collins out.

'What's going on, Jack?' Collins asked, turning, having preceded Lynn into the latter's cell. Such knowledge might have been his right. 'Don't take me for a cunt neither.'

'I'm not. If I get something going, I'll put you in,' he

promised. Lynn watched him closely to see whether or not he was convinced. 'I want a favour, Steve. That screw you got straightened over on the gate, the one who can do something about improving visits – any chance he could do one for me?'

'I would've thought so. You have to bung him. I mean, it comes to dough.' He hesitated as if uncertain about Lynn's having money available. 'What did you have in mind?'

'To be honest, Steve, I wouldn't mind giving my old lady a taste, 'it can be done. I'm forgetting what the memory's like when I come to have a wank.' He lowered his voice as if to emphasize his shame when he said, 'To tell you the truth, Steve, I was thinking of browning Brian.' He was sure that would convince him, as such information apparently put Collins in control of the situation.

With a sympathetic nod, Collins said, 'Know how it gets you, son.' He smiled. 'You know who it is over there who does it? 'S the PO, Gordon Walters. Don't fuck him for his money, Jack. It's gotta be there.'

'It will be, won't it.'

'Well, it's easy enough done. What you do is, you get your party to contact his party on the outside – I got an address back in m' cell. You tell him what you want and when. He'll tell you whether it can be done and how much it will stand you in.'

'He's all right though, Steve, is he?' Lynn asked. 'He's not likely to go the other way and nick me?'

'He's always been as good as gold with me. Times I've given my old lady one down on a visit. Don't worry, I'll put you in.'

The prospect of making love to his wife wasn't the prime object of the exercise, although he wouldn't pass up the opportunity if it presented itself. However, having Collins believe it was the object of the exercise. Lynn nodded thoughtfully. 'Good luck, Steve.'

53

It took Lynn over a month to arrange the details. He had to wait for his next visit to tell his wife what to do as it wasn't something he could write to her about. She was immediately sceptical, but finally warmed to the idea. The arrangements were easily made and cost eighty-five pounds. It would have been cheap at double that, Lynn decided, if everything went according to plan.

The deal arranged through PO Gordon Walters for Lynn to make love with his wife was laid on for their next visit, and Lynn's escape plans had firmed by then. Dolly was going to become a part of them and that was something for which he needed a little privacy in order to tell her what was needed.

Lynn was called out of the workshop and escorted across to the visiting block by two screws, his movements book going with him. Doors and gates were unlocked before him and locked after him in the familiar rigid routine. In the corridor where the category 'A' prisoners' visiting rooms were situated, the screws paused outside the first and one looked through the Judas hole. There was a visit in progress. As there were in all four of the rooms.

Alarm spread through Lynn. He wondered what was going on, whether something had gone wrong with the plan. Possibly the PO had taken his money with no intention of producing what he had promised. Lynn immediately began thinking of ways he could get back at the PO when he put in an appearance in person.

'Everything all right, Mr Berridge?' PO Walters asked as if he had no notion of what was happening in his sphere.

'A bit full up here, sir, 's all,' the screw who had been spoken to said.

'Yes, there was a mistake on the gate,' he replied. That was where all the visitors were controlled from, but any mistake there would have been made by him, as he controlled the flow of visits. 'Stick him in this one for now,' he said turning back along the corridor and pulling open the door of a holding cell. Dolly Lynn was already inside waiting for her husband. Lynn felt relieved. Motioning him inside, PO Walters said, 'You've got twenty minutes.'

Lynn was about to protest that the deal was for an hour of privacy with his wife. But he realized that to have protested would have cost him his visit altogether so he accepted the cheat.

PO Walters winked at one of the screws as he closed and locked the cell door after Lynn. He would wait a few minutes, give Lynn a chance to get at it before having a squint through the Judas hole.

Inside the cell Lynn clung to his wife tightly, enjoying her warm soft body pressed to his, smelling her perfume.

She voiced all of his doubts. 'I can't believe this is happening. I can't believe it, Jack.' She was anxious, apprehensive. 'I been walking round in a daze ever since the appeal. That just knocked me giddy. Now this ... I mean, I can't believe any of it. I can't believe any of it's happening ...'

'I know Doll,' he replied quietly. 'I feel the same.' He just wanted to stand there holding her, being reassured by her presence. They were silent for a few moments, then he whispered, his lips close to her ear, 'We're gonna make one out, Doll, me and a couple of others ...'

'Jack ...?' The information surprised her, but the firm grip he had on her held down her reaction.

'It's all right. 'S gonna be all right. I promise you. I'll tell you in a little while; 's one or two things I want you to do for me. Just relax now, love, try and relax. Come on, we only got twenty minutes.' He grinned. 'Though I tell you, the way I feel I won't last about two.' He ground his hips into her; at that moment his cock was hard and reaching. He began to caress her but could feel how tense she was. The circumstances weren't conducive to making love, and Dolly was a woman who had to feel at ease before she could get anything out of sex, even the prospect of the girls coming in at home and interrupting them would put her off. 'Take it easy, love, come on, it's all right,' he said, trying to reassure her, his hands running over her body as he did. Minutes seemed to tick away with the speed of seconds in his mind. He didn't like having to rush into things like this but there was no choice.

'No one won't come in, Jack, will they?' Anxiety furrowed her brow.

'No, 'course they won't,' he assured her. But she wasn't convinced. He pressed on regardless, caressing her large breasts. He put his hands up her jumper and quickly unfastened her bra; he had almost forgotten what nice breasts she had. He moved quickly on; running his hands down her thighs, he raised her skirt and brought his hand up over her tights and into the top of her pants. Her pubic hair was thick and bushy; his fingers moved on over it, found the opening of her vagina and met with some resistance. Finally she parted her legs slightly for him and as his fingers penetrated he found she was very dry. He persevered.

With his eye jammed hard against the Judas hole, PO Walters smiled in anticipation. He was getting an erection himself and at that moment wouldn't have minded changing places with the con. His colleagues were drooling as they stood waiting their turn to have a look.

Awkwardly Lynn eased his wife back with him onto the narrow bed, but she remained very tense. They didn't say anything to each other as he eased her tights and pants down her legs and over her feet. A sigh escaped from him at the sight of her, and his breathing quickened. She glanced nervously towards the door, and he pretended not to see the look as he knelt and put his mouth against her cunt. The taste and the smell evoked a rush of memories, of pleasure and pain. He moved his tongue against her as gently as he could but still his wife didn't relax. The seconds were going down in his brain like hammer blows. He moistened her vagina with saliva, knowing he would have to make love to her, forgetting her needs for the moment and simply answering his own before it was too late. A worm of doubt crept into his brain, and he questioned his own ability to fuck like this. His erection, which had been so demanding started to fade. Disbelief drenched him. He zipped open his fly and pulled out his shrinking cock, not understanding then what was happening, why he was losing his erection. He had an urgent need, and whenever he had had that on him before, he got and kept his erection until it had been answered. It was the fault of the bromide that was put in the tea, he decided, and began to get angry. He tried to get his limp cock inside his wife, but couldn't, hurting with frustration at the futile attempts. She caressed both him and his penis, but to no avail.

Their time ran out. Having failed to achieve sexual intercourse or sexual relief of any kind Lynn was left frustrated and edgy. His wife was in no better state. She blamed herself for the dismal result.

'I'm sorry, Jack... sorry, love,' she said quietly, on the verge of tears. 'I'm not helping, am I ...'

Lynn was so wrapped up in his failure to get an erection and carry it through that he wasn't even aware of his wife's problem, certainly he didn't know what she was saying. 'Jesus, that's never happened before ...'

'It's this situation, I mean, like this. 'S not natural ...' She didn't want to appear to put any blame on him, accepting that he had enough to cope with as it was.

'All that fucking bromide they stick in your tea ... what a time for it to happen.' He thought fleetingly of the asses he had stiffed since he had been inside. There had been no problem with an erection then. He wondered if he was going the other way. Finally his anger began to yield. 'I was looking forward to this. Cor, you don't know how much, Doll. Too much I s'pose.' He pulled her closer to himself.

"S my fault, Jack. I was so tense. I'm sorry.'

'I'll get back to my peter and get the raving popcorn, you see. Wish I could take you back there for a little while.'

'It is nice being with you like this, Jack, even if it's for such a short time.' She clung to him like a frightened child clinging to her father.

'We'll make a proper job of it when I get out,' he said in a whisper, his lips very close to her ear. It was time to tell her the things she had to know about the proposed breakout, before their time was up. "S one or two arrangements you gotta make for me.'

"S it gonna be all right, lovey?' she asked. It was her only question about the entire plan. The rest she would work at unquestioningly, do everything he asked.

'To be honest, Doll, I don't know. But I gotta try, 'in I? I mean, I got fuckall to lose.'

She pulled back from her husband slightly and looked at him, knowing the truth of this, knowing that prison was hurting and would go on hurting him all the while he was there. 'What d'you want me to do?' she said.

'Get Tommy to get us some cars. We'll want two. One to get us away from here, one for a change over. We'll want some clothes as well. Some for a big geezer, some for a much smaller one. And a bit of dough, 'f it can be got.' Things like passports and stuff for getting out of the country he could arrange easier himself when he was out. Although there wasn't that much for her to do, what there was was important. 'Can you do it all right, Doll?' If he thought for a moment that she couldn't he wouldn't have asked her.

She nodded.

He hardly had time to kiss his wife again before PO Walters returned to tell them this little session was over.

Both Brian Smith and Bob Mark grew more and more excited as the plans to make one out firmed and the date to try it drew nearer. They had decided on the first night of the new night shift. At times Lynn wondered if they'd ever reach that point without being tumbled. For his own part he was able to keep closed up but continually had to warn the other two. There were more than enough grasses about who would just love to have got a piece of information like that and put it into the screws.

It happened just as Lynn feared it might. How it happened he didn't know, a grass of some kind; or maybe he had been careless with the set of keys he was minding. All he knew was that it was on top with him.

Lying in bed after lights out, Lynn listened to the quiet on the wing. The quietness there wasn't the same as other silences: a con would cough, or ring his bell; get up for a leak, strike a match, or mutter in his sleep; they were all noises which echoed through the wing. As he listened he became aware of another noise, that of marching feet. It wasn't the feet of the single warder moving along the landing with the soft, almost indiscernible squelch of rubber-soled boots. There was more than one person out there. The movement stopped. The light in his cell suddenly came on and the door was simultaneously thrown open, startling him. PO Allen stepped briskly into the cell, flanked by Warders Westbury and Dobson. They looked like they meant business; all three stood with their arms folded and their legs apart in an aggressive, challenging stance.

'Up!' PO Allen barked. 'Get on your feet! Now.'

'What?' Lynn said, recovering himself. 'What's it all about?'

'Outta that bed 'fore we drag you out.'

Lynn didn't need another warning. He rose quickly and shivered in the chilly cell.

'Take those off,' Allen ordered, indicating the baggy vest and pants Lynn was wearing. 'Let's see if you're concealing anything on your person.'

Straightaway Lynn knew what was going to happen, 'M' prick's about all,' he said.

'Watch your lip. Just do as you're told.'

The two warders flanking the PO eyed Lynn menacingly, as

though hoping for some sort of resistance, which they were ready for. Lynn didn't resist, but pulled out of his vest and pants.

'Right, turn round, bend over, legs apart, let's see if you're hiding anything up your ass.'

'You go and fuck yourself,' Lynn protested. 'You want to look up my ass you get the MO up here.'

The two men glared at each other. After a few moments PO Allen said, 'Right, get them back on and get out on the landing and don't you so much as scratch your nose without I tell you you can.'

Lynn obeyed quickly, not because that would lessen his predicament, rather he didn't want to give them any excuse.

'I want every stitch turned over,' the principal officer told his subordinates.

Lynn had a desperate sinking feeling as he stood against the balustrade and watched the search in progress. It was as though nothing was worthwhile any more, everything was hopeless, he had lost and felt he might as well give up. He would like to have known who had grassed him, he would have topped whoever it was; then he realized even that was pointless.

As each piece of bedding, and furniture, and all his personal effects were turned over and thoroughly searched, so it was brought out of the cell and placed on the landing. Night-time searches were something screws sometimes did when they wanted to upset prisoners and cause them aggravation; this wasn't such a move, here they were definitely looking for something, and Lynn wondered whether he should help them out.

Finally the cell was empty apart from the half-full pisspot that stood in the corner. One of the screws was checking the walls for loose bricks, it was a pointless exercise as the black stippling on white walls would make the removal of bricks immediately apparent. PO Allen pointed to the pot on the floor – Lynn had used it to have a shit in rather than go to the recess before he had been banged up. Warder Dobson reluctantly lifted the pot, but there was nothing beneath it.

For a moment hope fluttered through Lynn as he saw the PO swivel on his heels and come out of the cell. Maybe they weren't going to find what they were looking for after all. He tried to keep his emotions off his face as Allen stood and looked at him. The principal officer reached over and took Lynn's plastic spoon from the table and went back into the cell.

Hope died in Lynn. It was on top.

With the spoon PO Allen fished the two homemade keys from the pot. His face – which up until that point was wrinkled with disgust – now broke into a satisfied grin.

54

Lynn spent eight days on the punishment block awaiting the arrival of the Visiting Committee. Attempting to make an escape, with which he was charged was a sufficiently grave offence for it to be dealt with by the Committee. Meanwhile he had been questioned several times about the proposed escape, who he had planned it with; who was going to help him on the outside. Lynn told them nothing at all. There was a chance Brian Smith and Bob Mark would try it on their own, though how they'd fare outside on their own he didn't know; probably both would be lost and shortly recaptured, but that wasn't any reason they should be denied their chance.

The evidence presented to the Committee was short and to the point. He was caught bang to rights; there was no denying his intention. On the back of his adjudication form where he was given the opportunity to answer the charge he had simply stated his original case that he was innocent, that he had been fitted up. He had nothing further to add. And he had been turned right round and escorted out. He didn't expect any result, and hearing the new chairman, William Honey, say to his colleagues before the door was shut: '... The evidence against the man is overwhelming, I think we all agree ...' he knew he wouldn't get one. The man wasn't even discreet enough to give the appearance of going through the motions. Whatever his sentence was, Lynn was resolved simply to try again and again to escape, wherever and however the opportunity presented itself.

In the adjudication room there wasn't a murmur of disagreement from either of the other two Committee members. The governor, the chief officer and POs Allen and McClean would have been in agreement too about the overwhelming evidence had their opinion been sought.

'The question is then,' Honey said, 'probably the single most important question when it comes to deterring miscreants within the prison system: how are we to punish the intractable prisoner such as this one?'

Mrs Marlow, a Committee member, said, 'The only answer, I'm afraid … though not very progressive … is total incarceration, total isolation.'

'I don't know if we can hope to be progressive with this type,' the governor put in. 'I think the very best one can expect is to defeat him.'

'Was there a psychiatric report?' Honey asked, without bothering to check through the pages in the file before him. He had a puffy face with eyes that were reduced to slits, capped with spiky brows.

'There is,' the governor said, 'but he was wilfully unco-operative. The opinion was, if I remember correctly, that he is dangerously self-centred, and has strong psychopathic tendencies.' Maudling had glanced through both the psychiatrist's report and the one made by the prison chaplain before adjudication. 'These, it seem, compel him to work wilfully against ordered society.'

'That's certainly borne out by his record over the past eight months,' Honey observed.

The governor, encouraged by the evident hard line of the Committee said, 'Personally I'd like to see him placed under special control. Oh, I know those units were designed for terrorists primarily, but this man is an unmanageable, I feel. Sensory deprivation is the only answer, I'm sure.'

Maurice Pollinger, the large, florid-faced third member of the Committee, who looked like a comic postcard impression of a publican, said, 'One can overcome one's objections to the IRA being put in such restraint – well, those sort of people deserve no better. But this man still claims he's innocent.'

Governor Maudling was about to respond, but Honey interjected, 'The appeal court has given its ruling, three judges eminently more qualified than we have decided his guilt. I think we can safely abide by that decision and keep a clear conscience. What do you feel, chief?'

The question threw Chief Officer Carne slightly, and he hesitated, wondering if they were fully aware of what they were talking about, if they realized that the Home Office had closed the special control units down. 'Well, the units worked, sir, there was no doubt about that. They broke the hardest of them, the few that had got put in them. But they came in for a lot of criticism.'

'Yes, that's why they were closed down,' Maudling said, a note of anger in his voice. 'But it's not those vociferous, woolly-minded liberals who have to cope with these people.'

There was silence in the room for a moment or two after that. It was as though no one had anything to propose that was a practical alternative to the units that were no longer available as a means of punishment.

Clearing his throat, Honey said, 'I suggest we give this man the maximum sentence, see if that doesn't dull his rebellious edge. Fifty-six days cellular confinement; forfeiture of all privileges; one hundred and eighty days' loss of remission. All agreed?' the chairman asked.

The Committee concurred.

'There is just one point, Bill,' Pollinger said almost reluctantly. 'How might we deter him in the future if the need arises?'

Therein lay the inherent weakness of giving anyone the maximum sentence in a system which paid lip service to liberalism. It was a question none of them could answer.

Lynn heard his sentence without a flicker of surprise. As far as he was concerned he might just as well have done his time on the block as in his cell; privileges weren't such that he missed them. As for the loss of six months' remission, it was meaningless in the context of the seventeen years which stretched before him, years he had no intention at that moment of doing.

He settled easily to his solitary routine of exercising, eating, reading, masturbating and sleeping, but with the light on the whole time. At night-time his clothes went outside the cell and were returned to him at morning slopout: this was to prevent his escaping, but it was a nonsense, as the only way out would be via the door, and his clothes were left in a neat pile outside the door.

He had been on the block for about a week after sentencing, and was in bed reading for a couple of hours after lights had gone out in the rest of the prison, when there was a sudden commotion of alarm bells, accompanied by the dogs barking and running feet, and shouts. Instinctively Lynn knew what had gone off; he felt both pleased for their initiative and disappointed, the noise suggesting immediately that they hadn't got very far.

Springing out of bed, he jumped up and caught hold of the bars of the window and pressed himself with ease to look out. Every prisoner whose cell overlooked the yard must have done the same; Lynn knew they were at their windows even though he couldn't see them. Shouts of protest came hurtling down from the wings.

'Leave them alone, you garity cunts!'

'They was only exercising.'

'Leave 'em be, you dogs!'

'Go home and catch your old woman at it.'

'Get down from those windows!' a voice boomed from across the yard, 'or you'll all be on governor's.'

'Go and fuck yourself, you dog!' came the reply.

What followed then was a game the screws played trying to catch whoever had called out the insult. They'd accuse someone of it, expecting him to answer with a denial or the name of the culprit.

Lynn couldn't see either Brian Smith or Bob Mark, but knew they must have been captured for things quietened down a bit outside. Then he knew for certain they were caught by the noise that swept through the block as they were brought in. He dropped down from the window and went to the door to listen.

Warders came along the central corridor of the punishment block like an angry swarm of wasps, driving Brian Smith and Bob Mark ahead of them. Both of the prisoners were scared, and at that moment unmarked. But both were realistic enough to know that that state of affairs couldn't last. They had after all hurt two guards in the escape bid, how badly they weren't sure; one of them they couldn't have hit very hard for him to have recovered quickly enough to have sounded the alarm. Brian Smith felt a scream rising through him, the sort of terrified scream he hadn't experienced since he was a child when he had learned to live with his fears and overcome his need to scream, knowing no one would ever answer them, certainly not his parents.

Angry, scrabbling fingers grappled with the lock on a cell door, delaying the escort as the warder pulled the door open. Bob Mark was hurtled into his cell. Warders would have dragged him into the cell, but there wasn't room for them all to go through the door together. Half of the dozen or so uniforms split off, following Bob Mark into the cell, the rest took the other offender on to the next cell. The last in thoughtfully pulled the door to: the deputy governor might wander round. It wasn't likely, but instinctive common sense told screws the doors of such cells weren't to be left open for anyone passing to look in.

'Thought you'd make one out, did you?' Warder Dorman said menacingly.

Mark didn't reply, his mouth merely moved in an agitated, spastic-like motion as he backed away until he came up against the far wall of the empty cell. The warders closed in on him, forming a tight semi-circle around him; their expressions were full of hatred, it was as though this man posed the worst possible threat to them. They were each more than a little afraid, not of him specifically, though they clearly recognized what damage he could do in one of his moods. What they were

483

afraid of was what he had done to their colleague tonight, what any one of the prisoners they helped keep locked up could do with this nothing-to-lose attitude if they were to relax their firm grip for a moment. Conditioning within the system had embedded that fear deep inside them, and when their grip slipped fractionally and something like tonight's attempted breakout occurred, all they could do was hit out blindly at that fear.

'You probably killed that officer you hit,' one of them said.

Another informed him, 'You ought to be topped for that, killing a prison officer.' It was merely wishful thinking.

'You fucking maniac, that would be too good for the likes of you ...' Their abuse was inadequate and didn't satisfy their feelings.

'You're a monster, that's what you are. A fucking monster ...'

Fear to match that residing in these men bearing down on him rose and touched panic trigger points in Mark. Without warning he rushed at them, trying to reach the door and escape this immediate danger. But the screws were ready for him. He wasn't able to break through them. They swung blows at him, fists and feet; some had sticks with them. There was a profusion of blows, a lot were going wide of the target or only glancing off him both because of their anger and the fact that there were too many in that confined space trying to hit the same target at once. But a lot were getting through and doing damage. All Bob Mark was able to do was cover his head and face with his hands and arms, seeking some protection, but even that was pointless when he sank to the floor. There they kicked him, their feet easily penetrating any barrier he tried to put up.

Three cells along all Jack Lynn could do was listen, angrily, helplessly. It was obvious that the would-be escapers were going to get some stick but Lynn hadn't expected it to go on for so long. There was no response to his ringing his bell; the morning came and he could get no information from the warder who unlocked his cell for him to slop out.

The first sign of anything was during exercise with three other prisoners who were on the block. They had been in the yard for about five minutes when Brian Smith was brought out to join them. He fell in line with the shuffling six paces behind Lynn.

At the first opportunity, Lynn turned and said, 'Sorry you didn't make it, Bri.' He didn't comment about his condition, there was no point. Brian Smith must have known how bad it was from the way he almost certainly felt.

'Well, at least we had a go,' he mumbled through his swollen lips.

'Yeah, you done all right ...'

'Eyes front there!' one of the warders yelled. 'Just keep moving.'

The five prisoners walked on in silence for a while, but Lynn couldn't keep silent, there was too much he wanted to know, not least why Bob Mark hadn't been brought out. Exercise was their only point of contact.

'Where's the other fella, Bri?' he asked, shortening the gap between them. Then as though Brian Smith hadn't heard the question. 'What happened to Bob?'

'I didn't see him after they separated us,' he said with difficulty. 'I think they gave him a lot of stick, Jack.'

Although Lynn had guessed that, the information disturbed him.

Throughout the whole of the day he was unable to get word on Bob Mark. Even Brian Lang, the block trusty, wasn't able to tell him anything about his condition, having been kept out of his cell. That night there was a lot of noise on the block, the sound of people making themselves busy, Lynn thought. Someone hurried along the corridor. A door banged. Someone said something in a muted tone. Something was going on. Another door banged. The impression left Lynn uneasy. Especially the cry he was certain came from Bob Mark.

With no means of telling the time other than by the natural succession of day and night and the bells which meant the commencement of something, everything was a between-times for the prisoners, but they learned to judge sections of the time. After the waking up bell, Lynn knew approximately how long it was before he was slopped out, and knew that this morning he was late. There was a lot of activity around the block, the coming and going of various parties, who he didn't know, but that uneasy feeling he had last night recurred. Leaving his finger jammed against the bellpush achieved nothing; he tried kicking the door, but his bare feet made little impression; there was nothing in his cell with which he could effectively bang. He returned to the bellpush. His finger was aching by the time the shutter was eventually opened. It was Warder Allison there.

'Why you ringing this bell?' he demanded tersely.

'My pot's full,' Lynn said defensively. 'Why ain't we been slopped out?'

'You think you're the only one on this block. Just be patient. There're more important things going on this morning.' He was about to close the shutter when Lynn stopped him.

'Mr Allison?' he appealed. 'Is Bob Mark all right? He was going on a bit last night.'

The warder hesitated, he glanced along the corridor uncertainly, then said quietly, 'Topped himself last night, he did. Hung himself in his cell ...'

'What ...' The words hit Lynn forcefully, momentarily taking his breath away. 'What the fuck you talking about?'

'Found him this morning. Just be patient, don't add to our problems.' He closed the shutter.

'Wait!' Lynn shouted. 'Wait a minute,' he pleaded, but got no response. He stood at the door, as disbelief swept over him. He blocked the information, trying to convince himself it wasn't true, that they were getting at him; then slowly and painfully an awareness crept through him and he knew it was true that Bob Mark was dead. But Lynn didn't believe it had happened as they said it had. 'They murdered him,' he said quietly at first. He repeated it, and again, the expression gathering momentum. 'Those fucking bastards murdered him!' The words rattled unheeded around his cell. Anger surged through him, demanding some release. He turned his rage loose on his cell rather than himself, hurling his pot, turning his bed over, pulling it apart, smashing the window, the protected light fitting, ending up by pounding the door with a broken piece of his table.

He was hoarse and exhausted and could offer no resistance by the time his cell was unlocked. He was taken out and into another cell. This one was stripped, not a single item in it apart from a pot. That was how Lynn would serve the rest of his chokey. He sat against the wall, his forearms resting on his knees, his head slumped forward. A screw looking through the Judas hole might have believed he was asleep, but he wasn't, despite his eyes being closed. He was crying and trying to hide his tears. He had thought a lot of Bob Mark, more than he realized, and it was dawning on him that perhaps he couldn't win, that the system was breaking him, despite his resolve that it wouldn't.

55

For two months while on the block Jack Lynn nursed his hurt and regret over the death of Bobby Mark, and nurtured his hatred for the system and those responsible, all the while trying to resolve his feelings with a practical viewpoint. He told himself there was nothing he could do about what had happened while he remained in solitary, and he was right. Protests would have gone no further than the governor; the only form his protest could take was an accusation against the warders on the block, which would merely have resulted in trouble for him. As would a physical attack on them. So he bided his time.

When he got back on the wing he found the subject of Mark's death a past issue. It had left a surface anger, but nothing Lynn could promote into a strident form of protest. For his part he would like to have had the entire wing, excluding the nonces, barricaded on a landing, or out on the roof tearing up the slates and hurling them, refusing to budge until the newspapers and television had taken up their cause, and the Home Office was obliged to have a full inquiry. But most of his fellow prisoners were apathetic, and Lynn suspected that Steve Collins had influence on the prevailing attitude, as he was still put out over not being part of the attempted escape. Who was Bob Mark anyway, just some simple lad who was category F and liable to turn it all in himself anyway? That wasn't the Bob Mark he knew, Lynn told the gathering up in the threes TV room. But it made little difference. Collins was doing the screws' job for them.

'They definitely topped him,' Lynn said adamantly, defeat edging into his voice. 'They done it all right.'

'No way will you convince me different,' Collins said

accommodatingly. 'But who's gonna believe it, Jack? I tell you, son, it's a nonstarter.'

'Someone's got to,' Lynn argued. 'We kick up enough fuss. We have a right to ruck about it.'

'They had a coroner's inquest, Jack,' David Morris said, fiddling nervously with his tobacco tin. 'Took his life while the balance of his mind was disturbed, he did. That was the verdict.'

'They didn't fucking well call me as a witness, did they? They didn't call Brian Smith.'

'You reckon it would have made any difference, Jack?' Alan Thompson said. He was one of the few who formed an opinion independently of Collins, and he was prepared to protest over the issue, but was being practical.

'There was no way he could've tore those cotton duck sheets to make a rope. I mean, he was a strong lad, sure, but 'you tried them, have you? Up my ballocks he did that and hung himself,' Lynn said. 'They give him too much stick, that's what. Hanging him like that was the only way they could cover it up.'

There was an uncomfortable silence as they sat with that truth resurfacing.

'You'll get us all nicked, Jack, that's what you'll wind up doing,' Collins said.

'How fucking hard's that?' Lynn demanded. 'Bob's dead.'

'You gotta be practical, son,' Collins said.

Lynn looked at him, checking his inclination to leap across the table and hammer him. The slag wasn't worth getting nicked for.

Shortly after that the meeting broke up, cons drifting quickly away to their cells in case Lynn should corner them and press them into action.

Smuggling a stiff out of his brief to ask him to do something was the only sensible course of action left open to him, Lynn decided, but that would be a slow process and would relieve none of the frustrations that had built up in him over the past two months; however, he was learning control and patience and cunning.

Micky Dunkerton, immaculately dressed in his prison uniform, with a clean shirt and wearing a tie, was lying on top of his bed reading when Lynn pushed into his cell. There was an awkward pause as the two men looked at each other. This sort of encounter was what most of them wanted to avoid, but they couldn't lock their doors against Lynn.

'Ready for the off, Micky, are you?' Lynn said.

'You wouldn't think.' There was another pause. He knew that wasn't what Jack Lynn had come about. 'Sorry I can't do nothing about a protest, Jack. But I only got one more day. Know what I mean?'

Lynn nodded. He understood Dunkerton's position; with only twenty-four hours before his release the man had too much to lose and it wasn't reasonable to expect him to put himself on offer. 'Silly ballocks'd nick you out of spite.'

'I liked Bob Mark. Bit simple, but a nice lad. I'd like to have helped, but you know. I'm even calling the screws "sir" now.'

Lynn nodded again. 'Got something in mind when you get out, Micky?'

'Draw a bit of Social Security for a few weeks; give the old lady a taste, if I can still get a hard-on. Then I s'pose I'll have to look for a bit of work. I mean, I'm a blagger, Jack. Someone'll put one up to me. What else can you do? Can't live on Social Security all your life like some of them parasites.'

'Hope you get on your feet.'

"S not hard, is it. Enough at it, know what I mean.'

There was a short pause. 'Any chance you'd take a letter out for me? 'S nothing in it for you, Micky – 's about Bob's death. I wanna see if my brief'll do something. I mean, 'you don't fancy it, 's all right.'

'No, I'll take a chance, Jack. Least I can do.'

Lynn felt a surge of relief, and some of the pressure eased off him. 'Good luck,' he said. 'He might be able to do something, m'brief.'

'They took a right fucking liberty with Bob Mark.' Dunkerton said. 'You gonna try and make another one, Jack?'

'You gotta try, Micky. Just go off your fucking head otherwise. Know what I mean?' He looked at him, realizing that the question had a purpose. 'Why, you got something in mind?'

'See if there's anyone about,' Dunkerton said, climbing off the bed.

Lynn checked that the landing was clear, then glanced back at Dunkerton as he lifted the top end of the bed. Removing the base cap from one of the hollow tubular legs he slid out one half of a pair of wire cutters and a hacksaw blade; from the other leg he took the second half of the cutters and the bolt which they fitted together with.

'I've had these about three years, can you believe, thinking about making one. But the time kept slipping away. Then I got m' parole. I didn't know who to give 'em to – I don't trust no one else, Jack, to be honest. If I left them here and they was found I'm yanked back in. They're safe enough. What about him?' he said, indicating a budgerigar in a large home-made cage. 'You want to have him transferred to your peter?'

Lynn didn't say anything but waited to see what he had in mind with this offer.

'There's a rope ladder in the bottom.'

'That's terrific,' Lynn said. It was like winning the football pools. 'Did you have one planned, Micky?'

'Well, only vaguely.' He gave Lynn the few details he had of the escape plan he had worked out.

The following evening after lights out Lynn went to work on the bars of his cell with the hacksaw blade, leaving the one on the extreme left of the window to fasten the sheet rope to. He had no fear of the strips of cotton duck sheets tearing as he lowered himself, taking extra care as he went past the windows of the cells below him. Where he dropped to the ground was in the exercise yard which put a fence between him and the wall. Although that meant extra work cutting his way through the wire there was he thought some advantage in that the yard helped to disguise the sheet rope that was hanging down the side of the wing. Cutting the wire was difficult. As he came out on the far side of the exercise yard he almost ran into a dog patrol. At that point he had no option but to go forward. He sprinted across the open compound to the lee of the wall, where he pressed himself into the shadow formed by the abutment. Alarm seized him as he looked towards the wing and saw as clearly as could be the sheet rope hanging down. The screw who was approaching couldn't be off seeing it. Light seemed to reflect from it like a beacon. He heard the warder talking to his dog. Either man or dog would hear his thrashing heart and the blood pounding violently in his ears; Lynn's mouth was dry and he tried in vain to moisten it; he felt more helpless and vulnerable at that moment than he had ever felt before in prison. He watched as the warder and dog passed no more than twenty feet from him. One or other of them needed only to turn his head fractionally to the right and they'd have seen him in the cover of that abutment.

Tension and anxiety slipped away from Lynn as he watched the warder go. He almost couldn't believe that his luck had held, but he felt drained, and was unable to move for a few seconds. When at last he did he unwound Dunkerton's rope from his waist, made certain the hook was securely fastened – whether the home-made hook was strong enough to hold his weight wasn't worth considering at this stage. He hurled it up the wall. It found a hold first time, catching on the barbed wire by one of the Y-shaped brackets that held it. With relative ease he hauled himself hand over hand up the rope, adjusting the blanket he had brought with him as he went. Getting the blanket out over the wire as he reached the top of the rope was the most difficult part of the operation. It meant hanging there by one hand, his feet dangling in mid-air – the thought sickened Lynn, who had no stomach for heights. It took three attempts to spread the blanket on the wire before he could pull himself onto it without tearing himself to pieces. But by this time the muscles in his arm were saying they had had enough and were about to give up. He struggled awkwardly onto the blanket. Barbs came through the folded cloth and cut into him when he rested on the wire. There was no way he could avoid it, his weight caused the rolls of wire to shift the whole time.

So preoccupied was he with keeping his balance on the shifting wires as he hauled up the rope to lower over the other side that he didn't notice the closed-circuit TV camera on the wall opposite as it swung round in his direction.

There were eight aspects of the perimeter wall shown simultaneously on the eight-screened console in the gate house. Jack Lynn was in frame on one of them as he lowered the rope down the outside of the wall. However, the warder on duty at the console wasn't where he should have been, but was at that moment coming through the door with a mug of tea. As he got back to his place his glance automatically traversed the console.

'Jesus Christ!' he gasped. Only his brain didn't at first register what his eye had seen, the sight being so unexpected. He spilt some of his tea in his panic as his hand shot out to the alarm button.

The bells starting up startled Lynn, causing him to lose his balance. He reached out, his hands clasping frantically at the wire. The barbs sank into the flesh as his hands took his weight. Finally he let go, the barbs tearing through his flesh. He hit the ground hard; he managed to get up as if intending to run, but couldn't for he had injured his feet. Even if he had been able to run there were about a dozen screws to stop him. He simply leaned against the wall, clasping his bleeding hands and grinning defiantly at them.

56

Lynn was up before the Visiting Committee for adjudication on his escape attempt. They gave him the maximum. Fifty-six days cellular confinement; loss of all privileges; one hundred and eighty days' loss of remission. He expected nothing less. However he was surprised when later that same day he was taken out of his cell and back along the block to the adjudication room, first stopping off to swop his shoes for slippers. Having been weighed off with the maximum, Lynn puzzled at what more they could possibly give him. All too soon it became abundantly clear.

Governor Maudling was behind his desk on his own when Lynn was brought in. Chief Officer Carne was present, along with PO McClean.

'You seem to be a man who is determined not to learn anything from experience,' Maudling said. 'Well, understand this. I am equally determined to break you ...'

'Like you done with Bob Mark,' Lynn interjected. The words just popped out. 'You done a t'rific job there, governor.'

'Quiet!' Carne ordered automatically rather than as though he really meant it.

Maudling raised his pudgy hand, indifferent to the interruption. 'Let him shoot off his stupid mouth, chief,' he said evenly, deriving enjoyment from this. 'He'll learn that every offensive remark, every display of disrespect will be to his cost. The fifty-six days' cellular confinement you were sentenced to this morning will be quite unlike any you have previously experienced. Firstly you will have no privileges whatsoever; you will have absolutely no contact at any time other than with warders on the punishment block; you will be in a stripped cell throughout the day, your bed only being returned for you to sleep at night. Your clothes will be removed from your cell at night; the light will remain on the whole time. You will be observed by a patrol every ten minutes day and night.' He paused for effect.

'That's terrific,' Lynn said defiantly. 'So what's different about that?'

The governor patiently raised his hand to silence him. 'The difference this time is that if any breach of discipline is reported to me, however minor, then your fifty-six days' sentence will begin from day one again, regardless of how much of it you have served. In other words, I want exemplary behaviour from you for fifty-six consecutive days before you will be released from solitary confinement.'

There was a brief silence. Then Lynn said recklessly, 'You got some fucking chance.'

A mirthless smile parted Maudling's thick lips. 'We'll see,' he said, like a man who knew he couldn't lose.

By the time Lynn had changed back into his shoes and had been escorted through the punishment block, PO McClean was waiting by the open door of his cell. He reached out and prevented him entering his cell. He was smiling a cold, humourless smile, while lines etched deeply into his masklike face.

'What we want from you is two months of impeccable behaviour,' he said, repeating the governor's demands. 'A wrong word to any of my officers or a wrong gesture, in fact if you so much as fart in the wrong tone you'll be back to square one. That understood?'

'That's all ballocks,' Lynn said challengingly. He believed at that moment that he could take anything they put on him, and for as long as they kept it up.

'You'd better get everything you want to say off your chest while you've nothing to lose,' the PO said reasonably. 'Tomorrow you'll only have fifty-five days to go.'

The two men exchanged uncompromising looks as each tried to assess the other.

'I'm going to enjoy watching you break, hearing you beg my staff not to put you on report when you slip.'

'I wouldn't count on it,' Lynn said.

'Inside. Not another word out of you.'

Lynn moved into the cell and the door was slammed after him. He stood waiting, half expecting the shutter to open and the PO to say something else. It didn't. As he waited Lynn experienced a curious feeling of isolation, something that hadn't happened to him before in solitary. He wondered why he felt that way now. Possibly it was because he had been told he was being isolated. He tried to dismiss the feeling. But it didn't go away; there was nothing in the cell with which he could distract himself, and the prospect of fifty-six days was suddenly a bit daunting.

The shutter opened and Warder Dorman appeared behind the grille. He didn't say anything, but simply looked in, then closed the shutter. It happened every ten minutes or thereabouts, and by the third day Lynn was beginning to be worn down by it. There was virtually nothing he could do which he wasn't seen doing by any of the warders opening the shutter: pressing, shitting, masturbating, walking, lying in bed. He began to tense instinctively as he heard the shutter slide back. The same lack of contact was evident when his food was passed to him. No longer did the block trusty bring it inside his cell, but gave the tray to the screw who opened the door and handed it in to Lynn. Except when Warder Oliver Dorman was on duty. He had the trusty put the tray on the floor, when he slid it inside with his foot as if Lynn was contaminated.

'Why don't you just throw it on the floor, you cunt!' Lynn screamed at him when Dorman did this at supper time. It was his first outburst for three days. Holding in all his anger and bitterness had caused him too much pain.

Dorman didn't respond immediately, but slammed the door as if ignoring the remark. But the shutter opened immediately. 'That's going to cost you the three days you've already done.'

'You no-good cunt!' Lynn shouted and hurled his tea at the warder, but the shutter was quickly slammed and Lynn had to live with a pint of tea on the cell floor until his bed was returned to him later that evening when he was given a bucket and a mop to clean up the mess.

In the exercise yard he was equally isolated, moving round in a circle within the wire for something a lot less than the hour he was supposed to have for exercise. He rarely saw other cons, not even at a distance, and when two went by under escort in the compound outside the wire Lynn felt elated. When one of them called out, 'How's it going, Jack?' he responded.

'T'rific.' He instantly regretted this, knowing it was to his cost.

'Inside!' one of the warders ordered. 'You're on report.'

That meant going back to square one, losing the ten days he had so far done. Lynn looked at the uniform contemptuously. 'You silly bastard. I can keep this up as long as you.'

He was put on report also for not getting out of bed quickly enough after the waking-up bell sounded in the morning; the cell was cold and having to stand around in his pants and vest waiting to get his clothes back wasn't appealing. There was no sense of justice here; whatever injustices prevailed in the penal system were magnified on this type of chokey. He was put on report for not folding his bed clothes neatly enough when putting his bed out. He was put on report for wilfully disfiguring prison property when he was caught keeping a record of his time by scratching the wall with a stone he had brought in from the yard. He had noticed a pattern in the way they were putting him on report, they were building up his hopes, letting him go a little longer each time before taking him before the governor. There was no defence that Maudling would hear. Lynn being on report meant that he was guilty, and the governor simply kicked him back without any argument.

Slowly he was learning to repress his feelings, but not

without considerable pain; he was learning to watch the whole time how he behaved. It required a great deal of work, a great deal of effort. When he thought about the process he told himself that the system wasn't in fact beating him, or wearing him down, rather he was merely being cunning.

Three weeks without going on governor's report gave Lynn a sense of achievement. He was shattered when after breakfast and second slopout of the day he was told by a screw that he was going up before the governor. He hadn't done anything, and protested the fact.

'I don't know about that,' the warder replied. 'I was just told to bring you up.'

It fitted the pattern, Lynn decided. He had had a nice run, just getting a little confidence, deciding he could maybe make if after all, when they decided otherwise.

'Your behaviour record is absolutely abysmal,' Maudling said as Lynn stood rigidly to attention, toeing the line in the adjudication room. 'Forty-seven days you have been on this type of punishment. Had you behaved yourself it would have been finished in another nine days. But you're a man who prefers to do things the hard way it seems. Out of forty-seven days your longest period without breaching discipline is currently twenty-two days ...'

'Yes, sir,' Lynn readily agreed.

Maudling removed his glasses and shook his head. 'No, sir. You've been making complaints against my staff. Allegations to the effect that members of my staff were directly responsible for Robert Mark's death.'

Lynn waited, fearing the worst. A knot of tension moved across his shoulders and up through his neck, making the back of his head ache.

'Whilst you are perfectly entitled to make complaints against staff, even one that brings about their suspension pending an inquiry, we do have legitimate procedures for it. You do not make complaints via smuggled letters as you did in the case of Officers Dorman and Jordan. Having illegal letters smuggled out is an offence against discipline. You will lose the twenty-two clear days.'

'But that was before I started this little lot, sir,' Lynn protested.

Maudling wasn't interested in that. 'Your fifty-six days' cellular confinement will begin from day one again. Understand that this has nothing to do with the fact that two officers have been suspended as a result of your action ...'

'You fucking liar!' The words burst out of Lynn.

'Take him away,' Maudling said, returning his glasses to his nose.

Reg Allison was one of the warders who escorted him back along the block. He seemed dismayed by Lynn. 'You shouldn't have been that way with him. He won't forget that.'

They reached the cell. Lynn looked at the old warder, accepting that his words were well intended. But he didn't respond.

'Why not toe the line?' Allison advised, as though that wasn't something Lynn had been trying, and as though trying brought its rewards. 'Be easier in the long run.'

Lynn nodded wearily and went into the cell. The door was slammed. He tensed, expecting the shutter to open. He wondered if he would ever get out of solitary. He recognized in himself that feeling of despair, of desperation that Bob Mark had had over his prison sentence.

Dolly Lynn felt helpless and frustrated over what was happening to her husband. She was doing everything she could to get something done about the treatment he was receiving, but it wasn't enough; she felt that she wasn't achieving anything at all. There seemed to be no progress resulting from her actions and her visits to the prison. Now she had this letter from Ronald Hazelwood, her local MP, asking her to call in and see him at his next surgery. He was very sympathetic when she had first called to see him after her husband hadn't got anywhere with his appeal, but he hadn't been able to do anything, despite getting on to the Home Office. He had listened patiently when she had gone to see him after she had got word from a recently released prisoner about the sort of treatment Jack was receiving. The MP had wanted to interview the prisoner who had brought her the news, but he had only been passing through town and she didn't know where to contact him. However, that hadn't lessened Ronald Hazelwood's enthusiasm for the case.

The MP's surgery was in a rundown shop with a curtained window in Kentish Town Road. The appearance inside the office was equally shabby. The furniture and furnishings were old and worn and had the appearance of having been donated by someone a long time ago. Sitting behind the small trestle table with its cracked linoleum covering was the MP. He was a thin, round-shouldered man in an old but expensive sports coat that had leather patches on the sleeves and cuffs. He had long, lank blond hair and wore heavy glasses. He rose and shook Dolly Lynn's hand warmly when she was shown into the inner office.

'I'm glad you could come, Mrs Lynn. Sit down, love.' He sat on the opposite side of the table from her and opened a thin correspondence file. 'Sorry if my letter alarmed you or raised your hopes unduly. But I thought it best you came in for a chat, rather than my simply telling you the position of things by post. Has the position changed at all regarding your husband since we last had contact?'

'No, I still ain't received no visiting order. I been down there again without one. Said I weren't gonna go away until I saw him. But it didn't do no good, they said I couldn't see him.' She paused, as if checking her tears. She was very disturbed about the situation with her husband. At times she even wondered if he was still alive; it was a silly notion, she told herself, but she remembered what had happened to Jack's friend, Bob Mark. She drew her hands down her tired face, massaging her dark-ringed eyes. 'They said he was in chokey still, and had all his privileges took away.'

'I'm afraid that was confirmed by my inquiries at the Home Office,' Hazelwood said, feeling slightly embarrassed at his evident impotence in this matter. 'Though I'm not sure they're allowed to stop his visits. He's considered a persistent troublemaker, Mrs Lynn, and as a result they seem to jump on him for every minor misdemeanour.'

'That ain't true, he ain't a troublemaker. I told you what he done, Mr Hazelwood, didn't I. He made a complaint about the death of another prisoner what's got two screws suspended. That's why he's getting all this stick, that's why.' Anger bubbled through her air of defeat.

'The Home Office did show me the catalogue of disciplinary charges against your husband, Mrs Lynn.' He wished there was something more he could tell her, something that would offer her comfort. 'I know there is an enormous bias in favour of the prison service at these disciplinary hearings. We are working at that, trying to get some reform, so that prisoners can be represented at their hearings by a solicitor.'

'But it's been over four months that he's been down the block, sir,' she said vaguely. 'I know what that's doing to him.'

'Let me get this right, Mrs Lynn,' Hazelwood said, his interest coming awake again when he saw the possible lever to put under the Home Office. 'You say he's been in solitary confinement for over four months? Is that what you are saying?'

'Yes, sir. And I ain't been allowed to visit him.'

'That's a different matter. I didn't fully understand that when you first came to me.' He had been through the prison rules often enough, knew that fifty-six days was the maximum a prisoner could be confined to a cell for punishment. 'I'll go back to the Home Office, Mrs Lynn, I'll tackle them again about this. See what they have to say. Certainly I'll endeavour to get his visits reinstated. Leave it with me.'

'Something's got to happen, sir,' she said ominously. 'Or Jack'll wind up hurting someone, he will. He won't be able to take much more of it. I mean it.'

'Try not to worry, Mrs Lynn. I'll get straight back on to the Home Office. Tackle the Home Secretary himself about your husband's case. I'll get some action on this if I can.' He thought perhaps he was being optimistic, but gave her his professionally reassuring smile.

57

During the time he had spent in prison Jack Lynn had got quite used to sleeping with the light on the whole time, and during his months on the block he had become used to the grille shutter sliding open every ten minutes or so as the screws checked up on him. However, even though his instinctive reaction whether awake or asleep was to tense now, what he hadn't got used to was the warders who reached into his sleep in the night, wrenching him violently into wakefulness. Sometimes they were real, sometimes they weren't; sometimes he was unable to distinguish between reality and unreality.

As he pulled himself clear of the shallow sleep that held him he found himself wet with sweat. The scream had ended, but he didn't think he had imagined it. He sat up in the narrow bed and listened. The punishment block was silent, save for the metallic sucking noise that seemed to go on the whole time; it wasn't anything but the atmosphere of the block, but it was always present at night and it disturbed him.

A marked change had come over Jack Lynn, both psychologically and physiologically. He was a very different person to the man who had been put down on the block six months ago. He had shrunk in stature, lost weight; his shoulders were constantly hunched and tensed in a defensive position; he blinked as though with an eye affliction, and he was very jumpy, starting at the least sound. The resolve to beat the system which he had set out with was gone; further, he denied to himself that it had ever existed.

He tensed, hearing someone move along the corridor outside the cell. The centre of his interest was frequently the door, and he would sit and stare concentratedly at it as he was now doing.

The shutter slid open and a warder appeared behind the grille. He stared in without speaking. Lynn stared back until his eyes began to water, then he averted them.

He wouldn't go back to sleep. He had no idea what the time was, but he would simply lie in his bed until the waking-up bell sounded.

The waking-up bell startled Lynn, even though he was listening for it. He rose instantly, having too much to lose to be put on report for lying in bed after the bell. Straightaway he began folding his bedding into a neat pile, glancing anxiously towards the door as if expecting to be caught out. These past few days had been very anxious days indeed for him. Having almost reached his goal he was terrified of being put back to the start. He had almost served fifty-six days straight off without committing any offence, but believed the screws were looking closely for something to pull him up on, some reason to kick him back, to make him start his chokey all over again.

The cell door opened and a warder said, 'Bed out!'

Smartly Lynn brought his bed out and placed it in an empty cell opposite his own, the blankets in a neat pile placed squarely on the end. Automatically Lynn reached for his pile of clothes as he came back across the thoroughfare, but didn't make it.

'Leave those. Did I tell you to touch those?'

'No, Mr Wright, I thought...' he began meekly. The warder who had opened his cell in the mornings for the past fortnight had always told him to get dressed first. This was it, he thought fleetingly, this warder would be the one to put him on report. He checked a tremble which started in his jaw.

'You're not supposed to think,' the warder said. 'Just obey orders.'

The uniform stepped into the cell, his eyes circling the empty space closely as he searched for possible infringements of the rules. Lynn watched anxiously, feeling a huge sense of relief when he was ordered to dress and slop out.

After breakfast Lynn received a surprise visit from the governor. Either the governor looking in, or his deputy, or the chaplain was supposed to be a regular occurence for prisoners on solitary, in fact Lynn had rarely seen any of them. He was sitting on the floor when the door opened.

'Stand up for the governor,' the warder ordered.

Lynn scrambled to his feet and stood to attention as Maudling and PO McClean stepped into the cell.

The governor looked him up and down, not displeased with the figure he saw before him. 'You're to be congratulated, Lynn. You have now managed fifty-four consecutive days without offending against discipline. That's quite an achievement. We're pleased with your progress.'

'Thank you very much, sir,' Lynn replied.

'It's taken you six months, when most prisoners would have learned a lot quicker. However. Two more days and you'll be able to return to normal routine on the wing. Doubtless you won't wish to repeat this exercise.'

'No, sir.'

The governor nodded his approval. 'In a closed society like ours, we simply cannot and will not tolerate disruptive elements. You must understand this. We will always find the means of breaking even the hardest, the most intractable prisoner. Good order depends on it.'

'Yes, sir,' Lynn said.

'Well done.' The large fleshy-faced man in spectacles nodded again, satisfied with his victory. He started away, then turned back as though forgetting the purpose of his visit. 'Incidentally, as you were so concerned about Robert Mark's death, you might care to know the result of the Home Office inquiry which you were instrumental in bringing about. It upheld the coroner's verdict that he took his own life while the balance of his mind was disturbed. It completely exonerated the two officers. I thought you might like to know.'

It was the supreme test for Lynn but he passed it easily. 'Thank you, sir,' he said without trace of disappointment or anger, all feelings of frustration and his sense of injustice totally subjugated.

Governor Maudling looked at him, questioning the sincerity of his response. 'Don't let yourself down these next two days,' he told him, then wheeled out.

Possibly the governor, pleased with his progress as he seemed to be, had told the screws not to goad him too much over his last two days. Lynn wanted to believe that, and certainly there seemed to be less pressure on him. Then he was seduced into believing that he would definitely make it out, and began to feel excited about the prospect: that was until he heard from one of the warders that the two warders who had been suspended over the Bob Mark inquiry were back on duty. Lynn quaked at the prospect, for he knew it would only be a matter of time before they got around to him.

Each time the door opened it renewed the fear in Lynn. His last two days seemed longer than the entire time he had spent on the block.

Dorman and Jordan got to him finally on his last night. Lynn was in bed curled in the foetal position. He was too frightened to sleep, though gave the impression that he was. He heard the key as it was carefully turned. His eyes came open in alarm, but that was the only part of him that moved. The door swung open and the two warders stepped inside, both taking up that familiar, menacing stance, legs slightly apart, arms folded.

'All right, get up!' Jordan barked.

'Move!' Dorman ordered when Lynn didn't respond sufficiently quickly for his liking. "Fore you're on report. You playing with yourself, were you?' he demanded as if that was an offence against the rules.

'No, sir,' Lynn said quickly.

'Right, remove your clothes, bend over, legs apart,' Jordan said.

Lynn had on only his pants and vest. He did as he was ordered. Meanwhile Warder Dorman began searching his bedding,

506

pulling it apart and dropping it on the floor.

'We suspect you have escape tools hidden here.'

'No, sir. Honest, sir,' Lynn said from his bent-over position, his feeling of desperation increasing. 'Or smuggled correspondence,' Jordan said. 'He's the one who caused our suspension, Oliver.' His colleague might not have known.

'Oh well, tell him the result of our paid holiday. He must be interested.'

'Reinstated, we were, without a stain on our character. That's what the record reflects,' Jordan informed him mockingly. 'Doesn't that please you?'

'Yes, sir,' Lynn agreed.

'You lying fucker!' Jordan thrust his baton hard up Lynn's anus and sent him crashing into the wall. 'All right, get up. Anything there, Oliver?'

'Nothing. Or he's a better man at hiding it than I am at finding it. Unless he's hidden something in his pot again.'

Jordan smiled. 'All right, pick it up.'

Lynn hesitated. There wasn't anything in the pot apart from what he had used it for a couple of times in the night. Finally he picked it up and turned back to the two warders with it, hating these two men for what they were doing to him, but hating himself more.

'Right, fish in there among them turds,' Jordan ordered. 'With your hand.'

Again Lynn hesitated, he looked at the uniform, then at the pot; then back at Jordan. He had the choice of simply obeying and getting out of chokey or throwing the contents over the warder and getting his fifty-six days all over again. He saw alarm pass briefly across Jordan's face at his hesitation. But there wasn't really any choice. So repressing his feelings Jack Lynn finally plunged his hand into the pot and fished around in the piss and excrement to the satisfaction of the two warders. They smiled, accepting that they had won, that the system had completely broken this would-be hard man.

Progress for Jack Lynn was swift now that he had started

507

thinking the way the prison authorities wanted him to think. He got his clothes back in his cell at night, got to sleep with the light out for the first time; even got onto the coveted working parties that moved around the prison doing jobs supervised by only a single warder.

The current working party Lynn was on was landscaping a small patch of ground outside the governor's office. Lynn and a prisoner from another wing were working together, digging holes to plant some trees.

'Dig fast enough, Jack,' the man said, 'we could tunnel out before silly ballocks even notices.'

'Be handy,' Lynn said accommodatingly. He didn't take him seriously.

The prisoner who was working with Lynn checked around, making sure the supervising warder wasn't within earshot or any of the other cons. 'You fancy making one, Jack? I mean, you seen that ladder in the maintenance shed? How hard would it be to do that padlock?'

Caution crept through Lynn as he said, 'Not hard, would it?' He wondered what he was getting himself involved in here. He didn't know this lad who he was working with, certainly he didn't know enough about him to try and make one out with him, even if he had had the inclination. Suddenly he saw what this was and became frightened. It was a get-up; they had put this con up to this to test him. He thought back, trying to remember what he had said, whether he had said anything that could be seen as conspiring to make a break. 'Old Bill who nicked me said to me, he said, "You can't do your time, don't do the crime." I mean, that's fair enough really. You're at it, you expect to be nicked sometime, stands to reason. The only chance you really got is doing your bird, doing it their way, know what I mean.'

The younger prisoner shrugged disappointedly, "S up to you. I thought you was a million.'

'Hold up,' Lynn warned as the white-coated warder approached. "S that deep enough, Mr Evans?'

508

'That'll do nicely,' the warder said, inspecting the hole. 'Just knock the stake in there first, then spread the roots out when you put the tree in.'

The two prisoners did as they were told. Lynn held the sapling as his partner shovelled earth over the roots.

'Jiggle it up and down, Jack,' Mr Evans said. 'Settle the roots in. It's going to be there a long time.'

'What sort of tree is it, Mr Evans?' Lynn asked, feeling compelled to make conversation, as though that was the only way to eradicate the doubts he thought they might have recognized in him.

'Copper beech. Ten or fifteen years you'll have a nice-sized tree there,' Mr Evans said casually.

The words didn't go casually past Lynn. They hit him forcefully as he remembered that he had all those years to do. The warder would have retired long before, but Lynn would be around to watch this sapling grow into a nice-sized tree.

Epilogue

Anger and hostility towards the hierarchy had surfaced among detectives on the Squad; it was more than usually apparent. Similar feelings were prevalent throughout the CID. The result of the extensive and prolonged corruption investigation which had been started by an outside force and concluded by CIB2 was that seven detectives who had ended up in the dock at the Old Bailey had been found not guilty. That wasn't the cause of the current ill-feeling, which had started when policemen, some of them senior officers, some retired, some who were suspended, had been arrested in highly publicized police raids on their homes, and had been charged variously with conspiracy to pervert the course of justice, accepting bribes, conspiring to sell bail and weaken evidence. Included among those arrested was Detective Inspector Maurice Head. DI Pyle had been fairly closely investigated but had managed to avoid suspension.

The reason why policemen were now angry was that despite having been to trial and got a result, a large number were facing disciplinary charges. These could mean anything from demotion to a small fine. But what they really meant was that policemen were subject to double jeopardy.

'Probably ninety-five per cent of CID are at it,' Pyle said conversationally. 'I mean, have at some time bent one, are bending one, or will bend one.'

'Oh, I don't know, Fred,' DCI Simmons said defensively. He was no less angry than Pyle over what had happened, then not only did his rank make him that much closer to the hierarchy, he wasn't facing a disciplinary board. 'That's a bit strong.'

They were at the bar of The Feathers. There weren't many

customers in at that time of the evening.

'It all depends how you book it, Tony. I mean, what most of them were doing is what most of us have done at some time.'

In an undemonstrative fashion the DCI conceded the point. He wasn't about to take his colleague for a fool, but the thought did briefly occur to him that Fred Pyle might have started working for CIB2, where he was being transferred to next month.

'There's nothing fundamentally wrong with the men who do the job,' Fred Pyle said. 'But I tell you if they aren't let do the job any way they can, there's going to be a serious breakdown in law and order. Especially now you've got all these people out of work with nothing to do but villainy.'

Pyle, like so many of his contemporaries had implicit belief in the end justifying the means. They knew very often who was doing the villainy, who they had to put away. Villains weren't governed by a set of rules when they went out and made one, they weren't subject to disciplinary hearings when they were most effective; detectives saw little reason why they should be hampered by rules of fair play when they sought to nick them. Most detectives had their own sense of morality in such matters, and detectives were honourable men after all.

'That's what's gonna happen, Tony,' Pyle said. 'It's all gonna break down. 'We get much more stick from the brass. The men in the job won't have any incentive to go out and feel collars. Not if they're going to get disciplinary over it.'

The chief inspector nodded. 'We'll get a result if we get nicked by you in CIB2, Fred,' he said.

'There's a good chance. Those other cunts,' Pyle said referring back to the hierarchy, 'are stopping good men going and getting a living. It won't be my game, Tony.'

He finished the scotch in his glass and motioned to the barman. There was time for another drink before he went off to his meet.